PRAISE FOR KRISTY WOODSON HARVEY'S

Lies and Other Acts of Love

"*Lies and Other Acts of Love* establishes Kristy Woodson Harvey as a major new voice in Southern fiction. This book stirred mighty emotions in me, yet left me with a sense of peace. A truly delightful read."

—Elin Hilderbrand, *New York Times* bestselling author of *The Rumor*

"A richly detailed, intergenerational tale of love, loss and loyalty. Harvey pulls the reader into the hearts and souls of her characters."

—Heather Gudenkauf, *New York Times* bestselling author of
The Weight of Silence

"Winsome and wise, *Lies and Other Acts of Love* shows us that true, strong marriages are forged as much out of pain as passion. Kristy Woodson Harvey treats both Annabelle, the young, naive heroine, and Lovey, the formidable matriarch, with skillful tenderness. Fans of Southern fiction, especially book clubs, will flock to this engaging, heartfelt story."

—Sonja Yoerg, author of *House Broken* and *The Middle of Somewhere*

"Richly drawn Southern characters . . . A story so perfectly detailed that we could imagine ourselves on a wraparound porch in the South with a tall glass of sweet tea. *Lies and Other Acts of Love* will grab you by the heartstrings and pull hard. A perfect story about the lies we tell and the secrets we keep—all in the name of love."

—Liz Fenton and Lisa Steinke, authors of *Your Perfect Life*
and *The Status of All Things*

continued . . .

Dear Carolina

"Kristy Woodson Harvey weaves a story around characters with rich, complicated lives we all identify with . . . Beautifully shows how a family comes to be. Not only by blood, but also by choice."

—Jodi Thomas, *New York Times* bestselling author of
Betting the Rainbow

"Southern fiction at its best. [*Dear Carolina*] shows us that love is not without sacrifice, and there's little in life that doesn't go down easier with a spoonful of jam. Beautifully written."

—Eileen Goudge, *New York Times* bestselling author of
The Replacement Wife

"*Dear Carolina* is like the Southern women within its pages and those who will love this book: sweet as sweet tea on the outside and strong as steel on the inside . . . Woodson Harvey is a natural."

—Ann Garvin, author of *On Maggie's Watch* and *The Dog Year*

"Southern to the bone and full of engaging characters . . . Captures your heart and doesn't let go; [Woodson Harvey's] keen insights into a mother's love will stay with you long after the last page."

—Kim Boykin, author of *Palmetto Moon*

TITLES BY KRISTY WOODSON HARVEY

Dear Carolina
Lies and Other Acts of Love

Lies and Other Acts of Love

KRISTY WOODSON HARVEY

BERKLEY BOOKS, NEW YORK

BERKLEY

An imprint of Penguin Random House LLC
375 Hudson Street, New York, New York 10014

This book is an original publication of Penguin Random House LLC.

Library of Congress Cataloging-in-Publication Data

Woodson Harvey, Kristy.
Lies and other acts of love / Kristy Woodson Harvey.—Berkley trade paperback edition.
p. cm.
ISBN 978-1-101-98706-3
1. Family secrets—Fiction.   2. Matrilineal kinship—Fiction.
3. Life-change events—Fiction.   4. Domestic fiction. I. Title.
PS3623.O6785L54 2016
813'.6—dc23
2015018199

PUBLISHING HISTORY
Berkley trade paperback edition / April 2016

PRINTED IN THE UNITED STATES OF AMERICA

10 9 8 7 6 5 4 3 2 1

Cover photo © Rafa Elias / Getty Images.
Cover design by Sarah Oberrender.
Text design by Kelly Lipovich.

Penguin
Random
House

For my grandparents, Joe and Ola Rutledge,
a living example of true, forever love

Acknowledgments

If a first novel is a dream come true, a second novel is a dream taking hold. Thank you to Katherine Pelz for choosing me for this unimaginably wonderful adventure. Life should come with an editor like you. To everyone at Berkley: You are phenomenal, and you make me look good. Thanks for all your hard work.

Bob Diforio, agent extraordinaire, thank you for your constant support and belief in me. It means the absolute world.

A million thanks to my Tall Poppy Writer friends who are not only absurdly talented but also unfailingly generous with their time, advice and support. You ladies prove that this is not a competition; it is a sisterhood.

Roxanne Jones, Julie Schoerke, Chuck Gold, Holley Pearce and Cindy Jackson, thank you for letting me do what I love. None of this happens without you, and you are so very appreciated every single day.

My mom, Beth Woodson, perhaps works as hard on my books as I do. Thank you for the hours upon hours you put in helping me in every imaginable way, and for reading—and loving—every single draft. My dad, Paul Woodson, thanks for always believing in me, even when I was down 0-5 in the second set. I love you both so very much!

My grandparents, Ola and Joe Rutledge, really are an example of what a lifetime of love should look like. Thank you for showing us all the way and for being the start of this wonderful family that I'm so proud to be a part of.

Penn Peninger, thank you for sharing your stories, for knowing that my asking which fabric you liked better as a toddler would lead to something, and for making the world's best peanut butter crackers.

Elizabeth Cook, thank you for giving a seventeen-year-old a newspaper column and making her realize that nothing felt better than stringing words together on a page.

Thank you to my two Wills for making every day amazing, for reminding me what matters and for celebrating the little things as if they are the big ones. You two are, quite simply, everything.

Dottie Harvey, Nancy Sanders, Cathy Singer and Anne O'Berry, thank you for (im)patiently waiting to read my next manuscripts and always making them better.

To the bloggers, bookstore owners, fellow authors, reporters and media pros who have embraced my books and me so fully, I wish I could name you all here, but I trust that you know who you are. Humbled does not even begin to describe how I feel at the way you have supported me. Thank you from the very, very deepest part of my heart for sharing this work I love so much with the world. You are at the top of the list of people I'm grateful for every day.

All of you readers are who I think of when I sit down at the computer. Those of you who have e-mailed me, written reviews, commented on my blogs, come to my events . . . There aren't enough thank-yous. Your kindness always came at just the right moment and is appreciated more than you can possibly imagine. You are helping me live my dream every single day. I hope something in these pages inspires you to live yours too.

Annabelle

∞

Storm Chasers

My grandmother, Lovey, says that there are two types of people in the world: the kind who flee to the shelters at the first threat of a hurricane, and the kind who wait it out, hovering over their possessions as if their fragile lives offer any protection against a natural mother that can take them out of the world as quickly as she brought them into it.

I come from a long line of the hovering kind.

As I sit across from my grandmother in her stately living room, the dimmed bulbs of the chandeliers reflecting off the scotch that I most certainly will not drink, I laugh as she says, "Well, why wouldn't I go to the beach? I've ridden out every other hurricane of the last half century there. Haven't blown away yet."

Her accent, Southern, proper, moneyed and with that particular Eastern North Carolina flair, is one that you rarely hear anymore. And I would listen to it forever. It is the voice in my head, imparting her wisdom, and I know it will remain so for the rest of my life.

She pushes the stylish bangs of her silver hair, cut increasingly shorter as the years have gone by, and I can't help but see that glimmer in her eye, the one of her mother, a grand lady whom I met only a handful of times but whose presence is stamped in my memory like the check endorser at my daddy's office. It is the same glimmer of my grandmother's sister, my great-aunt, one of those sturdy forces that, during the Second World War, moved with her war correspondent husband. While the bombs rained down on London every night, she refused to flee or even gather her children into the bomb shelters under the street. Instead, she bathed her small sons, scrubbed their dinner plates, laid her damp dischcloth over the sink and steeled her jaw against the Germans attempting to take her right to parent as usual. She sealed her fate by signing every letter to my great-grandmother, "I'll write you in the morning."

My own mom, nearly a foot taller yet lacking those long, thin, graceful features of my grandmother's, chimes in, "Mother, that is absolutely ridiculous. You will stay right here. There's nothing you can do if a storm comes, and I'm not going to sit around here wringing my hands that you're floating down the street in the rushing floodwaters."

I smile into my buttery scotch, as my mother has never been one to flee from the storm. At least once a day the city manager she handpicked to advise her on all political dealings will say, *Mayor, I suggest you refuse to comment on that matter.*

But she, like the women before her, is incapable of turning the other way, of snuggling warmly in the cellar until the tornado passes.

"Have you forgotten who's the mother and who's the child here?" Lovey asks.

It is then that I begin to wonder: Am I a storm chaser too? Would I walk to the market in spite of the shrapnel? Now I know. Sometimes it's best not to ask the questions if you'd rather not learn the answers.

Lovey

The Light

My momma always told me that honesty was the most important thing in life. But I've never understood why people are so hell-bent on honesty. It's not the truth that sets you free. The truth is the thing that destroys lives, that shatters the mirror. The truth is selfish and shameful, and better kept to oneself. In fact, I'm quite sure that the only things that paper-clip any of our lives together are the white lies. They are the defibrillators that bring us back when we were on the brink of succumbing to the light.

As I lie in my four-poster mahogany bed with the giant canopy, the one I made love to my husband in for decades, I raise myself onto my elbows and study his features across the room as the moonbeams stream through the crack in the curtains, pouring into the open, snoring mouth, revealing the secret that the teeth seen in the daylight are only another ruse, that time has taken yet another one of my husband's rights; the confinement to the hospital bed is not the only indignity.

He startles awake and, as so often happens in the middle of the night, turns his head from side to side, almost frantically, searching for me, the one who has been beside him since he was scarcely more than a boy. It is a clear reminder that, though I have always perceived myself as completely dependent on him, the leaning goes both ways.

"Lovey," he says, in his almost devastatingly lucid middle-of-the-night voice.

"Yes, my darling."

"Can I get you anything?"

I smile the heartbreaking smile of a master who knows she should put the dog down, allow it some peace. But the bile soars at the thought of him being gone from me, and I steel myself once again. "Not a thing, sweetheart. Are you all right?"

"As long as you're here, I'm perfect."

As he settles back down to sleep, to the snoring that is my morning rainfall, I remember the last time he whispered that in my ear, only days before the stroke, as we danced slow and close in the kitchen after a nightcap on the patio.

Short-term memories, I remind myself, not letting my mind wander back to those early years together, to the days we met, to the nights I knew I'd found my true love. Living in the past, I've always thought, is a sign of dementia. Slipping into those old memories, dwelling on the "what was" instead of the "what could be" means that it's almost over. And so I will myself to stay in the here and now, though it becomes harder and harder.

Tomorrow, I remind myself, *we have an appointment with that new neurologist. He'll have some answers. He'll have a cure.*

And as I relax back into a pile of down pillows, the thought, though I have willed it not to, crosses my mind: The lies that matter most are the ones we tell ourselves.

Annabelle

∽

Fanfare

My Lovey is the one who gave me my name. Annabelle. When she gave birth to my oldest aunt, the first of five daughters, she received Tasha Tudor's *A is for Annabelle* as a gift. She had dreams of petticoats and pantaloons and parasols and all of those other prissy "p's" that a woman dreams she might lose herself in when she is expecting her first child, those fantasies that can only ensue before one has experienced the realities of spit-up and cloth diapers and sleep deprivation of levels that boggle the mind. It became apparent five daughters later that the Annabelle in the story really was nothing more than a beautiful china doll, a representation of something that didn't exist in her hair-pulling, clothes-stealing, fighting-over-the-bathroom home.

But when I was born, all of that was going to change, thought my grandmother. I was a bit of a miracle baby, the result of a lot of prayer and some rather primitive, cost-prohibitive fertility treatments. So, this time, Lovey had those Tasha Tudor dreams all over again with a granddaughter that could be free from the burden of sibling rivalry. Lovey dressing me in the finest, most impractical fashion and saying, "'A' is for Annabelle, Grandmother's doll," is my earliest childhood memory.

I was telling my husband Ben all of this, lying beside him in our bed at Lovey and D-daddy's beach house.

Instead of responding, he turned his head, smiled and said, "We have to get a boat."

It was the same thing Ben had said to me every single morning of the beach trip, as we woke, the sun bathing wood-paneled walls, its shadow stretching and spreading like a dog after a nap. I turned over and kissed the rippled chest of my—unbelievably—*husband.*

He was so good-looking, so romantic, so unnaturally calm that I couldn't be ruffled by his only flaw, which is a flaw pretty much anyone would possess: A week with my extended family in my grandparents' oceanfront Atlantic Beach, North Carolina, home is too much for the man to take. Since Lovey, headstrong as ever, had insisted on veering into the storm, we decided we would all go. Mom, Dad, Lovey, D-daddy, Ben, and Mom's four sisters. We had visions of giggling over Pictionary in the candlelight. But, as so often happens, the storm passed right over with little fanfare, and we were left with a gloriously beautiful week of lounging.

I kissed Ben and said, "Take that gig you were offered in Raleigh. Nothing is keeping you here."

He smiled, revealing the dimples that lured me to him in the first place. "Not true. *You* are keeping me here. I'm afraid if I leave you hanging around the Shoals Club in that bikini one of the frat-boy bartenders will pick you up." He raised his eyebrows and pulled me in for a kiss that meant he had more than just kissing on his mind.

"So, TL," Ben said, using the "true love" initials that he had given to me the night we met. "Where do we stand on that boat?"

I swept my hair into a ponytail, my feet thudding on the hardwood floor, gritty with sand. I laughed, gave my husband a quick kiss and said, "Get a little rest. You deserve it."

I trotted down the bare hardwood steps. I had been coming to this house for so long that, in my mind, I could already see D-daddy sitting in his chair at the head of the table, buttering his toast. It must have been from the early morning that my brain was foggy because, when I got to the landing, where I could see the dining table below, his wheelchair pulled to the end, a uniformed nurse feeding him his cereal and wiping the milk drips with a bib, my breath caught in my throat.

Somehow, in the relaxation of vacation, I had forgotten about the reality of the present.

"Hi, Annie," my aunt Louise practically sang. She was sipping hot tea, sitting in a cane-back dining chair, her feet propped on a ladder-back one. The mismatched seats, collected from antique auctions over the decades, were one of my favorite things about the house. Louise's tan skin looked even darker against the raw wood paneling of the wall behind her. She was already in her bikini with a crocheted cover-up over top and, even from a distance, you could tell her body was perfectly sculpted underneath. "It's just because I never had babies," Louise would say, brushing aside the fact that, at fifty-three, she could still pull off the look better than most teenagers. She was a yoga instructor through and through, from her body to her soothing voice to her calm demeanor. It was amazing how different five sisters could be.

"Where's your suit?" she asked, glancing me up and down in my flannel pajamas with the multicolored polka dots. It was not my normal nighttime attire but perfect for the beach. In direct contrast to most older people, Lovey cranked the AC to sixty-five and nearly froze us all to death.

"I just wanted to run down and see what everyone was up to before I changed."

Lovey strolled in, mug in hand, looking so much like she had since I was a child that I forgot she was in her late eighties, not the same sixty-year-old woman she had been when I started coming here. I descended those final two stairs and leaned down to kiss Lovey on the cheek. Telescoping out from underneath her bathing suit cover-up were the legs that she said self-tanner made young again. I silently wished for her genes, free from the puckered, rippled skin of old age, as she said, "Get dressed, darling. We're going to the club. If we don't get there early, we'll never get an umbrella on the beach."

I kissed D-daddy on the cheek, the skin that was once taut on his robust, healthy frame now sagging and tired. I ignored the glassy look in his eyes, the thought that maybe he didn't know who I was. "Thanks so much for having us, D-daddy," I said brightly. "We're having the best time!"

"You're welcome," he said, nodding, still not making eye contact with me.

Forty minutes later, Ben in tow, we had managed to get the entire crew out to the beach. Ben was laughing as Lovey said, "Sally, he may be a millionaire now, but I'm still glad you didn't marry him. I never trusted that boy."

My aunt Sally, her blond hair held back with bobby pins, raised the eyebrows above her bright blue eyes at me and said, "Momma, I am certainly glad Doug isn't here to hear you say that."

"Why shouldn't I?" Lovey asked, her voice getting high and indignant, showing that spark that was my favorite thing about her. "I would think your husband would be happy to know that I'm glad you married him instead of Kyle Jenkins."

"Hey," I said. "Why isn't Doug here?" Sally was the breadwinner of her family and Doug hadn't worked in decades, so I knew his job wasn't the reason he couldn't come down for the week.

"Oh," she said. "Well, he just had some things to get done. It was kind of last minute after all."

"Ohhhh," Mom chimed in. "Didn't want to be here with all of us?"

"What?" Dad asked, feigning confusion. "I can't imagine why this wouldn't be Doug's dream vacation."

I smiled at my dad, even though he couldn't see me with his shirt over his face, his olive skin already darker from a couple of hours in the sun. He was holding my mom's hand, and they were as relaxed as I had seen them in months. Mom usually had a phone and an iPad attached to her, ready to attend to municipal business at a moment's notice. From pampered housewife to full-time city runner must have been a serious leap. But, as anyone who knew her could plainly see, this role was made for her.

Ben patted my hand, and I smiled at him, almost dozing underneath the huge umbrella that now ensconced most of my family.

"Where is that cute waiter?" Lovey said, looking around for anyone in khaki shorts and a white polo with the club's red insignia.

"You don't need one of them, Lovey," Ben said. "You've got me now." He winked at her, squeezed my knee and said, "Anyone want anything?"

I swung my legs over the side of the blue lounge chair and said, "I'll come with you."

"Waters all around," Lovey said. "Forty-six minutes until it's time for a little noon cocktail."

Ben and I held hands walking up the sand and then leaned against the weathered teak outdoor bar. He said, looking around, "Doesn't this place sort of remind you of *Dirty Dancing*?"

I shrugged. The morning tennis, afternoon swims and late-night band parties did seem a little like a throwback, something that surely didn't exist in reality anymore. But here it was, parents moving their kids to the beach for the summer for surf lessons and sea turtle camp, forging friendships that would last a lifetime. Maybe it was because it was how I grew up, but it all seemed a little enchanted to me. Down here, even as a kid, there was a sense of freedom and safety that was so hard to find in a world that seemed to be becoming scarier and less predictable by the minute.

"Nobody puts Baby in a corner," I said, smiling.

"I just can't imagine staying in a place like this all summer," Ben said. "Seems like kind of a snobby, unrealistic way to raise your children."

I felt my forehead wrinkle. I had always figured that I would spend my summers at the beach like my family had, raise my children on this same strip of sand that had raised me. "I guess it isn't the real world, but I think it's amazing to get to have this time that's so carefree."

Before I could elaborate, I felt a finger on my shoulder. I turned my head and hoped that my gasp wasn't audible.

I hadn't laid eyes on Holden Culpepper since the night I stormed out of his car more than a year earlier. In that instant, our entire past flashed before me, like the building was collapsing and I knew I was trapped. That completely forgettable face, with the mousy brown hair that was thick but somehow fell short of luscious or beautiful, was peering at me. It was like looking at a man come back from the dead. I couldn't remember the last time I'd even thought about him.

Oddly, the first thing he said to me, before we could even exchange hellos, was "Do you remember the night we met?"

I backed up nearly imperceptibly, afraid of where the conversation was going. But I remembered anyway. I was a freshman and he was a senior when I spotted Holden alone in the corner of a crowded fraternity house, music blaring, strobes flashing and smoke of every imaginable kind mingling through the orgy of dancers.

"That's Holden Culpepper," my big sister in the sorority had whispered, stumbling on grass-stained, five-inch heels. She was one of those girls that bleached her hair so the dark roots always showed through, the kind of girl that you knew would still be smoking a pack a day, stumbling drunk down the sidewalk at forty, while ruminating—loudly—that she hadn't found a husband up to her impossible standards.

"You know, his dad's the Culpepper Fund." Then she leaned in closer and, with her thick breath, said, "Apparently Holden's worth five million dollars already—and he's only twenty-one."

Casey would have been going after Holden herself, but she was already taken. She was dating her fraternity-president cocaine dealer, Jack, who was tall, dark, handsome and one hell of a dancer. "I like a self-made man," she used to say. I could always picture Jack's face on the front page of a newspaper, when he was all grown up, a captain of enterprise with a magazine-spread family, being dragged away to white-collar prison by his perky bow tie.

Holden, on the other hand, was precisely the kind of man a mother dreams her daughter will marry. Type A, straitlaced and possessing the kind of trust fund that generally only appears in *Town*

& Country. And he had been what I wanted. When I had been that superficial college girl, enamored of money and appearances, Holden was exactly the kind of catch I was looking to hook.

Coming out of my memory and back into the present, I squinted at Holden, realizing his question was still hanging there, the last summer item on the sale rack. "Sure." I shrugged.

"Well, you were right," he said.

"Right about what?"

"White lighters."

I smiled in spite of myself. I had walked to Holden that night and leaned beside him on a nonfunctioning radiator. I crossed my arms, looked down at his hands and sparked my lighter to the end of the cigarette hanging between his lips. He smiled out of one corner of his mouth and said, "Isn't that supposed to go the other way around?"

I had shrugged and leaned in close enough that my bare shoulder brushed his blue-and-white-checked one. He was wearing my favorite combination: neat khaki shorts with an oxford, Gucci loafers and a monogrammed belt buckle.

"I guess it should," I said. "But I looked over and saw what you were about to do, and I didn't want you to be cursed."

He looked confused, which made me notice a small scar over his eyebrow that lent his face something distinct. "White lighters," I said. "Don't you know they're bad luck?"

I had thought I was completely in control of that conversation until the moment he stunned me, saying, "White lighter or no, seems like this night has been pretty lucky for me."

"So why," I asked Holden, snapping back into the clear sunshine of the present, "was that white lighter bad luck for you?"

"I didn't catch a single fish today." He smiled nervously.

I couldn't decide if I was more pleased or confused by this

conversation. I would have imagined that Holden hated me, that he wished we'd never even met. But here he was, pleasant and joking, remembering with a smile what had transpired between us.

"Thanks for getting—well, you know—back to my mom."

I nodded. "Right," I stammered. "Well, it wasn't right to keep the ring."

The ring—the five-carat art deco family heirloom—was what Holden gave me, down on one knee at Jost Van Dyke, in the midst of one of the most famous New Year's parties in the world. The glow of the lights from hundreds of boats crammed into the tiny harbor was almost as intoxicating as the rum punch or Kenny Chesney's sweet voice on stage—an impromptu surprise from the star who was just a partygoer like everyone else that night.

It was a glorious beginning to what turned out to be a tepid engagement. Squinting at Ben's back as he ordered, I realized that Holden was talking again, and, already, I wasn't listening to what he was saying.

It was such a reminder of life with Holden after he had graduated from MBA school and the party was officially over. Every sentence out of his mouth started and ended with something about work or the market or a pain-in-the-ass client. I hadn't seen him in more than a year, and it seemed like pretty much nothing had changed. When he started ditching our plans and all of our friends because he was working almost every weekend, that was the last straw. I had begun to feel as though the dress had appeared much more glamorous on the runway than in real life. Or maybe it just didn't look as good on me as it did on the model.

That last night, heading down a Charlotte, North Carolina, highway on our way to his parents' for dinner, I had spent my day at inane cake tastings, dress fittings, florist appointments and, in short, had had just about enough. As he blabbed on and on and on about mutual fund performance, I said, "Your cruise control isn't working."

"Of course it's working," he said. "It's a brand-new Range Rover, for God's sake. You just hit this button." He leaned over me to instruct.

"I *know* how to do it," I snapped. "I've driven your car a hundred times."

"Well then hit the brake and try again."

I hit the brake, accelerated, and punched the button. The cruise control snapped into place, and, just as quickly as it had set, went loose again. I glared at Holden to show him my annoyance.

"You must have hit the brake," Holden said.

I don't know what it was about that exact moment that made me completely lose control. But the real issues in a couple's relationship are rarely the ones they fight about. It's the insignificant arguments masking the problems, piling on top of each other, gathering like raindrops that, combined together, finally cause the dam to burst. I zoomed toward the exit, flipped around on the overpass, and, before he even knew what was happening, was back at my house, slamming the door behind me. Holden rolled the window down. "Annabelle, what in the hell is the matter with you?"

I spun around and hissed back at him, "I didn't hit the damn brake."

That was pretty much the last thing I had said to Holden. Until now. "Well I'm glad to hear that work is going well," I said.

Ben turned around about that time, his hands full of six drinks. "Hey, babe," he said, furrowing his brow in concentration, trying to juggle all those plastic cups, completely unaware that he was about to come face-to-face with my ex-fiancé for the first time.

"Holden," I said, "this is Ben."

Ben gestured toward the cups. "I would shake your hand but——"

Before he could finish the sentence, Holden took a swing right at Ben's face. As Ben lost his balance, all six of those drinks went straight up in the air, raining down on the patrons of the crowded bar. I heard the general unhappy rumble as I felt my eyes widening and my hand come to my mouth. I glanced over my shoulder, surveying the damage, and saw Lovey laughing like she was reconnecting with old friends. I wanted to be horrified and indignant, but, when I saw Lovey laughing, that incredible, joyous laugh that takes over her entire body, I started too.

Ben shrugged his shoulders—he wasn't the kind of person to get ruffled easily—and said, "Dude?"

"You could at least have the decency to fall down," Holden shouted, drawing every eye in the place toward him.

I wanted to walk the twenty feet to the edge of the sparkling pool, dive in, and stay underwater until everyone had gone home for the night and had enough to drink that they had forgotten about this scene.

"I'm sorry?" Ben asked. "Did I do something to you? Do I know you?"

"You stole my wife, you prick."

Holden was quieter now, but still seething with anger like I'd never seen him. *That* was what I had been looking for when we were together. A little emotion. I wanted someone to get worked up over me—at least as much as he got worked up over the prime rate.

"I think you must be confused," Ben said. "I'm married to Annabelle."

Holden looked at me incredulously. "Yeah. I'm aware of that," he said. "And I'm *supposed* to be married to Annabelle." I'm sure Holden was wondering how our relationship could have meant so little to me that my husband didn't even recognize his name. Truth be told, I was wondering the same thing.

I glanced at Lovey out of the corner of my eye, now recounting the story to Mom, Lauren, Sally, Martha and Louise. They all started laughing, and, though I didn't want to, I joined them. I saw Holden walk to my grandmother and kiss her on the cheek. "Sorry, Lovey," I barely heard him mumble under his breath.

"It's all right, darling," she replied. "She's worth fighting for."

"It is not all right," my mother said through gritted teeth. I knew she would be mortified over the public humiliation. At least we were out of town, where the effect on her latest polls would be minimal.

"Boys will be boys," Lovey said.

"I'm so sorry," I said to Ben as Holden walked away. I put my hand up tenderly to his red cheek.

The bartender handed Ben a cup of ice, and he held it to his swollen eye. I was holding my breath, waiting for Ben to say something, knowing he must be angry. But then I started laughing all over again. "This would never have happened," Ben said, smiling as best he could with his frozen cheek, "if you had let me get a boat."

I rolled my eyes and felt myself exhale. He wasn't mad. Lovey walked over and said, "Well, Ben, I guess you and Dan have more in common than we could have imagined."

"How's that?" he asked.

"You are both willing to fight for the woman you love." She winked at him.

He smiled and said, "I was trying to keep it together so I didn't embarrass you. But if I'd known that's how you felt about it, I would have given him a fight that he'd never forget."

I leaned into Ben's side and said, "There's nothing to fight about. You've already won."

I looked at Lovey, expecting her to say something. But she had that faraway look in her eye, the one that was becoming increasingly familiar. I understood her reasons—no matter how silly they might have seemed to others—for not wanting to dwell on the past. But, even still, though she might not have talked about her memories, I could tell that now, more and more, Lovey was with us in body. But her mind was wandering to a happier time, with D-daddy, when life was simpler and the world was a little less of a fight.

Lovey

ℰℓℴ

Proper or Fitting

April 1945

Spring is so beautiful because that's when our Lord rose from the dead. From then on, Momma said, God made the chicks hatch and the birds chirp and those azaleas all around the church burst into bloom to remind us of the Resurrection.

That must be why spring has always been my favorite season in Bath. Walking barefoot down the dusty dirt road to my white clapboard church, sitting cross-legged by the river, dreaming about falling in love. I'd been in love once. Well, Momma said it was puppy love. I was just a little girl, she'd said, too young to know what real love was. I *had* been just a girl, far from the woman of nineteen that I was now. But I knew what it was to feel like every day was the first day of spring. The boy that made me feel that way might have moved away when his daddy was transferred to another parish. But I knew I'd always hold him in my memory, he'd be the yardstick against which I'd measure any other. No matter how far and wide the world took me, I'd never let him out of my heart.

Of course, the world hadn't flung me too far and wide yet. I'd never even left North Carolina, and I'd scarcely been out of the county. Daddy was a small-town farmer through and through, and, by all accounts, he expected me to marry a boot-wearing, tractor-driving vestige of himself who could take over the tobacco business.

But, from the time I was small enough to sit on his lap, dozing on his chest between stories about the trouble he got into on this, the very land he grew up on, I knew that I was destined for bigger things. I grabbed every last opportunity like a momma does a child too near the stairs, gripping it tight as I could so it couldn't slip away from me.

So, when I heard Daddy telling Momma over coffee, before they knew I was awake, "What sorta fool would let his daughter have her pictures taken like that? Splattered all over the newspaper for the world to see like some sorta harlot," my interest was piqued.

I peered around the corner, inhaling the smell of fresh bacon and coffee that had floated all the way to the tip-top of the fifteen-foot ceilings in my bedroom, just in time to see Momma shake her head. "I'd never let my Lynn do something like that. Doesn't seem proper or fitting."

How a large cosmetics company chose a backwoods map dot that no one had ever heard of as one of the towns where it would host a makeover contest, I'll never know. But it wasn't really my business to find out. All I knew was that it was advertised right there smack in the middle of the front page of that paper. I'd never in my life counted on being pretty to buy my bus ticket out of town. But I sure wasn't above trying it.

I'd never dreamed, like some girls do, of becoming a glamorous movie star, of seeing my picture on the cover of a magazine or flashing across a big screen. But when Daddy whistled and said, "Three whole weeks in New York City for the winner," my ears perked right up.

New York was a concept so foreign, such a bright and shining pinnacle, that I could scarcely imagine what being there might be like. I didn't even stop by the breakfast table for my toast that morning. I said, "Morning, Daddy. Morning, Momma," and skipped right out that kitchen door, the screen slamming behind me in the soothing cadence of near summertime.

I ran down the dusty street, barefoot as could be, totally outta breath, until I got to Katie Jo's house. Katie Jo was my best friend, and, for every buttoned-up, straitlaced, rule-following thing I did, Katie Jo did the most eye-widening, unladylike, derelict thing you could conceive. She smoked cigarettes and swished whiskey and did things with boys that made me blush just hearing about them. I liked living vicariously through her, imagining myself being that free.

Her vibrancy, the way she loved living her life, made her beautiful to me. So, when she came to the front door, her blunt, cropped hair with the split ends, her wide-set eyes and general tomboy appearance caught me by surprise. They weren't the features of great models by any stretch of the imagination. But, nevertheless, I exhaled, "They're having a modeling contest at Town Hall tomorrow. We have to go!"

Katie Jo sat down on a rocker on the front porch, and I sat down beside her. "Sweetie pie," she said, putting her fingernail up to her mouth, "I don't know if you've noticed, but—how should I say this?— I don't photograph so well."

I smiled. "Well, they're giving makeovers first, silly." I gave her my most enthusiastic grin, using the tone she was always using to trick me into one of her schemes. "Come on, Katie Jo! You gonna let something little like makeup keep you from getting to go to New York for three whole weeks?"

"New York City?"

I nodded, that grin popping up on my face like the daffodils on the first warm day. Wasn't a thing in this world I could do to stop it.

Katie Jo pumped her fist like those Rosie the Riveter posters down at the post office and said, "Well then, let's get our faces painted and our hair curled!"

The next morning, I snuck out before the sun. I'd told Momma and Daddy the night before that Katie Jo and I were going to take the bus to New Bern to catch a matinee. There was no point in getting them all worked up about this contest if nothing was going to come of it. Which it almost certainly wasn't. Katie Jo was waiting at the end of the dirt road. When she saw me, she started singing, "New York, New York, a helluva town, the Bronx is up, but the Battery's down . . ."

There'd been talk about changing the curse word in the song but I think it felt sweet coming off Katie Jo's lips, like the muscadine wine her grandmomma made in those big oak barrels in the tractor barn.

"There's no censoring you, is there, Katie Jo?"

She whistled. "There's no censoring you either. Pretty thing like you, you're gonna win for sure!"

Looking back, I know good as gold I was the poorest hick that crew had ever seen standing in that line—doesn't matter that by Bath standards we were right well off. They put me in a chair and applied my makeup and curled my hair and stood me in front of a man with a camera. I'd never had my picture taken by a professional before. Daddy had gotten Momma a Kodak 35, with Kodachrome film and all, so she could take a photo on Easter and Christmas. But that was only for special occasions. I tried to act comfortable, mimicking the laid-back way I'd seen the actresses smile and bat their eyelashes.

"You're a natural!" the photographer called, right before he shouted, "Next!"

The only thing I knew I was a natural at was picking corn, so I didn't give the contest a whole lot more thought. A month later, standing at the mailbox, the cool air starting to turn to the creeping warmth that, in another month, would scald, the mosquitoes could have flown right in my mouth it was hanging open so wide. *I'll have to get them to teach me how to put on all this new makeup I won*, was my very first thought. It was a ridiculous idea, that one, completely beside the point. I knew standing at that mailbox that there wasn't any way on God's green earth my daddy was letting me tear off to New York City of all places by myself.

All the same, I had never won anything in my life besides the English award. And it was like Edison discovering electricity. The light was on. And I didn't ever want to go back to the dark.

When my daddy got home that night, dirt under his fingernails and overalls covered with dusty straw and manure, I handed him the letter.

He curled his fist and said, "If you think I'm letting my nineteen-year-old daughter fly in some tin can across the country and fall in love with a damn Yankee, you've got another think coming."

"It's not across the country, Daddy," I replied. I had suddenly, in the moments after winning the contest, gone from a high school–educated farm girl to a worldly socialite. "It's just a couple of states away."

"I don't care where it is," Momma said, her voice high and tight, "you're not going."

"That's final," Daddy added.

I guess, looking back now, that burying my brother so young and losing those two babies she tried to carry afterward made Momma and Daddy cling to my older sister and me a little tighter than some other parents. It had changed things for me too. I had longed for a sibling to grow up with, but Lib was already eleven by the time I was born. I would see the other kids with their brothers and sisters, playing and running. And I'd beg Lib to play with me too. By the time I was old enough to be of any interest to her whatsoever, Lib was already off at Women's College. It broke Momma and Daddy's hearts that she was leaving them, leaving Bath, going out to make a bigger life for herself.

I'll never forget my momma and daddy's faces the day Lib came home and told them she was moving to London. "He's my husband," she was saying, bordering on hysteria, when I walked through the door from school. "This is the chance of a lifetime for him. Reporting on the *war*? This is something that country folks like us don't get to do."

Momma and Daddy were sitting across from Lib at our wooden kitchen table, Momma leaning on Daddy, sobbing into his chest. "She'll never make it back," she was saying over and over again.

Daddy didn't say a word, but you could tell by his eyes that he was terrified. I, on the other hand, thought Lib was impossibly brave. She was going to go off and have an adventure. She was going to a war, in another country. This was what living was all about. I didn't realize yet the supreme danger that she would be in. I didn't know what was happening in London. I didn't know how her days would consist of praying that she and her sons and her husband would make it through another night.

But I knew how Momma cried when she got those letters from

Lib. And I knew how she cried even harder on the days those letters didn't come. And I knew Momma and Daddy's tightening grip on me was palpable, almost suffocating.

I blamed my sister that day. Why couldn't she have stayed home with Momma and Daddy? Why did she have to be the one to go off? If she had stayed, maybe they would have let me have a life for myself.

I was too young to understand my parents. Too young to sympathize. I only thought they were trying to keep me from being happy by keeping me at home. And I had some living and some mistake making in me.

So I did what anyone in my position would do. I grabbed all the money I'd saved from under my feather mattress, packed my curlers, my best pumps and a few clean pairs of cotton underwear, the ones with the little line of lace trim around the top, and climbed down the drain spout before the sun came out. I left a note, just in case it wasn't obvious right off where I'd gone. My intention was not to kill my poor parents with grief and worry. I just kept thinking about Katie Jo. She wouldn't let a silly little thing like a "no" from her parents let her miss out on the trip of a lifetime. I was making my own decisions for a change.

With the gas and rubber rations, Momma and Daddy couldn't have driven to find me even if they'd wanted. And they would've had to dig up all those mason jars of cash buried around the yard to have bought plane tickets to follow me. And so, for the next three weeks, until I came home and they chained me to the fence post, I was going to be my own woman.

In 1945, the Waldorf Astoria was glorious. It was heaven on earth. Movie stars and presidents floated down the halls in the finest fashions, ate off of gold-rimmed china and danced to the best orchestras in the world. But I didn't know all that. I'd only ever seen Mrs. Bonner's boardinghouse in Bath with the one shared bathroom and the migrant workers in for picking season stealing a few hours of gritty sleep before getting back to it.

So those flyers with the black-and-white sketches couldn't have prepared me for walking into one of the grandest lobbies in the world. The Waldorf even smelled rich. Like perfume, flowers and hundred-dollar bills. My hair curled like Ginger Rogers's, with soft skin, full lips and the petite figure that youth allows, I didn't quite look like New York City high society. But I'd been primped, dressed, primed and educated by my chaperone, which was nearly as good.

"Your dinner is waiting in the dining room, Miss Hensley," the man behind the counter in the freshly pressed suit said. "Allow me to escort you."

I was so busy taking in the marble lobby and the women flitting about in sequined gowns that I hardly even noticed the orchestra playing and the couples dancing merrily. I grew up on a farm eating butterbeans and pork chops, so to slide my pristine pumps underneath a white tablecloth and eat lobster thermidor and foie gras, crown of strawberries and Key West turtle soup . . . No words do it justice.

In the midst of the finest food I'd ever tasted, I could tell a commotion of sorts was beginning. But I figured what I considered an excited rumble might be ordinary in New York City.

As all the diners started running for the lobby, my heart dropped into my stomach because there was no arguing that something was wrong. And I had the horrifying thought that the last thing I would ever do to my parents was disobey them.

Annabelle

∞

Fading into Him

True love is something you have to fight for. Lovey has been telling me that since I was a little girl. Sometimes you fight harder, and sometimes the person you love fights harder but, whatever the circumstances, if it isn't a love worth fighting for, it isn't worth having.

I realized that Holden still thought we were worth fighting for, as Ben said, "So you want to give me a little insight as to why I was punched out today?" Ben was lounging on our bed, towel around his waist, a frozen New York strip over his eye.

I grinned coquettishly, hoping he wouldn't be angry with me, though, truth be told, he was very seldom angry. "I just wanted you to have a little excitement in your trip is all. I hired that actor to shake things up."

Ben raised one eyebrow. "Uh-huh. Right."

"Well, you knew I was engaged. That was my engagee."

"That's all?"

I wanted to say something more, but in truth, there was nothing more to say. "Those sentences literally just summed up our relationship." I crawled up onto the bed, straddling Ben's waist and rubbing his chest. "It was nothing like us."

I wouldn't say that I fell in love with Ben so much as he consumed me. From the very first moment I laid eyes on him, I began fading into him, staining his skin with mine like new denim on a white cotton T-shirt in the wash.

He smiled and looked at me with that adoring smile. "TL," he said, "you are stupid beautiful."

I rolled my eyes and shook my head, leaning over to kiss him.

He exhaled deeply and said, "So, I have kind of a big question."

"Yes!" I exclaimed. "I'll marry you!"

He smiled. "How would you feel about moving to Salisbury?"

Salisbury was Ben's hometown, where his parents still lived. It was quaint and charming. But you didn't have to be a real estate agent to realize that quaint and charming equated to small. It meant settling down and living a regular life.

"Um," I started, not quite knowing how I felt but fully aware that I had taken vows that necessitated following my husband's passions, however crazy they seemed. "I thought you wanted to go on tour for another year."

I had never planned on going on tour. I had never planned on marrying a musician. And I had certainly never planned on living in an RV. Hell, I'd never planned on stepping foot in one. But I had done it.

In less than a week after I met Ben, I had gone from a swanky condo-owning woman engaged to a very eligible bachelor to a married, jobless groupie living in an RV. And I had never been happier.

I had always been the responsible one. I drove my drunken friends to parties and always went to class. I made good grades, accepted invitations from suitable boys and had a fractional share of the sexual activity of even my most prudish friends. So maybe that's why my time came all at once like that.

When I look back on my life, I think I'll always remember those months living in the back of that RV with fondness. Ben and I would lie there at night, his head on my stomach. "Oh I can't wait until there's a little Benabelle in there," he would say. Then he would look up at me anxiously. "Do you think?"

I would have been a young mother, much younger than I had ever imagined. But I was so swept up in that breathtaking love that the only thing that could possibly make it better was for another human being to come out of it. It's so unlike me, but I never once worried about raising a baby in an RV. That was the effect Ben had on me. For the first time in my life, I was glass half full. I knew it would all work out.

That's when Ben said, "I did want to go on tour for another year. But my dad needs me at the firm."

"Really?" Ben and his father were both CPAs, a totally strange job for my hippy-dippy, adventure-loving husband. But his idiosyncrasies were probably my favorite thing about him. "Doesn't he have like two other partners?"

"Three actually. But . . ." He trailed off. "But, it's bad."

I could feel my eyes widen as I got out of bed and arranged the sheets into some semblance of a made-up fashion. "Is someone sick or something?"

He cocked his head to the side.

I rolled my eyes. "Just spit it out." Then I put my hand to my mouth. "Oh, God. Your dad's not sick, is he?"

Ben ventured a smile. "No, no. It's just that one of his partners is on trial."

"Tax evasion?"

"They wish. Drug trafficking."

I felt myself wince. "Yikes."

Ben nodded. "Yeah. So he's probably going to lose his license, and Dad needs someone to work and something to boost the firm's morale and reputation in town."

I smiled broadly, putting my finger in my dimple. "So, like, the prodigal son and his blushing bride?"

Ben grabbed my arm and pulled me back into bed, kissing me passionately. "A new grandchild probably wouldn't hurt either."

When I walked downstairs later for a snack, I got the distinct impression that the rest of my family wasn't having as good an afternoon as I was. D-daddy was in his wheelchair, raising a banana to his mouth with a trembling hand, staring out the window toward the ocean. Usually when I saw him, I wondered what was going on in his head, if he was thinking or remembering, if he knew where he was. But, that afternoon, looking into his blank face, something inside me just knew he was gone.

Louise, Sally, Lauren, Martha and Mom were sitting around the table in their gym shorts and socks, hair wet from showers, while Lovey was sipping coffee, lipstick on, looking fresh and rested.

Louise was saying, "But if I have to go on another blind date, I'll absolutely lose my mind. Can't people just accept that I'm fifty-three and single? It's not a disease."

Lauren laughed, her green eyes sparkling, smoothed her blond hair back into a ponytail, and said, "That's good for you, but I could *never* be happy without a man." I realized that something felt off, like a dress that shrunk just the tiniest bit in the dryer. You could still wear it, but it didn't lie quite right.

Mom was saying, "Well, then we better get dressed and start cruising for men—" when I interrupted.

"What's going on in here?"

"What do you mean?" Mom asked in that strained, high, faux-happy voice she uses when she's trying to hide something.

"Oh, forget it," Lovey said. "Darling, I'm moving to assisted living."

She said it proudly, distinctly, with her head held high.

Sally's eyes filled with tears.

"Momma," Lauren said. "I still say you're plenty healthy, and you don't need to leave your home where you're comfortable."

The tears were running down Sally's face now.

"Stop it right now, you two," Mom scolded. "If she's ready to be out of that house, then she's ready to be out of the house."

"Yeah," Louise chimed in. "It's just a house." She turned to Lovey. "Besides, Momma, I hear that assisted living facilities are basically country clubs now."

"Oh my gosh!" Sally exclaimed through the tears. "You aren't getting rid of this house too, are you?"

"Honey," Lovey said, "you're making me feel terrible."

"No!" Martha exclaimed, shaking her head furiously, the sun reflecting off of her shiny jet-black hair.

Lovey shook her head. "I'm not selling the beach house."

I still hadn't said anything. But to say that some of the best memories of my life had happened around Lovey and D-daddy's breakfast room table wasn't an exaggeration. Those long talks with the women of my family, popping Hershey's Kisses into our mouths, had shaped so much of my growing. I thought of my room at Lovey's house, the twin bed where I'd snuggled under the duvet while she recited bedtime stories by heart. And the way her house smelled . . . Even though she never hung her laundry on the line to dry, her linen closet smelled like what I imagined sunshine must.

But, in the past several years, that house had changed for me. I'd walk in now and see D-daddy, confined to his chair in the dark living room, the TV dancing with movies that he loved as a young soldier, and nurses milling around bringing medicine, feeding him juice, checking his blood pressure. I wanted to pretend things were the same as always. But there was no mistaking that old age permeated.

Ben walked down the stairs, that steak still in his hand. As he reached the bottom step and smiled to say hello to us, he looked at the faces of my aunts and mom, pointed back upstairs, and said, "I don't think I got enough of a nap."

"Don't be ridiculous!" Lovey said. "You're family now, for better or worse." She sighed. "I'm just telling the girls that I think it's time for Dan and me to move to assisted living and sell the house."

Ben pulled out a chair and sat down beside me like this conversation was crucial to his future. "You can't sell the house!" Ben chimed in.

I glared at him, completely thrown by the unsolicited opinion.

"One of the best memories of my life is in that house," he said.

Mom laughed. "What are you talking about?"

"It was the first place Ann and I told anyone we were married."

Lovey smiled. "There are scandals and then there are *scandals*. When your granddaughter dumps her hedge fund manager fiancé and marries a musician she has known three days, that would fall into the category of the latter." She glanced over at Ben, who was laughing. "No offense."

He squeezed D-daddy's shoulder. D-daddy looked at him blankly, and I wondered if he knew who this man was sitting beside him at the breakfast table. "Do you remember what you said?" he asked D-daddy.

"What he *said*?" Louise asked skeptically.

Lovey laughed. "Well, sort of. He said, 'Mm.'"

Everyone around the table laughed, including D-daddy. That one-syllable grunt, maybe even more than his infectious laugh or quick wit, was the thing we all associated most with our grandfather and father. It meant he didn't approve of what you were doing, but he loved you, so he'd deal with it anyway.

"When she walked through my door holding the hand of a man I'd never seen, when we were all planning parties for her and Holden, I'd like to say I was confused," Lovey said. "But when you've been around eighty-seven years, there's not much left to confuse you." Lovey smiled adoringly at Ben. "But I loved you right off for how you talked to Dan and shook his hand and factored him into the equation."

Ben put his arm around me and pulled me close. I dropped my head on his shoulder, willing the tears not to come to my eyes, wishing that things could go back to the way they had been when I was little and D-daddy was so alive.

"I'd heard so much about him," Ben said. "I felt like I knew him already."

That rarely emerging voice piped up from the end of the table, shakily, but D-daddy's no doubt. "You couldn't have heard too much about me because I hadn't heard a damn thing about you."

Then D-daddy laughed and we all joined him.

"My thoughts exactly, Daddy," Mom chimed in, with a glee in her voice that only comes from D-daddy having a good day.

"But, Jean," Ben started, innocence in his voice, "you handled the news so beautifully."

"Oh, you weren't thrilled?" Lauren teased.

"All I said," Mom interjected, "was that we needed to have a wedding. I'm the mayor, for heaven's sake. People expect things from me."

That was the least of it. In reality, Mom had thrown a hissy fit like I'd never seen. The first words she said to my husband were, *You got married? You stole the privilege of having a wedding for my only daughter?*

"A wedding is a golden opportunity to get ahead in the polls," Martha said, laughing.

"And just think," Lauren said, looking at Ben. "That special day led to this special day." She pointed at Ben's now completely black eye, and we all laughed.

Ben looked down at me. "I'd take a million black eyes if it meant getting to be with you forever."

I smiled at him. "Well," I said, "good memories aside, I think wherever you feel most comfortable is where you should be, Lovey." I paused. "Where are you moving? Have you started looking for places yet?"

She waved her hand as if to say that this was a minor detail. "Well, there can't be more than a place or two that's even tolerable." She took a sip of the tea in front of her on the table. "Speaking of," Lovey said, "when are you two settling down and getting out of that RV?" Lovey shook her head. "It's rather unseemly."

I smiled at Ben. "Should we tell them?"

"Oh my God, you're pregnant!" Louise exclaimed.

I could feel that cloud unwillingly pass over me, but I smiled it away when Mom said, a panic-stricken look on her face, "She had three rum punches yesterday afternoon. I should hope not."

"No, no," Ben said, wrapping his arm around me tighter, knowing I would be upset from the baby comment. "You want to tell them?"

I smiled halfheartedly and, bracing myself for the reaction, said, "We're moving to Salisbury."

"Salisbury is a lovely town," Lovey said. But I could tell her mind was somewhere else.

Lovey always says that some things are out of our hands and that, if we're going to make it through this life, we'd do well to figure out what those things are.

"I think it's very mature of you to be so grown-up about your grandmother getting rid of her house," Ben said, as he crammed his shorts and T-shirt into my beach bag.

I shook my head. "It's only on the outside because, inside, I'm an absolute wreck." Then I shrugged, thinking of Lovey. "But, you know, there isn't anything I can do to change it, so it's probably best to just face it."

Ben wrapped me in that warm, sweet-smelling hug that had become my life preserver the past few months. "It's going to be okay, you know. It's going to be hard, but, at the end of the day, this is what's best for them. And we're all going to have to get on board."

I sighed. "I know." I kissed him, leaned back and said, "So, speaking of getting on board, when are we moving to Salisbury?"

Ben grinned. "What are you doing tomorrow?"

I rolled my eyes. "Then I need to get out of here immediately. I have some tanning to do."

I should have stayed pale. I should have suggested that we go ahead and leave the beach so we could get a head start on house hunting and unpacking.

On my way to the bathroom at the club that morning, I nearly turned around and walked the other direction when I saw Holden. But we were the only two people in the empty ballroom, so I couldn't very well act like I hadn't seen him. I ventured a wave and turned sharply to the right, like I was headed out to the terrace.

"Could we talk for a minute?" Holden called.

I looked around, as though he could possibly be talking to anyone else. I was going to say no. I was going to walk back out onto the beach where my family was telling old stories and attempting to skim board, wobbling and falling down like children learning to walk.

I was going to, that is, until Holden said, "Come on, Annabelle, I think you owe me."

He was right. I called off a wedding three years in the making with a thirty-second phone call and zero explanation. I owed him.

We walked inside the bar, chandeliers off and seating areas completely empty. I sat down on the couch, and he sat down right beside me. "Holden," I said. "Can't you sit across from me in the chair or something?"

If he heard me, he didn't let on. "Ann," he said, "I made a huge mistake letting you go. I want you back."

I laughed. "Holden, no offense, but I'm pretty sure I'm the one who let you go." I shook my head. "I'm *married*, for heaven's sake."

He snickered. "Please, Annabelle. You knew the guy for five minutes. Don't tell me you're happy with some washed-up, old musician."

I could feel the anger rising up my spine, vertebra by vertebra, as Louise would say. You could talk about me and you could talk about my choices. But when you talked about my *man*, things got dicey. I stood up, and I knew he could tell I was angry. "I've had enough of this. Maybe you should have been worried about me a little more when you had me." I wanted to walk away then, but I couldn't resist throwing one more jab before I turned. "Ben has the good sense to know how to hold on to what he has."

"I was immature and stupid, Annabelle. I've done a lot of growing up since then. I realize now that I should have treated you better."

I wanted to stomp away, but I stopped and turned back toward Holden, noticing that he was wearing the Vilbrequin bathing suit I had given him for his birthday my senior year. It was like knowing a bag of chocolates was in my pantry. I wanted to close the door and lock it away, but I couldn't resist finishing it.

"I should have fought for you then," Holden said. "But I was too ashamed. I let my pride take away the best thing that has ever happened to me."

I rolled my eyes, realizing it was difficult to look haughty in a somewhat sheer linen cover-up and flip-flops with bows on them. "This is never, ever going to happen, Holden, so I suggest you move on. It took meeting Ben to realize what I had been missing out on all this time."

It was a cold, callous statement, and, as soon as it came out of my mouth, I wished I could roll it back up like loose toilet paper. I wanted to say something more, to amend that horrible judgment, tell Holden that we did the best we could. But I knew that, in his mind, if the curtains were fluttering in the breeze, I needed to slam the window or it was going to come open again and again and again.

"He's going to hurt you, Annabelle," Holden called as I walked out of the empty bar. "Everyone thinks so."

I wanted to laugh indignantly, but the words pierced right through me, the spear he had thrown in retaliation for the arrow I shot. It was the first time I had considered what it might be like to be without Ben, how devastated, confused and completely alone I would be if he changed his mind. That was the benefit of being with someone like Holden. He was good on paper, decent husband material, and if it all went down the tubes, then, oh well. My attachment was minimal.

But to think about being without Ben was like losing my limbs. I loved him with a ferocity I'd never known before. I would look at him when we were lying in bed at night, him peacefully snoring beside me, and I would consider the fact that he was a good deal older. And I would start to panic. How would I ever live without him? How would the breath enter and leave my body if Ben wasn't there to regulate it?

And then I'd think of Lovey and D-daddy.

And I couldn't sleep a wink.

Lovey

♋

Bring Her Back Up

M y momma named me Lynn because it could be a boy's name or a girl's. She wanted me to grow up to do big things with my life, and she thought that having a name that could have been a boy's would make people take me more seriously.

But, it didn't much matter because, once Annabelle was born, she changed my name altogether. When she was a child, I used to say to her, "Oh, I love you," and, with those muddled little toddler syllables running together like they do, she would say back, "Oh, Lovey." From then on, that's what practically everyone called me.

I kept thinking of her as that tiny girl, sitting on the floor in the den at Dan's feet, playing with makeup in my bathroom, riding her bike around the front, circular driveway. The memories of this house were so pronounced for me, such a normal part of my daily routine, that I couldn't imagine being without them.

That's why saying you're going to move to assisted living and actually doing that same thing are very different matters. If I had ever been anything for my daughters, it was steadfast. I was brave and fearless. And if I wasn't, I never let it show. Maybe it was old age, the instability of it all, the loss of balance, the lack of memory, the persistent pain of the process of breaking down. Or perhaps it was removing the man who had made me feel invincible for all this time and throwing me into the river without so much as a float. But being alone in that house with him all night, every night, was the most terrifying experience I've ever had.

Every snore or gasp of breath convinced me that I would peek over the foot of the bed to see the man I had loved more than myself cold, blue and gone from me. Every creak down the hall or rustle of leaves from the trees was someone coming in to rob us, and, slow and decrepit from age, I couldn't get to the gun to defend myself—though no one could deny that my shot was better than the sheriff's. Every cell phone beep or TV flicker was the smoke alarm going off, and, though I may have been able to get myself out, my husband was a sitting duck.

"Oh, Momma," Lauren said gaily, sorting through a drawer of memories in the den, "surely we can get rid of some of these old clippings or letters or crumbling photos."

"I know!" Louise chimed in. "I can take all these old photos and scan them into one file so you can access them anytime you want."

"Or, I can have them all printed into one photo book," Martha said.

I nodded slowly to appease them, but knowing as well as my right from my left that I could never part with these things. Clippings of my girls' names appearing in dance recitals might not have seemed worth saving. But they were my memories. These drawers, overflowing with old bankbooks, receipts and never-filed photos were all I had left to hold on to.

I heard the front door creak open, and Jean called, "I'm here!"

I shuddered. Jean was the least sentimental, most cutthroat of the bunch. She would have dumped my drawers with all their memories into one black Hefty bag without a second thought and just left them right there on the street like a squirrel that has been run over.

"Momma," she said, "it's fine to keep all your stuff, but you can't move it all into a nine-hundred-square-foot assisted living apartment. It's not possible."

"I know," Sally said. "Why don't I take all of this home with me, and I'll organize it into a couple of scrapbooks for you so that it's all together."

"Well," I started. "I just don't know . . ."

"Come on, Mom," Jean pressed. "You know you don't even look at all this old stuff."

I peered down into the drawer on my lap and looked at the stack of papers and clippings in my hand. My girls looked in these drawers and saw a bunch of old junk. They didn't realize that this receipt from Penney's was for the pram that Dan surprised me with when we first found out I was pregnant with Sally. Or that I could just see Louise's happy little face when she brought me this kindergarten report card filled with "satisfactory" marks. I glimpsed a photo of Dan and the girls standing in front of our old house in Bath and realized that, as it is with all lives, the memories that filled these drawers weren't universally happy. But they were universally mine. I pulled out a boarding pass and smiled again, thinking how passionate Dan was about travel.

I looked at my girls, sorting through my possessions on the floor. "Fine." I exhaled. "Sally, put it all in scrapbooks. But don't you dare throw away one single thing."

"Oh, I won't, Momma. I promise."

Sally was as big of a pack rat as I was. "Jean." I glared at my youngest girl. "Now don't you even think about helping."

She laughed. "The good news for you is that with the election coming up, all my time will be dedicated to signs, speeches and debates."

I smiled at her, proud of my boldest girl's spirit and tenacity. She had lost three times before she was elected mayor. And, as it is in all purposeful lives, the falls taught her just as much as reaching the top. I turned over and looked at my husband, napping in his chair. And it made me think that we ought to shake things up. I knew right well that it made me crazy. But I finally said out loud what I'd been planning the past few weeks all the same. "Girls, I've decided I'm taking Daddy to Martha's Vineyard next week."

"Momma!" Sally said. "That's insanity. Why on earth would you do that?"

I shrugged. "He loves to travel and, who knows, a trip might perk him up a bit."

"Well, I can't go with you, Momma," Lauren said. "I absolutely have to work."

I caught Jean rolling her eyes at Martha. They were always accusing Lauren of acting like a martyr.

"I could probably go, Momma," Louise chimed in. "I could get one of the other teachers to take my classes next week."

Louise's yoga studio was her husband and her child all rolled into one. She had started it before yoga was the trend, and, between the vinyasa classes, chanting meditations and nutrition counseling, her business was bigger and busier than I think even she could have imagined.

Chartering a plane briefly crossed my mind. But then I thought of single Louise and divorced Lauren, and I worried, as I always do, that they wouldn't have enough one day. And so, as Dan and I had always planned, I mentally penciled it in the savings account register for my family's future.

"No, no, girls. I'll take a nurse."

"A nurse isn't enough, Momma," Sally said. "You need one of us to go with you. I'll see if I can get off of work."

Martha smiled. "I wish I could go, Momma, but my kindergarteners are just learning to read, and you know that's my favorite part of the year." It briefly broke my heart that Martha and John had never been able to have children of their own. But teaching gave her that connection with the children that she loved so much.

I know you aren't supposed to have favorites, but, when you get a little older, maybe it's that you quit thinking clearly and maybe it's that you quit caring so much about everyone's feelings. But I smiled, knowing that one of my girls didn't have a thing to do next week. "I think I might ask Annabelle to go."

"She's in the middle of moving, Momma," Jean said, shaking her head.

"What?" Martha asked.

Lauren rolled her eyes. "We all know what, Martha. Come on."

Louise interrupted. "Y'all don't know. This might work out perfectly, they might be married for seventy-five years, and you are all going to eat crow."

Sally smirked but didn't say anything.

Jean put her head in her hands. "Just pray, all of you, every night, that she doesn't have a baby with him. If she doesn't have a baby, then we're okay." She pointed her finger at Louise. "And you pray to your Buddha or whatever just in case."

I rolled my eyes heavenward, thinking that I could have been even more concerned about my daughter's choice of religion than Jean was about Annabelle's marriage.

"Momma, what do you think?" Sally asked.

I shook my head. "Nope. I'm not going to talk about the poor girl when she isn't here to defend herself."

"But she won't talk about it when she is here," Lauren said. "So it's not like any of us can put in our two cents."

"It's because she doesn't want any of your two cents," Louise interjected. "They're madly in love with each other. I don't know why y'all can't see that. The way they look at each other . . ."

Martha elbowed Jean and, in a loud whisper so we could all hear, said, "Hence the reason she isn't married."

Louise smirked. "Ha. Ha. Ha. Y'all are all so hilarious."

"There's just something about him," Sally said. "I know they're crazy about each other, but I just don't trust him."

They all looked at me again, and it took everything I had not to join in the Ben roast. I wanted not to think it, but I couldn't stop the question from rising to my mind: *Wonder how long it'll last?* I inhaled sharply, lecturing myself. It might not have been the future I had imagined for my girl, but she had done it. She had married Ben.

"Girls, all I know is that her ship is sailing straight without a cloud in the sky. And while it's that way, we'll all sail together." I sighed and smiled, thinking about the way my Dan always used to give me these words of encouragement when we were having a hard time with one of our girls. That's the most difficult thing about parenting: watching your children go down a path you're unsure of, letting them make those mistakes. But, oh my goodness, those mistakes are one of the most important parts of growing up. "And when it goes down . . ."

Five heads, all in unison, clearly thinking of their daddy too, nodded as I finished my sentence. "We'll swim to the bottom and bring her back up."

Annabelle

Full-Throttle

The way a man treats his mother is the same way he will eventually treat you. That is something that Lovey knew well. Her mother-in-law was as difficult as they come, but, even still, D-daddy loved and doted on her until the day she died.

I couldn't say how Ben was with his mother, because I'd never met the woman. I would venture to say that most people who have been married a year have met their in-laws. It's a pretty firm prerequisite for saying those vows. But, since Ben and I had eloped and left for his tour the next day, that monumental dating ritual had never taken place.

And, let me tell you, the longer I waited, the more nervous I became.

"Do you know," Ben said, as he flipped pancakes on the tiny stove in the corner of our RV kitchen, "that I am thirty-five years old, and you are the first girl I've ever introduced to my parents?"

I looked up from the *Yoga Journal* I was flipping through. "What? That's insane."

He shrugged, his back to me. "Obviously, they met my high school girlfriends because they lived in the same town. But I never really had them over for family events or anything."

I felt a little shudder run through my spine. What if he hadn't ever introduced his girlfriends to his parents because they were so judgmental? Or crazy? Or both?

"So," I asked, "why do you think that is?"

"I always knew I'd know when I'd found the right one—just like what happened when you walked in to hear me play that night. Until then, it seemed sort of pointless."

I stared at Ben's shirtless back, the muscles in his shoulders rippling as he turned the spatula. I couldn't see the long, diagonal lines that peeked out from over the belt of the khaki shorts slung low around his waist, but I knew they were there. And I couldn't believe that this man was even sweeter and more romantic than he was startlingly sexy.

I got up and put my arms around Ben's waist, pressing the side of my face into his back. I leaned into him and breathed deeply, like I could suck his scent into my lungs and never have to be without it again. He turned to kiss me, and I smiled. "I'm meeting your parents today."

I sat back down in a black-and-white-striped Sunbrella dining chair at the tiny three-person table. The RV ("coach" as the salesman had called it) was actually pretty swanky. Housed within quartz countertops and wood cabinets we had painted white were a stainless stove, microwave, sink and oven. Across the wall was a double refrigerator with freezer drawers. Truth be told, we ate out so much on that tour that we filled one refrigerator with groceries, and I took the other one for my shoes. Those were the only cold feet I had that year. The king-sized bedroom with the beautiful flax-colored linens may have been large by moving vehicle standards, but, any way you sliced it, closet space was minimal.

Ben handed me a plate of pancakes and stretched out on one of the couches that we had re-covered in white faux-ostrich leather with tufted backing, and said, "They are going to love you so much they aren't going to know what to do."

I nodded and furrowed my brow. "I sure hope so."

Ben winked. "Doesn't much matter. If they don't, it's too late now."

Two hours later, we pulled up to a house that I never could have expected. Knowing Ben like I did, his nonchalance about anything material, his pronouncement that money makes him uncomfortable, I was nowhere near prepared for this place. The huge RV slid right in the front driveway, and ten more would have fit. A black iron gate, complete with camera and keypad entry, ensconced in a huge gray wall led to one of the most gorgeous displays of French-style architecture I had ever seen. A flowing fountain stood in the center of a double-story middle with two curved wings, a beautiful U that made the entire compound, instead of seeming cavernous, envelop me and make me feel right at home. "Wow." I smirked. "So you'd rather live here than in the RV?"

"Don't be silly." Ben winked. "We're going to live in the RV in the driveway."

Before I could react, Ben's mother came running out the door, ringlets of auburn hair flying, lifting the bottom of long layers of chiffon so they didn't catch the wooden wedges underneath them. Driving up to this home, you couldn't help but picture the lady of the house in an austere Chanel sheath, heels, pearls and pristine blowout firmly in place. She would be lounging on a fainting couch, sipping a gimlet, while the butler opened the door.

I thought she would run to Ben, but, instead, before I could even get both feet out of the car, she had her hands on either side of my face and planted a kiss right on my lips. Coming from a family where a total stranger was lucky to get a lukewarm handshake, this full-throttle introduction felt a bit foreign. She pulled away, then embraced me in a hug and said, sincerely, "My daughter is so sophisticated and beautiful."

"Oh," I stuttered. I looked around, finally realizing she meant me.

I looked back at Ben's mother and studied her face, trying to find pieces of my husband's in it.

"Yoo-hoo, Emily," a neighbor shouted.

My new mother-in-law shooed me over in front of the gate and called back to an aging, gray-haired woman with two giant sheepdogs, "Isn't my new daughter-in-law beautiful?"

"Daughter-in-law?"

It bothered me for about a half second that Ben's neighbors didn't even know he was married. And that determination welled up in my chest again, that desire to prove everyone wrong. It may have been fast and it may have seemed unlikely. But Ben and I were madly in love, and that love was strong enough to carry us through the rest of our lives.

I could hear the rumor train flying down the tracks already, this harmless-seeming neighbor at altar guild with eight of her closest, loudest-mouthed friends, waxing poetic about Ben's new wife.

"I have been dying to tell y'all: Ben Hampton is married."

"Married? Well, I certainly wasn't invited to the wedding, were you?"

"I most certainly was not."

"Well, I feel terrible because the Hamptons went in on a party for all three of my children when they got married, and I didn't even know to ask."

"I never heard rumors of an engagement."

"I've never known him to go steady with any girl. I was positive he was gay."

Gasps.

"Well, obviously, she's some groupie he got pregnant."

Nods.

"That's the only explanation."

"So where's the baby? They've been married a year."

In unison: "A year?"

Before Emily could even answer her neighbor's shocked expression, my father-in-law sauntered into the driveway, pipe in mouth, suit and wingtips looking as though they were custom fit that morning. Now *this* was who should live in that house. "Ben, my boy," he said, puffing his pipe and slapping his only son on the back. "Congratulations on picking a fine bride for yourself."

I held out my hand, and he said, "I'm pleased to meet you, Annabelle."

This was more my kind of man. My parents would feel right at home with him. At least, my mother would. My father probably wouldn't even bat an eye at Emily's lip kisses. And it dawned on me that I, like Mom and my father-in-law, was the boring one in the relationship. And I needed someone like Ben in my life to temper me. For every ounce of me that was wound up, uptight, self-conscious and critical, he was laid-back, even keel and free spirited. I smiled, as every single moment like this since our wedding had reassured me of my initial thoughts when I met him: Ben and I were going to be together forever.

"Let's get you unpacked in the pool house," Emily said, putting her arm around me. Then she whispered, "Don't worry, we'll be on the lookout for a good rental in case your obnoxious mother-in-law starts getting on your nerves."

"I can't imagine that that would ever happen," I said. Sure, I had only known Emily for five minutes, but I could already tell that she was exactly like Ben.

The first thing I showed Emily was my refrigerator/shoe closet. She said, "You find in my line of work that the resourceful women are the ones who go the farthest in life."

After my yearlong groupie sabbatical, her comment gave me those nervous butterflies, a reminder that it was time to figure out what I was going to do with my future.

But I would worry about that next week. Because, as soon as I unloaded my few worldly possessions, I was heading to chaperone Lovey and D-daddy on their trip to Martha's Vineyard. Lovey was convinced that being in a place they visited every year, somewhere he loved, would bring D-daddy back, if only for a moment.

I was less sure.

But whether you've been married one year and have just moved to your husband's hometown or you've been married well over a half century and think something is going to unlock the vault of your husband's brain again, it's really the same thing that keeps you going: hope.

Lovey

&

Chance

My momma always thought I was part gypsy. I couldn't read palms or crystal balls, but, from the time I was little, I'd go anywhere and do anything, sacrifice whatever necessary to have a new experience. My momma never left North Carolina once, and she was just fine with that. But me? I wanted to see the world.

With Dan, see the world I did. He would hop on a plane at a moment's notice to practically anywhere, and I'd scramble to arrange sitters and jump right on board with him.

One of his favorite things was always taking the ferry from Boston to Martha's Vineyard. He loved the feel of the wind in his hair, the water rushing by, the cool early fall air in his face. While I was a born Pollyanna, I wasn't insane. I knew that even with a nurse to transfer Dan, and Annabelle (secretly) to help me, taking a car to the Raleigh airport, a flight from Raleigh to Boston, a cab from the airport to South Station, a bus from South Station to the ferry, the ferry to Woods Hole and a cab to our favorite inn in Edgartown, the Harbor View, was way too much.

But there was also no way a wheelchair-bound man was going to get into one of those tiny commuter flights on Cape Air that my darling husband was also so fond of. So we did some research, flew to JFK and took a rather large flight into Martha's Vineyard.

"Oh, Lovey, it's so cool," Annabelle said, grasping my arm tightly as we walked down the winding ramp. I wondered momentarily if they had had to put that out instead of the usual steps to accommodate Dan. But I stood up straighter, held my head up high and reasoned that, if you had lived as long and proud as Dan, concessions should be made.

She reached her hand forward and squeezed Dan's shoulder. "So, D-daddy. How you feeling?"

"Hungry," he replied shakily.

Annabelle raised her eyebrows at me, and I could feel the tiniest smile playing on my lips. Sometimes, I went days without hearing that voice, so even two syllables felt like a victory.

"D-daddy," she said, "if I remember correctly, you were awfully fond of the sandwiches at Humphrey's."

"Good tea too," he said, still looking ahead at the people filing into Martha's Vineyard's undeniably charming airport. The cedar shakes, the wooden beams . . . It was like a preview of what was to come, an indication that, yes, if the airport was this good, the rest of the island was incredible.

After a short ride in our handicap van, on our way down Edgartown's enchanting Water Street on foot, Annabelle and I were chatting, pointing out which stores we planned to visit, which items in the windows appealed to us.

I nearly fell right smack off the sidewalk when Dan, a few feet in front of us, pointed shakily and said, "Lynn, look!"

I turned my head into the North Water Gallery and, in an instant, was transported from the sidewalk in Edgartown to the ballroom of the Waldorf Astoria. I was nineteen again, slightly uncomfortable in the outfit the modeling contest had provided, feeling as though, farm girl that I was, I was wearing a costume, ready to take center stage at that Broadway show they gave me tickets to.

As the first bite of key lime tart melted off my fork onto my tongue, the sweet and sour fighting for position on my taste buds, I noticed that the noise from the guests was beginning to overshadow the lively songs of the orchestra.

When people began to shuffle in their seats and then, overwhelmingly, rush out the door, the alarm bells finally went off in my head. Was it a fire? A gunman in the restaurant? A mobster in our midst? I too rose from my seat and headed toward the lobby, trying to discern what was happening. Through the rumble of voices, over the din of the orchestra, I made out something distinct. "The war is over!" a man's voice cried. "It's over! We've won!"

My sister will come home, was my very first thought. The breath caught in my throat and, in the rush of the excitement, feeling as though my feet had left the ground, I let the crowd carry me along. To say that Times Square might as well have been Mars is an understatement. The lights, the buildings, the throngs of people everywhere you looked . . . For a girl who had known more cows than humans in her lifetime, it was startlingly wonderful, the rush of a lifetime. There I was, all alone, my chaperone having gotten lost in the crowd, looking up, up, up, marveling at the buildings around me, at the sheer energy of this place.

People were dancing, singing, throwing their hats. I didn't know what to do, all alone in a brand-new place. So I simply marveled, memorizing every detail. Even then I knew that, one day, my grandchildren would ask me, *Where were you when the war was over?*

And this unfathomably glamorous story is what I would get to tell them.

I felt that familiar ache in my heart, that soft pitter-pat that reminded me that I hadn't found the love that I would create those grandkids with yet. In the midst of my marveling, out of nowhere, a soldier, dressed to the nines in his whites, grabbed my arm, spun me into him, dipped me and planted a kiss on me that quieted the deafening noise.

"What's that photo, Lovey?" Annabelle asked, bringing me back into the moment.

We walked through the doors of the gallery and, as the woman dusting frames came over and asked, "May I help you?" I laughed as Dan said, "Yes. I'd like to buy this photo for my girlfriend here."

"Wait," Annabelle said, peering at the photo. "That's not you, is it, Lovey?"

I put my hand to the frame around the photo, the nurse in her uniform, the soldier in his, caught up in the kind of kiss that can only come from a moment of complete freedom. I shook my head. That photo of that couple's kiss might have changed the world. But my kiss that day changed mine.

"Oh, Dan," I scolded. "I can't imagine what that photo costs."

"I said I'm getting it for you, and I am," Dan said. He reached up to take my hand and put it to his lips.

We might as well have been back in Times Square for the rush it gave me to get a glimpse of my husband's old demeanor, his attitude, the way my pleasure mattered over all else. I almost expected him to get up out of the wheelchair and walk to the counter to pay.

The momentary thought that I had decided not to fly private in order to save money crossed my mind. *The girls can sell this photo later for whatever he pays for it now,* I thought.

I looked at the photo again and there I was, back in Times Square, breathless and shocked. I was trying to organize the fragments of my brain into one solid piece, scold this complete stranger for taking liberties with a woman he'd never met in the middle of all these people, for heaven's sake. But, in reality, I wasn't angry at all. My heart was racing out of my polka-dot dress, and I thought that, maybe, just maybe, in the most dramatic fashion, I had somehow stumbled right smack into the lips of a man I would be with forever.

I looked down at my shoes and said, "I don't know how you people do things up here, but where I come from, we certainly don't kiss total strangers in public."

I heard a gasp, and I looked up to hear Dan say, "Lynn?"

I put my hand over my mouth and laughed. "Dan?"

He wrapped me in a hug and kissed me again, this time with even more intention.

"What are the chances?" he asked. "How on earth are you?" He paused. "Because you look like nothing I've ever seen."

I could feel the golden glow emanating from my pores, a type of glee I didn't even know I could feel seeping out of every organ.

My Dan was back.

It was precisely the same thought I had standing in that art gallery that day, him chattering on with the owner.

"I'm lost here, Lovey," Annabelle said.

"I'm so sorry, darling. The picture isn't of us, but that's precisely how D-daddy and I got together. He kissed me in Times Square when the war was over."

"Wait. I thought you two grew up together."

Dan interjected, "In the rush of the celebration, I kissed the first woman I saw. And when I pulled away, it was her, that beautiful girl that I had carried in my heart since the day I waved good-bye to her out of the window of my daddy's Chevrolet."

I could see tears standing in Annabelle's eyes. I knew that those tears weren't from the heartwarming story; they were from having a man she loved like fury talking to her again. "When you know, you know, right?"

I nodded. "I knew when I was still that girl in pigtails. But coming back together like that, running into each other out of random chance and complete coincidence practically a world away from where we grew up . . . We knew it had to mean something."

Dan smiled up at me, and, in his face, I still saw a remnant of the boy I had fallen for a lifetime ago. Even the nurse pushing his wheelchair laughed as he said to Annabelle, "Don't believe a word she says. I would never, ever leave something as wonderful as being with my Lynn to chance."

As the woman behind the counter wrapped my photograph in brown paper, I glanced at it one last time. The utter shock and awe of that day, the freedom, the relief. The war was over. Dan was home. We were safe. I was having an experience a country girl like me never even dreamed of. Nothing had touched it until now, until, if for only a moment, my love had come back to me. Standing in the store that day, we may not have been kissing, lighting fireworks and making babies. But, all the same, holding his hand, knowing that he was the same man he'd always been to me, was totally exhilarating. And, even though I knew it'd hurt like hellfire tomorrow, I let myself think, like I always did: *Maybe this time he's back for good.*

Annabelle

∞

Exactly What He Wants

Lovey and D-daddy had a secret that kept them happily married for a lifetime: They made a deal that whoever left the other had to take the five daughters with them. It's hard to imagine it now, looking at my little Lovey. It's hard to think that, within her frail body, she would have had the strength and stamina for five children, cooking three meals a day, mounds of laundry, ironing a fresh shirt for her husband every minute and touching up five little church dresses every Sunday morning. Even with a parade of help, Lovey's life, while privileged, seemed like an awful lot of drudgery.

D-daddy might have been the one that went to work every day, rose through the ranks of the financial ladder. But Lovey was the one that held the family together. She was his walking stick, the extra hundred-dollar bill in his back pocket for emergencies. Her love for D-daddy was the thing that gave him the confidence to take the big risks that mostly paid off in their life together.

"It was two dollars," Lovey said, staring over the water, her coffee steaming in response to the unseasonably chilly September morning.

"What was, Lovey?" I asked, wrapping my arm around her thin shoulder and taking in the harbor. It was perhaps the thing I loved most about Martha's Vineyard. You knew that the money was all around you, but you couldn't quite spot where. Billionaire chiefs of industry captained twenty-five-year-old Boston Whalers, and hundred-millionaire heiresses walked amongst the crowd in fisherman sweaters and plain gold wedding bands. It was like Lovey always said: "When you have it, you don't need to flaunt it."

"Our marriage license," she said, smiling.

It was such a rare treat to hear Lovey talk about the past. She was so determined that her life would be over once she sank back and let the tide of her memories wash over her. I could almost picture them drowning her, stealing her last breath. I knew, without her having to say it, that she was terrified that D-daddy would outlive her. And, on this trip, I was almost as convinced as she was that maybe he could emerge from that semi-catatonic state in which he had been living the last three years, his brain revived and refreshed like a flower after the rain.

"Did you know that I paid for our marriage license?" she asked.

I shook my head and smiled. "I didn't have a clue."

"Dan only had a hundred-dollar bill and they couldn't break it. So I paid for the first thing we bought as a couple."

As she looked out over the water, I could tell that she was back in that day, seeing D-daddy, flustered, I'm sure, an ounce of that temper flaring, her soothing it instantly and him responding with that jovial laugh that had been my favorite thing about him.

Lovey looked back at me. "It was the best investment I ever made.

For two dollars, I got a husband, five daughters and someone to take care of me for the rest of my life."

We both laughed. My phone rang. I looked at the screen, held it up and said, "Speaking of."

"Hi, honey."

"Hi, TL."

I could tell instantly by his tone that something was off. "Everything okay?"

"Oh, yeah. It's fine," he said briskly. "Just missing you. Y'all having fun?"

I held Lovey's hand and smiled. "Oh, we're having a blast. It's chilly here but so, so beautiful. I'm sorry you couldn't come."

And I meant it. After being together nonstop for more than a year, getting into bed alone, no one snuggling me, no one's breath on my back, felt isolating and terribly lonely. I looked over at Lovey, thinking for the first time how she must have felt getting back into bed those first few nights with no one beside her, and I squeezed her hand again.

"Well, duty calls," Ben said.

I couldn't put my finger on it, but I could tell that something was amiss. He obviously wasn't in a rush to tell me, and I wasn't in a rush to pull it out of him while Lovey and I were having such a good morning. I spotted Kelly the nurse out of the corner of my eye, pushing D-daddy down the waterfront toward us, that semi-aware look like the world was a mystery that he was trying to solve.

"D-daddy is up and ready, so we're going to go get some breakfast," I said. "But call me later." I paused. "And, hey. Cheer up. If you want to talk about it, I'm here."

I thought of Lovey again, of the way she always supported D-daddy and made it easy to reach for those far-off dreams. A little pinprick of guilt, a bee sting after the initial shock, ran through me as I thought of how easily I let Ben give up that life on the road he loved, singing and traveling. It had been his decision to go back home, but, in that moment, I got the feeling that I should have fought him on it, encouraged him to do what he truly loved.

"I'm missing you like I didn't know I could," Ben said. "I just needed to hear your voice. I'm feeling much better. I love you all of it."

I smiled. "I love *you* all of it."

I put my phone back in my pocket, resisted the urge to check it again when it beeped, and gave D-daddy a kiss on the cheek, tightening the scarf around his neck, afraid that the wind would blow right through the body that age and infirmity had made so frail and bony.

"We were actually thinking of walking back to the Harbor View for breakfast, if that suits," Lovey said to D-daddy.

I watched her face, studying the tight lines of perseverance around her lips, the stony yet hopeful look in her eye that said she would never quit fighting, she would never give up hope. And, when D-daddy, as was the norm, didn't respond, that slight purse in her lips, that nearly unidentifiable shift in her eyelid, was the only thing that gave away her disappointment. As quickly as D-daddy had been there last night, he was gone today.

"I just don't understand it," Lovey said. "I can't figure out what brings him back like that and why he fades away again so quickly."

I shook my head trying to think of something to cheer Lovey up. I reached into my jacket pocket, my eyes widening at what I saw.

"You have got to be kidding me," I said out loud.

"What?"

"Guess who just texted me."

"Ben?"

"Holden."

"*Holden?*"

I shook my head, and, as irritated as I was by the contents of his message, I was happy to see that conspiratorial gleam in Lovey's eye.

"What on earth could he possibly have to say to you?"

I read: "I love you, Ann, and I meant it when I said I was going to do everything I could to get you back. I'm working every day on becoming the man you deserve."

Lovey stopped in her tracks. "Annabelle, what are you going to do?"

I laughed. "Do? I'm not going to do a thing. I'm married to the absolute love of my life. I've never, ever been happier. I'm going to ignore him and hope that eventually he'll go away."

Lovey and I sat beside each other on the front porch of the Harbor View, in matching rocking chairs, admiring the view of the harbor and the lighthouse. I grinned to see the dozens of men, all in matching navy blue Vineyard Vines fleeces, the item from the conference goody bag that became crucial in that last-minute change of weather from warm to chilly. They were chattering loudly, importantly on their cell phones, opening cases and closing deals, in a way that you knew they wanted you to hear them and be impressed.

There was a long silence while we both looked ahead again, all those matching sweatshirts peppering the lawn like sprinkles on a cupcake.

I broke the silence, saying, "If Ben were here, he'd be sitting right beside us, holding my hand, playing his guitar, telling us something funny." I pointed down toward the lawn. "But this. This would be life with Holden. I would be up here, trying to enjoy a cup of coffee, and he would be down there, talking a client down from a financial crisis."

Lovey smiled. "You may be right, darling, but here's the thing to watch out for: It's amazing how a man like Holden always seems, in the end, to get exactly what he wants."

Lovey

❧

My Best Friend's Gumption

September 1936

"Unkempt hair is a reflection of poor parenting," my momma was saying as she tied the red grosgrain ribbons in my pigtails. She was always trying to give me little pearls of wisdom here and there for when I grew up and had babies of my own. But I could hardly listen that morning I was so excited. All I could think was, *Fifth grade*, over and over again. I smiled at myself in the mirror, thinking of the comments from the other mothers in town.

"Fifth grade really is the hardest year," they had said.

"Now you know," Momma said, "fifth grade was tricky for Lib, so don't be surprised."

I smiled again. I absolutely adored school. The chalk, the blackboard, getting to be the teacher's pet, the one who got to bang the erasers clean after school. I had never made less than perfect straight A's, so fifth grade was going to be the challenge I was looking for.

"I have bacon and eggs ready and waiting," Momma said, smiling as she finished that last bow, satisfied that I looked perfect.

She put her hand up to the string of pearls on her throat. They were her grandmother's, a family heirloom, and one of the only things of value she had managed to hold on to when the Depression hit. Her wedding ring had gone, Daddy's pocket watch, the extra car. But we had made it through.

"As long as we can keep the house we'll be okay," Daddy had said over and over again. And we had.

There had been a few presentless Christmases, and I didn't care if I ever ate soup or grits again. But we had kept our home. And Daddy was so proud.

Later, at the table, I asked, "Momma, do you think Katie Jo and I will be in the same class?"

Momma rolled her eyes and exhaled. She didn't like me being friends with Katie Jo, not one bit. She peered at me over her plate, and Daddy peeked over his newspaper and laughed. "Just you don't start acting like her, Lynn." His smile was warm but he added, "Now, I mean it."

Momma sighed again. "There's only one class this year, so I'm sure you will be."

I had barely touched my eggs, but, all the same, I couldn't contain my excitement anymore. I kissed Momma and Daddy and said, "Can't wait to tell you about it!"

I ran down the driveway, that nervous energy breaking out humidly on my forehead by the time I got to the end of the driveway and Katie Jo.

She reached conspiratorially into the pocket of her jumper and smiled, handing me two pieces of hard candy.

I gasped. "Momma would never let me eat candy so early in the morning."

Katie Jo shrugged and smiled. "But she's not here."

I popped the first piece in my mouth, strawberry with a chewy center, and kicked the dust of the road out from under my saddle oxfords.

"You think there'll be any new kids in our class?" I asked.

Katie Jo groaned, "Who in their right mind would move here?"

I giggled. "What's so wrong with here, Katie Jo?"

"It's just so dull. I'm going to grow up and move somewhere marvelous. Maybe New York City." Then she shrugged. "Maybe Florida."

What seemed like too soon later, the stern, unsmiling Mrs. McLeary was saying, "No, no, you're an 'S,' so you go here. Move over a spot."

While Mrs. McLeary was discussing something with the sixth-grade teacher, as she was just beginning to line up her row of freshly washed children, shirttails slightly askew from the morning walk to school, Katie Jo darted out of line and stood behind me. We both giggled.

I couldn't imagine ever being as brave as Katie Jo. But thank the good Lord she was. Because if Katie Jo hadn't been her rule-breaking self that morning, my entire life could have been different. Katie Jo's spot behind me moved everyone up one space, and, as I would find out only moments later, put me beside the most beautiful, blue-eyed, blond-haired boy I'd ever seen.

"Who's that?" I whispered to Katie Jo.

She shrugged. "Never seen him before."

I looked back over, my first real crush grabbing my heart right out of my chest before I even knew what a crush was.

There we were, me in the fifth-grade line, him in the sixth, out front of the one-story elementary school, standing on the blazing asphalt. That massive flag waving was something to be respected almost as much as the cross itself. And the president was only a step below Jesus.

As we finished reciting the Pledge of Allegiance, little hands over so many beating hearts, Dan turned, those dimples gleaming, to smile at me. I heard Katie Jo giggle, and I guess I borrowed a little of my best friend's gumption that day. My ribbon-tied pigtails trembling with anticipation, I reached over and took Dan's hand. And that was it. My heart was stolen forever.

Annabelle

∞

Per-fect

Everyone needs a little struggle in her life because, when it's all said and done, it's the struggle that makes you strong. As I lay in bed that night after a beautiful dinner at the very upscale Chesca's, hearing D-daddy's snores through the doors of our adjoining rooms, I couldn't help but wonder if maybe Lovey was a little too old to have to struggle now, if she wasn't strong enough already. Maybe it was that she was so practiced at the life she was leading now, but she acted as if this horrible time seeing her husband in decline was business as usual. I was just his granddaughter, and, watching a nurse butter his bread and feed it to him, seeing the stares of the other patrons as she cut his meat, it took away part of that essence of D-daddy, that strength that he had, the way you knew he would always be there to protect you. Her entire world had collapsed in an instant, taking away the man that she had loved for a lifetime.

My mom and aunts, they whispered when she was out of earshot that she'd never move into assisted living. She talked a big game, they'd say, but, at the end of the day, she couldn't part with all her things. And, while we all agreed that that level of security would probably be nice for her, I felt like maybe she'd had enough change, that having the strength to live the life she was living and still hold her head high was enough to have to deal with without having to pare down all her worldly possessions and move somewhere new.

On our walk back to the Harbor View after dinner, I had said, "I don't know how you do it, Lovey. Taking care of him all day, every day must take an incredible toll on you. Traveling with him, taking him out to eat all the time . . ."

She had just shrugged. "I'm not going to hide him away like some sort of shameful secret. He might be an invalid, but he isn't dead."

She stood up a little straighter.

My heart ached to remember that Ben was thirteen years older than I, and that, chances were, I was going to be facing this same fate one day. I exhaled deeply and heard Ben's voice in my ear: *You can't worry so much, TL. Today is all we really have.*

I smiled and let myself go back to that wonderful night that changed my world forever.

After I'd slammed Holden's car door during the epic cruise-control argument, I didn't know things were over between us. But he wasn't the kind of man who would come after me when we were fighting. So I didn't waste my time looking out the window or dreaming of hearing footsteps on the concrete stairs up to my third-floor condo. As I picked up the phone to call my best friend Cameron to see if she wanted to go out, I realized it: I didn't care if I ever saw Holden again. I wasn't angry. I just really, truly didn't care. Had I ever loved him? I guess we always ask ourselves that question in the aftermath of what we think will be the rest of our lives.

Cameron answered the phone breathlessly, "You have to go out with me tonight!"

"I was planning on it."

As Cameron told me that this sexy guitarist whose YouTube videos she had helped go viral was playing at a tiny bar that night, it hit me that, though I was nearly positive I would marry him anyway, I had no real feelings left for Holden. But the thought of the calligrapher three-quarters of the way through addressing those engraved invitations was too much for me to take. The humiliation of having to send those Save the Date follow-up cards saying, *We regret to inform you that the wedding of Annabelle and Holden will no longer take place* was more than I could stomach.

"Whatever you want," I heard myself telling Cameron. "But you have to pick me up because I'm going to be in a condition tonight that you haven't seen since freshman year."

I realized how out of place I was going to look in the bar wearing the pink seersucker Lilly Pulitzer dress that Holden's mom had bought. It was entirely too prissy for me, much too "Sure, I'll stay home and iron your underwear, sweetheart." That dress looked like the woman Holden *should* marry.

I slid into the passenger side of Cameron's Camry (or CAM'SCAM, as her license plate said) and laughed at her getup. Frayed jeans that looked like she'd had them twenty years, a faded T-shirt with the armholes cut off and a deep V torn, a bandana wrapped around her head, and one feather earring. "Is this some sort of costume night?" I asked.

She looked back at me. "I don't know, pink princess. Is it?"

"I was trying to look like Holden's fiancée."

"And I'm trying to look like Ben Hampton's."

I nodded. "Can we smoke?"

She raised her eyebrows. "You haven't smoked in like a year. What about your fresh baby-making eggs?"

I groaned. "I know this is what I've planned since we were in kindergarten, but I feel like my life is going to end the day I walk down that aisle."

Cameron handed me a lit cigarette. "Duh. That's why I'm single." She smiled. "That, and that Ben Hampton is my soul mate." She sighed deeply. "We'll probably never marry, just pledge our lives to each other like Brad and Angelina."

I rolled my eyes. "Maybe you can wear vials of each other's blood around your necks too."

She sighed wistfully. "Maybe." Then she cut her eyes. "But you are aware that that was with Billy Bob, right?"

"I get *People*, Cameron. Of course I know that. But clearly your subscription isn't up to date."

"What do you mean?"

I laughed. "Brad and Angelina got married."

"No. Are you serious? That is so annoying."

"Yeah. Like forever ago." I gave her my best faux-supportive smile and patted her hand. "Listen, am I crazy to marry Holden? I mean, is my life going to be the most boring thing imaginable?"

"Holden is . . ." Cameron paused. "He's dependable. He's predictable. He'll never let you down. He'll never cheat on you. He'll always have his secretary buy you something amazing from Cartier for your birthday. I mean, he's kind of that guy that is great husband material." She paused again, and looked at me as we pulled into the parking lot. "But, damn, Annabelle. You're twenty-two years old. And you're the most amazing girl I know. You just deserve more than that."

I put my hand on the door handle. "This is going to be the worst thing anyone has ever said, but I think I just feel like, with Holden, I don't have high expectations for how my life is going to be. So if it turns out to be basically boring but easy, I'll never be disappointed."

Cameron put her head on the steering wheel. "Listen to yourself. You don't marry 'basically boring,' Annabelle. You marry 'can't live without.' You marry 'heart racing through your chest and feet lifting off the ground and want to rip each other's clothes off.' I mean, yeah. You have to be able to get along and have similar values and blah, blah, blah. But how could you possibly get through life without that passion?"

I looked at her for a long minute. And, not for the first time, I envied Cameron. She was so self-assured. She always knew exactly what she wanted. And, lately, now that college was over and I was supposedly an adult, I felt sort of lost. I didn't know what I wanted to do with my life. But I knew that life with Holden was something I was supposed to want. I sighed. I didn't want to talk about it, so, instead, I said, "I need a shot."

We both jumped out of the car and Cameron said, "Coming right up!"

I had never heard of Ben Hampton, never Googled him or had his YouTube video pop up on my sidebar. But when I walked into the sparsely attended bar, with a few ripped black leather chairs scattered around, and heard him crooning, he seemed familiar to me. He was so tall standing up there onstage, his hair as black as the guitar strap around his shoulder with these dark, piercing eyes. I'd never been the kind to get worked up over tall, dark and handsome. But, suddenly, I got the appeal. I sat down within his view, spellbound by his voice, suddenly self-conscious and wishing I looked more like rocker Barbie than bubblegum Barbie. He was so effortlessly cool, so sexy . . . But I wiped the thought away like a dry-erase doodle. I looked down at my left hand. I was engaged, after all, to hedge fund Ken.

At first I thought I was imagining it, but then Cameron whispered to me, "Your attire has so deeply offended my boyfriend that he keeps looking at you in disgust."

I didn't get disgust from his gaze. "Well, then maybe I should move out of his line of sight."

But when I got up, the strangest thing happened. Ben stopped singing, stopped playing and said, "Where are you going?"

I looked around, confused, and, as I was the only person standing, pointed to myself and said, "Um, me?"

He nodded. "Sit back down."

I sat back down obligingly, my heart racing in my chest. "I didn't know this was the freaking opera," I whispered to Cameron, mortified that I had been scolded.

"Excuse me, everyone," Ben said into the microphone, looking straight at me like a sniper on his target, like no one else existed, "I'm going to have to take five because I believe I just met my wife."

It was like jumping in the ocean. The noise all around me was suddenly muffled, and my lungs felt like they were filling with water.

Cameron whispered, "What the hell, Annabelle? How could you have stolen my boyfriend like this? We were meant to be together."

All I could muster was, "Apparently not."

He jumped down off the stage a few minutes later, took my hands in his and kissed my cheek.

"She's engaged," Cameron said indignantly, her hand on her hip.

He rubbed his fingers over the diamond on my left hand, never taking his gaze off of my face, and said, "Not anymore."

Maybe it was because I was twenty-two and unsure, or maybe it was because I was twenty-two and totally sure, but I followed Ben out of the bar a few hours later. I had to know more about him, I had to understand why I felt so immediately drawn to him. Under the flood of the streetlight that, instead of a dingy, moth-ridden fluorescent stream, seemed like an enchanted glow under the spell of Ben, I started to come to my senses, even through the tequila haze I was in.

"Wait," I said, suddenly feeling the two shots and two liquor drinks I'd had, "you could totally be a serial killer. I mean, this is nuts."

Ben walked toward me, a smile playing on his lips. I felt my back touch against the vintage CJ7 Jeep that my dad would have flipped for, my heart beating so loudly I couldn't hear anything else. He stepped closer, took my hand, and put it on his heart. "Would one sweet, beautiful girl make a serial killer this nervous?"

I leaned my head back against the window. "No . . . no. I guess not."

I'd never felt so totally out of control. I'd never done something so unplanned. And it felt so good I didn't want it to ever stop. I felt Ben's hand on my face, sweeping my hair behind my ear. I looked up at him and smiled, his sparkling eyes boring right through me. I felt like I couldn't breathe, totally overcome with wanting to be closer to him, to know him more. He leaned in and kissed me, my legs giving way. If it hadn't been for the car behind me, I probably would have fallen onto the asphalt. As I reached my hand up to run it through his hair, I heard, "Quit kissing my boyfriend, you slut," quickly followed by Cameron's loudest, drunkest cackle.

I laughed too as she made her way toward the Jeep, sort of sideways and peering. The combination of the drinks and the kisses had made me a little sideways too. "You," she said, falling into me, her mouth right on my ear, "have totally impressed me tonight."

She leaned away, looked at Ben, swallowed with intention and said, "I mean, this girl, she always does the right thing. I mean, seriously, you have no idea. She's like per-fect." She made a hand gesture to punctuate the last syllable.

Ben laughed, and Cameron squinted at him. "And you," she said, slurring, pointing her finger right in the middle of his chest. "I was in love with you until you pulled that sappy shit up onstage."

Ben put his arm around my shoulders. "Sorry to disappoint." He kissed my hair and opened the car door for me.

Cameron slid in right beside me, so I was in the middle of the front seat. I looked at her. "Whatcha doing there, sweetie?"

"Do I look like I can drive myself?" Cameron asked.

We both burst out laughing. "Oh my God," she said. "I love you so much. I'm so proud of you. I mean, seriously, I love you."

She hiccupped, and I leaned my head on her shoulder, smirking. "I love you too." Then I whispered, "Do we know he isn't a serial killer?"

Cameron shrugged. "He's so freaking hot."

I laughed.

"All right, girls," Ben said. "I don't know where I'm going."

"Doesn't look like it's going to be home with me," Cameron said.

Ben interlaced his fingers with mine. "Doesn't look like it. I think I've found the last girl I ever want to go home with."

I closed my eyes, feeling myself smile, and took a deep breath, wanting to memorize the moment. My best friend, the new love of my life. And then I groaned.

"What?" Ben asked. "Was that too much?"

"For me," Cameron said. "In fact, I'm probably going to barf on the floorboard. But I would assume she just remembered she has a fiancé that is busting up her plans to shack up with you tonight."

I slapped her leg. "That is so tacky, Cameron. I am not going to do that," I hissed.

"Rip off the Band-Aid, baby," Cameron said, producing two beers from her purse and handing me one.

We clinked the bottles, and I looked at Ben, feeling my heart melt. What *was* it about him?

"Hey," he said. "If you aren't sure, I can just take you home. You can sleep on it." He stopped at a stoplight, put his lips softly on mine and said, "But I promise you that I wouldn't let you dump your fiancé if I wasn't sure we were supposed to be together."

Cameron laughed. "God, you're really too much for me. We never would have made it. But Ann, she loves all that sappy horseshit."

I called Holden, feeling stone-cold sober. "The wedding is off," I said. "I'm sorry, but I can't marry you."

And do you know what he said back? "Is this about the cruise control?"

"Yeah, Holden," I said. "It's totally about the cruise control."

Then I hung up, Cameron cranked up the radio and the three of us sang "Don't Stop Believing" at the top of our lungs. We dropped Cameron off, and, before she half fell out of the truck, she drunk whispered, "Listen. Holden schmolden. Ben Hampton is a fooooxxxx. And you just know he's crazy awesome in bed. Text me later."

Then she slammed the door. "Will she be all right?" Ben asked.

I laughed. "Oh yeah. This is basically sober for her."

He put the truck into gear and said, "She's right, you know."

"How's that?"

"I am awesome in bed."

I raised my eyebrow. "Oh, yeah? You sure about that?"

He shrugged. "Wouldn't you like to know?"

It disturbed me how much I wanted to know. But I also got those nervous butterflies in my stomach because I hoped he knew I wasn't going to sleep with some guy I just met, no matter how taken with him I was. Which is why I was so relieved when Ben pulled into the parking lot under the bright yellow sign of Waffle House. "I'm in more of a sleep mood than a waffle mood," I said.

But Ben took my hand and pulled me out through the driver's seat anyway. And I realized that I would have followed that man anywhere.

We walked into the brightly lit restaurant and Ben called, "Hey, Hilda," to the aproned woman standing behind the counter with her pad in her hand. She had to have been in her seventies, and wouldn't have weighed eighty-nine pounds soaking wet. But she lit up like a schoolgirl when she saw Ben.

"Well, hey there, handsome," she said, her voice raspy from what sounded like decades of smoking. "The usual?"

He nodded.

"What about for the little lady?"

Ben looked me over. "Two eggs over medium, bacon, and coffee that's more cream and sugar."

I looked at him in astonishment. "That's exactly what I order. How did you know that?"

Ben shrugged. "I just know you. I can't explain it."

"So," Hilda said, handing us our coffee cups. "I ain't never seen you with a girl, Ben. I thought this whole time you came in here every night to see me." She cackled.

I laughed behind my hand and, inside, was bathing in relief. Ben was clearly a regular here, and he wasn't stumbling in with a different girl every time.

"You come here every night?" I asked. I couldn't imagine being able to keep a body like Ben's eating stuff like this.

"Well, I come every night I have a gig in Charlotte. Which is a lot of nights." He grinned, increasing those butterflies in my stomach. "What can I say? I'm a sucker for Hilda."

I smiled, feeling giddy and alive.

"So," Ben said. "You're the most beautiful girl I've ever seen. I'm assuming the fiancé dumping wasn't over cheating. And I assume you didn't really call off an engagement over some cruise control situation. So what's the deal?"

I took a sip of my coffee, feeling myself sobering—and waking—up. "He's just not the one."

Ben rolled his eyes. "Obviously. That's me."

I was so fully and completely charmed by Ben. And, when I looked in his eyes, it was like I knew him too. Sitting across the table, I instinctively felt that I understood him better than anyone else ever would, that I could see what was inside of him. "So," I said, taking my first bite of egg. "What's your story?"

"I have a feeling," Ben said, "that the only part of the story I'll ever care about again is just beginning."

"So this Waffle House late-night breakfast is the beginning of a Gabriel García Márquez–style love story?"

"God rest his soul," we said in unison.

"That was pretty creepy," Hilda interjected.

Ben laughed. "*Love in the Time of Cholera* is my all-time favorite book."

I gasped, mid–bacon bite. "Shut. Up. Mine too. My grandmother and I read it every year. She says it's a reminder of what true love should look like, of what you should find before you get married."

"My mom says that exact same thing." He paused. "Of course, she should've waited a little longer."

"Why is that?"

"Because my dad cheated on her."

"Oh no." I shook my head. "So they're divorced?"

Ben rolled his eyes and took another bite of waffle. "No. My mom's a sex therapist who believes that sometimes sex is just sex."

Even the word coming out of his mouth gave me those butterflies again. I shifted nervously in my seat as Ben smiled at me. I gave him a haughty look and said, "Just so you are aware. I'm not sleeping with you."

He gave me an amused look. "You're not?"

"No. I just met you, for heaven's sake."

He laughed, his fork in the air, mid-bite. "I know that, Annabelle. I told you: I *know* you." He shrugged. "But if you'll come home with me—just to talk"—he put his hands up as if surrendering—"I promise I won't put any of my irresistible moves on you."

He wiggled his eyebrows, and we both burst out laughing.

Watching the sun rise usually made me feel sick, gave me that panicked feeling that it was day again and I had yet to go to sleep. But, watching it rise out of Ben's bedroom window the next morning, after a night of talking until my throat was scratchy, my head resting heavily on his now contentedly beating heart, it made me feel unbelievably happy, as though the sun was rising on the first day of the rest of my life. I knew that, as improbable as it seemed, I had found my missing half in a bar, onstage, singing me love songs. Anyone over the age of twenty-two would have known for sure that a devilishly sexy, slightly dangerous musician would choose a new victim after every gig. But I knew when he looked at me that he saw the same thing I did when I looked at him: fire.

It was a Thursday night, and the dentist's office where I was the patient care coordinator wasn't open on Fridays. That meant seventy-two hours of pure, unadulterated bliss with Ben. Looking back now,

I'd like to say that I had misgivings, that I questioned how seamlessly it all came together. But I was either too young, too stupid or that potently in love.

I'd also *like* to say that Holden crossed my mind during that time, that the fiancé I had dumped with three sentences on the telephone was haunting my thoughts, the pain I had caused him weighing down my heart. But that would be a lie.

Lying in the grass in Ben's tiny backyard, looking up at the clouds, relishing quietly in the glow of those first moments of take-your-breath-away love, Ben said, "I always knew I'd know when my true love walked through the door. Period. And there you were."

I kissed him for probably the millionth time, rolled back over, and covered my face with my hands. "I can't believe I am doing this. I don't want you to think I'm the kind of girl who just goes home with guys she barely knows."

Ben rolled over on top of me, took my face in his hands and kissed me. "I don't think anything. I know you completely. I'm in love with you."

I bit my lip. I wanted to say it was crazy. I wanted to run away. I wanted to tear it apart and analyze and find all the ways it wouldn't work. But I couldn't. "I'm in love with you too," I said. "How am I in love with you? I just met you."

"Because I'm your soul mate, obviously."

I wanted to say I didn't believe in soul mates. I wanted to tell this guitar-playing god of a man that soul mates didn't exist. Only, they had to. Because, here I was, back in my Lilly Pulitzer and pearls, having just dumped the Gucci-loafer-wearing man of my dreams for a musician I didn't know the first thing about. We had to be soul mates. There was no other explanation for why I would have traded the life I had always dreamed of, thrown it away on a whim.

"Hey," he said. "Do you want to go snowboarding with me next month? I'm playing this gig in Montana, and it's going to be awesome."

"I love snowboarding. And Montana. And you."

"There's this bookstore in Missoula that you absolutely have to see. You're going to love it."

I turned my head to smile at him, loving the way his fingers lingered on my arm, the sun lingered on my face, the breeze lingered on our bodies. "Holden thought reading was a waste of time and that everything you needed to know could be found more efficiently via webinar."

Ben laughed. "That's why you and I aren't inviting Holden to Montana."

"Why are you going to Montana?"

"To celebrate my thirty-fifth birthday."

"Wait. You're thirty-five?"

"Yeah. How old are you?"

"Seventeen."

I could see his face turning ashen, and I felt a little mean. Before he could begin to stutter, I laughed. "I'm just kidding. Twenty-two."

He nodded. "Thank God. I don't need yet another felony."

It was my turn for the pale face. But before I could get too far into my fantasies of my maimed corpse hanging in Ben's closet, he laughed. "If you can dish it out, you've got to be able to take it, TL."

I rolled my eyes and shook my head. "Let's teach our kids to ski really early so they aren't afraid."

"Definitely," he said. "All three of them."

I bit my lip and nodded. "I'm an only child, but I have kind of a big, crazy family. I really want that kind of chaos in my life."

"Yeah. My sister and I aren't really that close. If you have two siblings, you'll probably be tight with one of them." He grinned at me. "I want to teach them how to play instruments when they're really little. Wouldn't that be cute?"

I smiled and kissed him. He was the most adorable human on the planet. The way he lit up when he talked about his music made me, quite honestly, jealous. And proud. "When did you get into music?"

He shrugged. "I don't know. I can't even remember a time when I didn't play an instrument. It has been my life's passion for practically forever. What about you?"

What about me? I'd always envied people who had some sort of talent that made them feel alive and fulfilled. But I didn't want Ben to think I was less interesting. So I kissed him again and said, "I think maybe you're my life's passion." And I meant it.

Those three days were the first time in years, maybe ever, that I'd truly felt alive. Food tasted like it was fresh from the ground, the air was cleaner coming into my lungs. The colors were more vibrant. And, as we walked around downtown Sunday afternoon, I realized that I was different too. I felt more beautiful, more confident, more positively glowing than I ever had in my life. I could feel passersby watching Ben and me, able to see our love as clearly as though it was written on the theater marquee we were walking under. And I realized that, improbably, Cameron had been right: I couldn't possibly live my life without this kind of passion.

On Sunday night, I felt like I had spent a blissful time in Never-Never Land and was having to fly back into my boring bedroom window. I avoided it all day, but, finally, at five o'clock, I ventured, "Ben, I have to go home."

He looked genuinely shocked, as though the idea that I'd ever had a life outside of this one had never occurred to him. "You are home, TL."

I laughed. "I have a condo."

"Sell it."

"I have a job."

"Quit it."

I looked down at my hand. "I have a fiancé."

"Marry me."

I smirked, but I could feel my heart racing. I wanted to spend the rest of my life with my hand in his, my lips on his, my skin on his. I wanted to take his name and breathe his air and sing his songs. Forever. But saying that to someone you have known three days is generally considered bad form.

"I'm serious," he said. "I want to marry you."

"Ben, come on."

He got down on his knee, right there on the sidewalk. "Annabelle," he said, "I knew when you walked into that bar that I had written every love song of my life for you." He softened a bit. "You're it for me, TL. I want to spend the rest of my life making love and babies with you. I want to be there when you fall asleep and when you wake up, when you're young and spry and when you're old and feeble. I want to take care of you when you're sick, be your shoulder to cry on when you've had a bad day, be the man who still thinks you're that beautiful, young thing even when you're ninety. I want to see your face when I'm taking my last breath and live one minute less than you so that I never have to be without you again."

I am not an emotionally gushy person, but that last part got me. I thought of Lovey and the deep, forever love she had with D-daddy. She had known from the moment she saw him as a ten-year-old child, so why was I questioning that I knew now at twenty-two? Moreover, I had always said that the most important characteristic in my future husband was that, at ninety, I could prance around in a thong and he would still see my hot, twenty-something ass.

I smiled and, trying to ease the intensity of the moment, said, "So what you're saying is that you don't want me to go home right now?"

He stood up and gave me one of those kisses that, in no time at all, had become like oxygen to me. I had so many questions. "Where will we live? What will we tell people?"

He smiled. "It will all be all right if we're together. Please marry me, Annabelle."

I thought of my mother's disapproving look, the disappointment Lovey would feel at me throwing away my so-called perfect life, the whispers all over town and the scandal of me marrying a man I barely knew. If Mom and Dad didn't disown me and refuse to pay for it, people would be buying tickets to see this wedding. But now that I knew what it was like to feel this carefree, this in the moment, I never wanted to go back to the way things were. Maybe it was dangerous and maybe it was reckless. But that was how I felt. So I smiled back and kissed Ben again. I nodded, threw my arms around his neck and whispered, "I can't imagine that I could ever love anyone like this. Of course I'll marry you."

And so I did.

Lovey

୭

The Best Gift in Life

My momma always said that a woman's most important job was taking care of her husband. And I had done that tirelessly from the day I walked down that aisle. But, at eighty-seven, packing, traveling and the mental strain of caring for a relatively helpless man were becoming quite a bit more taxing than they had once been. But it had all been worth it. For that half hour that Dan had seemed like his old self again, I would have traveled day in and day out for the rest of my fleeting time on this earth.

I thought about the photo of that day in Times Square, packaged tightly in my suitcase, surrounded by a cushion of clothing. I had the perfect spot for it, over the credenza in the den, right beside Dan's chair, where we could look at it together all the time.

"You ready to get home, Lovey?" Annabelle asked, shutting off her phone for takeoff.

I nodded, closing my eyes, smelling the smells of home, feeling the give of my mattress, hearing the whirr of the air-conditioning as it clicked on and shut off.

"Home," I repeated. It truly was the sweetest word coming off my lips. Much like "naptime" had been when all my girls were young.

Home was Dan's routine. Home was a revolving door of caregivers, our doctors down the street, the emergency room I knew, no worries about strokes or infections or tooth abscesses.

"You know, Annabelle," I said, "as much as I hate it, I think this might be our last trip."

She shook her head. "Don't say that, Lovey. You and D-daddy love to travel so much."

I smiled thinking of Dan, so dapper in his overcoat and top hat, holding my hand, walking through an airport, completely transformed, transported by being somewhere new. I turned to peek through the crack between the seats, almost expecting to see that same bright-eyed, shiny-skinned man he had been. When I turned, it was almost as if it was someone else sitting there, the sallow complexion, free from the suit he wore every day of our married life.

"We loved to travel," I said. And it surprised me when "He doesn't know where he is anymore" escaped from my lips.

Annabelle turned to look out the window, and I knew I had upset her. But pretending that things were all right didn't change them. Sometimes the truth just is.

Even still, I squeezed her shoulder and closed my eyes, remembering my granddaughter a year earlier, as happy as I'd ever seen her.

When she walked through my front door with Ben, only months before her wedding date with Holden, I knew instantly what had happened.

"You said you wanted a Love band when you finally did it," I had said as Annabelle sat down on the couch beside me.

Ben had sat down beside Annabelle, put his arm around her shoulder, squeezed her and kissed her cheek. "The weird part is that I found that ring ten years ago at an estate sale my mother dragged me to, and knew I wanted to give it to my wife one day."

I picked up Annabelle's hand and turned it over, examining each false screw. Not one line was out of place. No cuts. No lack of symmetry. Not even a hint that it had been resized. "Don't tell me it fit." Normally the ring would have been ordered to the perfect millimeter.

Annabelle smiled even bigger, if it was possible, so that I could see that her orthodontist had done a perfect job on even her back teeth. "What are the odds?"

"I didn't even know what Cartier was until I pulled this ring out for Annabelle. I just thought it was pretty."

Annabelle smiled sheepishly. "I guess I never saw myself getting married in Vegas, but it felt right in the moment, you know? Ben sang as I walked down the aisle, and it was just us. It was amazing."

I tried to push away the feeling that none of this was Annabelle, that that ring was the only thing that fit. This man and this life she was so swept away by seemed to be the wrong size. But I'd never upset my girl, so I didn't let on. I put my hands up over my face and shook my head. "So what do you think, Dan? Your favorite grandchild ran off to Vegas and married a musician she'd known three days."

"Mmmm," he muttered.

Annabelle and I laughed, the sparkle in our eyes matching, that a vestige of a man that we had both practically revered was showing itself. And I felt so sentimental in that moment that I let go of any anger I had at my granddaughter throwing away her perfectly orchestrated life of leisure. I knew what it was to be in love—even if it was misguided. And so did Dan.

"We can talk about the Holden of it all later, but what on earth did your mother say?"

Annabelle looked down at her hands and said, "Well . . ."

"No, no, no," I said. "If you are grown enough to run off and get married on your own, then you're grown enough to tell your parents on your own."

"If I may," Ben interjected. He moved around to one of the armchairs flanking the sofa, sat down and leaned over, his arms resting on his knees so that his face was only inches from mine. I found myself somewhat entranced by his dark eyes and the cadence of his voice. He reached over for my hand and said, "You are the most important woman in the world to the woman that is my world." I would have rolled my eyes, but he was so sincere that I believed him. Plus, looking over at Annabelle, I realized: *Why shouldn't he be in love with her already? What's not to love?*

"All we want is to get to revel in the positive energy of this experience, to be young and in love and unutterably happy." He nodded his head toward Annabelle. "She won't be happy until her family is happy, and I'll do anything in my power to keep her smiling." He gave my hand a squeeze. "So, please. I'm begging you. Help me give her the one thing I can't."

I raised my eyebrows. "You're good, kid." Then I squinted my eyes. "How many times have you been married?"

He shook his head. "Never. Never even been in love. That's how I knew TL was the one. I saw her, and I never wanted to be away from her again."

"TL?"

"True love," Annabelle sighed wistfully.

"Oh, mercy." I rolled my eyes, but, in reality, I thought it was sort of sweet. If I closed my eyes, I could put myself back in those days where love was more butterflies and love songs than grit and commitment.

Then I gasped. "Of course. You're pregnant." I shook my head. "Well, I'm just glad you ran off and got this whole thing over with."

Ben and Annabelle laughed. "I'm not pregnant, Lovey."

"Well . . . ," Ben said.

Annabelle smiled. "Okay. I can't promise I'm not pregnant, but I can promise that I wasn't pregnant before my wedding night."

The thought of her having a baby was what finally put the fear in me. A misguided marriage is bad. But you can get out of it with little fanfare. Once children are a part of the equation, there's an entirely new level of finality to the thing. As I picked up the phone, I hate to admit that, though I wasn't sure about him, I was fantasizing about seeing Ben's gorgeous eyes and Annabelle's perfect complexion on a little great-grandchild.

When I had called my daughter, she answered on the first ring, as she always did. I think she was panicked that one of us would die and she wouldn't be there. "Jean," I remember saying to her one day, "we all know how much we mean to each other. And that's the best gift in life. Because no matter when the final moment comes, we don't have to feel regret. We've loved as hard as we can."

I think it eased her mind, but not her predictability. She walked through the glass double front doors, into the entrance hall, and then she saw us. My tall, slender, fair-haired youngest girl stopped dead in her tracks, put her thumbs into the sides of the belt around her thin waist, took a deep breath and said, "Why do I get the feeling I'm being ambushed?"

They were the exact same words that came out of my mouth, not three hours after remembering that day, when Annabelle and I arrived home from Martha's Vineyard. After a plane flight and car ride, I arrived at my front door, exhausted, only to be greeted by my five girls, lined up, side by side, on the brick front stoop.

I glared at them, already knowing they were up to something, the way a mother always does. "What is this?" I asked. "Are y'all playing Red Rover?"

Sally stepped forward and hugged me, and I could see the tiniest quiver in her chin, giving away her tender heart. I sighed.

I sat down on the iron bench on the front porch, knowing I wasn't getting past that barricade of daughters any more than Dan was going to get up and salsa.

Lauren sat down beside me and said, "Momma, this is an intervention."

"A what?" My voice was high and squeaky.

"You know," Annabelle interjected. "Like on the show. 'Your behavior has affected me in the following ways . . .'"

I looked at all of them like they had announced they were joining a cult and taking me with them on their comet to heaven tomorrow.

"We're just worried about you and Daddy being here alone at night—" Louise started.

"Okay, okay." I cut her off. "I'll hire a night nurse or make arrangements for that dreadful assisted living. Is that what you all want? Could I please just get inside and lie down? It has been quite a long trip."

"That's the thing," Jean said.

And that's when I could feel my own chin start to quiver. I somehow knew before my youngest even said a word that my home wasn't my home anymore. I glared at Annabelle. "Did you know about this?"

She put her hands up in defense. "I promise I didn't know a thing."

I got up, pushed Jean aside and opened the front door. I gasped at how little furniture was left, the tears flooding to my eyes. Forty-five years of memories in this house, on this street, and—just like that—everything had changed. That seemed to be the theme of my life. "I can't believe you didn't even let me say good-bye," I said softly.

"Momma," Martha said kindly, "you would never, ever have said good-bye."

"You never would have been able to part with anything," Lauren said. "But we knew that this was what you really wanted."

"So we were only trying to help," Sally added.

Jean waved her hand as though she hadn't just destroyed my past in a weekend while I was lounging on the Vineyard totally unaware that my life was being pulled out from under my feet.

"Before you get all upset," Jean said, "why don't we get you and Daddy back in the car and go over and check out the new place."

"If you don't like it, we'll move all your stuff back," Martha said.

"They called," Lauren said, "and one of the new, remodeled units came available in the best place in town. We knew if we didn't get it now then we would never get one."

I was so angry I couldn't speak. *If you can't say anything nice* and all that was running through my mind as I got back in the backseat of the car. I crossed my arms indignantly. Annabelle was trying to calm me down, but I couldn't even hear what she was saying, seething like I was. I patted Dan's shoulder. "Our girls sure are something," I said. "We might have raised them a little too headstrong."

When we opened the door to our new light-filled assisted living apartment a few minutes later, my arm linked in Annabelle's—she was the only member of my family, after all, that hadn't completely betrayed me—we gasped in unison. Though I had shakily decided that I would move, I hadn't even begun to look for places. In my mind's eye, I had pictured worn laminate countertops and sterile, white hospital linoleum tile floors, inpatient white walls and sheet glass windows with those thick, black frames.

But this place, with its hardwoods, marble countertops, breakfast island and modern bathrooms complete with soaking tubs and lifts felt more like a spa than a nursing home. And the floor-to-ceiling French doors and windows leading to our private balcony illuminated the entire living space. I put my hand up to my mouth. "Oh my goodness," I said, examining the waterproof lift remote by the tub. "I'll be able to take a bath again." Then I looked over at my husband. "So what do you think, Dan?"

He said nothing in response.

"We can get up every morning and have our breakfast on the balcony overlooking the little lake," I added.

"Yeah, D-daddy," Annabelle said. "You and Lovey will be dining al fresco all the time."

He looked up at Annabelle expectantly, like he was waiting for something else. And she smiled proudly as he said, "I think that'd be nice."

The best part about the apartment was that it was filled with all my things. The Fabergé eggs collected on a glorious trip to Russia, the Herend from Hungary, Dan's German Lugers from the war. The first antique chest we had ever bought together was perched in the corner of the small living room, a new TV hanging over top, and, of course, Dan's chair, his lifeline of the past few years, was right across from it.

"So what do you think?" I asked my husband again, not exactly expecting a response but so practiced at figuring his needs into my daily equation that I didn't know what else to do.

"I think my chair looks nice."

All my girls laughed, I'm sure from a mixture of relief and happiness.

"Do you think you can stay here?" I asked Dan.

He looked up at me in that slack-jawed way that filled my heart with pity. "Yeah."

"Well, girls," I said. "Your daddy has spoken."

I would have sooner dropped those Fabergé eggs out the window, one by one, with tiny, experimental parachutes than admit that they had been right. I guess, at eighty-seven, I'd never expected a fresh start.

Annabelle

∞

Be Like Lovey

Leaving your husband for too long is dangerous. According to Lovey, that's when affections stray. But I disagreed with her. I thought that being apart, at least every now and then, gave people a chance to miss each other. And I had missed Ben like I didn't know you could.

When I pulled back into the driveway of my pool house, I heard, "Oh, thank the Lord, my girl is home!"

That's probably something you would expect your husband to say when you return from a five-day trip with your grandparents. Instead, the first person to greet me at my temporary pool house residence was my mother-in-law, Emily.

I gave her a hug and said, "I missed you so much!"

"I missed *you* so much," I heard from behind me.

I turned and jumped into Ben's arms, wrapping my legs around his waist and kissing him.

"Wow," Emily said. "I'm a little jealous. His greeting seemed more enthusiastic than mine."

I laughed. "Maybe it seemed that way, but what I think I actually missed most was your warm quinoa cranberry salad."

Emily started backing away, grinning like her scratch-off ticket was the five-thousand-dollar winner. "Well, then I'll go whip some up right now!"

"I'll come help you in a minute," I called after her.

"I don't think so," Ben said, taking my hand in his and raising his eyebrows suggestively.

I smiled, thinking that I was the luckiest girl in the world. A husband love stories are written about, a doll of a mother-in-law and a home so gorgeous I didn't think I'd ever want to leave it. Who would ever want to have their own house when the one they were in came with a pool and three free meals a day?

"Let's go celebrate your return," Ben whispered in my ear, sending shivers down my spine.

I lit up and then, remembering, scrunched my nose. "I'm having my period."

I could see the disappointment in his face, and I knew it was about more than just sex. "Oh," he said. "Again?"

"Yeah, again," I said, hearing the irritation rising in my voice. "Every month." Then, trying to take the edge off, I asked, "Did you miss that day of sex ed or something?"

He ventured a half smile and said, "I guess I was just hoping . . ."

I shrugged, trying to remain unflustered, trying to ignore the fact that my calm, relaxed, adoring husband was putting an undue amount of pressure on me. I probably should have said something of that nature to him, because I'm sure he didn't mean it. But I didn't because I didn't want him to think I was being silly. Instead, I replied, "Well, obviously I was hoping too."

I couldn't help but hear my mother's voice in my head. *Annabelle, it's too soon to have a baby. I know you think he's the love of your life, but, for heaven's sake, you two barely know each other. Give it time, get in your routine, build that strong foundation. That is the most important thing. A baby needs totally committed and completely ready parents.*

I gritted my teeth even thinking about that, of how skeptical she and my dad had been about the fact that I had married Ben three days after I met him. If I was honest, I'd yet to find anyone—even Cameron—who wasn't a little leery of it. But to us, it was a great love story, the mark of how unutterably sure we were that we were the one and only to each other.

I had said to my mom, "It took you and Dad like a decade to have me. I don't want Ben and me to have to go through that." I had crossed my arms. "Why can't you just be like Lovey? Why can't you see what we have? Can you not just be happy for me?"

Sure, I was acting like a child, but, in reality, I sort of was one. And it pierced right through me when she had said, "Lovey isn't happy that you threw away your perfect life on some fly-by-night guy you barely knew. She just has the sense to know that you're going to figure out what a mistake it was in your own time."

I had walked out then, tears burning in my eyes, crossed between the indignation that no one could see how perfect Ben and I were and that far-off fear that, oh God, what if she was right?

As I walked through the door of the pool house, Ben kissed my neck, and all of that worry and all of those ugly moments floated away. Ben. I even loved to say his name. I turned and kissed him.

"I need to jump in the shower and get this plane grime off of me," I said.

"I need to shower too," Ben said, raising his eyebrows. He kissed my cheek, then my neck and whispered, "Seems like a shame to waste all that water . . ." He was grinning at me so boyishly that I couldn't be mad anymore.

"I think that sounds amazing," I said.

I turned and ran toward the bathroom, Ben laughing and following behind me. I loved squeezing soap into the ridges of his tight abdomen, those dimples in his cheeks coming out as he leaned over and kissed me, so much taller than I. I felt myself relax. I felt my body meld into his, free from the stress of whether it was going to fail me yet again, of whether next month would bring yet another negative pregnancy test. In those moments with Ben, for the first time in a long time, I felt like I was right where I needed to be.

Lovey

❧

A Thing About Marriage

May 1945

I'd been warned against wasteful spending my whole life. So, the entire time I was in New York City, I sent my parents one telegram. It read, *Celebrated victory in Times Square STOP Home May 28 STOP Love you STOP.* In those days, you quickly became experienced at saying everything you needed in the ten-words-or-less telegram price break.

I never heard back. Needless to say, I had no idea what to expect on the final leg of that trip back to reality, back to where I'd come from. I cried the entire plane flight home. Partially, I'm sure, I was sad about leaving a world that had charmed me more quickly than a soldier on leave. But the real tears were for the actual soldier on leave that I was flying away from. Conveniently, Dan's family had moved from Bath just up the road to New Bern. "Had to come all the way to New York City to find each other again," we were fond of saying. We weren't neighbors, exactly, but weekend visits were possible.

"I'll write you every day," I had said when our lips parted.

"No need," he said breathlessly. "As soon as I talk to your parents, I'll be asking for your hand."

I smiled thinking about that, the rain clouds of my tears finally drying up in the midafternoon sun streaming through the window. His love was all I needed.

I'd certainly never wanted to be a model, so this contest, this win, this picture in the magazine, it truly must have been orchestrated by someone much greater than I was to fling me back into the arms of my Dan. I had had my picture taken a few more times during the trip to document how marvelous winning this contest was, and how fantastic the cosmetics were too, of course. Me at the theater, me dancing at the Waldorf, my hair blowing at the top of the Empire State Building.

They told me I had potential; they could maybe even offer me a contract. But I wasn't a model. And I wasn't a New Yorker. I was a farm girl. I wanted to be a wife. Dan's wife. And, as I had discovered on that trip, I wanted to be a student too. I wasn't sure if I'd ever get to travel the world. I may never stand atop the Eiffel Tower or sit on the steps of the Great Pyramid of Giza. But I hadn't been valedictorian of my class for nothing.

I had practically whispered to Dan over tea at the Plaza that I thought I might like to go to college. He had lit up brighter than the chandeliers above us. "I didn't want to say anything, but I'm going to college too." His face fell and then it lit up again. "You should go to UNC. Gosh knows, you're smart enough."

I smiled into my tea even thinking about what Daddy would say if I told him I wanted to go to the University of North Carolina.

"Dan, honestly, don't you think that's a little improper? I was assuming I'd go to Women's College just like Lib did." I knew Momma and Daddy wouldn't like it, but they couldn't very well pay for Lib to go to college and not do the same for me.

He shrugged. "But then we have to be apart. If you go to UNC, we can be together, we can get married."

Married . . . It was that sweet thought that I held on to as I closed my eyes, preparing myself for what it was going to be like to be home again. I didn't know what to expect when I walked through that door. Coldness. Screaming. The punishment to end all punishments. *But,* I reminded myself in my white gloves and best traveling suit, *I am a grown woman now. I'm going to be married soon.* What could they really do to me?

I walked through the door to silence. Complete, deathly silence. "Momma," I called. "Daddy, I'm home."

"In here," came Momma's voice from the kitchen.

She was standing by the stove, the radio droning in the background, her apron tied around her petite waist. Daddy was in his dinner chair, reading his paper.

"Hey, baby," he said when I walked in, not bothering to get up.

"We've got fried chicken, okra and mashed potatoes for dinner," Momma said. "Hope that suits."

After weeks of the finest cuisine flown in from all over the world, I would like to say that my palate had become more sophisticated. But I was still a down-home girl at heart.

The cuckoo clock chimed from the dark, paneled den, and everything around me felt eerie, like the foreboding music in a picture before the murderer makes his kill. They didn't ask about my trip, and I didn't tell. It was as though I had walked down to the corner grocery for sliced bread and come back.

About halfway through dinner, I couldn't take the suspense any longer, and, so, I finally said, smiling, "I met a man."

That did it. Daddy banged his fist onto the table, his napkin clenched inside. "I told you we should go after her, Lily Ann. I told you she'd meet some damn Yankee and be gone forever."

Momma's face was white. To the outsider it might seem like she was afraid of Daddy's anger. But I knew better. She was afraid of me. Coming home and saying I'd met a Yankee was only a step off saying I was marrying a Catholic.

"Calm down, Daddy." I laughed. "He's from New Bern. Do you remember Dan from school?"

Momma nodded. "Really? Dan?"

I nodded. "He's a soldier now."

Momma exhaled deeply, and Daddy actually smiled. "A soldier, eh? Must be a fine fellow. I like a man who isn't afraid to fight for what he believes in."

It was my turn to smile. "Well, I think you'll like him a lot. You remember his daddy used to be the preacher at our church. And Dan has grown up so handsome." I could feel myself swooning at the table over the hand that had spent the month in mine, the lips on my cheek. We kissed on the street corner, and I felt like I was starring in my own show. A famous starlet meets her true love, and, emboldened by passion and the forward-thinking ways of the city, she isn't even afraid to kiss him in *public* of all places. *Oh my Lord,* I remember thinking, *being young and in love is the best feeling in the world.*

"I'm so glad you found somebody you like," Momma said.

"He's actually going off to college now that the war's over." I paused. You could tell by the change in their faces that they knew what was coming. "And, well, I was thinking that I might like to go to college too."

Daddy sighed and Momma said, "Did you really not miss us at all? You just want to run off again to college?"

"Momma," I protested, "I'm not running off and leaving you. I'm bettering myself. I want to go to college, be a teacher, make a difference."

"But—" Momma started, but Daddy cut her off.

"Sweetheart, it isn't fair for us to keep Lynn here like she's in prison. Lib went to WC so it's only fair that Lynn gets to go too."

"Well, actually," I began nervously. "I was thinking that I might go to UNC."

I think both of my parents were stunned speechless, so I continued. "Dan is going there, and we thought if we could both go, then we could go ahead and get married, live in married student housing. We could be together while we're getting an education."

Daddy laughed ironically. "I can't believe that you would even mention something as crass as going to a men's college."

"But it isn't a men's college," I said, shifting in my chair, trying to keep my tone in check. "It's coeducational."

I've never been as shocked as when Momma said, "But she wouldn't be going as a girl. She'd be going as someone's wife. I think that's different."

I smiled at her, so grateful for her support. "Right," I said. "I'd be living with my husband there, so it wouldn't be inappropriate at all."

Daddy looked at Momma warily, and she nodded her approval. Holy hell and hallelujah, I had pulled it off. I was going to college.

Only, I found out the next day it wasn't going to be as simple as all that. I thought Dan looked a little pale as he was opening the passenger-side door of the car, but I didn't say anything.

"Guess what!" I practically sang as he got behind the wheel. We were going to get ice cream at that same shop where we'd had our first kiss as kids, to tell Haney that, in the most unlikely way, we had found our way back to each other. I thought it was impossibly romantic.

"What?" Dan asked, his enthusiasm not quite as strong as mine.

"Momma and Daddy went for it. They said if I was going to UNC as your wife, then I could go."

Dan pulled the car over on the side of the road, put it in park and looked at me. He turned, took my hand and said, "Lynn, it didn't go as well with my parents."

"What do you mean?"

"They told me that it wasn't suitable or proper for a man to get married until he was educated, settled in his business and had enough money in the bank to provide for his family . . ." He turned and looked out the window. "They've always said that, but I thought once they saw how in love I was they would change their minds."

"Oh," I said, feeling the tears coming to my eyes, the glee of my morning so instantly replaced with an intense sadness.

"They said they wouldn't pay for my college if we got married now." He paused and looked back at me. "So I'm not going to go."

"Not going to go!" I protested. "Don't be ridiculous, Dan. Of course you're going to go."

"But I love you, Lynn."

"And you'll love me four years from now. You go to UNC, I'll go to WC, and when we graduate, we'll get married. Plain and simple."

"But, Lynn, can you wait that long?"

"Sure," I lied. I reached over and kissed him softly. "We have our whole lives to be together. What's four years in the scheme of things?"

I realized a few minutes later that the ice cream at Haney's shop didn't taste as sweet when it was mixed with the first lie I had ever told the man I loved.

Annabelle

∞

We're Living

The Lord gives and the Lord takes away all on His own time. And there isn't anything a man or woman can do to really change that, according to Lovey. There wasn't any other good explanation as to why a twenty-three-year-old who'd never had so much as an imperfect checkup still wasn't pregnant.

It had been only a little over a year, sure. But something inside Ben and me as a couple just needed that little person to complete our family. In retrospect, I wonder if that deep longing for a child of our own was a bit of a cop-out, an insurance policy in case we realized that everyone was right: We hadn't known each other well enough to get married. If it were only the two of us, it would be easy to walk away. If another person were in our lives, it would keep us together, would force us to tunnel underneath the ground of those hard years and come out the other side as in love as we ever were.

I could picture this tiny, energetic son of ours, twirling in the grass at music festivals, listening to his daddy sing onstage and wanting to be just like him. I could see myself, a crown of flowers in my hair, rocking a brown-eyed baby girl on my lap underneath the stars outside the RV.

At one of those very festivals where I was dreaming about our little mini-mes, an agent approached Ben about cutting a demo.

I was so excited I could scarcely breathe. Maybe it's because I was so intoxicated by the sound of his voice onstage, but I knew that Ben could have been someone really important in the music world.

"You know," he said to the agent, as I was sure he was about to sign on the dotted line, "I really appreciate that. But I just sort of make music for fun."

It was our first real fight.

Back in the RV, I'd said, "Are you crazy? Do you know how many people wait a lifetime for an opportunity like that? How many people scrape and fight and claw to try to get anyone to even listen to them? And you have it handed to you on a silver platter and say, 'no thanks'?"

Ben shrugged. "I love music, and I don't want that to change. Albums and tour dates and pressure . . ." He waved his hand. "I don't want all that."

"But, sweetheart," I said, softening, changing my tactic, "you could do what you love for a living."

He shook his head and peeked it into the refrigerator, emerging with a beer. "We're living right now, aren't we? Besides, I just want a simple life."

"Sure, Ben, yeah. I mean, we're living. But what about when we're older, what about when we have kids? You could be up there onstage every night and selling albums every day and paying for our house and private school and college funds just by singing."

Ben looked at me in bewilderment. "Private school? Are you kidding me? There's no way our kids are going to private school."

I had taken my private school education for granted, just always assumed that my kids would go there too. And, in reality, the only kids I had considered having were with Holden, so there wasn't much of a question. But I knew that where our kids went to school wasn't really the issue that night. So I said, "I guess we can cross that bridge when we get to it."

"The bridge to public school," Ben said under his breath.

I couldn't understand it then. Maybe I was too young or too naïve, but I couldn't reason out why someone would throw away his chance at fame. Now I realize that being happy isn't about any of that. And that happiness is something you have to hold on to no matter what. But, that night, I said, "Are you seriously that unmotivated? Or are you afraid of failure? Or what? I do not get it."

Ben sat down beside me on the couch and tried to pull me to him. But I was too worked up to give in. "It's not any of that," he said quietly. "I have everything I want. I finally found the woman of my dreams, and I don't want to risk you or this happy life for anything."

I shook my head, knowing I couldn't stand my ground against an argument like that. I leaned over and kissed him. "I love you," I whispered. "I just want you to get what you deserve."

"I love you too," he said. "And, maybe you don't get this, but our happiness in our little life is the only thing that matters to me."

In the entirety of that wanderlust year, it became the only thing that mattered to me too. There was no shortage of beautiful women fawning over my husband, but never once in that entire year did I ever feel anything but glorified by him. He would stare at me as he sang, dedicate his newest love songs to his only true love. And I could scarcely wait to get him alone again to show him my appreciation. It was a dream year, like wading through the fog and mist with no real responsibilities. It is a chance I'll always be glad we took, because when in your life do you ever get to be that carefree and that in love?

I hate to admit now that we really didn't talk about the future, as evidenced by our private-school fight. I wasn't sure when he'd be ready to stop singing or where we'd make a life when we got finished. My brain had spent a lifetime as a clogged drain of questions, stray hair and fingernail clippings and matted dirt preventing me from just being in the moment. And I was making up for it.

But those days were over—at least for now—I reminded myself, lounging by the pool, eating grapes, clearing yet another text from Holden. I'm here and I love you, it said. If you change your mind, my door is always open.

I sighed. I didn't want his damn open door. I looked over the pool and considered the idea that, while it was lovely to be waited on hand and foot and spend my days hanging out with my mother-in-law, I needed a job.

My phone beeped again. That meeting in NYC that you always loved so much is next month . . . Sure would be nice to have a pretty girl on the plane with me.

I rolled my eyes. Maybe that was a part of the problem. When I knew I was going to marry Holden, working was almost out of the question. He traveled constantly on business, and it went without saying that part of the responsibility of being his wife was wining and dining and shopping with the other spouses. But that wasn't the life I chose. And I felt pretty certain that in any life, without a bigger purpose, I was always going to feel bored and antsy.

When Ben got home that night from the CPA grind, the shocked expression on his face was no surprise. It was the first night since we had moved in that I was waiting for him fully clothed. "What gives, TL?" he asked, loosening his tie.

"I need to talk to you."

He sat down beside me on the couch, pulled me close and hoisted my legs onto his lap. "I love talking to you too," he whispered into my ear.

When I didn't return his steamy kiss, Ben pulled back. "Oh," he said. "You're serious."

I smiled. "I've just been thinking that I can't hang around here all the time."

"You ready to move on? Or get our own house?"

I shook my head. "No. I think I could stay in this pool house comfortably for the rest of my life and have your mom wait on me . . . but I think I need to get a job."

Ben smiled. "That's awesome! Have you found something you really want to do?"

I looked skeptical. "I don't have a clue what I really want to do."

"So why are you getting a job? I'm making plenty and we have like no bills."

"I just feel like I need to do something with my time; I need a purpose."

Ben rubbed my shoulder. I knew he was trying to be supportive because he was always supportive. He only wanted what was best for me. "But, TL, you'll be pregnant soon, and there's no use in stressing yourself out with a job unless it totally fulfills you, you know?"

Every logical cell in my body knew that he was trying to take the pressure off of me, to let me know that I didn't have to do anything just because I felt like I *should*. But I could feel myself getting angry anyway. "Oh, so being a CPA fulfills you?"

Ben shook his head. "No. It's a job. But I do it because I'm your husband, and I like taking care of you. And my dad needs me. And making both of you happy fulfills me, so revision to my previous answer. Actually, being a CPA does fulfill me."

He had responded to my snap as coolly and calmly as I could imagine. But, for the first time in the fifteen months I had known Ben, I needed him to argue with me. I had to feel him waver just an inch from that sheet-glass countenance of his. "And quit saying soon I'm going to be pregnant. I'm not pregnant, and the last thing I need is you reminding me that I'm failing at my only responsibility."

Instead of fighting with me, Ben lowered his eyes to the ground, making me feel a hair off of Hitler, and said, "TL, I love you madly, and I think you're the perfect woman. I don't need a baby from you to be happy or fulfilled or anything. Let's just not worry about it."

What I needed to do was cry. I needed to crawl into my adoring husband's lap and sob about the baby I had dreamed of and how scared I was to even find out why it had yet to appear. We could be adults, talk through it together, and make a plan for either moving forward or putting it on the back burner. But, instead, I stomped off into our bedroom, like the relative child I was, closed the door rather forcefully and yelled, "I told your parents we'd have dinner with them at seven."

Friends always asked me if it was hard having a therapist as a mother-in-law. Until that night, I had always answered, "No." Until that night, it had always been easy and normal and like any other mother-in-law. But, until that night, I had been transparently happy. As soon as we sat down outside in the gorgeous iron coral chairs around their outdoor dining table, Emily said, "Oh no, kids. I sense some tension. Should we talk it out?"

"Everything's fine, Mom."

"Well, are you having enough sex? Because you know if you aren't having enough sex—"

"Jesus, Emily," Ben's father Greg interrupted.

"They're grown-ups, Greg. They're married."

"I know, Emily, but no one wants to talk to his mother about . . ." He paused and waved his fork around in a circle. "That."

"Well, I was simply asking," she said, turning toward Ben, "because—"

"Yes, Mom," he interjected before she could go any further down her line of psychological questioning. "We have lots of sex, if you must know."

I could feel myself looking into my salad as though it was a criminal in an interrogation room, and I was the bad cop.

"Yes," she started up again, "but sex for *pro*creation and sex for *re*creation can sometimes feel different. You don't want to feel like you've lost all the fun of it on the quest for baby."

I knew my face was redder than the tomatoes on the plate, but I turned to Ben and said, "You told them we were trying to have a baby?"

He shrugged, his fork and knife in midair. "I didn't know it was a secret."

"Great," I said, thinking that if it wasn't enough for the two of us to be thinking something was wrong with me, now the entire family thought something was wrong with me.

"If it makes you feel better," Greg said, "I didn't know about the baby."

I laughed ironically. "Probably because there isn't a baby to know about."

I could feel tears gathering in my eyes, and I was beyond embarrassed. I wanted to stop them, so I looked down in my lap and gulped my water.

"Oh, pumpkin," Emily said. "We think you are absolutely glorious. You don't need to have a baby to prove that."

I nodded and swallowed, hoping the tears standing in my eyes weren't obvious. "Oh, I know," I said. "It's just that Ben is so perfect and has been so incredible that I want to give him something in return, and this is the only thing I can think of that he can't have on his own."

Greg looked at his son and said, "Sport, you're on your own here. I'm going to my study."

"TL," Ben said, an amused look on his face. "You are my entire world. The sun rises and sets around your face. All I could ever want from you is you. Nothing in heaven or on earth can change that."

"See what I mean?" Emily said. "It's no coincidence that procreation and pressure both start with *pr*."

I actually laughed at that in spite of how uncomfortable I thought it was to talk about sex with Emily.

That night, we put the procreation on the back burner. And my husband and I discovered that fighting with your spouse is the best thing you can do—as long as you get to make up.

Lovey

Grounded

You can have a big house and two cars and closets full of clothes, but, if you don't have Jesus, none of it means a thing. So, from the time I was a little girl, hands down, the most important thing in my life has been my faith. I believe in God like most people believe in gravity. I can't see Him, but I know He keeps me grounded. When you're as old as I am, you learn that every day isn't perfect and that life can be sunshine and roses one minute and gray skies and thorns the next. And you better never leave home without your umbrella because one minute the birds are chirping and the next it's thunderheads and downpours—or vice versa, thank the Lord.

But you couldn't have told Annabelle that the day I went to meet her new in-laws any more than you could have told me that one day we'd be talking to people on the telephone in our cars. And if you can't imagine it, it doesn't exist.

"Oh, Emily," I said. "I am so thrilled to hear that y'all are Episcopalian. It just does my heart good."

Emily turned to Annabelle. "You'll have to start going to ECW meetings with me, Annie."

That brunch table certainly proved that religion knows no bounds. That was the thing about Emily. She was so uniquely who she was, and, just when you thought you had her figured out, another surprise was just around the corner. In a flowing maxi dress with a thick, handmade woven leather belt around her waist procured from some obscure village and crafted by a woman who would otherwise have had no income, Emily looked more like one of those non-denominational hippies. I, in a sunny yellow, perfectly tailored suit with a pillbox hat and pumps, looked every bit an Episcopalian. But the eleven a.m. cocktail bound us both as members of a church that knows alcohol's proper place in Southern society.

"In fact," Emily said, breaking me out of my thoughts, "let's all go to church together in the morning!" She turned to me. "You will absolutely adore this church. It is nearly as old as the town itself, built in the late seventeen hundreds. It's full of amazing architecture and incredible stained-glass windows."

Jean said, "I have a speaking engagement tomorrow afternoon, so we might not be able to make it."

"Mom," Annabelle said, "couldn't you try to reschedule? This is the first time we've ever been together as a family, and I think it would be nice to go to church." I gave Jean a stern look across the table. Annabelle needed us all to come together as a unit to affirm that what she and Ben had done was acceptable. And we should, even if we didn't really think it was. Because families have to stick together.

The next morning, I had promised myself that I wouldn't be one of those pathetic old women who comes to church and sniffles into her handkerchief the entire time, the kind of woman who makes you wonder whether she's suffered great loss or is atoning for great sin. But my sniffles into the same linen and lace pocket square that I had carried down the aisle at my wedding were for the former. In all our years of marriage, I had never sat on the pew of a church without my husband.

Even after the stroke, the caregivers had him up, dressed, and in the handicap van at 9:40 sharp so we wouldn't be late for the start of the ten a.m. service. And now, here I was, spending the night away for the first time in years and going to church without him for the first time in our marriage. I tried to act like the tears were an allergic reaction to the stunning flowers by the altar, but my family, they knew better. Annabelle, with Ben's arm wrapped around her shoulder, his fingers stroking the bare skin of the top of her arm, took my hand and leaned over to whisper, "He wouldn't want you to sit at home and rot for the rest of your life, Lovey."

I knew it was true, but, all the same, it felt wrong. I closed my eyes to take a deep breath, and, in that instant, I was transmitted back to my hometown church, a white clapboard chapel as beautiful in its austerity as this one was in its opulence. And there, in my hat and itchy dress, squeezed in between my parents in a packed pew, I saw fourteen-year-old Dan sneak out the side door right before his daddy took the pulpit for the sermon. I waited a respectable beat before leaning over and whispering to my mother, "I have to use the restroom."

Before she could object, I was making a beeline for the door. In retrospect, it couldn't have been a secret, like we thought, that Dan and I skipped out on the sermon to steal a few moments alone. We would walk down the downtown sidewalk, hand in hand, toward the ice cream shop that, on summer days, had a line around the corner. Haney wasn't open on Sundays, but he lived above the shop. If you snuck around back, you'd find him, bad leg propped on a milk crate, listening to a preacher on the radio, drinking out of a coffee mug that we didn't realize until years later was always full of whiskey.

Some of the kids in town were afraid of Haney, his gruff demeanor and slow-to-smile temperament. But those secret Sunday rendezvous created a bond between us. Haney had lost his wife in the car accident that cost him the nerves in the lower part of his left leg. Dan and I always thought he saw a glimpse of his former life in us, sneaking away to hold hands for a few breathless moments in young love.

"Y'all just go on in and help yourself," he'd say, without even looking at us. "Leave your nickel on the counter."

He wouldn't smile or even look our way most days. And it was a relief not to see him dragging that leg behind the counter, leaning on one brace while he scooped the ice cream, the weight on his good leg. But I knew those Sunday mornings meant as much to him as they did to us because, every time I'd go in the shop on other days, Haney would give me the tiniest smile, and, when he did, his eyes twinkled with our secret.

The tiny ice cream parlor had only four red stools, and, most days, getting a seat was out of the question. But on Sundays, Dan and I had them all to ourselves. I would sit down, legs dangling, ankles crossed, and giggle as Dan said, "What will it be for the little lady today?" even though he knew it was always chocolate.

He handed me my cone and sat down on the stool beside me. I could tell he was anxious about something, but I could only assume that it was nerves over the never-ending lectures he got from his momma for missing church. But it was worth it—especially that day.

"I can't believe school is starting back in a week," I ventured.

"I know. Last year of junior high for me."

"Yeah." I nodded demurely. "Then it's off to the big leagues. You'll probably forget all about me."

He looked at me seriously. "I'll never forget you, Lynn." He paused and said, "You've got a little ice cream on your lip."

I grabbed my napkin out of my lap, but before I could wipe away the offending drops, his lips were on mine. It goes without saying that I've had a special place for chocolate ice cream ever since.

That memory had cheered me right out of my black-veil-wearing depression. And, at that exact moment, a tall, slim man who looked to be in his early thirties walked down the aisle in the most glorious vestments. He had that adorable hair with enough soft curl to make him look boyish but not enough length to make him look unkempt. I'll admit that the vestments did make him look even more regal, but, combined with his warm eyes and gentle pat on my shoulder as he walked by, I thought that if I'd been fifty years younger, this man could have been just the right kind of charming.

I was entranced by his sermon, a moving dialogue that spoke to both the spirituality and the levelheaded nature of the typical Christian: what God is telling us and a step-by-step plan for figuring it out.

Over lemonade on the lawn, in a perfectly pressed collar, the man who I had discovered was the new associate pastor walked over to where Annabelle and I were chatting, and, though I knew she was married, I couldn't help but think how I had dreamed of one of my daughters or granddaughters marrying the pinnacle of the perfect Southern man, a vestige of my late father-in-law: an Episcopal priest. I didn't want to, but there just wasn't a thing I could do to keep from thinking how this was the kind of man my Annabelle *should* have married.

"Hi, Annabelle," he said, reaching over and taking her hand in both of his.

Then he looked to me. "Mrs. White. We're so pleased to have you with us today." He smiled like a little angel, this wholehearted grin that made him even more endearing. "We'd love to have you visit with us anytime."

He put his hand on Annabelle's arm and said, most confidentially, "I'm not sure if you'd be interested, but I'm looking for someone to help Junie out." He nodded his head toward a little lady that must have been my age. "It would be something to get you out of the house just until you found the right job."

My heart was racing. If he'd asked me, I can tell you right now what I would've said. But, Annabelle, she didn't say yes right away.

"Well," Annabelle said, a hair flirtatiously, "I better walk through those four steps, make sure the Holy Spirit is telling me that's the right thing to do, and then I'll let you know next week."

He laughed. "Glad my sermon had an effect on you."

Annabelle swore that I was insane, that my long-standing Episcopal minister dream had made me crazy. But, standing between those two kids on the lawn with the lemonade, I'd say that sermon wasn't the only thing that had an effect on her.

Annabelle

∞

Perfect Seeds

The first year of marriage is the hardest. Lovey always told us that adjusting to living with another person, no matter how much you love them, can be tricky. But I think when you get married in three days, the first year of marriage is like that glorious first year of dating. Your nerves prick when his hand brushes your leg, you count the seconds until you are together again. You frivolously worry if you've texted him too much that day and play games with yourself: *I'm not going to say anything back to him until he texts me twice in a row.* Or, *I'm not going to look at all of his Facebook pictures again until I've finished this load of laundry.*

When you've only known each other as long, that first year is magic. So, it's the second year, or, if you're us, about eighteen months in, when the dew finally wears off and the grass loses some of its luster. But I don't think either of us could have acknowledged that that's when we started to hit a bit of a rocky patch. It is only in retrospect that I can even see the shift, the minor turn in the earth that gives you vertigo. We weren't fighting or anything. It was just that, all of a sudden, a relationship that we both knew was going to be endlessly thrilling became mundane.

Maybe it was that Ben was back working at a job that, to put it mildly, didn't get his creative juices flowing like they once were. When he wasn't singing, I wasn't his muse, and, quite frankly, I had a bit less time for musing anyway. My new boss, Father Rob, affectionately nicknamed Priest Charming by his parishioners, had taken what was supposed to be a part-time job and made it full-time demanding.

I was more than a little intimidated walking into the church office that first day. I loved the look of the Saint Catherine House, its aging brick and white picket fence, the idyllic little flower garden. The impossibly tall ceilings inside, huge, light-filled windows and comfortable furnishings made it feel more like home than work. But I didn't have a firm grasp on my actual responsibilities, and my doctrine was a little rusty, since I hadn't been a regular church participant since high school. But I was excited to be getting out of the house and doing something, *anything* that felt like it had purpose. Plus, it was a great way to take my mind off of not being pregnant.

"Oh my Lord, I'm so happy you're here," Junie said as soon as I walked through the door my first morning, my arms overflowing with homemade muffins of every kind. That they were homemade by Emily could be our secret. Junie rushed to hug me, squishing the muffins into my chest, and, as I laughed, Priest Charming appeared from around the corner, raised his eyebrows at me in surprise and laughed too.

"Junie, do we need to watch that video on sexual harassment again?"

That was the moment I realized that this job was nothing like I thought it was going to be. I had assumed Rob would be as stuffy and uptight as his clerical collar.

I had also expected to get right down to business, to engross myself in spreadsheets and contact lists and bulletin proofs. But, instead, Rob said, "Okay. Let's get in the car."

"Where are we going?" I asked, imagining myself at some poor parishioner's bedside, solemnly holding the prayer book as Father Rob read him his last rites. So I was more than a little surprised when he said, "Strawberry picking, of course."

I thought maybe that was some sort of first-day-on-the-job welcome or something, but, when Junie said, "Better you than me," I realized that seemingly unrelated field trips must be a part of the job description. As Rob opened the door of his Audi convertible for me, he said, "Don't you love the first strawberries of the year? I think strawberries instantly make it feel like summer."

I nodded. "I *always* say that. And not those grocery store, middle-of-winter strawberries either. Real, ripe, minute-old strawberries." I put my seat belt on as he pushed the top down, and, though I was wondering how an associate pastor could buy an Audi convertible, I kept the thought to myself. Instead, I asked, "Is there a reason we're going strawberry picking?"

"I'm sure there's a reason," Rob said. "I'm just not sure what it is yet." He grinned at me.

"I'm confused."

"Well, every night before I go to bed, I ask the Holy Spirit to put something on my heart that I should do that day. So every morning I wake up with a distinct urge to complete some task—sometimes mundane, sometimes off the wall."

"So how do you know that it's a message from heaven? I mean, how do you know it isn't just the aftermath of a dream or a random thought?"

He shrugged. "Haven't you ever just known, Ann?"

I looked at him sideways when he called me Ann. It seemed sort of intimate for someone I barely knew. But, then again, Rob didn't seem like the kind to feel uncomfortable. And, of course, I "just knew" all the time. I instantly thought about Ben. "So do you ever get done with a task and think, 'Well that was pointless'?"

"Oh, sure, all the time." Rob pulled into a parking space outside of Patterson Farm. "But I never, ever think that about that first-thought-of-the-day task."

Rob and I each got a Patterson Farm cardboard basket with its open top and wooden handle that fit right over your arm for picking. It made me think of Lovey and how she would take me strawberry picking when I was little. I would keep those empty picking containers, wrap my dolls in blankets and slide them into the baskets, pretending they were my own precious babies. It was the first time I had thought about my empty uterus since breakfast.

About halfway down the first row, I said, "Doesn't it feel sad just leaving some of these behind, or picking them, realizing they're bad, and then throwing them back."

Rob nodded and was quiet for the first time that morning.

Since I tend to ramble in uncomfortable silences—at least when they're uncomfortable on my end—I continued. "I mean, they all start from the same perfect seeds, but then when they grow, some never even get to reach their full potential of being spread over pound cake with homemade whipped cream."

My boss laughed. "Thanks, new Girl Friday."

"For what?"

"You just wrote my sermon."

And that's when I realized that, though I might have stopped inspiring my husband, that didn't mean I wasn't still a muse.

Lovey

ᆋ

The Nicest Boy

May 1949

My momma always said that you didn't stop dating until there was a ring on your finger. So, I didn't want to, but, to appease her, I went on the occasional date when I was at WC. Well, more to the point, I went on hundreds of dates with Dan and a few with other boys. I'll admit that it got harder and harder to see the other girls come home with rings on their fingers, leave school early to get married. There were even a few that left school and got married because they were pregnant—but we didn't talk about that out loud. Just behind our hands in hushed tones after she was gone.

Dan and I dreamed of our wedding day. When he went home for Christmas break, he negotiated with his parents that he would work for one year after college, get his feet on the ground, and we would get married. It was longer than either of us wanted to wait, but it was better than the five years that his father's parents had demanded of him.

Dan was coming to pick me up that night, and I couldn't wait to see him, to go dance, to feel his strong arms around me, our lips on each other's. With only a couple of weeks until graduation, we could see the light at the end of the tunnel. And I had found a teaching job in New Bern, where he would be working as a banker, and a group of girlfriends to live with. At least we would be in the same town now and could see each other all the time.

Dan handed me the telegram before I realized that there were tears in his eyes. Before I could even finish reading it, I was sobbing. "If they had just let us get married. Why didn't they let us get married?"

"How could this happen again?" Dan asked. "Don't they think I've served my time?" He punched the hood of the car, and I didn't blame him. I wanted to too.

Dan hugged me close to him. "Will you wait for me, Lynn? Please, please promise that you'll wait for me. We are getting engaged the minute I get home, my parents be damned. They can have their house and their money and their rules." He kissed my head and lowered his voice, looking down on me. "All I want is you."

We cried a lot that night, but Dan told me not to be scared. "I won't be fighting this time, Lynn, so you don't have to worry."

"They aren't fighting now," I cried. "But what about later? What if the war heats up? Oh, I can't bear the thoughts of knowing that you're in danger."

He had kissed me passionately and said, "I promise that I will come home to you. And when I do, we'll get married. And I'll spend the rest of my life taking care of you and making it up to you."

I was supportive. My parents were not. Since Dan wasn't going to New Bern, it seemed silly for me to. So, instead, I went back home. I was twenty-three already, and most of my friends were married, having babies, starting their lives. And I was so jealous I could scarcely breathe.

That first night back home I realized I had made a huge mistake. I should have gone to New Bern with my other single girlfriends.

I was sitting on the living room sofa, crying my eyes out because my Dan was gone. The love of my life was on the other side of the world. War had brought us together and war had torn us apart again. It didn't seem fair.

"Look," my daddy said. "I know you're brokenhearted, Lynn, but we think it might be time to move on."

"Move on?" I spat through my tears. "I will not move on. Dan is the love of my life."

"Of course he is, darling," my mother soothed. "But, in the meantime, the nicest boy wants to take you out."

I glared at her. "Momma, have you not been listening? I'm in *love*, for pity's sake. I am marrying Dan the moment he gets home. I'm waiting for him. I'm not dating a bunch of people I'm not interested in. I did that in college because you made me. I'm done now. In my mind, I'm married to Dan already."

She shook her head. "Darling, I don't know how they do it where you've been, but, 'round here, I think you know there's no such thing as going steady until there's a ring on that pretty finger. Nobody's gonna pay for that cow when they can get the milk for free."

"First of all, no one is getting my *milk*, Momma. So let's just get that straight." I fluffed my hair. "Second of all, there will be a ring on my finger before you know it."

"Well," Daddy interjected, "I was telling Ernest's daddy all about you being summa cum laude and all that time you spent in New

York, and I promised him a date when you got back home after graduation."

"Ernest . . ." I thought with my finger against my lip. "Ernest *Wake*." I shook my head. "Daddy, no. No way."

Ernest had been nicknamed Booger in middle school because, far past the age when children become self-aware, he still picked his nose during class. He had curly red hair, freckles, glasses and bad teeth.

"He's quite the catch, young lady," Momma said.

"No, Momma," I said, stomping my foot softly. "He's *rich*. Not a catch."

"Well," my daddy tried to soothe, "I promised him a date, so you'll need to go out with him."

"This isn't some impoverished country, Daddy! You can't just marry me off to some rich man, trade me for a couple of cows."

"Oh, don't be ridiculous." Daddy sniffed through his laughter. "They'd have to give me some chickens too."

"Besides," Momma said, perhaps feeling slightly more empathetic than Daddy, "no one said a thing about marriage."

And they hadn't. Not yet.

Annabelle

A Special Place

Whatever you're doing, whether it's the job of your dreams or washing the dishes, make sure you're the very best at it. Because being your best and working the hardest always leads to better things, Lovey says. It's advice I've always tried to follow. And starting my new job at Saint Paul's was no different.

There was going to be a lot of on-the-job training because, before I worked for Father Rob, I didn't know much about what a priest did. I mean, obviously, they give a sermon on Sundays and are in charge of morning prayer and visit a lot of sick people in the hospital. But, beyond that, I had no idea what the day-in, day-out life of a priest was like. And I still don't. Because I can tell you, unequivocally, without even having anything to compare it to, that most priests don't do the kinds of things that Saint Paul's Priest Charming did.

My second week of work I walked in moderately more prepared, having realized that every day was going to start with a new surprise.

Only, that morning, when I got to work, Junie was there but Father Rob was nowhere to be found. "Oh, good," she said when I walked through the door. "We've beat him here, so maybe we can actually get some work done."

I laughed. "Why is it that men always seem to be the distraction and it's the women that get it all done?"

She shook her head. "I don't know, but I've been around eighty years, and I've seldom seen that not to be the case." Junie paused, opened a file drawer, her aged hand shaking the tiniest bit, and said, "Do you think you could teach me how to use the e-mail?"

Before I could even begin to panic about trying to teach an eighty-year-old who still procured lickable stamps because she thought the self-stick kinds were a fad, the phone rang. "Good morning, Saint Paul's," I said unsuspectingly.

"Annabelle, this is Lucy Simmons."

I rolled my eyes at Junie. This was going to be good. I could tell already. "Good morning, Mrs. Simmons. How may I help you?"

"Um, well, yes, I suppose it is a good morning. But . . . well, did you know that Brian Peterson is a chef?"

I couldn't imagine how this was relevant to my life. "Well, I suppose I did know that." I didn't know what else to say.

"Well, then, wouldn't you say that it seems a little unfair that he won the chili cook-off, while I, an untrained chef, placed second? I mean, I would venture to say that my chili is the best chili anyway, but to lose to a professional chef seems to violate the rules."

"Well, Mrs. Simmons, I'm not sure that there were any official rules, per se. We raised eleven thousand dollars for the job skills training program, which I think was really the point of the contest."

She paused. "Well, sure. But I just don't think that seems right. Maybe I could talk it over with Father Rob and see what he thinks, but I would suggest that maybe for next year you have some official rules in writing."

I looked around for Father Rob, assuming that this was a joke. He was testing me, seeing how I would handle the parishioners' more ridiculous requests. "Well, I'm sorry, he's not in right now, but I'd be happy to take down your number and have him call you later."

Priest Charming roared into the office, his collar over a T-shirt and shorts, but before he could say a word, I put my finger to my lips, widened my eyes and shook my head. This was a message I could see getting lost. Instead of putting down her number, I wrote "Mrs. Simmons" and circled it, showing it to him. He mimed a noose around his neck.

As she said, "Could you just repeat that number back to me so I can make sure you got it right?" I replied, "Thanks so much for your feedback. Have a blessed day!" I hung up.

"A blessed day?"

"Yup. When things get really irritating around here, I tell people to have a blessed day instead of blessing them out."

Junie laughed. She never laughed. The irritating phone call had been totally worth it.

I turned to Rob. "You might want to get down some official rules for next year's chili cook-off."

Rob smiled, shook his head and handed me a pair of gardening gloves. Junie and I shot each other a knowing grimace. I pretended to be annoyed so that she and I would have that bond, but, truth be told, I looked forward to a fun surprise at the beginning of the workday.

"So," I said, as I climbed into the passenger seat. "Are gardening gloves my only clue?"

Father Rob smiled. "Mrs. Taylor is one of our most faithful parishioners, and she sprained her ankle last week."

I could feel my brow wrinkling. "I'm not certified in any way to be a caretaker."

He laughed. "She's fine, but she has an award-winning garden, and I woke up this morning feeling like we should go prune her roses."

"That's fine with me, but I won't be held responsible for any damages. I don't know the opposite of green, but that's what color my thumb is."

Father Rob laughed again, but I stayed serious. "This is not a joke. I can kill any plant, anywhere."

My phone beeped, and, looking down at the screen, I felt myself grimace. The new message on my Facebook wall read, *Happy nineteen months to the most beautiful girl in the entire world. You are the love of my life and I can't wait to celebrate with you tonight!*

"Oh, no," I said out loud. "No, no, no, no, no."

"What?"

"Ben just wrote this hideous, lovey message on my Facebook wall."

I fully expected to have to explain why that was a problem, but, instead, Rob said, "Oh, no. Why would he do that?"

I shook my head. "I hate that so much."

"Oh, I know." Rob made a gagging sound. "It's like 'Hey. I know we're sitting across the room from each other, but I wanted to tell you I love you.' So insincere."

"Exactly!"

My phone beeped with a text from Cameron. Are you and Ben getting divorced? I hear writing on each other's Facebook walls is the first sign. And it makes me vomit.

I laughed and turned to Rob. "My best friend is also appalled by the Facebook shout-out."

"Why don't you just take it down? Can't you do that?"

I sighed, thinking of sweet, sweet Ben and how he would do just about anything to make me smile. "I don't want to hurt his feelings."

I realized that it was probably bad form to be talking to my boss about something so personal and trivial, so I said, "Poor Mrs. Taylor. Probably going to have a yard full of formerly award-winning roses totally dead by tomorrow."

Fifteen minutes later I found out that the yard wasn't the only thing I wanted to kill. "Not like that," Mrs. Taylor was griping, for probably the tenth time. "I'm over here in this chair, foot all akimbo, and you can't even manage to prune my shrubbery properly."

It wasn't the gracious, warm thank-you I had expected. How Father Rob smiled through it all I don't have the slightest idea, but he whistled and took it all in stride while I couldn't have felt less happy. We were kneeling over in the dirt, our backs to Mrs. Taylor, sweating, replanting a couple of bushes.

Perhaps it was because our gardening skills weren't enough to complain about, but Mrs. Taylor, presumably to my rear end, said, "So why is it that none of you young people around here ever volunteer?"

"Well," I stuttered, "I just moved here, so I'm not totally sure, but I think everyone is just so busy with work and kids."

What would you call this? I felt like asking her. I swallowed the lump in my throat and clipped those bushes a little harder as I remembered my own childless state. On the bright side, it made me think of Ben. Fun, gorgeous Ben. We had planned a special date that night, just the two of us, and, though I was still a little concerned about Cameron's mostly joking text message, I couldn't be more ready for a night out.

It was the first time in my life that I had had even an ounce of trouble making new friends. I had acquaintances and was invited to the girls' events, but I hadn't felt that special spark with anyone yet, that sixth sense that this person was going to be a lifelong friend.

"Well, I need someone to chair the Spring Fling," she continued on. "Laura Anne has just stepped up and done everything this year, so I couldn't possibly ask her again. Do you know of anyone?"

I turned awkwardly to look at her. Mrs. Taylor peered at me, and, Father Rob, wiping a stream of dirt across his sweaty forehead, said, "I can't think of a better person for the job than Annabelle. She's an ace with the organization and handles anything that's thrown at her like a total pro."

I turned back toward the bushes and shot him an evil look. "I know you're my boss and a pastor," I hissed at him, "but that doesn't mean that the devil can't still find a special place for you."

He laughed and said louder, "In fact, I think it would be great for Annabelle. It will give her an opportunity to meet all kinds of new people."

"Well, then it's settled," Mrs. Taylor said, shifting so that the sides of her flabby body spilled over the frame of the chair. "I'll call you about our first meeting."

When I told Ben about it over a candlelit dinner at La Cava that night, thankful for the first time in months not to be pregnant, as a rich cabernet numbed the stress of the day, all he could say was, "Please, let's not become one of *those* couples."

He didn't have to elaborate. We had spent many a moonlit night lying under the stars on the top of the RV, talking about how our lives were going to be different. We weren't going to be one of those boring, by-the-book couples who settled into suburbia and joined the PTA and had sex once a month. But, as I took another sip of wine, I felt a sinking feeling that, here we were, living in Salisbury, steadily employed and already volunteering for things we didn't care a thing about. We needed to shake it up—and fast.

I didn't mention the Facebook thing to Ben, not wanting to hurt his feelings. And it shouldn't have been a big deal. But I couldn't count the number of times Cameron and I had rolled our eyes and said that having to share your "love" with your Facebook friends was so fake. And I couldn't shake the feeling that it was a sign that something was amiss.

Our waiter, tall, thin and prematurely gray, approached the table, and, in a tone that said he and Ben went way back said, "Our special tonight is penne a la vodka with shrimp. I highly recommend it." He turned to Ben and said, "Laura Anne had it earlier this evening and said it was fabulous."

"O-kay . . ." Ben said the word like it was two. "I guess I'll have that."

"Make it two," I said, smiling generously. When the waiter was out of earshot, I said, "Who the hell is Laura Anne? Mrs. Taylor was talking about her earlier today."

Ben swigged his wine and said, "Weird. She's a girl I went to high school with. Classic overachiever. Kind of annoying."

I nodded. "Oh. Well, things don't change. Mrs. Taylor said Laura Anne is the only one who ever helps her with the volunteer stuff."

"Anyway," Ben said, "tell me more about this event. Are we going to have our pictures on the front page of the *Salisbury Post* as the town's most philanthropic new couple?"

I sighed. "Can't we go on the road again?"

Ben shrugged. "Dad's partner should be back from his 'sabbatical' in six months. And then I'm all about it."

"Sabbatical?" I whispered.

"Court-ordered sabbatical," he whispered back.

Ben's mom picked us up in the Subaru station wagon she had had since he was in elementary school, and I felt like I was a kid again as we giggled and held hands in the backseat. Even when you live alone, sometimes it's nice to have a couple of hours to really talk and reconnect.

That night we lay in bed and whispered about nothing and everything all at once until the sun came up. "I'm so glad I found you," I told Ben. "Being with you has made me free."

He stroked my face, kissed my mouth and said, "You are the only woman in the world to me, TL. Nothing is better than knowing I get to be with you for the rest of my life."

It was exactly what we needed. And, as I drifted off for a couple of hours before I headed into work, I felt so content that, no matter where the future led, my forever was lying beside me.

When I woke up that morning, I had an e-mail from the other man who wanted to be my forever.

Good morning, lovely. Just wanted to inform you that I'm booking a Paris trip for two weeks from now. You know no one does Paris quite like I do. Give me a chance to wow you. We can rebuild what we had. I love you.

Just like Cameron had said only a few hours earlier, I thought I might throw up.

Lovey

✺

Little Lies

It was a woman's responsibility to replace herself and her husband times two, according to my momma. And that was even more important for me, since momma only had Lib and me to carry on the family. I listened, but there were an awful lot of times when my five girls were growing up that I thought I must have been insane. *Who*, I would ask myself, *would sign up for all of this time after time after time?* But now that the tantrums are over, the fights about late nights out and car dating and boys and outfits and shoes, and Dan walking through the house counting how many lights had been left on, I'm so happy that I have my five girls—and that they have each other.

That afternoon, sitting at my squeaky-clean new assisted living apartment, there they all were, crowded around their daddy, doing their best tricks to get his attention even though he didn't know if he was in North Carolina or Timbuktu.

"I think he knows what's going on and just can't express himself," Sally said.

The thought made me shiver. I hated when she said it. I couldn't think of much worse than being trapped inside your body like that, aware of what was going on but unable to interact, thoughts cruising through your mind like always but unable to get off at the port of your mouth.

"Sally," Lauren, who was my feistiest child, scolded, "Momma hates when you say that."

Louise shrugged her shoulders, a perfect fourth child. She waved her hand. "He doesn't have a clue what's going on. And he's just perfectly content to sit in that chair and watch his black and whites."

I nodded, not sure if I agreed. But I had to convince myself that was true to chase away the nightmares of being trapped inside myself, screaming and screaming with no one able to hear me or help. "He's such a good patient," I said. "And that's something to be thankful for."

"Yeah." Jean laughed. "Because I think we all know it could easily have gone the other way."

She grabbed a handful of Hershey's Kisses and placed them in front of her feet, where she was sitting cross-legged on the floor. Then she handed the bowl to Martha, who was sitting beside her in the semicircle, flanking the chairs where Dan and I were sitting.

"Hey, Daddy," Martha said, like he was going to answer. "Do you remember that time that Bobby Franco came to pick me up in his T-Bird convertible and didn't get out of the car to open my door?"

"Oh, yeah," Lauren said. "He beeped the horn, didn't he?"

Martha nodded. "And Daddy flew out of that house and told him he better get the hell out of his driveway and never come around his daughters again until he had learned some damn manners."

We all laughed, and I felt that familiar mix of pride and sorrow that so often filled me these days. We had had so much life together. It burned like turpentine for it to be gone, but I was so grateful it had happened. My Dan had been a lot of things in his life, but, without fail, the constant was that he was a complete gentleman. From our first date to the last time I saw him on his feet, he opened my door, pulled out my chair, stood when I left the table and always treated me with respect. Well, almost always.

"Could we please stay on task, girls?"

Jean exhaled sharply. "Momma, none of us cares what we get. Just pick who you want to give everything to."

"I call the ring!" Sally and Louise shouted at the same time.

Then Sally added, "For sentimental reasons, of course."

Dan had bought me a five-carat diamond after Jean was born, one carat for each daughter. It was a mea culpa for putting me through so much.

And I well, well deserved it.

I wouldn't say to them that day—or any day—that Jean was getting that ring. It symbolized so much more than she would ever realize, and, as much as it had been a carat for each girl, that ring was really about Jean. And I wanted her to have it.

Jean shook her head. "I'm not talking about this anymore, so let's talk about something else or let me get back to writing campaign contribution thank-you notes."

I smiled at her, internally musing at the irony that she was by far the most attached to me, the most horrified by the thoughts of my being gone.

Trying to change the subject, never wanting these family moments to be too fleeting, Louise said, "Can you imagine if you had married Ernest Wake, Momma? None of this would be happening right now."

Lauren looked up at Dan, who had been fiddling for ten minutes with an old letter we had handed him. I had no idea what he was doing, but I would have bet the cases of gold coins he kept in the credenza beside him that it wasn't reading.

"Daddy, you made short work of that old Ernest, didn't you?"

To my surprise, he looked at her, smiled and said, "Yeah."

I put my head in my hands. "Oh, girls, if you could have been on a dinner date with him." I rolled my eyes. "The way he sent his food back, and talked down to the waiters. I was beyond mortified. It was so dreadful."

"So why didn't you just refuse to go?" Lauren asked.

I smiled and shrugged, thinking of my parents, of how hard they worked for everything they had, of the way they scrimped and saved and sacrificed to make sure that my sister and I had as many advantages as we could. I would wrap myself in my bedclothes during the most frigid winter nights, huddling by the roaring fire in my room, the heat rising rapidly through the tall ceilings that were our only reprieve from the scalding summer heat. "It made my momma and daddy so proud that I was dating Ernest Wake. Plus," I added, looking over in Dan's direction, "Dan had been called back to the service, and it wasn't like we had e-mail and cell phones. I didn't have any good way of knowing where he was going or when or if he was coming back." I swallowed hard, realizing that it wasn't all that different now. "At my age, I didn't have too many good prospects, and I knew that Ernest and I would have a nice life together if, God forbid, Dan didn't come back."

"God, that's depressing," Louise said. "Hence the reason I'm not married."

"Well, it was a different time, Louise," I said. "You know that. An unmarried woman didn't have a lot of good options. Sometimes marrying for love wasn't in the cards."

"So you may as well marry for money," Martha said, laughing.

I made all my girls smile with one of my trademark phrases: "It's as easy to love a rich man as it is a poor one."

"Speaking of," Lauren said, "I've been meaning to tell y'all about the new man that I'm dating."

"Oh my goodness, who?" Sally asked.

Lauren smiled, and I could sense just a hint of that maliciousness in her getting ready to escape. My stomach gripped like I'd had too much Metamucil just about the time she said, "Kyle Jenkins."

All eyes turned instantly to Sally, as Kyle Jenkins had been the man we thought she would marry. She had dated him for five years and then, one night, after he had asked Dan's permission to marry her, he dumped her with no explanation whatsoever. He tried to get her back, but she had already met Doug. Sally had decided that, while brilliant, good-looking and destined for the kind of fortune that girls dream of, all she really wanted in a partner was someone who would be kind, steady and would never hurt her like that again.

I braced myself for the reaction of my other girls, and it didn't surprise me one bit when Louise said, "Don't you sort of feel like he's using you? Like you're the Sally replacement?"

Sally shook her head and said, "Don't be ridiculous. I think it's great."

But you didn't have to be trained in reading body language to realize she didn't think it was so great.

"He is so wonderful," Lauren said, as though none of her sisters had even spoken. "He's smart and charming and so, so funny."

"He's a great dancer too," Sally added.

"Lauren, that's so weird," Jean chimed in. "He's never even gotten married. You have to know that he's been in love with Sally his entire life."

She waved her hand. "I think that's absurd. When we saw each other at the club over the summer, we really hit it off." She smiled. "It's so difficult to find a man who can really take care of you these days."

It was the tiniest jab at her sister, a reminder that Sally's stay-at-home husband had rarely held down a job for more than a few months over the course of their marriage. But, as a stay-at-home wife, I thought they diminished Doug's role in the family way too easily. He was a good man, and they were happy. Who could ask for more than that?

I always defended Lauren when the other girls ganged up against her, but, this time, there was little to defend. She had made her choice, they had formed their opinion, and that was all there was to it. It had to have bothered Sally that her sister was dating the man I always suspected was the love of her life. But she was as cool and calm as I'd ever seen her, and, if it bothered her, she didn't let on.

"Okay, then," Lauren said, glancing at the diamond Tiffany watch she had inherited when her former mother-in-law died. "Kyle and I are meeting for dinner in Chapel Hill tonight, so I better go home and get beautiful."

Jean rolled her eyes at Martha, Lauren kissed her daddy and me, and, just like that, she was out the door and on the elevator. It was as if she wanted to make sure we were talking about her when she was gone.

"She is such a bitch!" Jean said, as soon as Lauren had closed the door.

"Jean," I scolded, trying not to smile. "Don't say that word and especially not about your own sister."

Louise nodded her head, taking a sip of the kombucha mess that she was rarely without. She was always trying to get Dan and me to drink it to improve our immunity and gut flora. But I liked my gut flora the way it was, thank you very much. "Momma, I don't know how you can defend her all the time. She is such a hideous person. How did you raise her and all of us in the same family?"

"Now, girls . . ."

I looked over at Sally. She hadn't said a word, but she was whiter than Ernest used to be in his swim trunks on the first day of summer. For someone who had held it together so beautifully while Lauren was in the room, her countenance immediately shifted when her sister walked away. "I can't believe that he would actually do this to me," Sally whispered.

"He?" Martha asked. "What about your wicked witch of a sister?"

And I didn't need to hear any more to know that, sometimes, no matter how good a girl seems, all of us, from top to bottom, need to use our little lies every now and then.

Annabelle

❧

In Your Head

If you do something you love, you never work a day in your life, according to Lovey. One of the great things about my new job was that, while it put a check in that "employed" box, it was about the furthest thing from work I could imagine. My days were jam-packed with fun activities that, even when they were dreadfully annoying, like that day with Mrs. Taylor, were much more exciting than pushing paper around a desk and intermittently checking Facebook, making sure I didn't need to hide any more offensive messages from my husband.

Plus, if I wanted to flit over to Greensboro, the midpoint between Raleigh and Salisbury, for lunch with Mom and Sally, Rob didn't care one bit. Although my hours indicated otherwise, I was still technically part-time, after all.

I was practically salivating over the black-eyed-pea cakes that I knew I would order, smiling thinking of how much fun it was going to be to laugh with my family—especially since Ben's newfound "real" job had him working so much. It was definitely a switch after being together nearly nonstop for a year.

The minute I saw Sally, though, I felt the day take an unexpected U-turn. I slid into the oversized, mercifully tall booth, sized just right to hide Sally's pained face. My mind wandered to the first natural place: Lovey and D-daddy. But, when my mom's face came into view, where she looked at me from beside her sister, I felt the tension dissolve a little. I knew her well enough to know that her expression was out of feeling her sister's pain, not her own.

Sally pinned on a fake smile and said, "Well, hi, Annie."

I shook my head. "Absolutely not. What's going on?"

"Nothing," Mom said.

I crossed my arms. "I'm twenty-three years old. You can't 'nothing' me anymore and think I'm going to buy it."

Right then, my phone beeped. I looked down expectantly, hoping it was something sweet from my husband. Instead, I sighed and rolled my eyes, setting my phone on the table.

"What's up, buttercup?" Mom asked.

"Holden is what's up. He won't freaking leave me alone."

As Mom said, "You know I hate that word," Sally burst into tears like I had just announced that I had received a text from my oncologist. I looked at Mom, stupefied. Sally had always been sensitive, sure. But Holden texting me here and there wasn't anything to cry about.

I took a sip of my tea, told the mystified waiter that we might need a minute and said, "Okay. Now 'nothing' definitely isn't going to cut it."

"Don't you dare get involved with him, Annabelle," Sally sobbed. "If it means changing your phone number and closing your e-mail and moving to a new house, you get away from him." She pointed her finger at me. "Don't let him get in your head."

I shook my head, feeling my eyes widen. "I'm not," I said. "I promise. At first I was being mean, but that didn't work, so now I'm just ignoring him."

Sally shook her head. "That's what I should have done with Kyle."

"Kyle?" I mouthed to Mom.

Then I nodded, remembering Kyle Jenkins, the absurdly handsome man who was always eyeing Sally at the Shoals Club. We all knew that, for him, she was the one that got away, the reason he never married or had a family.

"Lauren is dating Kyle," Mom explained.

I took another sip of my tea, still feeling a little bit confused.

"No, no," Sally said, sitting up taller and composing herself. "She should know. Someone should learn from my mistakes."

The waiter reappeared, and, at what seemed like a very inconvenient time, we ordered our food. I was literally on the edge of my seat, waiting for these random ingredients to mix in the cocktail shaker and become something cohesive.

"People like Holden, they get in your head," Sally said. "You think it's all well and good, but they wear you down over time."

Mom pushed her hair behind her ear and said, "No, Sally. Holden was never like Kyle. If anything, Kyle was more like Ben."

That made my breath catch in my throat. I still wasn't sure how the frames of this film were going to fit together, but I knew unequivocally that I didn't want Ben to be like Kyle when, as I was starting to see, these tears my aunt was crying were over him.

"Wait," I said. "I'm so confused. Why is Kyle like Ben?"

"Kyle was the absolute love of my life," Sally said. "We had that instant, burning passionate love that you dream about all your life." She shrugged. "And then he just dumped me."

"And so you married Doug," I said. Doug certainly wasn't a

head-turner like Kyle, but he was a good man. He was always there for all of us and the first one to make a joke or lift you up when you were feeling down. I had always thought that Sally and Doug's marriage was as solid as it got.

"And Kyle decided he wanted me back. He wrote me letters, called me at work. A time or two, he even showed up at my office."

My mom shook her head.

I leaned back the slightest bit, so the waiter could put those black-eyed-pea cakes I'd been so excited for in front of me. And I wondered again why we would be in the midst of such an emotional crisis in the middle of a restaurant.

"And then what?" I asked, popping my fork into my mouth, thinking through my anxiety that the food really was tasty.

"He wore me down," she whispered.

"You had an affair?" I whispered back, wide-eyed.

Mom laughed quietly. "More like a marriage."

I glared at her. "That's mean, Mom. And what does that mean?"

"We've been seeing each other on and off since 1989."

I almost spit my black-eyed-pea cake right across the table. I didn't want to, but I laughed incredulously. "So the reason he looks at you like you're on fire is because you *are* on fire."

Sally looked down at her hands. "I'm so ashamed."

"Does Doug know?"

"Oh, Lord," she said. "Doug has known forever."

"And he's okay with it?"

Mom rolled her eyes. "The whole thing is utterly absurd."

I shook my head and put my hand on the table. "Wait a minute. Is that why Doug didn't come with us to the beach? Because you were sneaking out with Kyle?"

Sally scrunched her nose in a gesture that revealed everything.

I stared at her in disbelief. "Let me get this straight. You mean to tell me that the man you have been seeing on the side since before I even existed—who your husband knows about—is dating your sister?"

Sally nodded. "Kyle told me that he had had enough and that I had to choose. Of course, I don't want to break up my marriage, so I chose Doug." She inhaled. "It has been like living without water, but I chose to stick it out."

"So he—very maturely—chose to start 'dating' Lauren," Mom said, making air quotes.

My phone rang. It was Ben, and, even though I missed him like crazy and wanted to talk to him, this was like one of those really great stories in *Us Weekly* that you don't want to read while you're waiting in line at the grocery store but you can't possibly resist.

"How could you even want to be with someone who would do that to you?" Mom asked, shaking her head. "You're a grown-up, and they're playing this ridiculously childish game with you."

"No, no, no," I said. "Forget wanting to be with him. How could you be married to a man who was okay to sit back and let you have an affair for your entire life together?"

Sally leaned back heavily on the bench and sighed. As if Mom and I had never even asked her a question, she said, "What if Momma knows?"

Mom shook her head.

"Lovey knows everything," I said.

Sally gave me a downtrodden look.

"What?" I asked. "She does. She knows everything; she just has the decency not to say it."

Mom gasped. "That comment on the beach!"

I nodded furiously.

"Oh, God," Sally said, laying her head on the table. "About how she was so glad I married Doug and not Kyle." She sat back up. "I've been worrying about Lauren telling her, when, in reality, she has known the entire time."

"Wait," Mom said. "So you think Lauren knows?"

Sally laughed cruelly. "Hell yeah, she knows. She's playing the most vicious game of chicken with me that I've ever encountered."

"Ohhhh," Mom said knowingly. "So her parading around bragging about how rich and charming and funny he is is her seeing how long it takes to break you."

"This is the most dysfunctional thing I've ever heard," I said.

I was sort of impressed, though. I mean, here was this squeaky-clean woman that you would never imagine had even had sex were it not for the children to prove it. And yet, here she was, gallivanting all over the state in the midst of a totally torrid affair for decades without anyone being the wiser. I looked at her milky skin, relatively wrinkle-free and, despite the circumstances, generally unworried in appearance. I thought of Ben, of the physical pull my body felt toward his, of the gnawing feeling in the back of my mind I always had knowing that I was away from him. I craved his touch and his attention. And so, in that way, I could relate to what Sally was going through.

I just had no idea that it could still be happening to a sixty-year-old.

I shook my head again. "So what are you going to do?"

She sighed heavily again. "As twisted as it is, I think it's going to work."

"What is?" Mom asked.

"This ridiculous little game Lauren and Kyle are playing." Sally shook her head. "I want to be with Doug and be happy—"

"But you can't," Mom said.

Sally shook her head and, in a near whisper, said, "I'm so desperately in love with Kyle."

In spite of the terrible circumstances, I smiled. It made me happy to know that, even after all these years, Kyle could make Sally feel like a desperate schoolgirl in love. Because I never wanted that feeling to end with Ben.

I had always thought of my aunt Lauren as the villain of our family and, trust me, I thought what she was doing was evil. But maybe her intentions were the purest of all of us. Instead of letting Sally hem and haw and finish off her life unsettled and unsatisfied, she was pushing her to choose the man she knew had been first in her sister's heart all along.

I looked at Mom, "Did you know about this?"

She shook her head.

Then, to Sally: "Did Lauren?"

Sally shook her head. "I'm assuming that Kyle told her."

"Seems like a pretty risky move," I said.

Sally's face was suddenly wrought with horror. "Oh my gosh," she said. "She does know, right? I mean, they aren't actually dating? This is just a game." She looked down at her hands and whispered, "Isn't it?"

Mom reached over and patted her hand reassuringly. "Lauren is tough. No doubt about that. But the thing about her strength is that she uses it on those who are trying to hurt the people she loves. She would never turn on us." She paused. "We're sisters."

I shook my head. "Seems like a pretty risky move all the same."

Then, as my phone beeped with yet another text from Holden, Mom said, "You, of all people, should understand the crazy lengths people will go to for love."

Lovey

❧

Rather Serious

July 1951

No matter how you feel, when a man takes you out on a date, you act polite, gracious and warm. Sometimes, following Momma's advice took more effort than others. All I could think about that night, in the most perfectly manicured garden that one could ever hope to see in real life, surrounded by women in summer dresses as colorful and full as the flowers, was how socially inept Ernest Wake was. At that summer party on the farm, studying Ernest's red hair and pale, freckled complexion, I thought, not for the first time, that he wasn't particularly good-looking. He wasn't particularly anything, come to think of it—except for rich. He was the heir to a banking fortune that my mother had prayed for every night since I was born. And, at twenty-five, I was way past my prime, well on my way to becoming an old maid who had a better chance of becoming president than finding a suitable mate.

According to whispers around town, Ernest was my last chance. I would by lying if I said I didn't feel the pressure. But I'd also be lying if I said my heart wasn't over the ocean with the boy who had stolen it first and held on to it with the perfect grip for all those years.

That night, celebrating summer surrounded by gloriously manicured acres of farmland, in a yellow floral dress with just the right amount of crinoline underneath and a pair of pristine leather pumps that I still had from the contest, I sipped my punch demurely, holding the arm of Ernest, trying to sort through whether I was sickened or excited over the rumors that tonight would be the night he asked me to be his wife.

All I could think of was Dan, the man I had kissed good-bye two years ago, the man I had received sporadic letters from—as he was at sea with little access to mail. I had promised to wait for him, but I couldn't predict when the Cold War would be over. I couldn't predict whether that war would turn from cold to hot. I couldn't predict, I thought, with a lump in my throat, whether he would even make it back. The thought turned my blood to ice water as I said, "Oh, I agree that the new theater downtown is positively marvelous."

I had seen the grieving widows and mothers sobbing into their black lace handkerchiefs, pouring themselves over the pine boxes, crying, "And all this for what? For *war?*" If this Cold War turned hot, I thought again, and that was going to be the end for the greatest dream of my life, I wished we had married before he'd left, his father's wishes be damned. Then I could mourn in public for as long as I liked; I wouldn't have to worry about hiding my emotions in my bedroom, where they were appropriate.

I took another sip of my punch and decided that I had had too much to drink. As a sailor in naval whites breezed through the door,

I smiled, thinking that he resembled my Dan. Of course, every tall, lean man in a starched uniform has a similar look. I peered up at Ernest and felt that familiar panic that this dull man with all his money was the rest of my life, coupled with the disdain that my Dan had had to go, while Ernest's family's considerable assets had conjured a way out for him. I didn't know much about sex—besides what Katie Jo had described, of course—but I couldn't stomach the thought of ever having to undress the man whose arm I was holding.

When the sailor reached the gate and removed his hat, scanning the crowded yard, I gasped. "Dan," I whispered under my breath.

He couldn't have heard me, but, at that moment, his eyes locked on mine, and I thought my heart would burst with joy. My arm slipped out of Ernest's, and I wanted to run to Dan. But my feet were still glued to the moist yard, as if they were unsure whether what I was seeing was true or a figment perfectly shaded by my champagne imagination.

Dan sauntered over, his shiny patent leather shoes glistening in the late evening sunset. He took my hand in both of his. A display of affection larger than that would have been inappropriate.

"You're here," I said.

"For you."

"Excuse me," Ernest interjected. "I'm Lynn's date. And we're rather serious." He raised his eyebrows. "Don't you have a boat to get back to?"

It was so rude that I nearly smacked him. But, though the rumors around town were that my mother had spent twenty-five years grooming a spinster, she had at least taught me manners. "I *am* here with Ernest," I said, rolling my eyes the least bit so that he would understand. "Maybe we could catch up later on?"

"We could," Dan said. "But I've waited long enough."

With that, I heard myself squeal with delighted surprise as he leaned over and threw me over his shoulder like a sack of potatoes. I put my hands behind my back to keep my skirt from flying up, and, as Dan ran down the dirt path and to the road, Ernest hollering, "Put her down right now," we were both in the kind of hysterics that make your stomach hurt.

When Dan finally dropped me at the edge of the road, he fell into the tall grass, wiping his brow and feigning exhaustion.

"That was quite an entrance," was all I could manage through my giggles.

I sat beside him on the grass, and he said, "Some pompous shrimp isn't going to tell me that I can't see *my* girl." He kissed my hand. We stared at each other a long moment, and I could see the horrors of war written in the fresh lines of his skin. They started when he was fighting, but the anxiety of the what-ifs of the Cold War had deepened them. But that light in his eyes, that love burning like a kerosene lamp when he looked at me, was still the same. "I've been counting down the hours until I get to ask you this," he said. With that, he propped up on one knee, put his hand in his pocket and produced the most beautiful diamond with baguettes flanking it. I couldn't imagine where he had gotten the money to buy it, knowing that this was decidedly against his parents' rules, but if he had proposed with rolled-up tinfoil, I would have been short of breath all the same. He picked up my left hand. "I first held this hand fifteen years ago, when I was just a kid. And all this time later, every time I see your gorgeous face, the life and love that springs from my bright and beautiful girl, I feel like that same restless boy trying to reel in the catch of his life."

I could feel the ecstatic tears coming down my face.

"You are the only woman in the world to me. Life isn't worth living without you by my side."

I gasped, wiping the tears from my eyes, and said, "Well, ask me already."

He sighed. "Before I ask you, there's something you need to know." He paused and took a deep breath, and I could feel my heart racing with fear. I had heard the stories of soldiers coming home with love children in foreign countries or marriages made out of the desperation of war. So when he said, "I've already asked your father," I laughed.

"Well, of course you have," I interjected. "You're a perfect gentleman."

He shook his head.

"No, Lynn, you don't understand." He furrowed his brow. "He said no. He said he'd already promised your hand." He rolled his eyes. "To *Ernest*."

I put my hands on his shoulders, shifting to my knees in front of him, and sighed. "But, all the same," I whispered, "I've already promised my heart to you."

He smiled. "Please marry me, Lynn. You're all I want forever."

As my lips met his, urgently, passionately, I made a deal with God, one that I've kept all these years: If He would just let me marry this man—if, this time, He wouldn't take him away, I would stand faithfully by Dan's side until my last breath.

When you make a decision, you have to stick with it. Being wishy-washy hasn't ever gotten anyone anywhere. But, though I tried, I wasn't as resolute as my momma.

"I never should have done this," I said to the nurse that second week in the new assisted living apartment. "I think we need to go back home."

Every night since we had been here, Dan had tried to get out of bed, convinced that the house was on fire and he had to get the children. "You get Sally and Lauren," he'd shout. "I have Louise, Martha and Jean."

I'd try to soothe him, but he was so much stronger than I was, so out of his head, and unaware that his legs, if he tried to get up, would fail him like an injured mare. And then where would we be? Head injuries and broken hips would race through my mind as I pushed the call button, thankful to be on the second floor, only steps away from the night nurses.

"You know what, honey," the nurse said to me, her hot pink scrubs seeming too cheerful for my downtrodden mood.

"What?"

"I think that Ativan we're giving him to calm him down is keying him up."

"You think that could be it?"

She nodded. "Sure do. We'll try something else tomorrow night."

I sat down on the edge of the bed and stroked Dan's hand.

"It's okay," I said. "I'm here. And remember what you said? You said that anywhere we were together, we were home."

Dan had been looking at me the entire time since he calmed down, but it finally seemed like I was coming into focus.

"So, the girls . . ."

"The girls are fine, sweetheart. The girls are grown and gorgeous and doing splendidly."

He exhaled deeply. "I'm so sorry, Lynn. I'm so sorry."

I shook my head and stroked his cheek, dually thankful for and confused by these middle-of-the-night moments of lucidity. The calm after was almost worth the storm of these hallucinations that no neurologist in the country could seem to diagnose or cure.

"It's okay, sweetheart. You can't help it."

"That's not what I'm sorry for," he said, turning his head away from me, toward the bed we had shared for decades before he had been relegated to this one.

I felt my heart sink, a painful truth rushing back, a secret that, in the midst of caretaking and the fear and uncertainty of the day-to-day that is old age, seemed to ebb a bit.

"Do you remember our house in Bath?" he asked.

I smiled. "Remember it? Why of course I remember it. I brought all my babies home there."

He turned to look at me again. "All of them," he agreed. "You were so brave, Lynn. So strong. I'll never forget you saying, 'This is the only way this can happen. Either you're in or you're out.'"

I remembered. But I didn't smile. That had been one of the worst nights of my life, leaving that house in Bath.

"Oh, Lynn, I'm so sorry," he said again, noticing the change in my expression.

"There's nothing to be sorry for," I said. "This is my life, and I wouldn't change any of it."

I thought, *Well, maybe this part.* I couldn't help but feel like life had stolen something so irreplaceable from me, left the foundation but blown over the home with all the memories inside. "They were good years, weren't they, Dan?"

"They were all good years," he agreed. "Even the bad ones."

He smiled at me.

I turned away for a moment, thinking of all the things I wanted to say to him. In the day-to-day living, the breathing in, the breathing out, the one-step-in-front-of-the-other things, I had counted on him more than I could ever thank him for. But in the crisis moments, in those instants when the reins had to be taken, the emergency brake pulled, he looked to me. I wanted to talk about it more, sensing that this could be my last opportunity. But, when I looked over, he was snoring again, the straining and sweating and wild-eyed abandon of a half hour ago replaced by the innocence of dreaming.

What he was dreaming of, I couldn't be sure. But, in my heart of hearts, I hoped beyond hope that it hadn't all been for naught. I prayed that the dreaming was of me.

Annabelle

∽

A Dot on the Radar Screen

Y ou should never worry about moving to a new town with your husband, according to Lovey, because, in reality, your husband is the only friend you need. That was a lovely sentiment, but, as I was learning, maybe not a totally true one. I loved Ben madly. But I needed friends.

It bugged me that, though I had made loads of acquaintances, I still hadn't formed any great, call-you-on-the-phone, let's-grab-lunch kind of friendships with a single person in Salisbury. All my life, through school and college and summer camp, I had been a people collector. They liked me, I liked them, and I formed instant bonds easily.

So, while I wasn't thrilled about spending my Sunday afternoon getting primed, pressed and primped for what was going to undoubtedly be a very boring baby shower, I was going to go. I was going to smile and be chipper and politely sip champagne and toast a mother-to-be that I had met exactly once.

"So, how do I look?" I asked Ben, twirling in a pale pink dress with a pleated skirt that I thought looked very shower appropriate.

Ben raised his eyebrows at me. He stood up, put his arms around my waist and pulled me in for a kiss. "I don't think I like that," he whispered, his forehead resting on mine so that those lips, juicy and delicious as hot Krispy Kreme, were right in my line of sight. "I think you better let me take it off so we can find something else."

I was ready to ditch the party altogether, when I heard the three soft raps on the French door that meant Emily was ready to escort me.

Ben gave me a downtrodden expression and whispered, "Tell her you can't go."

I shook my head and very, very reluctantly pulled away from him. "You better be here, ready and waiting, when I get home," I said.

"Ready and waiting for what?" Emily asked when I opened the door.

"Um," I said, "the mail."

"It's Sunday, love bug. The mail doesn't come."

I tapped my palm against my forehead in faux aggravation with my silly memory. Emily, quite predictably, was wearing one of her flowing skirts, a fitted T-shirt over it and a belt wrapped around her waist. She was carrying a present wrapped in fabric.

"What's that?"

"Cloth diapers," she said, "wrapped in a reusable burlap sack."

"How lovely," I said, thinking of the sterling silver teething ring in the pink toile paper under my arm.

I was afraid I had misjudged the shower, my gift, and the attire, until we pulled up to the hostess, Kimberly's, home. It was a large, two-story brick house with a circular driveway that held nearly all of the guests' cars. A sprawling backyard connected with the enviably green golf course, and they blended so seamlessly I wondered if the greenskeeper was also their yardman. The front door was decorated with the largest pink bow I had ever seen, a labyrinth of different shades and textures so fine that I was certain it had cost more than my gift. The front urns, instead of being filled with small boxwoods, were overflowing with long, pink stems of every variety imaginable. I tried not to be impressed. And we hadn't even opened the door yet.

"Hello, lovely girls," Kimberly said, opening the door, handing us each a glass of champagne with a satin ribbon tied around the stem and tiny pink cranberries floating in it.

She kissed us, and I noted that even her home smelled pampered. Instead of cooking smells or cleaning products floating in the air, it was a blend of restful relaxation, notes of flowers and chocolate, like even the house didn't have to do anything but look and smell beautiful.

I looked around the high-priced baby shower, realizing that it was obviously given by a childless friend. I smirked at how totally inappropriate the theme was: exotic cheeses with wine pairings. I wondered if she didn't realize that a pregnant woman could have neither. One look at her face, though, told me that this soiree was a stab, as understated as the linen tablecloths, at her friend for betraying her—and, by extension, nights of drinking on the patio until sunrise—for motherhood. I took a bite of my Blythedale Camembert and said to Emily, in a tone that she would understand, "This really is so lovely."

Kimberly, in a Diane von Furstenberg wrap dress so tight I could see her belly button, came out from around the corner to refill my half-full champagne glass and, looking at Jill, the mother to be, said, "Oh, isn't she just glowing?" Her mouth smiled, but her eyes looked as if another woman had just stolen the last size 6 Brian Atwood pump from the Barneys shoe department sale.

I smiled. "You know, she really does. She's so tiny."

"So," Kimberly said, pushing the bra-strap-length platinum hair out of her face, "are you and Ben planning on having kids anytime soon?"

I shrugged, a gesture that revealed nothing, but obviously insinuated to Kimberly that we weren't planning on it.

The light returned to Kimberly's green, heavily lined eyes as she said, "Oh my gosh, me neither." Then she added, "Hey, we should get together sometime, you know, for coffee." She winked at me. "Or cocktails."

Before we could set a firm date or time, Jill's mom appeared at Kimberly's side and asked, "Do you think Jill could have some water?"

"With all of this delicious wine around, why would anyone want water?"

Jill's mom laughed, but I think Kimberly was only partly kidding. She was by far the most spoiled of the group with the least home training and as infertile as concrete, as I later learned. But she was looking for a new friend and so was I. She was feeling me out to see if I was worth investing her time and energy in, to see if I had a few good years left in me before I too would abandon her for life with baby. That had given me a little lift.

I spotted Mrs. Taylor out of the corner of my eye and raised the champagne glass to my face to hide my, "Oh, good Lord, no," to Emily.

But we had been spotted. As Mrs. Taylor, cane and limp firmly in tow, lumbered over, Emily said, "Love you, shug, but you're on your own," before whirling in the other direction and waving toward basically anyone else in the room.

"Mrs. Taylor, you're looking well," I lied. In reality, she was shoved into the largest size of St. John knit suit like a sausage into a casing, breathing heavily from the mere effort of walking across the room.

"Oh, Annabelle," she said. "I do absolutely adore that dress." She set her empty champagne glass on the perfectly coordinated and labeled cheese table, where it stuck out like a piece of licorice in the sugar jar. "Wherever did Ben find you?"

I didn't respond because, though I couldn't quite identify why yet, I felt like she was lining the trap with peanut butter, waiting for me to walk right in and take a bite.

But nothing could have prepared me for what she said next. "You know we all just always thought he would marry Laura Anne."

I hope I didn't look as stunned as I felt. I felt that familiar nausea return to the surface. I wanted to walk away, but I didn't want to give her the satisfaction of having caught me off guard. So I said, smiling politely, "Well, every past girlfriend made him the amazing man he is today."

She opened her mouth to continue, but I put my finger up, saying, "Excuse me, I need to make sure I remembered to put the card with my gift."

I felt my breath catch in my throat and, looking around at the smiling, straight-haired girls all around me, realized that I didn't have a single real friend in the group. Any of them would have asked me about my weekend or what Ben and I were doing for Labor Day. But I couldn't whisper to any of them about my encounter with Mrs. Taylor. Not one person in that room would laugh with me and say, "Oh, who cares about that anyway?" And now I knew why. They weren't my friends. They were Laura Anne's friends. And those two things, totally unbeknownst to me, were as at odds as detoxing and McDonald's.

I went to stand around Jill and watch the gift opening. I tried to catch Emily's eye, but she was bubbling over like the champagne in her glass about something or another to a friend on the couch. I tried to look interested in every pink baby blanket and monogrammed onesie, but the reality that my husband hadn't told me about an ex who was as prominent in town as Cheerwine billboards was nagging me too much to enjoy myself.

I snuck out the door, knowing that I wouldn't be missed, sensing Kimberly's irritation from across the room that someone had thwarted her plans. Gift opening wasn't a part of this non-baby baby shower agenda. I texted Emily, **Had to jet,** and took off the pumps that were sticking into the damp earth of the golf course. It couldn't have been more than a half-mile walk home, but, instead of giving me time to cool off, it only gave me time to become increasingly agitated. How could he not have told me? How could he let me walk around this town thinking I was the only woman who had ever been a dot on the radar screen when everyone was saying behind my back that he should have married Laura Anne?

So I did what I always did. I picked up the phone.

"You are so old and so boring that I don't possibly want to listen to anything you have to say," Cameron said.

I smiled. "I just found out that my husband dated this girl that I'm always hearing about, and he didn't even tell me. Can you believe that?"

Cameron laughed. "Of course I can believe that. Look at him, for God's sake, Ann. He's gorgeous. I'm sure he's dated everyone."

"Yeah. But this bitchy woman from town said everyone always thought they'd get married."

"Who gives a shit, Annabelle. He didn't marry her. He married you."

I paused for a second, feeling nauseous again, realizing that, between work, Holden texting me every five minutes, now this Laura Anne thing, and not being able to get pregnant, my emotions were getting the best of me—and my stomach lining.

I sighed. "Fine. You're right. I mean, I know you are." I kept walking, wondering if the damp golf course grass was getting chemicals in my bloodstream.

"Does he know about every little fling you've ever had?"

I sighed again. "No, Cameron. He doesn't know about every little fling I've ever had. Okay?"

"Well, then count your blessings that you were the one to finally tame that hunky, sickeningly sweet man and cut him some slack."

"I hate you. I hate it when you're right. And I need you to come visit immediately."

"No way. Too boring."

And with that, Cameron was gone. Some people would probably be offended, but Cameron was Cameron. You loved her or you hated her. And she couldn't care less either way. I smiled, thinking back to our conversation right after I broke the news to her that Ben and I had eloped.

"I would like to be sorry," I said, when she called seconds after receiving my text, "but I think we're good enough friends that you can appreciate my overwhelming bliss."

Cameron sighed. "I'm not that mad about Ben, but the fact that you didn't let me be your maid of honor is totally unforgivable."

I smiled and could picture a ten-year-old Cameron, blunt pixie cut, baggy jean shorts and 2 percent body fat, saying, "Gag. Who would ever want to have to wear one of those horrible dresses and be in a wedding? Don't you dare ever ask me, because I will say no."

I had reminded her of that moment outside our fifth-grade

lockers, and she said, "I thought that was the beauty of best friends. I thought you knew when 'no' means 'yes.'"

I had laughed at my friend and said, "When we have a big party to celebrate later on, I'll have a special corsage made for you to wear around the party, and the favors will have a little card inside saying that you're the maid of honor."

"Ugh, I don't want to have to wear some stupid *flowers*."

That meant she was thrilled. Ben had wrapped his arms around me from behind and kissed my neck. I giggled, and he said, "I just finished a new song for you that I want you to hear."

"How is it possible that you stole my life?" Cameron had said. "I mean, honestly, I am never taking you out ever again."

"Well, the good news is that I'm married, so every other man now belongs to you."

"Yup," Ben said in my ear. "You're mine all mine until the day I die."

"I think someone else already wrote that line, sweetheart," I said, kissing him.

"Gross," Cameron said. "I need to go now. I have to go wedding dress shopping so that I can wear a big white dress to your party and steal your day like you stole my man."

"Knock yourself out," I said. "You'll make it about ten minutes in that crinoline."

Cameron sighed deeply like she'd been defeated. "You're right. I'll never survive."

"I love you, sister I never had."

She had sighed. "Fine. I love you too. But you owe me some serious nights out as payment for this life-altering slight."

It occurred to me, walking through the golf course that day, remembering that call with Cameron, that I could use a serious night out too. Before I could get through the front door of what had been a sex-filled love nest when I left and was now a frigid den of lies, "Why on earth didn't you tell me about you and Laura Anne?" was cascading out of my mouth in a tone that matched my crossed arms. I knew deep down that Cameron was right. He married me. So why did anyone else matter? But, probably because I had spent the day at a baby shower, I was sad and frustrated, and I needed to take it out on someone.

"Did Laura Anne tell you that?" Ben asked.

"No," I said, pouring myself dramatically onto the couch. "That bitch Mrs. Taylor told me. And then I looked around the room and finally realized why I—me, the person who has always had a million friends in every corner—have yet to get close to one single person in this entire town."

Ben sat down beside me on the couch and said, "Oh, TL, everyone in town knows that Mrs. Taylor is just a bitter old gossip. The only reason she would have said that is to get a rise out of you." He squeezed my knee supportively. "And now you're giving her just what she wants by letting her."

He pulled me up, even though I was still limp as a week-old vase flower, and pulled me in close. He kissed my head and said, "You have plenty of friends here. It just hasn't been long enough for you to get that close to any of them yet."

I nodded and leaned my head on his shoulder. "I just don't feel that initial 'click' with anyone, you know?"

"Oh, yeah. I know," he said, raising his eyebrows suggestively. "I know all about what that click feels like."

I wanted to give in to his dimples and sweet humor, but something inside me couldn't let him off the hook that easily. "Why didn't you tell me y'all dated?"

He shrugged. "It never came up, and it didn't matter anyway. We said we weren't going to talk about exes."

"That's technically true," I said. "But, when Holden gave you a black eye, I didn't say, 'Oh, yeah, he's just some annoying guy I went to college with."

Ben rubbed my leg. "But, babe. Come on. Laura Anne didn't punch you out by the pool."

I rolled my eyes. "No, you're right. She didn't. In fact, I've yet to meet her. I'm not even sure she exists."

Ben's expression changed to that one I couldn't resist. It was that look that reminded me, no matter what the circumstances, that he worshipped the ground I walked on. "TL, I fell for you so hard and so fast I haven't taken a breath to look back. Why talk about the past when the present is everything you've ever dreamed of?"

I rolled my eyes, but I could feel myself softening. He kissed me and said, "I wasn't expecting you home for at least another hour, so I'm only about halfway through *Die Hard*." Then he winked. "But I could be persuaded to pause it for later."

I willed that prickle of heat up my spine to go away, not quite ready to make up this soon. "Ugh," I said. "I'm going to take a bath."

I walked down the pristine white runner in the hallway, glancing over at the sunset blanketing the pool, tucking in our little corner of town for the night. I could feel my anger beginning to dissipate when the phone I was still holding in my hand rang. And I was mad all over again.

"Oh, hi, Mrs. Taylor," I said, as though she hadn't totally shaken my world an hour earlier.

"Annabelle, darling, I wanted to talk to you about the Spring Fling, but you ran out before I got the chance."

I could feel my eyes rolling toward heaven. Maybe I was asking

God to help save me from this woman. I was supposed to "just pick the art" for this party, yet, somehow, I had managed to get so many jobs that the title of "chair" was affixed to my forehead with superglue, though no one ever actually asked. In my head, I screamed: *Leave me the hell alone. I can handle one damn fund-raiser.*

But, instead, I said, "I'm so sorry I had to rush out. Ben wanted me to come home. You know how it is with newlyweds, hard to be apart for even a second!" It was a lie, but I hoped it emphasized to her that we were such a perfect couple that all of what he and Laura Anne had was totally eclipsed by a single night at home.

She laughed in that haughty way. "Well, I just wanted to let you know that I'm sure the gala has gotten to be a lot more than you bargained for—"

It *had* gotten to be a lot more than I had bargained for between soliciting corporate donations, getting auction items, negotiating with the band, the food, the flowers, the bar, the artists . . . But I would never, ever have acted like I couldn't handle it, so I said, "Oh, no. Not at all. I'm thrilled to do my part."

"Well, what I was *saying* is that it has been so much work for one person that the committee and I decided to get you a co-chair."

I actually felt sort of relieved. "Oh, great! Who did you have in mind?"

"Only the best party planner in town, sweetheart."

I could feel the lump growing in my throat, and that nausea rising again, this time coupled with a lump that meant I was in serious danger of crying. I knew who the best party planner in town was without even asking. But I thrust myself onto the sword anyway. "Oh, who is that?"

"Why, Laura Anne, of course."

Lovey

◈

The Exact Man

July 1951

A girl's wedding day should be one of the most special of her life. But I didn't have any grand visions of my wedding day, no matter what Momma said. I wasn't expecting a cathedral full of socialites and out-of-season stems like Consuelo Vanderbilt. I didn't anticipate an orchestra or five-star food.

All I wanted was a beautiful day, in my mother's lace wedding gown, in the church that I had attended my entire life. Afterward, a little champagne punch and showing off my new wedding band to my closest friends would do.

Katie Jo, sitting on my pink bedspread, looked at my engagement ring hesitantly, as though I was wearing a live snake that may jump off and bite her. She sighed. "I can't say that I'm particularly excited that you're getting married. But I *am* particularly excited you're not marrying Ernest Wake."

I nodded in agreement.

"Would you have really done it, you think? At the end of the day, could you have made yourself?"

I shrugged. "I'm not getting any younger, and I want kids, so I might could have if I had known for sure that Dan wasn't coming back." I felt a shudder run down my spine. "Although the idea of having to make a baby with him is like drinking snuff spit."

We both laughed.

"So what's it like?" I asked.

"What's what like?"

"Sex, of course," I whispered, though we were the only two in the house. I could feel my cheeks turning pink at the mere mention.

Katie Jo stopped and smiled. "Well, I guess it depends. If you just aren't so nervous, then it's wonderful."

"Are you ever nervous, Katie Jo?"

She laughed. "Oh, no, darling. I think I was born without the ability to be nervous." She winked. "Which is why it's always so wonderful for me."

I thought of Dan, that familiar heat, that pain of desire rising through me. I had waited my whole life to give myself to a man. And I just knew that he would be worth waiting for.

"Are you still waiting until you're married?" Katie Jo asked. "I mean, I'm not ever getting married, so I couldn't possibly have waited, but you've almost made it."

I grinned at her. "I don't think I can wait."

She gasped and hugged me. "You have to tell me every detail!"

"Ew, Katie Jo."

"Honey, that's what best friends are for."

And I was so grateful for a best friend because, only a few hours later, after telling my family about the engagement, I certainly wasn't grateful for them anymore.

"Lynn, let's just go back and talk this whole thing out," Dan called from behind me as I stomped down the dirt driveway to nowhere in particular.

I crossed my arms, planted my feet in the dust and spun around. "I'm not talking to anyone. If they don't want to be a part of our wedding, then they won't be a part of our marriage either."

"Sweetheart," Dan said, finally catching me in a hug.

As I leaned into him, I thought of how nice it was to feel the strength of those gun-carrying arms around me. I inhaled his after-shave, imagining the shape of the bare torso underneath that starched white shirt.

"You know they have to be stunned. They were expecting you to come home and be engaged to this other man. Imagine how they must feel."

I put my arms around his neck and kissed him again, this time more passionately.

Between kisses he said, "I'm sure if you just give them a little time, they'll come around."

Dan's hand trailed down the back of my shirt as I contemplated *a little more time.* And, all of a sudden, I realized I was out of time. I wanted to feel the heavy weight of him on top of me. I wanted to put my lips on the skin underneath that crisp shirt.

I had waited twenty-five years. And I wasn't waiting one more minute.

I threw my lips on his, my breath vanishing into his lungs, lost in the dream of his body and my body becoming one, of our lives and our hearts converging in a swift, passionate motion. "Can we go somewhere?" I whispered.

He smiled down at me. "Anywhere you want."

I raised one eyebrow suggestively. "I mean *alone*."

His eyes widened in surprise. "Lynn, but you've waited all this time."

I smiled and shook my head. "I can't wait any longer."

I could tell the promise of a lusty evening was getting into Dan's head, overtaking his rational thought. And feeling his desire for me made me want to do it even more.

But he stood up taller, straightened his shirt and said, "No. This isn't right. I want to make love to my wife."

I pushed my lip out into a pout. But then I lit up. "So do."

"So do what?"

"Make love to your wife."

He paused.

"Let's go get married right now. At the courthouse."

He shook his head. "This thing with your family will blow over before you know it, and you'll always regret not having them at your wedding."

"I'll always regret not spending every possible second as your wife."

We kissed again, and Dan took my hand and squeezed it. "I want you to have the exact wedding you want."

"I have the exact man I want," I said. "And that's all that matters."

I learned later that the wedding night is nothing like all those girls described it. It wasn't scary or painful. And, like Katie Jo had said, I wasn't nervous one bit. This was my Dan. And it was perfect. Giving my body to the man I'd pledged my heart to fifteen years earlier was the best feeling I had ever had. I was finally a woman with the confidence to prove it. And this life, this man, was going to be my forever. Love was grand indeed.

Annabelle

∞

Mad Game

Lovey always says that the right outfit can totally change your outlook. No matter what her financial situation when she was younger, she always made sure to buy one new, fabulous outfit every season, complete with shoes, hat and bag.

I had never been much of a shopper but had definitely inherited Lovey's taste for the finer things. Like her, I would rather have one gorgeous designer outfit than ten from the mall. But, looking through my closet, nothing seemed quite gorgeous enough to be Spring Fling worthy.

It was the first time in my life I wanted to buy a dress to impress another woman. But, upon occasion, you know you are the amateur at the Masters, so, instead of looking like a total rookie, you get the same putter Tiger's using.

The thing about Laura Anne was that she was sort of like one of the saints. I heard about her all the time, and I believed that she existed. But I had never actually seen her. You would think that would have been difficult, given that we co-chaired the same event. But, somehow, we managed to coordinate the entire thing via e-mail and never actually made it to a meeting together.

It gave me plenty of time to build up Salisbury's star quarterback—and my husband's ex—in my mind. I had her pictured as tall, at least five eight or so, with those blue eyes so rich you think they must be colored contacts, and long, naturally blond hair that perfect shade that is luscious and stunning without looking like a floozy. She also, of course, had a perfect body in my mind and, for better or worse, she did my physique a lot of good. In the weeks leading up to that event and our first meeting, I became quite the runner and yoga goddess.

I told myself it was because I didn't want to come face-to-face with my husband's ex without him thinking that I looked better. But, in all honesty, I think it had less to do with what Ben thought and more to do with what everyone else thought. I was so tired of hearing about this perfect, infamous Laura Anne that I needed to prove I wasn't the consolation prize.

My paycheck seemed to go as quickly as it came, and I certainly wasn't going to ask my new husband for the kind of money I was planning on dropping on my attire. So I did something that I had always been too proud to do until that moment: I called Lovey.

"Hello, my darling Annabelle," she said when she answered. I loved that my eighty-seven-year-old grandmother read her caller ID.

"Well hello, my darling Lovey."

"How's life in Food Lion country?" It was a special question from my grandmother because she and D-daddy had made a good part of the fortune they had amassed on the grocery store's stock.

"All is well, Lovey. I just wanted to tell you that I am chairing the biggest gala of the year next weekend."

Lovey gasped. "You need to get here immediately. I must buy

you a new dress for your formal introduction to Salisbury society."
She sighed. "I know all you young people have gotten casual, but in
Salisbury they *dress*."

I smiled. I don't know if she instinctively knew that's why I was
calling or if the offer was her own idea. I said, "Oh, Lovey, I couldn't
ask you to do that."

"Darling, I insist." I could hear her flipping through the pages
of her calendar. "I have bridge on Monday, book club on Tuesday,
D-daddy has a doctor's appointment on Wednesday . . . How about
Wednesday afternoon? Thursday I'm having my hair done."

"Do you think that's enough time before the party?"

"Oh, heavens yes," she said. "I'll order everything I think might
work from Neiman Marcus, and I'll have Sun here in case we need
any alterations. Easy breezy!"

I laughed. It really was something to have had the same tailor so
long that she would make house calls. "Well, I can't say no to that,
Lovey. I'll call Mom and see if she can meet us."

I took the day off, realizing that I was a little bit sad that I wouldn't
be there for that morning's adventure. How many people could take
a day off of their job and feel like they wished they were there? I was
feeling so blessed that it had all fallen into place so seamlessly. My
husband was a god who worshipped *me*, my job was so fun it didn't
feel like work, and I was going to look hot Friday night. Father Rob
and I talked all the time about counting our blessings, about being
thankful for the present without the "if onlys." But, until I had my
baby in my arms, I'm not sure I could fully embrace anything else.
After the gala, I promised myself again, *we will go to the doctor and find
out what's wrong.*

When I got to Lovey's, she and Mom were sitting on the floor,
flipping through old photo books. To see an eighty-seven-year-old

cross-legged is sort of like spotting a tiger in the wild. It made me happy that, like Lovey and Louise, I had started a daily yoga regimen.

"Well, we've found what you should wear," Mom said without even getting up to hug me.

Lovey nodded and pointed to the book. She and D-daddy were posed casually, his arm around her shoulder. She was holding a swaddled, infant Mom, while my aunts hovered around in their Easter bonnets, squinting uncomfortably in the sun. "I wore that to our first party in Raleigh, right after we moved," Lovey said. "So I think it's fitting that you wear it to your first party in your new town."

It was a stunning black sleeveless dress with a thin ribbon around the tiny waist, just the right amount of flair, and just the right amount of skin. Mom pointed to where the dress was hanging on the door, and I gasped. "It's perfection!"

"Well, go try it on," Lovey said. "This old thing would love to think its dancing days weren't over."

As I sucked all the air out of my stomach, I couldn't imagine that, after just giving birth, Lovey had been tiny enough to fit into this thing.

Mom and Lovey managed to get it zipped, which was nothing new. The "two-person dress" was something we all wore more often than not. Assuming, of course, that it didn't produce bra fat, VPL, or any other travesty of too-tight clothing, it was the perfect recipe for looking your best at any event.

As expected, Mom said, "Just go on the three-day diet, and it will be perfect."

The three-day diet was a dreadful grapefruit and hard-boiled egg situation with the occasional spare square of toast that was guaranteed to produce at least a five-pound weight loss in record time. And five pounds could easily turn a two-person dress into a one-person one.

When I produced my egg and fruit combination at work on

Thursday, Father Rob came down the hall immediately. "What is that stench?"

I smiled sheepishly. "Hard-boiled egg."

He shook his head. "I will take you to lunch. You can't possibly eat that."

I sighed. "I don't really mind boiled eggs, for one. For two, I have to be crazy thin by tomorrow. Thinner than Laura Anne," I added, under my breath.

Father Rob laughed. "You're nuts. And you're thinner than her anyway."

I brightened. "For real?"

He shrugged. "Seriously. You're Heidi Klum, and she's someone's mom in the carpool line."

The momentary sting of wishing I was someone's mom in the carpool line was soothed by the spine-straightening thought that I was like Heidi Klum. "For someone who's abstinent, you sure do know what to say to a woman."

He winked. "I'm abstinent by choice, not because I don't have mad game."

I laughed so hard it shook the table, and that damn egg rolled right onto the floor. "Now look what you've done!" I said through my giggles.

He took my hand, pulled me out of the chair and said, "Perfect! Now let's go get some real food, Heidi." He looked me over and said, "You're looking much too thin."

I put my hand on my heart. "You can keep my paycheck this month. That was all I needed."

We walked through the double doors of Sidewalk Deli and into the building, the tall, white fountain in the middle and the walls painted with outdoor scenes; real, iron balconies affixed to the bricks. I inhaled, "Ahhh, food smells so good."

Rob laughed, reached in his pocket and handed me a penny, as had become our custom when we came to the restaurant together.

I was closing my eyes as he said, "Wait!" He winked. "Be careful what you wish for."

I closed my eyes and tossed my penny, making the same wish I always did. *I wish I would get pregnant!*

"Do you want to tell me yours?" I asked as we stepped into line.

"If I tell you," he said, "it won't come true."

A few minutes later we were sitting at one of the black iron tables with the glass top, and Father Rob was putting his pickle spear on my plate. "So, I'm coming to your party," he said between bites of the roast-beef-filled Bell Tower. I was having a particularly torrid affair with the grilled pimento cheese that might as well have been handmade crème fraîche for as decadent as it tasted after two days of near starvation.

"That's so nice!" I said, swapping sandwich halves with him and licking my finger. "But you hate parties."

He nodded. "I do. But I think you're going to need moral support. Anyone on the edge of anorexia over an ex-girlfriend needs a shoulder to lean on."

I nodded. "Maybe you could make up some stuff within her earshot about how gorgeous and brilliant and talented I am?"

"I could," Rob said, taking a sip of his sweet tea. He grinned. "But I wouldn't be making it up."

You have to take care of yourself or you won't be able to take care of anyone else. And, that day, I needed some downtime, preferably a day of glamour-inducing pampering. But I was forced to realize that I made a commitment and I must honor it.

So far, things weren't going too well. The flower arrangements were too short, the van that was supposed to deliver the tables and chairs had broken down, and the band, waiting to board a delayed flight on the other side of the country, *hoped* they would make it on time.

So I did what I did best in a crisis: I called Ben.

In direct contrast to the "Sure, TL, I'll run pick up those tables and chairs in my dad's truck," I received a "Sorry you're in a pinch, babe, but there's no way I could possibly leave work right now."

Ben's constant care and attention was a little like water running down the drain. When it suddenly backed up, it took a few minutes for the reality to set in. I ended the call, threw my hands up in the air and said, "So what the hell am I going to do now?" to no one in particular.

A familiar voice from behind said, "The devil got you down, Ann? Or is it the deviled eggs?"

I laughed and turned to see my boss, looking scarcely older than a high school kid in a T-shirt and shorts.

I shook my head. "Someone has to go pick up all the tables and chairs because the rental company can't get them here."

Before I had finished my sentence, Father Rob was dialing the phone. "Hey, Junie. What's up?"

I smiled, thinking of Junie on the other line, rolling her eyes at her young boss asking her what was up. He nodded and said, "Could you round up a bunch of our youth group in need of service hours? And make sure you get some big guys with trucks."

He hung up and looked around. Before I could even say thank you, he said, "Mrs. Taylor is going to have a conniption when she sees those stubby flowers."

I sighed. "I know. And the best part is that this will somehow all be my fault."

"Wait. Where is the hallowed Laura Anne?"

I smiled pertly. "Where is she ever?"

Rob said, "Well, I guess when it comes to fixing the flowers, I'm the best you've got right now." He looked around the room, surveying every element like it was a member of his flock in desperate need of saving. And then we got to work.

We had fixed the first arrangement in a very long line, when I heard a voice I knew as well as my own say, "Oh my God. It's worse than I thought."

"Cameron!" I squealed.

In her cutoff jean shorts and white T-shirt, she was ready for work. Cameron had grown up in her mom's flower shop, and, though she didn't want to do that for a living, she had true, raw creative ability.

"Cameron, this is Rob. Rob, this is Cameron," I said as they shook hands.

Cameron raised her eyebrows.

"He's the priest I work for."

Her face fell.

"Oh, good," Rob said, looking toward the driveway. He grinned at me. "I'll go help the boys unload. Seems like that's more in my skill set than fluffing flowers."

Cameron and I both laughed. "All that talent," she said. "Totally wasted."

I sat down in the lone chair under the tent because Cameron was already working away. These were her arrangements now. "It's not a total waste. I mean, he can get married and everything."

Cameron shrugged. "Yeah. So that means still a total waste for me."

I laughed. "So, what on earth are you doing here?"

"You've been talking about this stupid party forever. I thought maybe I should come help you out."

That was the thing about Cameron. She was rude and sarcastic, but she had the biggest heart, and, at the end of the day, was always the first person to help you out in a pinch. "And, don't worry, I brought a very appropriate dress to wear tonight so as not to embarrass you."

I laughed. "You wouldn't embarrass me. I can't believe you're staying."

"Oh, yeah," she said. "After the number of times I've heard the name Laura Anne, I wouldn't miss this for the world."

That night, I scanned the crowd, searching for the leggy blonde who was growing taller, whiter teethed and more regal by the moment. So, when a perky, bordering on shrill voice behind me gasped, "Oh my gosh, you must be Annabelle. Finally!" I expected to have to look up to respond.

You can imagine my surprise—and relief—when I turned to find a girl, barely five feet tall, with a brown bob, embracing me like we were old friends. "Oh my Lord," she continued, seeming to scarcely stop to take a breath, "that is the most gorgeous dress I have ever seen, and you are the only girl I have ever met who is as beautiful in real life as in her wedding picture."

I wanted to hate her on principle. I wanted to despise her simply because she had dated my husband, because she had been there first. I'm not one who has ever been much on flattery, but there was something about her face that seemed so honest and open. As much as I didn't want to, I could see instantly why she was so dearly loved.

True beauty was intimidating, but soft, nice-featured cuteness wasn't a threat to anyone. And I felt myself breathe for the first time since I put on Lovey's ridiculously tiny dress, realizing that I hadn't needed to worry all this time. She was really no competition.

An older man I recognized from the club came by, leaned down to kiss her on the cheek and said, "Beautiful job as always, Laura Anne."

"Oh, thanks," she replied in that fairy-tale princess voice, "But it was really all Annabelle who put it together."

It was a nice acknowledgment because it really *was* all Annabelle who had put it together.

Cameron appeared behind Laura Anne's head and rolled her eyes.

Laura Anne sipped her champagne and said, "Listen, we have been super swamped lately, but Jack and I must, must throw a party for you and Ben." Before I even had a chance to respond with a polite "thanks, but no thanks," she said, "I mean, obviously Ben knows everyone already, but all our friends are just dying to welcome you to town. We're thrilled to have you here!"

I thought she might burst into song right then and there, and I couldn't fathom in my wildest imagination that Ben had ever been with anyone so . . . perky. I wanted to say that a party wasn't necessary, but the truth of the matter was that I had already met everyone in town, and they hadn't quite taken to me, to put it mildly. As much as I hated it, I needed everyone to know that I was in Laura Anne's good graces because, as was becoming increasingly clear, that's what it was going to take for everyone to finally acknowledge that I was Ben Hampton's wife, not the other woman.

I tried not to laugh as Cameron made a face like she was gagging and then disappeared. A moment later, I felt an arm around my back and turned to feel Ben's soft lips on my forehead. "So I see you two have met," Ben said, looking amused. He raised his eyebrows at me as if to say, *See why we didn't work out?*

As if on cue, a tall, handsome man in a perfectly fitted tux appeared at Laura Anne's side and squeezed her shoulder. "Jack," he said, waiting for me to hold out my hand for him to shake. "It's a pleasure to meet you."

You didn't have to ask Jack any questions to know everything about him. He had been to prep school and attended college somewhere that money, good looks and partying are as important for acceptance as grades and SAT scores. I caught a glimpse of the oversized diamond on Laura Anne's tiny finger and wondered if she had already scoped my simple Love band. I wondered if she wished Ben had locked it on *her* finger and thrown away the key.

"So, Jack," Laura Anne said, handing her husband her empty champagne glass, wordlessly defining that she needed more and clearly displaying the power dynamic between the two of them. "I was just telling Annabelle that we'd like to have a little celebration for them."

"Oh, that's not necessary," Ben interjected, but I squeezed his hand.

When Jack said, "Oh, no. We insist," he didn't argue again.

All I can say, looking back now, is how deeply I wish I hadn't squeezed his hand.

Lovey

ℒ

Old School

One of the most important things a girl can be is a good judge of character. Even now, I can tell in less than a second whether I trust someone. Your eighties are rough on the gait, eyesight, hearing, smelling and tasting, but, somewhere in there, your trust muscle gets worked like a bride by a personal trainer until it's strong and ready to take on anything—even that size-too-small Vera Wang.

That's how I knew instantly that I didn't like the look of that Laura Anne. She seemed sweet enough, sure, but I could tell that underneath that sparkling gymnast exterior was a conniving Real Housewife waiting to get out. But I never had the opportunity to tell Annabelle that because, days after that party, they were already thick as thieves. Taking morning runs, playing weekend tennis, planning couples getaways to the mountains.

I can't count the number of times I've seen best friends turn out to be the worst enemy a girl can have. *Never with Katie Jo and me,* I thought, smiling, remembering that I needed to call her the next day.

I felt an arm around my shoulder and heard a voice say, "As lovely as you look, you must have been on the egg and grapefruit diet too."

I looked up to see a pair of charming dimples wrapped in a gorgeous tux.

I put my finger to an exceptionally well-tied bow tie. "So you don't have to wear the collar?"

He shrugged. "Nah. I like old school, but I'm not married to it."

I looked across the room at Laura Anne and Annabelle, chattering away like field mice. "What do you think of her?"

He got this sort of faraway look in his eyes. "Oh, Annabelle is a miracle. She's so . . .." He paused, looking down at me, smiling. "Honest. There's such a purity about her heart. I don't know what I ever did without her."

I raised my eyebrows, wondering if he meant he didn't know what he did without her in his office or his life. "I meant Laura Anne."

Rob laughed that easygoing laugh of his, and I couldn't help but think that he seemed more alive than most people. "Oh, Lynn, don't do that to me." He gave me a thin-lipped smile that told me exactly how he felt about her. But all he said was, "God loves all His children. We're all in His image."

I felt a kiss on my cheek from behind and did what can only be described as a triple take. "Hi there, little Lovey."

"What in God's holy name are *you* doing here?"

Holden shrugged, a couture tux able to make even the plainest of men suddenly look a little like Leonardo circa *Titanic.* He adjusted his tie. "You know I've always been a huge fans of the arts."

"Uh-huh," I grunted. "You're a fan of something all right," I said under my breath.

"Excuse my manners," I said. "Father Rob, Holden. Holden, Father Rob."

Rob was so tall Holden had to look up to him. "So, what brings you to Salisbury?" Rob asked.

Holden looked wistfully across the room at the tiny waist and flowing hair of a granddaughter that I could say without bias was a stunning sight to behold. Rob's gaze followed Holden's, and he said, "Dude, that's kind of a weird way to look at your sister."

Holden raised his lip at Rob. "Sister," he practically spat. "Annabelle is the love of my life," he said, at precisely the moment that Emily appeared by my side.

"Oh," she said, patting the feather peeking out from her loose bun. "So you're the one that gave my Ben a black eye, huh?"

Rob said, "Wait. What?"

Then, finally, Annabelle stopped laughing long enough to peek in our direction. I'm not sure if it was the sight of Holden, or the fact that he was waxing poetic with her mother-in-law that made Annabelle turn so instantly white. But, either way, though two men who claimed Annabelle was the love of their life were under the tent that night, I couldn't help but notice that it was Rob who ran to her rescue.

Annabelle

∞

Sold Out

The best gifts in life are often the most unexpected. And, to be sure, becoming friends with Laura Anne was unexpected. In a matter of hours, her signing me on as her cohort had earned me four invitations from her circle of friends. And, for someone who had felt so utterly alone in her new town, that was a very happy occurrence.

"So it's kind of ironic, right?" Father Rob asked as soon as I got to work the next week. "You were so stressed about meeting Laura Anne, and now you two are"—he paused and then, in a singsong, tween voice, he said—"besties!"

I laughed, and Junie sighed audibly from her desk.

"What's the matter with my favorite little month over there?" Rob asked.

She shook her head. "It's just that someone in this office has to get a little bit of work done."

"I'm so sorry, Junie," I started, but Father Rob put his hand up to stop me.

He walked around to where Junie was sitting, took the pile of papers from her hands, and set them back on the desk. "Junie, my love, the work of the church shouldn't be such a burden."

"Well," she said crankily, "someone has to file all of the parishioners' donations and keep track of the pledges."

Father Rob perched on the corner of the desk, his hands out in front of him as if painting a landscape with his bare fingertips. "Just picture it . . . a world where the work of the church is the work of the Holy Spirit. The work of the church isn't filing and paperwork and mundane e-mails. It's extraordinary callings and saving the poor and oppressed from their distress."

I smiled at Junie, who was rolling her eyes at Rob, who was clearly goading her. "Well," she said, her voice crackling, "that's all well and good, but the Holy Spirit can't pay your salary if someone doesn't get all this paperwork done."

Rob hopped down from the desk, gave Junie a solid pat on the back and said, "Well, then, thank the Lord for you."

I could see the tiniest smile escaping from the corners of Junie's mouth. She didn't want to be, but you could tell that she was endlessly amused by her new boss. He had given more vibrancy to these last decades of her time on earth than she would have imagined, like a menopause baby forcing a retiree out of the loathed last third of hobby-filled life.

"Junie, would you like to come with me to interview some new musicians?"

"Musicians?" she croaked like a frog. "We've already got an organist."

"Yeah." He scratched his chin. "But, in the spirit of the good old Holy Spirit, we're going to jazz up the ten thirty service a little. Make it a little more fun and family friendly."

Junie shook her head. "I won't have any part in it. When Mrs. Taylor comes in looking for a neck to wring, the autopsy won't be mine."

He turned to me and winked. "Ok, then, Annie, looks like it's you and me."

He held his arm out and, as he escorted me to the church, said, "So, are we going to talk about that pale fellow that showed up at the party?"

I could feel my eyes turning toward heaven. "What was that? I mean, what sort of ex-fiancé just shows up unannounced like that when a person is happily married?" I could feel the shame and anger rising toward my face.

"On the bright side, that little song he sang—and the proclamation of love beforehand—ensured that everyone in this town knows your name."

I put my hand up to my forehead as if shading the sun from my eyes. "I honestly can't even talk about it. I'm trying to pretend it never happened."

He said, "Yeah. You're right. I won't remind you."

Then, as if by total accident, he started singing under his breath, "I can't live, with or without you . . ."

"Stop it," I said, slapping him on the arm with the back of my hand. "It's not even a little funny." But I laughed anyway. Holden had heard that Ben had won me over by singing to me at his show. I think he was trying to even the score a bit, pay us back by mortifying us like he had been so deeply embarrassed.

"Actually," he said, "he doesn't have a bad voice. Do you think we could get him to sing in our new band?"

I laughed again. "You know, in reality, I deserved this. I mean, I embarrassed him, he embarrassed me. Now we're even."

I thought of my inbox full of messages from Holden. I kept thinking that they were going to stop, but, so far, he had been very persistent.

"What did Ben say?"

"Pretty much nothing," I said, trying to push away the nagging feeling that Ben should have taken care of the situation somehow, when, in fact, it was Rob that had pulled Holden off the stage and defused the situation saying, "All right, a beautiful singing telegram from Ben to Annabelle, with love."

The crowd had laughed and clapped, but Ben had seemed like it was pretty much business as usual.

As we watched a very talented guitarist strum in the sanctuary, I said, "So, do you actually think you're going to pull this off? I mean, the older members of this congregation are going to have a fit if you mess with their service."

He shrugged. "My calling in life is to bring people to Jesus, to show them how much better their lives would be if they were completely sold out for Christ." He shrugged. "Changing this service is what I'm supposed to do, so I can't help but know that there's some great purpose here."

I smiled and, thinking of my sheltered little life, of how worried about my social status I'd been, started to feel a bit like a sellout of a different kind.

Four hours later I was wrangling myself into my most stylish, skinniest jeans, noticing they felt a little snug, and saying, "I know you're tired, honey, but this will be fun."

Greg and Laura Anne had invited us to be their guests for supper club at Kimberly's house. You couldn't help but notice that befriending Laura Anne had immediately improved my social status. Ben walked to me, interrupting the very ambitious zipping I was trying to do, and kissed me. I lingered for a long moment, my lips on his, and he said, "But I can think of so many more fun things we can do right here, all by ourselves."

I thought of my top dresser drawer spilling over with lingerie and how little use it had gotten over the past several weeks. And so I said, "Honey, I promise, we're *not* going to become one of those couples."

It struck me, as I plucked a sleeveless silk top, the perfect weight and dressiness for a casual dinner, that we already felt a little like one of those couples. That can't-breathe-without-touching-you passion was still there in spurts, but it broke my heart a little to realize that, contrary to what I had believed such a short time ago, I could, in fact, survive the day without making love to the gorgeous man I had pledged all my days to.

He kissed my neck, wrapping his arm around my waist, and whispered, "You're all I want for the rest of my life."

I turned and kissed his mouth again, upturned in that sincere smile that always drew me in so fully.

"Who needs friends?"

Two hours later, sipping chardonnay on Kimberly's slate patio, I remembered that, actually, I needed friends. Maybe the statute of limitations on only having to have your husband is a year because, since we had moved to town, this was the first time I felt like I could breathe. Laura Anne was balancing on the arm of the very sturdy outdoor chair on which I was perched, saying, "It is so, so fun to have a new BFF! It's like, from the second we met, I just *knew* we were going to have so much fun together!"

From the looks of the girls surrounding me, I could tell that they were as jealous as if they were a room of single girls searching for the perfect man, and I was flaunting my sparkling, six-carat forever. But I had been to high school, and I had seen *Mean Girls*, so I knew as well as a person could that, if the queen bee says you're her new best friend, the other girls will hate you behind your back, sure. But they'll be stuck on you like a mosquito in a spiderweb to your face, because, in reality, you're now their best shot of becoming really, truly "in."

I should have watched that movie again, though. Because, somehow, basking in the glow of the attention of my new friend group that night, I forgot that the leader of the pack would just as soon eat you as share her throne.

Lovey

Why Men Stray

Momma always said that you have to find the right balance in life between depending on your husband and maintaining your independence. But, truth be told, because I relied on Dan for my money and so much else, I never felt all that self-sufficient.

I learned quickly after moving into that assisted living facility that I had been quite independent, after all, despite how I felt. And now, all that was gone. Maybe it was the fact that someone checked on me every hour or that, for the first time in my life, it wasn't my responsibility to coordinate the housekeeper and the yardman, the laundry and the ironing, the meals and the caretakers. I should have felt a sense of reckless abandon, a crushing weight dissipating into thin air.

Instead, I felt an overarching sense of uselessness. For sixty years I had been a wife, which translated to cook, cleaner, laundress, ironer, errand runner, mother, caretaker, feeling soother and sometimes gardener. And now, here I was, totally free. And I felt like I was losing my mind. Mercifully, when I got up from the sofa where I was reading probably the fifteenth book that month, I turned on the bathroom light, and, in that particular mix of spark and noise, the bulb over the sink blew.

I had bridge that afternoon, and I couldn't very well do my makeup when one of the bulbs was out. Whistling all the way, I walked purposefully to the tiny utility room, slid the lightweight stepladder over my arm like a purse and grabbed a light bulb. Sure, I could have called maintenance, but it was a light bulb for heaven's sake. Dan was the invalid; he was the one that needed the care. Not me.

I climbed up the three small steps carefully, twisted out the old light bulb, screwed in the new one and headed back down. One, two . . . I never got to three. The third step had escaped me, and, instead of landing steadily on it, one of my feet slipped. Struggling to regain my balance, my foot twisted underneath me and, before I knew what was happening, I was on the ground amidst the sound of shattering. I looked over, expecting to see that light bulb in a million pieces on the tile floor. I gasped. Seeing the bulb perfectly intact, I realized, as I tried to hoist myself from the floor, my leg determined not to allow it, that the shattering sound hadn't been the bulb. It was me.

My mind raced with fear, remembering that Dan was alone in the den. I tried to call for help, but no sound would come. It was like that nightmare where the gunman is chasing you and you're trying and trying to scream, to no avail. I don't know if it was the fear or the swift rise in blood pressure that severe pain can trigger, but that's the last I remember of that afternoon.

On the bright side, while I was catching up on my beauty rest, I had the loveliest dream . . .

It was May 1952, and I was perfectly coifed and made up, wearing an overworn yet expensive A-line dress. I could barely climb the four stairs that led from the driveway to our tiny front porch. I was sore, throbbing, exhausted. But, most of all, I was inexplicably ecstatic. I looked down at her again.

"She's just so perfect," I said to Dan, wistfully. "Those little lips and those tiny eyelashes."

As we reached the top step, Dan set my valise down beside us, put his arm around me and leaned to kiss the cheek of the first addition to our family.

"She's so small," he said, for probably the millionth time.

I wanted to say, *She didn't feel so small when I was birthing her,* but I refrained.

Those were the waiting room days, where the woman toughed it out alone as the man paced around outside, puffing the cigars that he was supposed to be handing out.

It's better now, I think, when men get to be in the room, when they get to experience that earthshaking moment when their child takes his or her first breath. And, even more important, when they can actually see what their wife goes through when creating this little miracle.

But, back then, we still liked the ruse. I had given birth only ten days earlier, but there I was, makeup on, hair fixed, tiny pumps on my feet, hat jauntily pinned to the side. It was most definitely a different time, one where women preferred to be adored for their perfection as female specimens to being adored for their hard work in childbirth.

"Do you see what I was saying now?" I asked Dan.

He looked around and laughed. "Yeah, I can't believe I was so worried about us having a big house. We could tuck her in the back of the closet and never know she was here."

Sally opened that tiny mouth and let out a wail, as if to say that she wouldn't be forgotten. "Are you hungry, little girl?" I padded gingerly off to the nursery, still determined that I would only nurse in private. My husband didn't need to see what he thought of as one of my most sexual organs being used for something else entirely. Of course, by about the second month, and especially the second child, that romantic notion of keeping everything the way it was so as not to disturb my husband's world was pretty much out the window.

My mother was horrified by the entire thing. *Girls bottle-feed nowadays, Lynn,* she said. *Don't ruin yourself with breastfeeding. That's why men stray.*

But it felt like the right thing to me.

"How long?" Dan asked.

I shrugged. "Probably thirty minutes or so."

"Really?" He lit up. "That's all?"

I cocked my head to the side, examined his face, and realized through Sally's stilted cries that we were definitely not talking about the same thing. Though I felt totally nauseous at the thought of sex, I smiled devilishly and said, "Oh, honey, I wish it didn't have to be, but it will be months before we can do that again."

Thank God, I thought, closing the door behind me. *In case you hadn't noticed, I just pushed a human out of my body.*

I think I might have been starting to wake up about that time, the searing pain nearly knocking me out again, but I fell back into that dream just long enough to think: *Ah, yes. Those were the days. Just the three of us in a small, simple home where the only lies we had told were the tiny white ones.*

Annabelle

Throwback

Never let anyone see you sweat. Lovey says that literally and figuratively. She has never been too fond of getting all gross at the gym where everyone can see you outside of your primped perfection. But, in a larger way, she was a master at teaching all of us to keep our cool no matter what. And I needed that advice that morning.

"I completely understand your concern, Mrs. Jamison." I mimed a talking hand at Junie. "Yes, I can understand how the drumming hurt your husband's ears." I nodded, though she couldn't see me. "Well, the wonderful thing is, Mrs. Jamison, if you're annoyed by the sounds of the children allowed to stay in the service, you can always go to the eight o'clock or the nine fifteen like you usually do. It is only the ten thirty that has gotten more contemporary."

I hung up a few minutes later, wiping sweat from my brow. That was the sixth call I had received that morning about the new contemporary service. It was only in its second week, and attendance was up more than 30 percent. Families with children loved the music, the laid-back atmosphere and being able to let their little ones enjoy the sermon too without the scornful looks if they accidentally dropped a crayon. The church's oldest, most faithful parishioners, on the other hand, were about to have a stroke. Literally.

Father Rob breezed through, pulling on his sport coat. "Another complaint?"

I nodded. "You're looking snazzy. Where are you off to?"

He looked uncharacteristically stressed. "I'm heading to an afternoon conference." He paused, as though he were thinking, turned back to me and said, "Hey, why don't you go home for lunch now."

I looked at the computer. "It's ten forty-five."

"Yeah. But you've had to deal with all these complaints. Take a long lunch. Go home and rest."

I shrugged. "Don't mind if I do."

Going home for a leisurely cup of tea, a sandwich, and maybe even enough time to whip up a batch of my hubby's favorite toffee cookies for dessert sounded like it would hit the spot. I *had* been a little stressed that morning. I rustled for my keys in the bottom of the monogrammed L.L.Bean bag that I used to tote my work essentials. In a flash I was around the corner and in my driveway. I could feel my heart flutter excitedly when I noticed Ben's car was there too. If the thought crossed my mind that he hadn't called me, it ran out just as quickly with the justification that I was rarely able to come home for lunch—and especially not so early.

Smiling at the happy coincidence, I pushed the door into the galley kitchen and called, "Honey, I'm home," expecting to see Ben. When he wasn't there, I headed toward his office, calling, "Ben?"

"Oh, hang on a second," he yelled from our bedroom. I started up the steps and stopped at the tiny bathroom right in front of me.

I opened the medicine cabinet and applied some of my favorite cherry Carmex to my chapped lips before turning the corner to our bedroom and saying, "Do you want me to make you a sandwich?"

I had felt a little neglectful lately. Ben was working insane hours. Combine that with the fact that Laura Anne and I were always grabbing drinks, treating ourselves to a long dinner or catching an early movie, and Ben and I hadn't had any time at all to ourselves. A leisurely lunch would be just the thing we needed to get us back on track.

Ben was lying down, the covers mussed. I was pretty sure I had made the bed before I went to work. "Oh my gosh, are you okay?"

"Oh, sure," he said. "Just lying down for a second. I didn't sleep well last night."

I looked around the room, sensing that something was off but unable to put my finger on it. Emily's housekeeper had become, by extension, our housekeeper too, and she was in the habit of redecorating a little here or there in between the dusting and vacuuming. I guessed that that was it. I crawled in bed beside him, kissed my husband and laid my head on his chest. "I have a long lunch. Do you want to go out?" I raised my eyebrows at him suggestively and unbuttoned his top button. "Or we could stay right here."

"Oh. Um." Ben paused. "I'm playing golf this afternoon, so I actually have to get going here in a second."

I stuck out my lower lip and said, "You didn't mention anything about golf."

He shook his head. "I totally forgot. It's with a new potential client."

I brightened. "That's great!"

I had sensed something off with my husband ever since we had moved back to Salisbury, right around the time that I had gone to Martha's Vineyard with Lovey. I knew the Holden thing had to be bugging him nearly as much as it was bugging me. And, of course, being tied to a desk all day and barely even picking up his guitar had to have been frustrating.

I sat up, sensing that his somber mood had returned and decided to let him rest for a bit. "I guess I'm going to go down and make a sandwich," I said.

"Then are you headed back to work?"

I yawned. "I don't know. Father Rob is out, and I can easily do the newsletter from here, so I might just work from home this afternoon."

I kissed him quickly and skipped down the steps, so excited for a childhood throwback to peanut butter and jelly for lunch.

I could hear Ben rustling around upstairs, and a few minutes later he came down with his airplane golf bag on his shoulder. I had bought it for him for his birthday the year before when he was going on a trip with his friends. It was basically a huge black duffel that zipped all the way around his entire golf bag, with the clubs inside, so that nothing fell out in flight.

"What are you doing with that?" I smiled. "Going on vacation without me?"

He shrugged. "Just had a few extra clubs I'm taking to the course today. This seemed easier than lugging them all down." He scooted out the back door without so much as a good-bye kiss, shouting, "Running late. Sorry."

"That was weird," I actually said out loud.

I went back to my peanut butter spreading, thinking he sure must have been nervous about that client. As I carried my plate into the living room for the rare treat of a little trashy daytime television, I felt that nausea grab hold of me again. I had been nauseous kind of a lot lately. And my pants were feeling a little tight . . .

"Oh my God," I said out loud. I dropped my sandwich on the coffee table and sprinted upstairs saying, "Please, please, please!"

Maybe my penny-in-the-fountain wish would come true after all. I grabbed one of the pregnancy tests from the enormous stash I kept in the bathroom cabinet. I followed the directions, set it on the sink, and walked out of the room. I paced up and down the hall twice, not nearly the five minutes the package said. But, when I peeked in, one eye squinted shut, I saw it. Two lines.

"Yay!" I squealed. I could feel the tears in my eyes, the breath catching in my throat. This is what we had been waiting for all this time. If anything would put the pep back in our marriage, it was this little baby.

I jumped in the car, assuming Ben was playing at the club only a few blocks away. I debated. Part of me wanted to go to the baby store and present him with a tiny gift that night over a gorgeous dinner. But the other part of me couldn't contain her excitement. He had to know right now.

I paused at a four-way stop where I was about to go straight. Only, when I looked to the right, I saw Ben's Jeep stopped on the side of the road. Before I even had time to wonder if he had broken down or run out of gas, he leapt out of the front seat, lowered the tailgate, and unzipped the golf bag.

I just sat there blinking and blinking, my eyes focusing in and out as if readjusting to the light. My body went numb, and my heart couldn't decide whether to pound or stop. It was the most ridiculous thing I'd ever seen, something that I'd never have believed if I'd heard it from a friend. And, though it is normally Lovey's voice that I hear in my head at moments like these, this time, it was Rob's: *Be careful what you wish for.*

Lovey

The Other Road

A proper Southern woman doesn't make a big fuss about herself when she's sick or hurt or down. It's better to suffer in silence than be a burden to others. And, of all the things she taught me, my momma embodied that one the very best.

I thought of Momma when I said to Jean again, "You are not to call her. She will feel like she has to run down here and see me, and that's the last thing she has time for."

Jean put her hand on her hip and said, "She will kill me if you go in for surgery and she doesn't even know."

"She won't make it in time anyway, so why stress her. We'll call her when I'm out."

"I know, but . . ."

"But what?" I snapped. "I'm not going to die in surgery, Jean. For heaven's sake. Who would look after your father?"

"Don't even think about dying," Dan chimed in from the foldout chair bed beside me. He reached over and took my hand again. "What would I do without my girlfriend?"

Jean looked at me in awe, for probably the tenth time that day. As soon as the assisted living nurse arrived for her hourly check, Dan was awake, alert and fully present. When the paramedics arrived, and I started coming back into consciousness, he was shouting at Kelly, one of our regular nurses, from the bed, "No, not that robe. She'll want the pink one for the hospital. And make sure you get her slippers too."

I was certain I was still dreaming, my subconscious floating back to a simpler time when my husband was in charge, when he was the breadwinner, decision maker and protector, and I was the grocery shopper, dinner cooker and pigtail braider.

By the time I was fully conscious again, sitting up in my hospital bed, oxygen in my nose, morphine pumping through my veins with the same breathtaking vengeance as an epidural after hours of labor, I realized that, indeed, it had been true.

"I don't think we'll be prepared to make that decision until we've had a second opinion," Dan was saying to the nurse. "If there's some way to set it while it heals and avoid the surgery altogether, we'd obviously choose that option."

It was about that time that Jean had arrived, sprinting at her high school track pace, completely out of breath.

"Surgery?" I asked.

But before I could get an answer, she burst into tears. "Are you in so much pain, Momma?"

I held my arm up. "I am in no pain of any kind, darling. Now what in the world is wrong with me?"

"It's your hip, Ms. Lynn," Kelly, Dan's nurse, said. "You broke it when you had your spill."

"Damn stepladder," I said under my breath.

It was one of those moments that we all inevitably have in our lives. One of those times that we wish instead of veering right we had veered left, instead of taking the interstate we had chosen the back road. I looked at Dan and then back at Jean. And I suddenly realized that, if we could all erase those moments we wish we had taken the other road, what a disturbingly different world it would be.

Annabelle

So Soon

Lovey always says that expectations ruin relationships. I had tried to apply that advice in my marriage with Ben, take things day by day, for what they are, and not place any unrealistic ideals on him. But, sitting there behind the steering wheel, blinking and blinking, I realized that, yes, I had a few expectations of my husband. And they weren't all that unrealistic.

I bet you could count the number of women who have ever wished to see a dead body in the back of their husband's car on one hand. I mean, it's a pretty twisted lady who wants her husband to be a murderer. But, with a body, there can be an explanation. Maybe he was framed. Maybe someone planted the body in his car. I could picture myself, hair fluffed, running down the streets of some court-room drama, the fearless, undaunted jail widow determined to prove her husband's innocence.

Or maybe he was a murderer and landed in that cell rightfully. At least in that scenario there's some sort of closure. Second-guessing your judgment, sure. Mourning the person you thought you knew, absolutely. But the truth is out there, and there's no decision to make. He's gone for fifty to life whether you decide to forgive him or not.

When your husband unzips his travel golf bag, though, and there's a body in it, but, instead of a cold, blue-lipped remainder of someone who has wronged him, out steps a tiny, wedge-heeled, mid-thigh-length-dress-wearing vestige of your brand-new BFF, the situation is a little less black-and-white. I could feel my face scrunching in confusion only seconds before my eyes widened. I gasped, my hands glued to the steering wheel.

I wanted to think that maybe they were planning me a surprise party and didn't want to give it away. I wanted to think that she had run by to borrow something or ask him a question or make plans for the weekend. But there's only one scenario so dire that it necessitates your husband carrying your five-foot friend down the stairs in a golf bag. And it can only end in the confessional—or the graveyard. Either way, I can guarantee you Jesus ain't pleased when you tell him what you've done.

My first instinct was to peel away from the curb and slam into them both. But I got my composure. No one wants her baby to be born in prison. As Laura Anne sat up, her legs still trapped in the zipped black bag, she laughed like she had just been crowned prom queen all over again. I snapped six or seven photos with my iPhone like I was going to have to prove this to the insurance company. Maybe it was that I was going to have to prove it to myself later on when I saw Ben again and couldn't possibly imagine that a love so deep could actually have been so fleeting.

As I was about to turn the corner and confront them, watch them stutter and stumble like the last drunk leaving the bar, my phone rang. I tried to press "Decline," inadvertently hit "Accept" and said, "Mom, this isn't the best time. Could I call you later?"

"Lovey fell," she said. I could feel the anxiety rising in my stomach.

"What do you mean she fell?"

"She was up on a ladder, and she fell. They don't know if her hip broke and caused her to fall or if the fall made her hip break."

I gasped. A hip break wasn't good. My other grandfather had died of pneumonia after a hip break. My life with Lovey flashed through my mind. Sitting on the counter while she made me those fantastic, lumpy, chocolate milkshakes that were the only real antidote to a sweltering summer day. Lovey pacing the length of the fence during my most heated tennis matches like an anxious father outside the delivery room. Lovey bringing me a piping hot cup of coffee, a cold towel, two aspirin and an amused smirk the morning of my very first hangover. When I closed my eyes, I could see her laughing, that great, uninhibited laugh that took over her entire body. And I sped away from the stop sign toward Raleigh, toward Lovey.

"She's going into surgery," Mom said, and I could hear Lovey hollering in the background.

"Darling, now listen," she said, "I am going to be fine. Don't you dare get yourself all in a tizzy. The last thing I need is you flying down the highway trying to get to me."

"Too late," I said. "I'm already on the interstate." That nausea rose to the surface, and I realized, finally, that it wasn't just my anxiety. It was my child. Even though it should have made me feel more afraid of what I would do without Ben, incongruously, realizing that this child I had prayed for was right there made me feel like it was going to be all right.

But that didn't change the fact that my eighty-seven-year-old Lovey was going under the knife. What if I didn't make it in time?

What if I didn't get to say good-bye to one of the most important and influential women in my life?

"Annabelle, I'm serious. I don't *need* you."

"Well, Lovey," I said, cringing at the thoughts that I had just kissed the same lips that *Laura Anne* had kissed, that I was pregnant with that man's baby, "I just might need you." I could feel the tears coming to my eyes as I said, "So you damn well better not die."

"Oh, honey," she said. "Don't worry one bit about that. I talked with God this morning while I was lying there waiting for the ambulance, and He says it isn't my time."

I laughed through my tears. Lovey spent every Sunday in the front row of the Episcopal church, the same prayer book she'd gotten at her wedding on her lap. I wasn't a bit worried about where she'd go when she went. I just wasn't ready. Especially not now.

"Lovey, what on earth were you doing up on a ladder?"

"Why shouldn't I be on a ladder?"

"Well, because you're eighty-seven years old?"

"That's offensive," she snapped.

"It's not offensive, Lovey; it's true. You could so easily have met the same fate as Dr. Juvenal Urbino."

The mere mention of the name was like a steamroller flattening me into the pavement. I was back in Waffle House, talking about *Love in the Time of Cholera*, back in Ben's apartment, in his bed, basking in the glow of pure satisfaction and sticky, potent love.

She snickered. "Please. Of all the characters in that book, I think we all know I'm not him." Then under her breath she said, "Damn fool up on that ladder trying to get a *parrot*."

I turned my head to change lanes and realized that my pulse had slowed a bit. Talking to Lovey made me feel like she was going to be okay—and like, somehow, a ruined marriage and single motherhood wasn't the worst thing that could happen to me. My breath caught in my throat and I faked a bad signal, knowing I couldn't hold on a minute longer. The pipe burst and the devastation and humiliation all came flooding out in one big sob. Ben was the love of my life. My forever.

I had never expected forever to end so soon.

W hen it comes to family, if someone on the outside tries to criticize, they'd better watch out. But sisters? Well, they're allowed to talk about each other just a little. So I smiled when I walked into the hospital waiting room and heard Martha saying, "Of course Lauren couldn't possibly make it."

As we all exchanged hellos, I was thankful that the tears staining my face could easily have been for my grandmother. "I mean, really," Martha continued. "Like her wedding planning is so much more important than everyone else's job. This is your *mother* for God's sake."

Sally rolled her eyes. "Let's place bets on how much she's going to help during the recovery and rehab process."

Mom laughed. "Right. I'm not holding my breath on that one."

Martha pushed her glasses back up her nose, and, looking down at the newspaper, said, "She had to have all those horrible transfusions during the last surgery. I think one of us should get some blood ready for her just in case."

Sally shook her head. "That's the dumbest thing I've ever heard of. Do you know how well blood is screened before it's used for transfusions?"

Louise, uncharacteristically ruffled, looked up from her crossword puzzle. "It was screened well in 1984 too, but people still got AIDS because we didn't know what it was yet." She fiddled with the turquoise stud in her ear and said, "Well, I'm certainly not standing in line to do it. I think the blood is fine, and I always pass out when I give."

Sally crossed her arms. "I have low iron. They won't even let me give blood."

Martha shrugged. "We all remember the Broughton High blood drive incident, right?"

Mom sighed and stood up. "I'll give the blood, okay? It's not that big of a deal."

I linked my arm with hers and said, "I'll go with you to talk to someone about that."

It would have been as good a time as any to tell her. But the truth was so bad, so convoluted, so scary, that I couldn't face it yet. In fact, I think I was in denial. I was captaining the ship, and I could see the water filling it, yet, somehow, I hadn't faced that it was, in fact, going to capsize. Maybe it was the thrill of knowing that I was going to get to be a mother, or maybe it was that I have the tendency to try to be strong when everyone around me is crumbling. But I was something bordering on chipper that day.

Mom and I approached the nurse's station, and Tammy, the head nurse on duty that day, smiled from behind the desk. I think we were her favorite patient family. "What can I do for you girls? Is that sweet daddy of yours still in there with your momma?"

Mom nodded. "Yup. And just as clear as a bell today." She smiled. "Tammy, I was wondering if I could give some blood for Momma in case she has to have a transfusion."

She bit her lip. "Well, you can. But it has to go through the same screening process as everybody else's, so it's unlikely that it would be ready in time to use for her surgery."

Mom nodded. "Well, can I do it anyway so I don't have to go back there and deal with those lunatics?"

Tammy laughed. "We can always use some good blood. What type are you, sweetie?"

"B, I'm pretty sure," Mom said. "I try to give blood a couple of times a year."

Tammy nodded. "Well, your mother is A positive, so she can't take your blood anyway. Looks like you're off the hook!"

Mom grimaced. "Daddy is A positive too, so maybe he could give for her? Martha is dead set that some family blood will be waiting in case of emergency."

I laughed, and, before I could even think about the ramifications of what I was saying, I blurted out, "That's impossible. If they're both A positive, you can't possibly be B."

"What do you mean?"

Tammy waved her hand. "I'm sure there's just some sort of mix-up. Maybe your daddy isn't actually A, or you're not actually B."

Mom didn't say anything, but you could see the slight change in the color of her face.

"How do you know what D-daddy's blood type is anyway?" I asked.

Instead of answering, she put her finger up. "I'll be right back."

I followed her to the waiting room and watched, perplexed, as she snatched her wallet out of her pocketbook and rifled around while saying, "What blood type are you?" to her sisters.

"I'm A positive," Louise practically sang. "I remember because, obviously, I'd never be anything less than an A plus."

"A negative," Martha said.

Sally rolled her eyes and tapped her pencil on the newspaper she was now holding, I assumed trying to fill in the answers Louise couldn't on the crossword. "I'm O. The damn universal donor." She sighed. "Please tell me you are too. Could you store some blood for me? I'm always nervous I won't be able to get any when North Korea bombs us to smithereens."

Mom pulled a card out of her wallet and said nothing, practically stomping back to the nurse's station. "See," she said to Tammy, thrusting her Red Cross blood donor card in her face. "B."

Tammy nodded. "Well, people make mistakes all the time. It's probably just a card that got printed wrong."

But I think we all knew right then and there that the Red Cross didn't make a lot of blood-typing mistakes. So we must have been wrong about D-daddy's blood type. Mom walked back to the waiting room, in a bit of a huff. I could tell she was trying to look calm, but that was a bothersome discovery to say the least. I tried to think, sitting quietly by myself. Could my mom have been adopted? I looked from my mom to her sisters and back again. The four women in that room had different hair color and even different eye color, but that was it. They were the same height, the same body type, the same facial bone structure. They even, all four of them, had the exact same nose. There was no conceivable way that they weren't blood. So that was that. She was just wrong about D-daddy's blood type. I pulled out my phone and checked my e-mail. But, as I trashed one message after another, I couldn't delete the nagging feeling that something wasn't quite right.

Lovey always says that the clothes may make the man, but the jewelry makes the woman. And she certainly had enough to go around. When I woke up six mornings after arriving in Raleigh, completely nauseated, mostly from the pregnancy, partly from the fact that I had to go back to Salisbury and face the music, I was thinking about borrowing some of Lovey's jewelry.

Ben was home, waiting, having no idea that I knew what he'd been up to. I should have been going over in my mind what I was going to say, what I was going to do. But I felt like my entire life was hanging by one thin spider silk. If he admitted the affair, it was going to break immediately. If he didn't admit it, I would know that he was lying and be forced to make a decision, to tangle myself in the web. Either way, my marriage and my husband were irrevocably changed. So, instead of playing it out in my mind, I thought about jewelry.

I didn't know what I would do yet. Would I leave? The idea of being without Ben, even after how devastated I was, seemed like a fish trying to breathe out of water. And there was the baby to think about. I put my hand to my stomach and immediately felt sad. Even if I stayed, this baby, which had been made out of so much love, would never get to experience the perfection of what Ben and I had had.

That was the night that we had decided was a great time for Laura Anne and Jack to throw the "welcome to town" party she had insisted on hosting for us. Of course, when I agreed, I had no idea that she and my husband were sleeping together. The offer would have seemed less sincere.

I should have canceled the party, but I wasn't ready for Ben to think something was amiss yet. Not before I had made up my mind about how our future would look. And, if I was going to go down, I was going to go down looking good. I had had another one of Lovey's cocktail dresses fitted for the occasion, that, thank the Lord, still fit, paired with Christian Louboutins that I had put on my credit card.

And Lovey's lockbox, a treasure trove of jewels that were too fabulous to even be seen in the light of day, was the only missing piece.

I couldn't put my finger on what, but, in one way or another, I just knew that Lovey had been lying about my mom her entire life. But, in reality, I didn't have any proof that my suspicions were valid. And I needed jewelry. I needed a piece so statement making that it said, *I don't care if you're sleeping with my husband, you whore. I'm still better than you.*

That was a pretty serious thing to say with a piece of jewelry. So I went to the nursing home room where Lovey was finally recuperating, and, after a few minutes of small talk said, "So, Lovey, how about letting your favorite granddaughter wear your David Webb elephant bracelet tonight?"

Lovey laughed a little longer than usual, which made me know that she was still on a bit of pain medication. "So that's the one, huh?"

I winked at her. "Is there really anything else?"

I thought of the thick gold bracelet, the elephant's trunk straight up in the air, creating a locking clasp, the diamond and jeweled head that was so shining and bright it seemed to have its own light source. It was probably the most expensive piece in Lovey's collection. More than her massive diamonds or the huge emeralds that used to cascade down her ears and almost onto her shoulders. And it was the kind of piece that even the woman in the room who wants to pretend she doesn't think you're amazing absolutely must comment on.

So, sure, a bracelet wasn't going to change the fact that I had to face—and, even worse—be nice to, a woman who had taken a sledgehammer to the glass-front armoire of my life. And it wasn't going to change the fact that I was pregnant, and, for all intents and purposes, alone. But it would be *something*.

Lovey laughed again, "Sure, darling. Just be careful. It's insured, but you and I both know it's completely irreplaceable."

She pointed to the laminate nightstand and said, "Just make sure you ask for Melissa. She knows how to get into everything."

I grabbed Lovey's keys, kissed her and D-daddy good-bye and thought again that there was no way that those two, the most faithful and loving people I'd ever known, were hiding something as huge as their daughter's parentage. It had to have been some sort of mistake.

In the long, marble lobby of the bank, smelling of ink and fresh bills, I spotted Melissa right off behind her teller stand. She was short and broad and the kind of girl that you would have described as athletic or stocky. Her blunt haircut was just right for making her seem like she had cheekbones, and, no matter what, she was one of the nicest girls I knew. "Annabelle!"

She flew out from behind the long line of teller stands and embraced me in a hug, which felt good after the few days that I had had. And it made me miss my old life, where I was comfortable, where I had friends and acquaintances and knew everyone in the grocery store. That was a good thing because, no matter my feelings about it, I was going to have to move back to Raleigh if I left Ben. There was no way I could raise a baby on my own without my parents' help. The thought of that was unutterably depressing. Melissa and I exchanged pleasantries, and I said, conspiratorially, "I'm here to borrow one of Lovey's bracelets, and she said you were the one who knew how to get to all the good stuff."

She laughed, grabbed her huge ring of keys and, entering the vault, passing over all of the small doors, made her way to a huge opening at the top. She stood on a small stepladder, put her key in first, then mine, and turned. I stood on my tiptoes to help her remove the massive drawer that contained many of Lovey's prized possessions.

"I better get back out there," she said. I could lock the box with only my key.

"Thanks," I said, anxious to get digging in the gem mine of Lovey and D-daddy's lockbox. Dozens of matching navy blue felt bags held triple and quadruple strands of pearls with diamond clasps, sapphire clasps, ruby clasps. Earrings of every shape and size, stone and cut, rings from every decade of D-daddy and Lovey's life together, and bracelets so heavy your arm was more toned after wearing them.

I smiled as I removed the trinkets, hearing D-daddy say, "When you have this many girls, you have to have enough jewelry to leave behind. So you can't have one fantastic bracelet, you have to have five."

If that was true, then Lovey and D-daddy could have had a dozen girls, no problem.

I sifted through all of the jewelry but wasn't able to find the precise piece I was looking for. I piled them all back up, locked the door, and sighed. As I did, I realized that I probably should have just picked another piece. But if it wasn't in the lockbox, that meant the treasure was probably in Lovey's jewelry box at home. I'd swing by there when I left.

"Did you find what you were looking for?" Melissa asked.

I shrugged. "Lovey was going to let me borrow her bracelet to wear for this party I'm going to, but I don't see it in the box."

Melissa smacked her gum. "Well she has two, you know."

"Ohhhh," I said. "It must be the wrong one."

She grabbed her massive key ring again and stepped into the vault, holding her hand out for Lovey's keys. "This key is for the big one, but this key is for the little one."

I nodded, searching my brain for some sort of memory, for some inkling that Lovey had told me about another box, had told me to look somewhere besides the usual place. I started to tell Melissa it was okay. I started to tell her not to worry about it. But, before I even had a chance, she had inserted Lovey's key, was fitting her key inside too, and the small silver door swung open.

"Thanks, Melissa," I said. "I'll only be a minute."

"Take your time, shug."

I lifted the thin metal handle and slid the drawer out of its cubby slowly, putting one hand underneath to support its weight. I wasn't doing anything wrong, I reminded myself. I was simply going to look quickly for the bracelet, put the things back and leave. Plus, it wasn't like I cared about rummaging through Lovey and D-daddy's stock certificates and bearer bonds.

I set the drawer on the floor, opened the lid and was surprised and delighted to find that, perched right on top, was the prize I was hunting. I started to put the box away and leave when I realized that, far from boring paperwork, the drawer was filled with memorabilia from Lovey and D-daddy's life together. Old passports, wedding pictures, train tickets, snapshots of my mom and my aunts. I pulled out each memento, so happy that I was able to see all of these beautiful things. I put my hand to my stomach and took a deep breath. No matter what I decided about Ben, it was all going to be okay. Because I had this amazing, close-knit family that would stand by me and support me and help me raise this child. It was a moment of total comfort.

In the bottom of the box, in a neat stack, were five, perfect birth certificates, in age order. Sally, Martha, Lauren, Louise, Jean. Underneath was a nondescript-looking white envelope, the edges yellowed with age. I opened it carefully to find another birth certificate with my mother's name on it. I unfolded it, and, as I opened it, it seemed that another paper was stuck to it, almost glued. I rubbed the pages between my fingers, the way I would have a pair of fresh dollar bills. What I peeled from the back of the birth certificate was a carefully completed—in Lovey's neat print—"Application for a Copy of a North Carolina Birth Certificate." It was stamped "Copy." I didn't think much of it, figuring that Mom had gotten an extra birth certificate when she was married or traveling, and put it back in the box. As I folded the form, a checked box caught my eye. I didn't even mean to read it; I didn't mean to look.

But, there it was, unavoidable, on this form in Lovey's own handwriting. Under "Your Relationship to the Person Whose Certificate Is Requested" the box was checked "Parent." And under the column marked "Record Changes," "Adoption" was checked.

I felt my breath catch in my throat, slammed the lid to the box, slid it back into its spot and ran out of the vault. "Thanks, Melissa," I called, trying to rationalize in my mind what I had just seen.

"See you later, shug. Tell your momma and them I said hey."

"Sure will."

I walked out of the bank, my head lowered to avoid talking to anyone I passed on the way out. I felt like the bank was being held up at gunpoint and I was just standing there, watching a robber hold innocent people ransom, and not doing a thing about it.

I must have read it wrong, I kept reminding myself. I didn't see what I thought I saw. Or maybe I just didn't understand it. All of those questions I had had at the hospital flooded back to my mind, all at once.

With every step, I reasoned it out yet again. *Mom's blood type means she can't be Lovey and D-daddy's child. But she looks exactly like her sisters. There's no way she's adopted.*

But there it was. In the box. Lovey had filled out a form. She had checked that she was the parent. And she was requesting that a change be made due to her daughter's adoption. *Her daughter's adoption.* I gasped and stopped dead in my tracks in the middle of the parking lot. And then I started walking again. D-daddy wasn't my mother's father at all. But there was no doubt that my mother and her sisters were the thickest blood you could imagine. So there was only one explanation. Lovey had cheated on him with another man and he, in his infinite mercy, had forgiven Lovey. He had taken her back and taken her love child as his own.

My phone rang, and I saw "Mom" flash across the screen. How could I be normal now, knowing full well that I was the bearer of a secret so massive? I wished so hard that I'd never opened that lockbox, that I'd never seen that birth certificate. But that's the thing about a secret that haunts your dreams and fills those empty spaces in your mind. Once you know a thing so huge, you can never un-know it again.

Lovey

Uprooted

In her old age, my momma always used to say that the nursing home was practically like the country club. She was lying. I know now that it doesn't matter who you are, where you're from or what you say when you're with your friends. When you get old, you do not think that the nursing home is practically the country club, and you most certainly do not want to have to live there no matter how short term your stay might be.

If you had ever told me that I would be pining for my tiny assisted living apartment, I wouldn't have imagined it. But there I was, flipping through my datebook as if any of my plans were still relevant, confined to a double bed with itchy sheets, hoping that they could fit me in for two physical therapy sessions that day. I may have been in the kind of pain that one never forgets, but that didn't matter. I had seen the other patients in their beds, the ones who had come here for therapy and never gotten out. That wouldn't be me. I'd rather be dead than dependent.

I looked over at Dan, the snoring, open mouth, wishing that I could reach the cord to turn off the fluorescent box light shining on his sleeping face. And I remembered that what we want and what actually happens are often two different things. I rolled my eyes at the pair of pleather-covered avocado green chairs flanking a rather nice high-definition television. The cinder-block walls, while cold, had a fresh coat of white paint on them, whose smell did an adequate job of blocking out the nursing home stench, that of death, decay, old age and any number of bodily fluids.

Luella, whom you could just tell by her confidence and regal air was the backbone of her household and a pillar in her community, rushed in, her white nurse's shoes squeaking on the faux-hardwood floor, which, I must admit, did an above-average job of imitating the real thing. "Miss Lynn," she said, "you got to pick out you and Mr. Dan's meals for the next few days so we can bring you what you like."

I nodded. "Thanks, Luella."

"Mmm hmm." She pulled the chain over Dan's head and turned to fluff the pillows behind my back. I watched her, in awe of the grace, agility and speed in such a stout package.

"Miss Lynn, you want me to take you to the bathroom before I get on down the hall?"

This was perhaps the greatest indignity. But I could feel in my bones that I was mere days away from transferring my own body weight to my walker and shuffling to the bathroom right beside me on my own.

I nodded. "Unfortunately."

Luella laughed like we were old friends swapping stories about cute things our grandkids had done. "Miss Lynn, it ain't nothing to be ashamed of. We all got to go, and we all do it the same way."

I nodded, supposing that was true. "Luella, when I get back to assisted living, will you come be one of Dan's nurses on your off hours? I'll make sure you're well taken care of."

Luella smiled, her shiny teeth, all in a straight row like so many soldiers, making me wonder if she had good genes or even better dentures. "I sure would, Miss Lynn. My grandbaby's trying to get through college, and I could use the extra money to help him out."

I placed my good leg on the floor and groaned a bit as the bad one woke and hollered at me for disturbing its peace. It wasn't that still pain that I was used to feeling in my old age, not a dull ache or a heartbeat throbbing. It was a rushing, circular pain, like runners around a track, active and ever changing so that getting used to it was an impossibility.

"You controlling your pain, Miss Lynn?"

"I'm pretty sure it's controlling me," I said. "Tell me something else to keep my mind off of it."

"Well, my daughter's pregnant again."

I tried to smile through my grimace and said, "Congratulations."

"Not really. My husband Ray and I cain't understand that girl. This will be her fourth baby by two different fathers, and she ain't thought about marrying a one of them. She's a good girl, but it's like she missed that chapter of the Book or something."

Sally crossed my mind. My sweet, beautiful adulteress Sally. I had no doubt that she would keel over like a sailboat in a strong wind if she knew I knew. But mommas always know. I had spent so many sleepless nights worrying about her actions, wondering what I could have done differently as her mother. But at the end of the day, it was like I said to Luella, "We can have them in Sunday school every week and in that front row where the preacher's sneezing on them. But we can't control our children any more than we can control that last breath."

As if on cue, Sally stepped through the door, saying sunnily, "Hi there, Luella." Then she added, "I can take Momma to the bathroom. I'm sure you have tons to do."

Luella nodded. "I'll come check on you in a bit, Miss Lynn. And don't you worry. When you get back across the street, I'll come look after Mr. Dan." She winked at me. "I can tell already you won't be needing any looking after."

I looked at Sally, her eyes flashing. And it occurred to me that, though I didn't agree with her choice, though I wondered how someone so sensitive could wound the people around her so fatally, she was undeniably happy. Maybe it was that she never had to reach that point in life where loving someone becomes mundane. Because, the entire time they were together, the man she loved was always a secret, always a thrill. Like the rush Katie Jo used to get from sticking a bottle of fingernail polish in her purse, my Sally must have been addicted to that feeling of first-time, brand-new, might-slip-through-your-fingers love.

But the thing that no one ever tells you about being in love is that, for every percentage that person makes you feel what you expect—that deeply rooted, grounded security—they have double that power to make you feel uprooted, wandering and totally lost. I had felt it, and I didn't have to ask my son-in-law Doug to know that he had felt it too.

But, of course, I didn't say any of that. All I said was, "I am so glad to see you, my darling girl."

And that's the thing about your children. No matter what they do or how much you disapprove or how much you wish you could change their actions, you love them madly all the same. At the end of the day, that's the only choice that truly matters.

Annabelle

∞

Genetic Mutation

You can be the sunshine or you can be the cloud. And, if you can possibly choose, the sunshine always wins more friends. Without fail, even when the going got really tough, Lovey was the sunshine. Mad at her as I was, old habits die hard. I might not have agreed with her choices, but her voice was still the one in my head, guiding me, ironically, to the right thing. So, before I walked into work that morning, I channeled my inner Lovey, put on my best sunshine face and crossed my fingers that I could make it through the day sans emotional breakdown.

"I can't wait to tell you what we're doing this morning!"

Father Rob was so excited that I momentarily forgot about the fact that my husband was having an affair with my only friend in town. My Lovey was not anywhere near the person I thought she was. She was still laid up in a nursing home recovering from her broken hip, so I couldn't even have a conversation with her about it. And, to top it all off, I was pregnant. That was a lot of things to forget.

D-daddy was, predictably, back to his mute, sleeping-twenty-hours-a-day self after the exertion of coming back a bit during the emergency, surgery and hospital stay. I was facing so many personal crises that I was that poor, frightened deer in headlights. I knew I needed to run, but both of the directions that had previously been so safe were blinding and terrifying.

"I can't wait to hear," I said, but Rob already knew me too well to accept my fake enthusiasm.

He cocked his head. "What's wrong?"

I raised my eyebrows. "How much time you got?"

He grinned even wider, and it was almost as if he was having to control himself from jumping up and down. "I have two hours because we're going to go see Lovey!"

I shook my head vehemently. "I just got back from Raleigh, and, furthermore, I'm not sure I can deal with her right now."

I have to admit that I felt a little guilty when his face fell. "Can't deal with Lovey? Is she not the same since her surgery?"

"You could say that."

"Well, it's not uncommon for older people to be very cranky for a couple of weeks while the brain is recovering from the trauma of being put to sleep." He paused. "Hey, have you had any surgery lately?"

I didn't want to, but I smiled the tiniest smile. "I am not old, mister."

He squeezed my shoulder. "All I know is that the Holy Spirit commands me to Lovey's bedside today, so I must go. Should you choose to accompany me, there will be snacks and a box set of all of James Taylor's hits."

I couldn't remember if I had told him how much I loved James Taylor, but, when you got right down to it, pretty much everyone with functioning ears loved James Taylor. His voice had such a soothing yet masculine quality, kind of like drinking champagne while lying on an animal skin by a crackling fire. I shrugged. "What can I say? You had me at snacks."

For how terrible I was feeling, it was hard to believe that I lost myself in that drive, in the Bugles and Reese's cups, the "Up on the Roof" and, of course, "Carolina in My Mind."

"Can I ask you a question?" I asked.

"You may."

"Do you drink?"

He shrugged and looked at me. "Sure. I mean, I'm not staggering around the bar or anything, but a couple of beers or a glass of wine with a good meal."

"So why is it that some Christians don't drink? I mean, Jesus turned the water into wine, people."

Rob laughed. "Do you want to talk about what's really bothering you?"

He was so good at reading people—especially me. I sighed. "My D-daddy isn't my D-daddy."

His face turned somber, and he reached to pat my arm supportively. "Oh, Annie, this must have been so difficult for you. For his body to be here, but his mind, the thing you loved about him most . . ."

He was so sincere that I felt terrible when I couldn't control the laugh escaping from my throat.

Rob looked puzzled.

I shook my head. "No, no. You're right. It sucks so bad that he's living like this, but, to be honest, I came to terms with that a long time ago. His mind has been gone for years, and there isn't a thing I can do to change that. So I have chosen to love him for who he is now, accept the good days and the bad and move on." I inhaled deeply. "I mean literally, biologically, my D-daddy isn't my D-daddy, and, so far worse than that, he isn't my mom's dad."

Though I had promised to keep it buried tightly inside without so much as an "X" to mark the spot, I could hear the whole story rushing out of my mouth like an overzealous bride into the Kleinfeld sale. I had lived with all of these terrible secrets for days and had no one to turn to. I certainly couldn't confide in Lovey or Mom when I was so confused about them, and I was making excuses to scarcely even look at Ben much less tell him about the sordid past I had possibly discovered.

"Now wait just a minute," Rob interjected. "So what you're saying is that Lovey had an affair and that affair became your mom and no one else knows?"

"All I'm saying is that Mom's blood type couldn't possibly have originated from two A positive people, and she seemed pretty darn shocked about the whole thing. I found some paperwork Lovey filled out for the adoption of my mom. And I can't think of another possible explanation."

"Maybe she was adopted and they didn't want to tell her."

I pursed my lips and shook my head. "She looks exactly, to a T, like her other four sisters. There's no way they aren't related."

Rob turned down the radio and said, "Let's not jump to conclusions. I mean, remember that black baby that was born to two white parents a few years ago and they determined that it was some sort of bizarre genetic mutation?"

"Yeah," I said out of the side of my mouth, "a genetic mutation that that mother paid a whole lot of people to create."

Rob laughed, and, as comfortable as I was with him in that moment, I decided to finally ask him a question that had always crossed my mind. "Don't be mad when I say this."

"I won't."

"And don't question my faith because you know that I know that I couldn't tie my shoes without Jesus."

"I know." He grinned at me.

"But what if, I mean, seriously, what if Mary was just an unbelievably impressive liar? I mean, what if she was so convincing and convicted about the Immaculate Conception thing that everyone just believed her, and our entire faith is based around a beautiful teenaged girl who didn't want the whole town thinking she was a slut."

Now that I was pregnant myself, I felt very close to Mary. And we were kind of in the same boat when we got pregnant. We could be as excited as we wanted, but the popular opinion wasn't going to be so good. Father Rob paused for a minute and then burst out laughing. I could tell he was just trying to appease me when he said, "You know there, Ann, you make a good point. But I tell you what. Even if Mary is just the best liar in history, I'm going to love her anyway. Because she gave the world the greatest gift it has ever known." He cleared his throat and took his eyes off the road for a beat too long as he said, "Same with Lovey."

I looked him in the eye, and it was a moment that will linger in my memory forever. Because, in that instant, I knew that no one would ever see me as clearly as Priest Charming.

Some things in life are better left unsaid. And I'm pretty good at figuring out which things those are. But the blood-typing incident was generally all I could think about. It was a trick my mind was playing, obsessing over my mother's DNA, when, in reality, I should have been obsessing about my husband's infidelity and how on earth I was going to attempt to raise a baby on my own.

I had told Rob to go back to Salisbury after our visit with Lovey. I would get my mom to bring me back in a few days. It was a great excuse to stay away from Ben. But I underestimated how oddly alone I would feel watching Rob pull out of the driveway.

I wasn't ready yet. Not to face Ben, not to admit that I had been wrong, not to disgrace my family, and, most of all, not to consider what being a single mother was going to be like. So I stuffed the pain away, hid it under my pseudo-detective skills and bandaged it up by finally responding to Holden's messages.

How's Lovey? he had texted me while I was sitting in the nursing home that day, trying to seem normal and nice while Rob was joking with Lovey and D-daddy and being generally adorable. I was about to burst wide open to say something to Lovey. But it was pretty clear that, though there would probably never be a perfect moment, this one was about as far from right as you could get.

She's doing as well as a person who just broke her hip can be, I typed back, rapid fire, I'm sure shocking the daylights out of him after months of no response. Then, in what was an extremely calculated move, I added, I'm in Raleigh visiting her now.

Any chance I could buy you a cup of coffee?????

In spite of myself, I smiled. I've always been a hopeless romantic. Flowers, candy, candlelight, poetry, anniversaries, long walks on the beach, chick flicks. I love it all. It is my one greatest downfall. And, though Holden couldn't get my blood pressure up quite like Ben, he was a master of the romantic gesture. He could whisk you off to Paris at a moment's notice in a limo filled with champagne and flowers, and organize a surprise party so grand you couldn't imagine how you didn't know. It was a very tempting quality for someone seduced by romance.

Mom always accuses me of having a man "waiting in the wings," of dating one but having my backup plan all lined up and ready for when that relationship inevitably ripped at the creases. That was how I knew Ben was the one. I didn't have a backup plan. At least, I didn't think I did.

That propensity to always have another man lined up has earned me some flak in my life. "You need to learn how to be alone," one friend would say. "You need to find yourself to find happiness."

All I knew was that my *self* was much happier when she had a man doting on her.

I looked down at my phone. I may have married Ben for love. Mad, passionate, can't-bear-to-blink-without-you love. I had married for love, and look where it had gotten me. Miserable. Disgusted. Living with a man I knew I had to let go of. But I knew that, once I did let go, all of those Cinderella dreams I had had since childhood would be over. It was in that moment, when I texted back, I think that would be nice, that I realized that, more than rushing home to attend to Lovey in her time of need, I didn't confront Ben and Laura Anne that day when she was climbing out of the golf bag, because I had nowhere else to go. It wasn't that I didn't want to see them squirm in their disgusting lie; it was that, if I didn't have Ben, I didn't know who I was.

Where?

I could practically taste a latte but realized that I couldn't drink caffeine. And I certainly couldn't risk being seen in public with Holden. Of course, my husband didn't have much of a leg to stand on if he found out, but I didn't want to embarrass my family by gallivanting around town with an ex when I was, presumably, happily married.

Your house.

His response was so uncharacteristic I laughed out loud: ☺

A few minutes later, lying on my back beside my childhood swing set, wondering if my son or daughter would like playing on it one day, looking up at the clearest blue sky, trying to decide what I wanted to achieve out of this meeting with Holden, I couldn't hold it in any longer. Mom was on a meditation kick, and I knew I shouldn't interrupt the "oms" floating around in her head. But I couldn't help it. I was hoping that she knew all about what that adoption box meant and that I wasn't going to have to live the rest of my life walking around hiding something from her. "Did you ever figure out who made the mistake with the whole blood type thing?" I asked. "That could be kind of a big deal in an emergency."

She barely turned her head, squinted one eye at me and said, "Momma said I was wrong about Daddy's."

She turned back and closed her eyes again, but I had a feeling that I had disrupted her chi with my question. I wanted to keep prodding. But she must have believed Lovey's lie. And I guessed that was okay.

Sleepy and finally relaxed in the fresh air, I closed my eyes, the sun feeling warm and soothing on my tired skin. As I opened them again, a thin cloud was floating across the acres of blue, a wispy layer that took me back to my childhood, to D-daddy's office. To the truth.

I was rolling an iron car back and forth in front of the mahogany desk that was hyperbolically huge, reserved for mob men in the movies. A puff of smoke that looked precisely like the cloud floating above my head ascended from D-daddy's cigar. Perhaps it's because smell is most closely related to memory, but that warm, woodsy scent of tobacco always relaxes me and puts me back into the safety of D-daddy's office, into the lap of a man too big and strong to ever fail.

Louise was sitting across from him, her legs up on the desk. She was babysitting me that weekend, and we had just finished having lunch with D-daddy and Lovey.

How they got on the topic I couldn't tell you, but D-daddy was saying, "One of Truman's advisors made a speech in South Carolina at the end of the war about how the fighting might be over but not to be fooled: We were in the midst of a cold war." He paused, chewing on the end of that sweet-smelling stick. "It must have been 1946—no, 1947—and our mayor, who had been at the speech, decided then and there that the town had to snap into action." I remember D-daddy laughing here, his blue eyes gleaming in that way that made you remember how unstoppably good-looking he had been in his youth. "Kooky fellow, that old mayor . . . Anyway, instead of making emergency kits or building bomb shelters, he used city funds to tattoo blood types onto the entire town. That way, if we were hit, and people were running around in the midst of blown-off arms and burning buildings, the rescue crews would know which transfusions to give right off the bat."

D-daddy had laughed again here, taking another puff of his cigar, the smoke billowing. Through that hearty chortle he had said, "If the Soviets had decided to nuke us, the cockroaches would've been lucky to survive." Then he'd taken off the suit jacket that I never saw him without, pulled his neatly starched and pressed shirt out of his pants and lifted it two inches to reveal a distinctive "A" on milky white skin that hadn't seen the sun in decades.

"Why we all agreed to that insanity, I'll never know. But the horrors of war can make men do strange, strange things."

I remember learning in science class that the more we remember a memory, the more distorted it becomes in our mind. I'd never thought of that black "A." It was hidden in the recesses of my consciousness, waiting for a moment when I would need it. I wasn't going to say anything to Mom, of course, but my heart sank all the same.

I closed my eyes, going through it again, picturing the piece of paper in the hospital with Lovey's "A+" on it, D-daddy's tattoo of the same. And I could see that Punnett square I'd looked up online, burned into my memory. The possible offspring from two A positive parents were A positive, A negative and O negative or O positive. That was it. No B.

But, on the other hand, one A positive parent, with the help of an AB parent or a B parent could create a B offspring. A B. Like my mom.

Everything I had known about Lovey, everything I had thought, how I had revered the way she stood by D-daddy through thick and thin, the way she had taken care of him tirelessly for the years he was confined to that chair had changed now. Because theirs hadn't been true love at all. It had been a marriage of deception, a relationship filled with lies, affairs and an illegitimate daughter. It hit me all at once that the man I had thought nearest to God wasn't even my biological grandfather. And, like that tattoo needle, the thought seared into me, making a permanent impression.

Lovey

ىل

A Souvenir

August 1951

"Honeymoon" is the most beautiful word in the English language. I figured Momma must have been right when she said that because as Dan and I boarded the plane in New York, where we had stopped over for a couple of days, I could scarcely contain myself. *Imagine,* I thought, *me, on a Pan Am flight to Cuba of all things.* We were dressed in our daytime finest for the occasion. I was wearing my best traveling suit complete with a wide-brimmed hat with a thick, satin bow tied around it. I could still practically see in my mind's eye the beautifully wrapped package with the colorful poster inside. "Fly to Cuba via Pan American World Airways System." That could only mean one thing: I was officially a world traveler.

I had been on a plane before, I reminded myself, walking a little taller through the airplane's corridor, Montaldo's hatbox firmly in hand, purse draped casually over my arm. *But that had been TWA.*

"Imagine," I whispered to Dan. "Getting to fly on a real-life, double-decker airplane."

Dan squeezed my gloved hand as a flight attendant in her gray-blue suit, hat perched jauntily atop her head, walked by. "This will be the first of many, many flights like this one. Don't you worry, my beauty."

I sat down in my spacious leather seat the color of fresh cream, opened my ashtray and lit a cigarette, my husband leaning over to kiss me. I hadn't smoked before our wedding, but Dan had picked up the habit during the war, and I thought I was unfathomably glamorous, puffing and exhaling in long, slow drags. Dan and his father had gone on and on about real Cuban cigars, from Havana, no less. And I couldn't wait to see Dan, fedora atop his head, lounging by the private beach that the flyer touted, puffing on a real Cuban cigar.

"What do you think it will be like?"

"What do I think what will be like?"

I smiled and tapped him on the arm. "Cuba, of course."

"My parents said that the Hotel Nacional is absolutely splendid," Dan said.

It was a generous gift, especially for in-laws who were less than thrilled with not only their son's elopement but also his choice in brides. But I would win them over one day, I reassured myself often. And, if not, so be it. I had Dan now, and that was all the approval I needed.

My parents, on the other hand, as soon as they had been invited to Dan's family's sweeping Victorian in the heart of New Bern's downtown, situated right on the Neuse River, had forgotten all about their thwarted plans to marry me off to Ernest Wake. They wanted me to have money, sure. But if I could have money *and* love? Well then, so much the better.

I had stared so long at the brochure for the hotel that I practically had it memorized. *Rendezvous of the Americas,* I thought again. The phrase was almost as romantic as Dan's proposal had been.

I squeezed Dan's hand over the armrest as we took off, sailing up higher, higher and higher even still until we were cruising, leaving behind our old lives as single people, climbing to heights that I hadn't yet dreamed of, much less experienced. Two flight attendants wheeled a table, complete with white tablecloth, toward us, popped the top off of a bottle of champagne with much ado, and said, "We hear congratulations are in order, lovebirds."

I could feel myself blushing, realizing that this whole affair had me feeling like a girl of eighteen again, not the woman of twenty-five that I actually was. "Oh, that looks absolutely marvelous," I said, realizing that this dream of a trip hadn't even really started yet, and I was already dreading it being over.

"Did you know," I said to Dan, "that Betty Grable and Rita Hayworth have stayed at the Nacional?"

He smiled at me adoringly. "The Rockefellers too."

I sighed. "There's just no telling who we might spot."

And though the celebrity sightings were less numerous than I had dreamed, the display of fruit on the chest in our room was like nothing I'd ever seen. At home, fruit was muscadine grapes, strawberries, and an apple and orange here and there. But sitting here, on the dresser in our vibrant room, was practically a harvest of things I'd never heard the names of. Mango, papaya, kiwi. And yet, they had Coca-Cola just like home.

Slipping into a bikini the exact color of those Pan Am uniforms

232 Kristy Woodson Harvey

with tiny white print all over, I said, "Oh, Dan, I can't wait to get down to the pool." I had already become comfortable undressing in front of my new husband, something that I couldn't have even dreamed of in the previous months. But the moment we were pronounced husband and wife, we became one flesh, after all. And, free from the misshaping and stretch marks of childbearing as I was, there wasn't much to hide.

"I suggest that we have cocktails and the biggest lunch we can dream," Dan said, squeezing my hand.

As we sat down under one of the black umbrellas flanking the pool and admired the glamorous awnings over the cabanas, I couldn't help but stare through my sunglasses at a conspicuous group of men, in full suits, eating lunch by the pool. They were talking loudly, clearly Americans, and, just by the way their cigars teetered on the edges of their ashtrays between bites, you could tell they were important.

"Dollar-a-year men," Dan leaned over and whispered to me.

I nodded, trying to be impressed but unable to control the thoughts that dining across from America's political elite was one thing. Rita Hayworth was quite another.

Our starched server with the thick accent came to the table, and, tossing my menu to the side gaily, I said, "I believe I'll have a bowl of coconut ice cream."

"Coconut ice cream?" Dan questioned, laughing. "For lunch?"

"I'm on my honeymoon, darling. It's hot. And I'd like to have ice cream." I pulled my sunglasses down so he could see the twinkle in my eyes. "Ice cream has a very special place in my heart, if you'll remember."

Dan smiled. "Well then, ice cream it is."

I had never had coconut ice cream before, but it topped anything

I'd ever eaten ten to one. "Fields of white velvet," I said to Dan, licking my lips and pointing my spoon in the direction of the bowl. "That's what this ice cream brings to mind. It is the most delicious thing I have ever tasted."

"Well then, I believe you should have another bowl."

I heard my momma's voice in the back of my mind. *Lynn, desserts are for special occasions, and then only one.*

But this was the most special occasion. So I said, "You know what, my love, I believe I will."

I thought that that ice cream would remain my most vivid and special remembrance of that trip. That is, until a few weeks later when I realized that Dan and I had brought back a souvenir that we would cherish for the rest of our lives: Sally.

Annabelle

~~~

Ants Marching

S in is rarely hardest on the sinner. I know now that Lovey's right about that one. Because, while I was up all night, every night wondering, stressing, plotting and planning, Ben slept as soundly as a worriless child in that bed beside me.

How he and Laura Anne snuck around without worrying they'd get caught, I'll never know. Because, as I pulled into Holden's driveway that day, my butterflies had butterflies. I wish I could have said that the jitters I was feeling that day were out of love. But they weren't. They were out of fear and anxiety. They were out of the worry that I would get caught, that someone would see. And I was only drinking coffee, for Lord's sake—decaf, at that.

I had taken my parents' extra car to Holden's. They thought I was on my way to Salisbury, but I was going to make an unexpected pit stop. As Holden's back door pushed against its springs and slammed shut, I instantly felt more comfortable. It was all the same—in the sunroom, at least. The sofa with the cashmere Ralph Lauren Black

Label blanket thrown casually across the back. The bookcase filled with prizewinning, hand-carved decoys and antique guns leaned against the wall. The smell of Old Spice and pine and Labrador mixing together into a cologne of well-bred, moneyed masculinity.

And then there was Holden, in shorts and an oxford with rolled-up sleeves, Gucci loafers and, for a hint of something new, the monogrammed belt buckle had been replaced by Hermès's signature "H" buckle with an alligator strip running around his taut waist. Holden stepped over the threshold from the kitchen to the sunroom to embrace me. He held me for a long time there and kissed my hair, somehow instinctively knowing that trying for more was too much too soon.

"My house instantly looks better when you walk through the door," he said.

I smiled, feeling a familiarity about it all that was somewhat comforting.

"Can I get you a drink? Maybe a Veuve Clicquot?"

"What are you doing with Veuve Clicquot lying around?"

He turned, his hand on the refrigerator door and, looking wistfully past me into the space behind my head said, with a prophet's voice, "I hoped that you would smell it and come back to me."

We both broke down into a fit of laughter, and, even with my life gone so terribly wrong, it felt so good to laugh. I leaned over the marble island as Holden poured and handed me a wineglass. "No champagne flute?"

He shook his head. "I went to a wine tasting recently and they told me that champagne flutes are made for aerating bad champagne. Good champagne should be enjoyed from a wineglass."

I thought of Ben, a brand-new guilt surging, a pain stabbing right through me like a shard of glass in a hurricane. I thought of the RV, of the laughter and the love and the simplicity of that life and how I wished that I could lasso that moment and pull it back to me.

But I can't, I reminded myself, standing up a little straighter, my shoes tapping on the hardwood floor as I slipped them off and curled up in a chair in the adjoining den, directly across from the piano. Holden sat down at the keys and began to play, periodically looking over his shoulder at me. "So, you know how I feel about you, right?"

I walked over to him and set my glass on the piano, remembering that I couldn't drink it. I couldn't help but roll my eyes at that business-as-usual comment. "Yes, Holden, I know how you feel about me."

"So is it forward of me to ask why you've come here today?"

I shrugged even though he was focusing on the concerto flying from the keys like a horse jumping over its hurdles. "I'm not really sure," I said. "I guess I've gotten your texts, and I've read your e-mails, and I'm wondering what you're really hoping to gain from all of this."

His fingers stopped all at once, ten ants marching home to their queen suddenly stomped by a careless human shoe. He turned on the slick, black bench and said quietly, "You. I'm hoping to gain you."

I sat down on the bench beside him, and he put his arm around me. I could feel the tears coming as I laid my head on his shoulder. His comfortable, predictable, even-keel shoulder. He rested his head on mine. "I want another chance, Annabelle," he whispered. "No big to-do that you don't want. No my mother pressuring you into wearing pink seersucker. None of that. I just want you for who you are, and I don't ever want you to change. I want you to be the mother of my children."

That simple sentence was all it took for my misting over to become a huge puddle on the floor.

I could see his eyes glazing over, as he whispered, "What's wrong, Ann? What's going on?"

I sniffed and composed myself. "I'm pregnant," I said simply.

His head popped up, and I could see the shock pass over his face. He stood up so quickly I nearly fell over. He began pacing the length of the living room. I figured that being pregnant with another man's baby was enough to scare him away and that, now, no Ben, no Holden, I was really, truly alone.

His shock turned to confusion, and he said, "So what are you doing here? I mean, does Ben not want a baby or something?"

I bit my lip. "Ben doesn't know."

True mystification was written all over his face, but then he steeled his jaw and, in that classic, Holden way, that decisive, confident manner that I needed most, he said, "Don't tell him."

"What do you mean, don't tell him?"

"Don't tell him. If he knows, there will be custody battles and the baby being shifted from place to place and all sorts of confusion."

It made me realize how little I had actually considered this. I had to tell Ben, didn't I? I couldn't keep a secret this huge from Ben. Or could I? He hadn't been terribly concerned about keeping a huge secret from me.

My thoughts shifted to Lovey. Had she been at this same crossroads? All of a sudden, I began to understand her a little bit better. Because, now, it wasn't about me, and it wasn't about Ben and it wasn't about Holden. It was about this precious little baby and what would be best for it.

I thought of my mother and how she had never had any doubt about who her parents were. And she was happy. And, though I knew it was wrong, I nodded all the same. "Okay."

Then I started crying again. "Holden, this won't work. I mean, I won't be divorced for a year at the minimum, and I'm going to be pregnant and having this baby with you . . . Our families will absolutely die. What will people say? What will they think?"

"I don't give a shit what people think," he said. "We'll move. I'm sick of Raleigh anyway."

My heart was starting to warm to him, to realize that, for all his faults, this was a man that was capable of being a rock for me when I needed it most. That's when I made the mistake of glancing down at the Love band adorning my left finger.

I had made a vow. I had promised to love Ben and cherish him and be faithful to him until the day I died. And he had broken that vow. And now, sitting in the tapestried den of my ex-fiancé, I was the one who felt broken. "Where will we move?"

He shrugged. "I don't know. But we'll just go. And our families will be pissed, but, wherever we go, the people there won't know. We'll just act like we've been married the whole time. And, when it's legal, we can sneak off somewhere, just the two of us, and get it done." He cleared his throat and looked down at my stomach. "Just the three of us, I mean." He winked at me. "I think a little return trip to the BVIs might be nice."

I thought of that trip with Holden, the night we got engaged, the joy I had felt at the Christmas-card-perfect life that I had won for myself. And how I had thrown it all away on a fling that hadn't ever really loved me. The weight of all of my bad decisions suddenly felt like it was suffocating me. I had to get outside and get some fresh air. I started toward the door with Holden following behind me. "Where are you going? I think we have a few more details to iron out here."

I shook my head. "I know, Holden. But I have so much to deal with between now and then. I just need to go."

In the way I needed most, he said, "Okay. I'm here whenever." He paused. "Do you want me to get a crib or something?"

I looked back at him, my hand on the car door already and said, "For right now, let's just wait. Just don't tell anyone." I turned back and added, "Can you just wait a little longer for me?" I put my hand on my belly. "For us?"

He grinned like his horse had just won the Derby and said, "Oh, Ann, I'd wait for you forever."

I sped out of the driveway and down the highway, angry at the uninvited tears crashing my party. As I drove, music blaring in the background, I sobbed for the person that I had pushed away the most: my husband. And for this baby that we had made out of so much love.

Somewhere along the two-hour drive from Raleigh to Salisbury, I composed myself, and I thought about my options. I had spent so long thinking that the only choice was to leave Ben, but what if that wasn't it? What if I could stay? What if we could move away and go back to that simpler time where we first fell in love and we were both so happy? What about that option?

The pride surged in me, and I thought about Doug and Sally. I knew that I could never be that woman, that I could never live with a man when I knew that he had someone else filling his heart and his bed, knowing that I wasn't enough for him. I couldn't bear the thought of having to face Laura Anne forever, of her knowing that she had battered my ego and humiliated me, that she had taken from me everything I thought was real.

Having to go to Laura Anne's house for the party she threw us, smile politely and thank her graciously, had been unthinkable enough, especially considering that I couldn't drink. I would say it was one of the hardest nights of my life, but, in other ways, it was one of the proudest too. I kept my composure, I didn't kill either of them, and I made it through almost two hours before claiming a migraine—I don't get migraines, but Laura Anne doesn't know that—and having to go home. Ben had given me an odd look, but never said a word about my fake condition. In fact, in the car, he said, "Oh my gosh. You don't think this headache could mean you're pregnant, do you?"

I flat-out lied with a simple, "No."

And I knew that night that I couldn't bear the thought of being the woman that stayed and took that from a man, even one that she was convinced was the other half of her soul.

Worst of all, I couldn't imagine the humiliation if Ben didn't want me anymore. What if I gave him the option to rebuild what we had and he chose her anyway?

The hardest thing for me about the affair was that, though I was so seethingly angry with Ben, I still loved him so madly. He had been my entire life, every laugh, every heartbeat, every tear had been with him and for him. And, oddly, it didn't seem like he loved me any less. When I saw him standing in the doorway of the pool house, waiting for my headlights to pull up, I broke down again. And it was Ben, as always, who pulled me onto his lap, stroked my hair and whispered, "Everybody needs a good cry every now and then, TL."

And then I started crying even harder because I knew that I wasn't his TL, at least not in the way I wanted to be. I knew our marriage was over, and he had no idea. The man who had changed everything about my life would be gone from it soon. It was as though everything I had put my faith in on this earth had fallen into a mythic hand that had closed and crumbled it all in one fell swoop.

I composed myself, picked my head up from Ben's shoulder and looked at him.

"What's the matter with my girl?" he asked, nuzzling my neck.

I looked into his eyes, and I knew it was the right moment. I needed to tell him something. About the baby. That I knew about the affair. But, instead, I said, "It's just so hard to see Lovey like that."

"I know, sweetheart. But she's going to be fine. She has so much love around her, and, when you're surrounded by love, what else do you really need?" He kissed me. "After I found your love, I haven't needed another single thing."

And that's when it hit me. What if I had my facts wrong about Ben? What if Laura Anne zipped up in his golf bag that day hadn't meant that he was cheating? What if it was something else entirely, something that the four of us would sit around a fire pit and have a good, long laugh about in the near future?

And there I was again, back to questioning everything, back to feeling like the axis of my life was tipping so far to the left that I was on the verge of falling off of the world. For a moment, I had hope. Maybe there was another explanation as to why Ben had to sneak Laura Anne out of the pool house. And maybe there was some other explanation to the whole blood-typing, birth certificate fiasco. Maybe it was nothing more than a mistake, a slip of the pen. Another explanation for anything, at this point, would be a very welcome change.

Lovey

One Big Secret

In life, you have to be prepared for the surprises, good and bad, and take them in stride with grace and humility. But I never saw it coming that day. I was lounging in the elevated nursing home bed, sipping a cup of coffee with impossibly fresh cream that Luella had procured from the farmers' market, thinking that this nursing home gig wasn't so bad after all. All of my meals were prepared, Dan was taken care of and, even though I was as ready to get out of here as a two-week overdue woman is to give birth, there was such a sense of safety in knowing that, in an emergency, a team could be assembled for Dan as quickly as I could push a button.

I had talked to each of my girls that morning and was thrilled that all five of them would be coming that weekend. The love they had for each other, that bond, it made me so happy. But, in the quiet moments, it made me a little bit sad too. Even after my sister Lib and her husband had come back home, when the war had ended, we'd never been close. Through all of those years of her living in

Charlotte and me in Raleigh, only a few hours up the road, we had never seen each other more than once or twice a year, never grazed beyond the niceties of conversations about children and work, cooking and keeping the house. Sometimes I ached for that missed opportunity, wondered what kind of sister I could have had if either of us had made the effort.

But, happily, I had been there a few days before she died. It had been unexpected, her death. Although, certainly, at ninety-four, death is always an expectation. Her last words to me were, "Lynn, I know I was never much of a sister to you. But I've always loved you so much. I've always prayed for you and the girls and been so happy for your happy life."

Even as she said it, I wondered if my happy life had driven a wedge between us. I wondered if I had confided in her more, if we hadn't been so busy keeping up appearances, if our paths could have collided in a more meaningful way, if we could have had even a fraction of what my girls had.

As well as my own face in the mirror, I knew there was no use harping on what might have been. And, besides, there was a silver lining. On the very bright side, where He hadn't given me a close relationship with my real one, God had given me a sister to navigate every up and down with. In fact, I had spoken with Katie Jo that morning. While I was laid up in bed, she was getting in a new one. "I have a new beau," she had said, giggling as though we were fourteen again.

"A boyfriend?" I had asked, feigning shock. Katie Jo had married once, years and years ago, but never had children. And that was just as well because her marriage began after I had Sally and ended before I had Louise. She swore she'd never do it again, and, truth be told, some birds just shouldn't be caged.

"And, oh my Lord, he really is a boy, Lynn. It's almost embarrassing."

I laughed, the pain pulsing in my hip. But, in that moment, I envied her. I looked over at Dan, confined to his bed, me confined to mine. And I realized that maybe I'd had my last adventure. But not Katie Jo. Her last adventure would coincide with her last breath. That's how it was always meant to be. "Do tell."

"He is seventy-two, Lynn. Can you believe that? What would a seventy-two-year-old want with an eighty-eight-year-old?"

I laughed again. "Oh, mercy, Katie Jo. You know, I can't imagine any man worth his salt that wouldn't want you."

She promised to visit. I hoped in the deepest part of my soul that I would see her again before one of us was gone. Hearing my best friend's voice, the way we could still pick up right where we left off, had done my heart good. And I realized again that we might not have had the same momma and daddy. But, in my mind, Katie Jo would always be my sister.

I looked over at Dan again. He was dozing between frames of the black-and-white film on the screen, and I knew that everyone else in the world, everyone besides me, would say that my comfort in having a team to save him at any moment was an idiotic, cruel thought. Why, they would wonder, would I want to revive a man who had virtually no quality of life? But the thing about a long marriage, the overriding factor in an existence where you became one flesh with a man and never looked back, is that, no matter the personal cost, no matter the reasonable reality, you can't bear the thought of being away from him. As incongruous as it may seem to the outside world, to the person with whom their body and mind has been joined for longer than a good many people are on the earth, not having them there, in any state, feels as impossible as staying on the ground without gravity.

I was nearly dozing off myself when the door slammed and both Dan and I popped up, alarmed. I couldn't even question who it was before Annabelle peeked around the corner.

My family had been as faithful as hunting dogs about coming to visit us while we were here, realizing that, when you're basically confined to a bed, the days seem too long even for someone who knows that her hourglass is almost out of sand.

"Hello, my darling girl," I said, trying to sit up.

My smile faded quickly when I saw her closed body language, the way her normally relaxed and shining countenance was wrinkled and worried. "I know, Lovey," was all she said.

My mind raced, and I could feel myself going pale because, in all my life, I'd had only one big secret. I looked over at Dan; he was gazing back into the television screen, completely unaware that the one thing we had tried the hardest to hide for more than fifty years might be out in the open. But that was impossible, I reassured myself. There was no conceivable way that she could know.

And so, taking a leisurely sip of my coffee, trying to calm myself, I said, "I have no idea what you're talking about, darling."

"I know about Mom," she said.

I could feel my pulse racing again, realizing that it contributed to a vile throbbing in my hip. *Calm down,* I told myself. That could mean practically anything. Maybe Jean had been caught doing something illicit with campaign funds and Annabelle thought I knew. Or maybe one of my only daughters that I believed to be squeaky clean was also having a little fling.

"Darling, what in heaven's name are you talking about?" I took another sip of my coffee, as casually as I could, though my heart was beating out of my chest.

"I saw the paper," she said, crossing her arms indignantly. "I saw that form you filled out about Mom being adopted."

I was racking my brain. I had burned those forms immediately when the new birth certificate was issued. "What form, sweetheart? Maybe you should sit down. Are you feeling all right?"

Annabelle laughed cruelly. "I wondered why someone as smart and methodical and prepared as you are would possibly risk keeping that form and getting caught. But now I see. You didn't know it was in the lockbox, did you?"

I had been in that lockbox thousands of times. And I always looked at those birth certificates. I compared them to make sure that they were perfect. I counted pictures to make sure that each girl had the same number. I had created a spot where all five of my daughters would go after Dan and I were gone and never have a single question. I knew for certain that there wasn't any sort of form in that lockbox. She was bluffing. I could feel myself calming. "Annabelle," I said. "Why don't you come sit by me. You're not making any sense."

That look she gave me, it was so mean and so hideous that I couldn't believe it could even come from those big, beautiful eyes of hers. They were all beautiful. Every last one of the children and grandchildren in our family. But Annabelle was in a class all her own. Long and lithe, with skin that seemed to have an otherworldly glow. To see her so angry, the shadow on that gorgeous face with those impossibly high cheekbones, was the shock of my lifetime.

"It was stuck, Lovey. Practically glued to Mom's birth certificate. The others might never have even noticed it. But it felt thick to me. And when I rubbed it together, that second piece of paper started to peel off. That piece of paper that you didn't even know was there."

I was finding it difficult to catch my breath. I looked over at Dan again, as if he was going to spring to life and save me from this inquisition. It had happened before. When I had needed him, even in this state, he had seemed to come back and take charge once again. But this time, just blankness. If I had been younger, I could have thought of an explanation. If Dan had been well, he could have smoothed this over. But she had seen the paper. She knew.

But then Annabelle said, "I can't believe that you could cheat on D-daddy," and I felt a flood of relief wash over me.

Daughters and granddaughters have a complicated relationship with their mothers and grandmothers. There is a vicious kind of love there, one that I would venture to say, while not as pure and untainted as their love for their fathers and grandfathers, goes deeper. It is the kind of love that ebbs and flows, fights and forgives. It is the kind of love that takes the bullet, recovers in the ICU and lives to tell about it. And I realized right then and there that I had two choices: I could stand in front of the firing squad and take it. Or I could tell the truth. I looked over at my husband, completely indefensible in his current state, and felt that rush of pity come over me.

And so I made the decision that any wartime wife worth her salt would. "I can't be sorry for anything that led to the creation of a daughter and a granddaughter so sensational and first in my heart."

I hadn't admitted anything, so, in that way, I hadn't actually lied. But I hadn't totally told the truth either. But, like I've said before and I'll likely say again, those little white lies are the only things that make any of our families what they are. When the truth would be too large a pill to swallow, a tiny omission of fact here or there keeps the peace like nothing else I know.

"How could you do that, Lovey? How could you lie like that forever? I mean, does Mom even know?"

"Calm down, love. Your mother is a perfectly happy, grown woman, content in the knowledge that two parents love her unconditionally. And there is no reason for her to ever have to question that."

She shook her head. "I thought you were better. I have always had you up on such a pedestal, that you were there for D-daddy no matter what, that you had the kind of love story that would go down in the history books. I had you pictured as this steel magnolia who stood by his side faithfully no matter what. But you were no better than anyone else, after all."

Before the lying and deceitful part, I would say she hit the nail right on the head about what kind of wife I'd been. And then she shocked me again, spinning around toward the door and saying, "You're no better than Ben."

And, with that puzzling and horrifying sentence, my girl was gone.

Annabelle

Feet over Head

Lovey always says that North Carolina is the best state because its inhabitants really live by its motto: "To be, rather than to seem." Back in the car, my hands frozen on the steering wheel, I could see that motto, protected by one of those binder sheets and snapped in between its three rings, gracing the pages of my fourth-grade North Carolina project. That was going to be my motto too. I wasn't going to sit in the front row at church holding the hand of a man who was thinking of someone else. I wasn't going to brush the hair and tie the shoes of the children of a man who was with someone else when I was away. I put my hand over my stomach protectively and felt my heart sink. But, then again, I had this baby now, this little person to think about and worry about. This precious angel that deserved to have a mother and a father, no matter the cost to me. And, whoever this baby's father, I was going to *be* its mother.

I don't know why I had chosen that day to confront Lovey. Maybe it was that it had been a few weeks since her hip break, and I thought she was stronger. Maybe it was that I couldn't stand to bottle up all these secrets for one more second. One was going to come pouring out, and, for now, that seemed like the safer one to let loose.

And now I didn't know where to go. I couldn't go to my childhood home; I hadn't even told my mom I was coming to Raleigh, lest I cause suspicion. And now, knowing what I knew, what Lovey had admitted, I certainly couldn't go back to Ben. I abhorred the thought of being like the woman I had always loved so much, of living the rest of my life in a lie, acting like my marriage was one thing when it was really something else. No matter what I chose, my entire life was going to be a lie anyway. And, quite frankly, hiding the real father of your child was a substantially larger deception than having an affair.

I realized in the midst of my inner monologue that I was driving in the direction of Holden's house. And who cared, really? My entire life was a sham, and I deserved better. And then I had a troubling thought: *She never actually admitted it.*

But Lovey had said she would never be sorry for anything that led to the creation of her daughter and granddaughter. And there really was no other explanation.

I could feel the tears coming down my cheeks again as I pulled into Holden's driveway. I hadn't even turned the engine off before he was out the door, chewing the sandwich that he, completely predictably, had come home for lunch to eat. Already a multimillionaire in his late twenties, but God forbid he spend eight bucks on lunch.

He swallowed and hugged me. "What's the matter with my girl?" He peered over my shoulder into the backseat. "I'm less excited because I don't see any possessions back there to indicate that you're moving in here with me." Then he asked again, "What's with the tears?"

I knew I would never tell him about Lovey and D-daddy and Mom. It was too big a secret to ever share, knowledge that needed to be held under lock and key with twenty-four-hour security. I knew how distraught I was that D-daddy wasn't really my grandfather, so I couldn't begin to think how Mom would feel to know that she wasn't truly his daughter. I could picture her entire childhood a thin stream of water from a green garden hose, evaporating as quickly as it hit the pavement on a sweltering August day.

So I said, instead, "I've decided to finally tell Ben I'm leaving him."

His face lit up. "And . . ."

I leaned my head on his chest again. His safe, familiar, boring, uncomplicated, chest. I could hear myself saying to Lovey less than two years earlier, *He's my Ernest Wake.*

But he wasn't my Ernest Wake. He smelled great and dressed well and, though not gorgeous like Ben, was perfectly genetically suitable for producing another generation without the worry of getting teased at school. I had no doubt that he would weather what was going to be a pretty terrible storm with me, and that he would raise Ben's child like his own and give it every opportunity and every bit of love that he could.

And, in a different way from how I had loved Ben, I did love him. It was a familiar kind of love, not the kind that makes your heart race but the kind that makes you feel safe under the covers when you're saying your prayers at night. The kind that, when he calls on the phone and says, "I'm sorry, sweetheart, I have to work late," you don't drive to his office and spy through the window to make sure he's telling the truth. Because honesty is as important to him as never wearing seersucker after Labor Day.

"And, if you'll still have me, I'd like to give it another go."

He hollered, "Woo-hoo!" throwing the crust of his sandwich into the yard, picking me up and spinning me around in the concrete and brick driveway.

He leaned forward to kiss me, but I put my hand up. "I'm not going to be that girl," I said. "I may be leaving him, but I don't want to be a cheater too."

"Whenever you're ready, Annabelle, I'll be here waiting with your favorite flowers all around the house and a chilled bottle of Veuve Clicquot—or two." He winked at me. Then he paused. "Wait. I guess that won't really work. Maybe sparkling cider?"

And I knew he would. I was positive that he would have the florist deliver fresh vases of hydrangeas, peonies and white roses every single day until I arrived on his doorstep.

"I'll figure out where we're going to live so you don't have that on your plate on top of everything else. Colorado?"

I scrunched my nose. "Isn't it kind of cold in Colorado?"

"I just thought because you loved to ski so much." He shrugged. "Well, whatever. I'll find the perfect place and get back to you. And I'll start interviewing nannies."

"Nannies?"

He looked at me like I was dense. "Yeah. For the baby. So we can travel and stuff?"

I shook my head, realizing that, in the fog and distraction of what I was going to say to Ben, I had momentarily forgotten about the baby.

"Do you need new clothes? Let's get you a new diamond—something bigger and better than my grandmother's."

I put my hands on his shoulders, smiling at his excitement, surprised that I couldn't see how much he loved me before when it was obviously there the entire time. "Holden, relax. It's just me. I don't need a thing."

I knew I should have added, *Except for you*. But, as hard as I tried, the words were stuck like a hamster in a tube too small. I tried to back them up, move them forward, topple them feet over head. But they wouldn't budge. And so I said, "I'll keep you posted."

"I'll keep you posted too. I'll find the perfect place."

I felt those anxious tears rising in my throat. I wanted to thank him. But, suddenly, the idea of moving, of uprooting my life, of getting a divorce, of having a baby born in the midst of that, of trying to make a new life with a man that was comfortable, sure, but wasn't necessarily the love of my life, was too overwhelming to face. So I just nodded.

And with that, I got back in the car and sped out of the driveway. I examined the house as I passed by, the white, two-story brick with the pretty flower border along the cobblestone path and the three-car garage. The oak trees in the front yard were stately and beautiful. It was a perfect specimen of an old Raleigh home, of the kind of place where you couldn't wait to see a pink or blue bow as you pulled up the driveway. There was a huge backyard with the perfect corner for a swing set, a shed for toys galore and a bright, sunny spot for growing vegetables. The master bathroom was huge with two sinks and a separate tub, and the kitchen was out of a chef's imagination. It was everything I could ever want, everything that I knew Holden would find for us wherever we made a life together. And yet, I couldn't really see myself in any of it.

But I've done the heart-racing thing, I reminded myself. And it hadn't worked. So safe and secure would be just fine. It wasn't about me anymore. I had a baby to think of now.

I looked down at my phone and noticed that I had three missed calls from Rob.

"Shit," I said under my breath, frantically dialing. I had been so convinced that I had to get to Raleigh right that moment before I lost my nerve to tell Lovey what I had found out, that I had forgotten to call Rob and tell him I wouldn't be in until the afternoon.

"Please don't fire me," I said, as he answered.

He laughed. "I'm just glad you're all right. What on earth is going on?"

I looked at the phone and said, "I don't feel like I can tell you over the phone with the NSA and God knows who else listening in. I'll fill you in when I get there this afternoon."

I said it like it was nothing, not even realizing that I felt totally safe trusting Rob with all of those deep, dark secrets that I thought were better hidden away. I merged onto the highway and said, "I'll be there right at two."

It occurred to me, as I set the cruise control, that, while marrying Holden and having security for my baby seemed like the best option, of everything in Salisbury, I knew I'd miss my job the most.

Lovey

Gypsies

August 1951

My momma always told me that you should never stop holding hands, that just holding hands could keep a couple connected through the hard times. And Dan had never held my hand that tight before. He knew how nervous I was about seeing his parents again.

And the expansive front porch of their massive waterfront home in New Bern's picturesque downtown didn't help my nerves. I was a simple farm girl raised on fried chicken and vegetables I picked myself. It also didn't help that the light drizzle falling on the sidewalk had made my flowers wilt and my hair grow. And suddenly the polka-dot dress that I had been wearing the night Dan and I reunited in New York felt all wrong. I ran my free hand over my hair, trying to salvage what I could of my style.

"Don't worry. They're going to love you," Dan whispered as he turned the doorknob and crossed the threshold.

You couldn't help but look up in the grand foyer, flanked by the living room on the right and the dining room on the left. The chandeliers in all three rooms were like something from a movie set. Crystal fixtures so huge that it made you wonder how many men it took to hang them. I didn't have long to stare, though, before Dan's mother was practically running into the entrance hall, throwing her arms around her son's neck, breaking his grip with mine. She was much taller than I had remembered, much taller than I was, which made her even more intimidating.

And her joy for her son, when directed my way, turned into an icy handshake and, "Well, hello there. I guess you married my Dan."

As though I had hog-tied him and dragged him down to the courthouse, him fighting tooth and nail to break away from all five feet of me.

"Honey, I'm home," Father White called as he entered the back door, his voice dripping with that Southern, aristocratic accent that Dan also possessed to a lesser extent. He hugged me warmly and said, "Well, my dear, didn't you grow up nicely? How are your folks?"

Relief flooded over me like warm bathwater. At least someone in this family would act civilly toward me. I nodded and said, "Very well indeed. Thank you for asking."

Then he kissed his wife and said, "Sorry, darling. I had a few sick I needed to visit before I came home for supper."

She replied haughtily, "I know duty calls, but, for heaven's sake, the meal is going to be a mess if we don't sit down."

Jane tapped a buzzer with her foot, and two uniformed maids swept through with an array of food so beautiful that I thought I might could eat it, sick as I felt.

"Well, yes," she said. "We would have liked to invite your parents to dinner to get to know them. We don't want them to think we're ill-mannered. But when you run off and get married like some sort of gypsies, it's rather hard to follow society protocol."

"Oh, well. They remember you fondly and certainly don't think you're ill-mannered, Mrs. White."

She looked me up and down like something the cat dragged in and said, as though I had grown up in a tent in the woods, "I should suppose not."

"Mother," Dan said. "We will have a lifetime to celebrate together."

"Would have been nice to dance at my own son's wedding is all . . . ," she said under her breath.

Father White leaned back from the table and lit his pipe, its sweet smoke filling the air and overpowering the smell of the roast on the table. "Now, darling, just you calm down. You've got two more chances with two more sons."

I smiled politely and said, "This roast is just delicious. I can't thank you enough for having me."

Jane looked up from her plate dully and said, "Well, you're my daughter-in-law."

The subtext that hung in the air was, *I didn't have any choice but to invite you.*

With that she set her napkin on the table, scooted out her chair and said, "Dan, I could use your help with something in the kitchen."

The nausea was rapidly returning. I expected there to be a few bumps in the road when Dan and I ran off and got married. That was reasonable. But I hadn't expected such coldness from my new mother-in-law. I took a sip of my tea, swallowing hard, trying to keep the tears lodged in my throat from coming down my face.

Father White got up and took Dan's seat beside me at the table. With his pipe still in the corner of his mouth he said, "Now don't you mind Jane. She can be a bit of a bitch."

I could feel my eyes widening. I'd heard my fair share of cuss words—you had to when you were best friends with Katie Jo—but I couldn't imagine one coming out of the mouth of this handsome, dignified man who was a preacher, no less. I couldn't help but laugh.

He put his arm around my shoulder and squeezed, taking a puff of the pipe that smelled so good I wished Dan would start smoking one too. Then he whispered, "You know, darling, sometimes the shoe just fits."

From that moment on, he was sealed in my heart as one of my all-time favorite men. Good, kind, true, witty, handsome and well-to-do, Dan's father was the pinnacle of men to me from that lunch forward. As soon as I found out I was pregnant with Sally, I hoped against hope that she and any other daughter I ever had could find a man just like that.

Annabelle

∞

Absolutely Everything

There are going to be ups and downs in every life. And, if you can hunker down and hold tight through the challenges, Lovey says another victory will be right around the corner. It was a bit of consolation during that terrible time, but, looking back now, I don't know how I possibly could have lived like I did for so long, pretending that everything was normal and okay, when, in fact, I was an absolute wreck. Every time I looked at Ben's lips I could imagine them on Laura Anne's body. Every time I heard him breathe I imagined his breath in her ear, his whispers for her like they had been for me such a short time ago.

I had avoided him at every turn since that day I saw him with Laura Anne, pretending that the door I had slammed to my affection, leaving him out in the cold, was over the stress of Lovey's injury and my new hours at the job that, in reality, felt like my only saving grace.

In such a short time, my singular obsession had snapped like a taut rubber band from the family I would make with Ben to how to get out of this thing most gracefully and transition into the next step, missing as few beats as possible.

I didn't know how I could live my life knowing that I had never told Ben he had a child. The part of me that still loved him, that still wished we could have that fairy-tale life together, knew that he had a right to know, that he would be a wonderful father and that he should get to make a mark on this life that he created. But the other part of me thought that Holden was right: No baby deserves to be unstable and shuffled around, feel torn between his parents. Just like with clothes off the rack, which, in all likelihood, I would never wear again once I was with Holden, sometimes, none of the options available seem to fit quite right.

I had shown up at work right at two, as promised that day I left Raleigh and Lovey. Rob had sent me home immediately, and I was so grateful. Exhausted from the two-hour drive and the confrontation with Lovey, the pounding in my head from the things I had said to her, the words that I wished I could take back, I left the church and went to the pool house to take a bath, the cool cloth on my head feeling clearing and calming in direct contrast to the steaming tub of water. I wondered if I should even be taking a bath. When I had called the doctor, the nurse had said, "Congratulations! But it's so early now. We'll see you in five weeks to check how everything is coming along." *Five weeks.* It was coming up. Soon this would all be real. I couldn't avoid it anymore.

The nurse had said, "In the meantime, no alcohol, no sushi, no fancy cheeses. Just swing by here to pick up your prenatal kit and vitamins." She hadn't said anything about taking a bath.

So I lay there, completely still. And I just thought—or plotted, more like it. Somewhere between a cartographer and a big-screen villain, I plotted my next course, worked through what I would say and what I would do.

I knew that I could pull the trigger now, let the bullet of the truth that I knew so well fly at Ben. Because I had Holden to run to. I had a man that was going to stand by me even in this horrible scenario. And I was grateful. Because, pregnant with someone else's child, who was going to want me now?

I would push aside my anger at Lovey because, as Rob so astutely stated, she had given me everything good and true in my life—even if the truth wasn't exactly as I had seen it. And I understood her better now. A child changes absolutely everything. She would ultimately, I knew, be the one to help me heal, to help me love again, trust again, to lead me through this maze of unanswered questions with the sage wisdom that only a dump truck load of life experience can provide.

I was beginning to feel better, in control again, in charge of my future and my destiny, when I heard the back door close tightly and Ben's footsteps down the hall.

I slid my toe up to the silver lever on the tub and pushed down, the water beginning to flow out. My body, made buoyant by the gallons surrounding me, was suddenly heavy, the pull of the water on my skin feeling like a man bearing the weight of himself down on top of me. It occurred to me how long it had been since I had given in to the lure of Ben, to the calming, soothing satisfaction of total, blissful, thoughtless freedom. I was already pregnant, after all. What was the worst that could happen?

Pushing the thoughts of *her* out of my mind, of the other woman whose total demise occupied the vast majority of the spaces that used to be full with loving Ben, I decided that, since I wasn't completely ready to move on yet, my plan not fully intact, there was no use in him getting so suspicious, of wondering how our love life had gone from full saturation to bone dry in a matter of weeks. And, as the last of the water gurgled its way down the pipes and out to the sewer, I called, "Oh, Ben!"

I had forgotten how easy it could be to completely lose myself, to feel that love well up in my cells and flow in and out of my bone marrow. It must have been the thing that overtook my need to control, that superseded the strategic agonizing. It was like living and breathing itself, the essence of everything good. And, when it was over, when we were both lying there, my head on his beating heart, his fingers trailing lazily down my relaxed back muscles, though I hadn't planned it, though it hadn't been plotted down on paper for my ideal timing and my perfect, graceful exit, with my bags packed, in the light of day, trudging home to my future, I couldn't hold it in any longer. Like one thin, straight line out of a fresh Elmer's bottle, my words marched across the blank expanse of his chest. "I'm leaving you, Ben."

No emotion, no tears, not even a crack in my voice to indicate the devastation I felt would undoubtedly hide out in the deepest crevices of my ability to love for the rest of my life.

Ben bolted upright, and, in an unlikely response, began to dress. Calmly, evenly, he pulled on his boxers, then his pants, then his shirt. He buckled his belt. And, in the spaces between his silent dressing, I also pulled on my skirt and tied my disheveled hair behind my neck.

As the seconds turned to minutes that felt more like hours, he finally said, "Why would you even joke about something like that?"

"I know, Ben."

"Know what?"

"About Laura Anne."

He started stammering, the way that men do when they've been caught in the trap and are trying to decide whether to lie down and die or to see if they can chew their leg off without bleeding to death before help arrives. "I . . . I have no idea what you're . . . what you're talking about."

As the tears pooled in his eyes, I have to say that I was surprised. I had become so accustomed to hating him, seething inside with rage that someone I loved and trusted with every cell in my body could betray me so handily, that I guess I only assumed that he felt the same way toward me. And then I knew he had decided to lie down and die after all. "But, TL, you can't do this to me. You're the love of my life."

"Can't do this to you?" I asked, still calmly, still evenly, still emotionless. "Maybe we should review the facts of the case here. I'm pretty sure I wasn't the one cheating on you with my ex." I felt a sting of guilt because no one could possibly deny that keeping the knowledge of his child from him was one of the worst things that you could ever do to a person. And then there was the truth that I had my entire life with another man and Ben's baby planned out. It was harder to be indignant, remembering.

He shook his head vigorously. "No, no, no, no. It was stupid. I was feeling sad about not having a baby, but I didn't want to upset you, so we started talking and it just happened. But I don't love her. I don't want her. I never loved her. I only love you."

It was the first time I had ever seen Ben bordering on hysterical. And I was so happy I almost cried. I hadn't been wrong all this time. He had truly loved me.

Maybe it was because I had been living with the secret for so long, but I was finally the calm one while he was the one unraveling over the outcome that was now out of his hands. "Everything has changed for me now. There's no way I can be with you knowing what you're capable of."

Ben hugged me and rested his chin on my head. I didn't hug him back. "We can start over again. We can get out of here, go on tour again, be back to that all-over-each-other couple, me singing to you and you loving me."

"Yeah, but see, here's the thing. Now that you've been that with *her*, it's ruined for me."

"You can't leave me, Annie. I'll be alone forever. I'll wait for you until I die. You are the only one for me, I swear."

It scared me how cold I felt toward him now, how quickly that burning passion had dissipated. But it is, after all, fire that forges steel. It made me wish that I had confronted him about it when I first found out, that we could have had a chance to repair it while my insides still felt raw and oozing, before the skin had healed back over and made the body forget that it had ever felt anything to begin with. "Then I guess you should have thought about that before you started carrying your girlfriend down the stairs in a golf bag."

I could see his eyes widen a fraction. I knew he didn't want to give himself away, to let me see his shock. "That long?"

I nodded. It was stunning even to me that I had known for weeks without cracking. Although, clearly, he knew the wind had shifted.

I was getting ready to walk away when I felt something trickling down my leg. I looked down and saw a line of red making its way from my thigh to my ankle, a kindergarten teacher's perfect mark on the blackboard. "No!" I said. "No, no, no!"

I looked up at Ben, wishing that anyone was there but him. "You have to drive me to the hospital!"

I was frantic, marching out the door ahead of him, not even worried about the trail of red that I was leaving on the white carpet.

He grabbed my arm. "What is going on, Annabelle?"

"I'm pregnant!" I shouted.

His eyes widened. "Mine?"

"Who else's would it possibly be? You're the cheater. Not me."

We rode to the hospital in silence, and I already knew before the ER doctor said, "I'm so sorry. There's no heartbeat."

"Oh my God," I said, choking back my tears. "Is it because I took a bath?"

He gave me a puzzled look and patted my hand like I had totally lost my mind. "No, sweetheart. It wasn't anything you did. And everything with you looks perfect on the ultrasound. This is just nature's way of taking its course. Sometimes it isn't meant to be. But you shouldn't have any problem with pregnancy in the future."

I should have been relieved. I should have been able to breathe now that my ties to Ben were gone. That I didn't have to choose between telling the complicated truth and living a lie, that I didn't have to be an unwed mother, that I could move on now, be free.

But I didn't. I felt devastated. Minutes earlier, there had been a living thing inside of me, and, now, with a swoosh of blood and little fanfare, it was just gone. It was one of the only things I could think of that could actually supersede my anger at Ben. And we cried together, for all that we had had, and the even more that we had lost.

I let him hold my hand on the way to the car, and he said shakily, "Annabelle, we can try again. We can start over. I'm still me. I'm still that same man that you fell in love with."

Before I could even get out of the car or answer, Emily was rushing down the driveway. She was the last person I wanted to see, another reminder of how the life I had led was going to be gone, the rug pulled out from under me with all these people that I had loved riding away on it. Her face was ashen as she hugged me. "Honey, I'm so sorry."

"I'm assuming you knew the whole time?" I asked it like a question, but I knew that not much got past Emily, especially when it was happening under her roof.

She shook her head. "I had no idea you were pregnant."

"That's not what I'm talking about."

She opened her mouth, and I could tell she was going to lie, but then her expression shifted, and her eyes filled with tears too. "Please, Ann, you are my daughter. You mean everything to all of us."

I put my hands on my hips. "So you're going to stand there and tell me that you believe that I mean everything to your son?" I paused and gave her my most sarcastic look. "I guess I always just assumed a man I meant everything to wouldn't screw his girlfriend when he was supposed to be committed to me."

She shrugged. "But he never cared for her. Sometimes sex is just sex."

I threw my hands in the air. "Well, I'm glad you feel that way. You two can just take your free-love, no-consequences, no-apologies selves and do whatever the hell you want to. I, for one, am out of here."

Ben grabbed my arm, and I couldn't help but say, "I thought this was the thing you hated most about your dad, the one thing that you would never do."

He looked down at his feet and back up at me. "Sometimes we become what we hate."

I rolled my eyes, but I couldn't help but see my own hypocrisy. I had thought about letting Holden be the father of my child. I had considered never even telling Ben. The very thing I hated most about Lovey. *Sometimes we become what we hate.*

As I slammed the door behind me, I planned to go straight to Holden. I would be back in his house like I had never left, back to my safe, stale, contrived life. I sat in the car at the stop sign for a long time, willing myself to pull off toward the highway, to drive toward the life that felt like it had all but been prearranged for me, like Ben was the rest stop I had pulled into on a detour toward my fate. But, as cold and closed off as I felt in that moment, I still knew what it was to be truly loved. I knew what it was to feel like one lifetime wasn't enough. And I knew I'd never have that with Holden. But maybe someone else would. I heard the engine turn over as if I hadn't been the one to turn the key. And when my car started down the road, I realized that I had no idea where I was going to go.

I couldn't go home. I wasn't ready to ruin my parents' lives just yet by telling them that they had, in fact, been right about Ben—and everything else, really. We had gotten married too fast. We hadn't known each other well enough. It was all just a fairy tale, minus the happy ending. I thought back to that night in the bar, to those days following, to how exuberant I had been, how certain that Ben was what I had been waiting for. And, in a lot of ways, he had been. What we had shared was incredible and passionate, the kind of love that romance novels were written about. Romance novels, the steamy kind. Not epic love stories. I was relieved when the tears finally came, when I could cry for what I had lost. Ben called and called and texted and texted, but I didn't have to answer him anymore. It was over. We were over. And I didn't owe him anything. He deserved to wonder where I was, to wonder if I was okay. And he should have known by now that I wasn't.

Driving down the tree-lined streets of Salisbury's historic district, the setting sun reflecting off of its beautiful, oldest homes, pulling into one and then knocking on the door of The Oaks Bed & Breakfast, is perhaps one of the lowest points of my life. But I didn't have anywhere to go. Rob was my only real friend in town, and I certainly couldn't stay with him. And I wasn't ready for the humiliation of admitting what had happened to anyone, not even the priest.

Lucky for me, the room was warm, the bed was soft, and, despite the pain in my stomach and the even stronger one in my heart, I awoke to the smell of breakfast cooking, which meant that, against all odds, I had fallen asleep. I realized that I had been dreaming of Paris, of strolling down the riverbank and laughing, sitting at corner cafés and eating baguettes and cheese. I had been totally, utterly alone in a foreign country, and I had been as happy as could be. It was as comforting as the incredible breakfast I gorged myself on. Physically, I was feeling a little better. Less pained, though still very, very empty.

It wasn't terribly surprising that I was the only person in the restaurant that morning. And, knowing that I couldn't face the truth for a little bit longer, I asked the slender, aging woman who brought my plate, "If I stay here for two weeks, could I get a special rate?"

She smiled. "Of course. Are you here for a special occasion?"

I laughed ironically. "Well, I'm not sure that being too afraid to tell your family and friends that you're divorcing your husband is a special occasion, but, unfortunately, that's why I'm here."

She patted my hand, sat down across from me and said, "That's how I got here too. You just stay as long as you like."

It may not have been Paris, but the bread was almost as good. And the airfare didn't cost me a dime.

There's no such thing as "out of the blue," and surprises are very rare. Because, if we fine-tune that voice in our heads, that one that's talking to us all the time, we already know what we thought we didn't. So I guess I shouldn't have been surprised to see Ben sitting on a bench in the garden of the Saint Catherine House, where my office was, that morning when I got to work. In the shade of the ancient trees, surrounded by cheerful flowers and chirping birds, Ben seemed almost innocent, like maybe we could start all over again, go back to that dark bar that night and rekindle what might have been.

But then he said, "Annabelle, you can't just freeze me out like this. We're madly in love with each other. Don't throw it away on something stupid."

It made me realize the wide and gaping sinkhole that stood between what he thought was stupid and what I thought was stupid. Lying in bed at The Oaks the night before, I thought I could get over it. I thought that maybe Ben and I would have a chance to pick up the pieces and move on. But seeing him sitting on the front lawn, as handsome as he'd ever looked, the devastation rimming his eyes, I knew that time could never heal this wound, that I could never move forward in good conscience and have a family with a man that I didn't trust.

"I guess it's a good thing we didn't have a child together," I said, unable to catch the tears from streaming down my cheeks.

Ben shook his head. "Don't say that! I wish we had. You know I wanted this baby more than anything." He looked down at his hands. "We still can. You heard the doctor. We can get pregnant again. Then maybe you would be willing to fight for this. For us. Why aren't you willing to fight for us?"

I crossed my arms. "Ben, this is crazy. You're standing here acting like *I* did something to *you*. I'm not the one that cheated. I'm not the one that couldn't make it two years without sleeping with someone else."

I could see the tears filling his eyes. "But you have to forgive me, Annabelle. You're the only woman I've ever loved. You know I don't love her. You know this wasn't about love."

I shook my head, feeling the anger rise up in me. "No, Ben. No, actually. I don't know it's not about love. I don't know what it was about, but, whatever it was, it sure as hell wasn't devotion to me." I paused and took a deep breath. "And, furthermore, if you can't talk to me about what's bothering you, and you're going to run off to Laura Anne every time you're upset, then we don't have a marriage at all."

He reached out and took my hand. "But we can work on that. We can go to therapy. Build our communication skills."

I thought about Lovey, Mom, my great-grandmother and my great-aunt, those pillars of strength and stability, the women who would fight through anything to make good on their promises, the women who would do whatever it took to keep their families together. Lovey had made some mistakes, sure. We all do. But she had kept her family together. Holding Ben's hand, standing across from him on the lawn, it made me sad to know that I wasn't the woman that they were. I wasn't as strong or determined. I wasn't going to ride out the hurricane and see what happened on the other side. Because, right now, at this point, I had very little skin in the game. No children. No joint property. No retirement funds. No complications. I could get out now and never have to regret, years down the road, when the bomb eventually went off again—and it would; you could just see it in my family members' faces—that I had stayed and made a life with a man who couldn't give me what I really needed.

I sat down beside Ben on the bench and, with a final surge of love, kissed him for the last time. I rested my head on his shoulder, the sore space in my abdomen making me tired, the anger I felt toward Ben floating off into the sky like the seeds of a wish flower. "I just can't, Ben. It's not going to work."

He put his head in his hands, and you could tell by the way his back moved that he was crying again. "Oh, God. I can't believe that I made the one woman I have ever loved hate me so much."

I rubbed my hand up and down his back. "I don't hate you," I whispered. And I didn't, not really. I was mad at him. I was humiliated that he would put me through something so publicly scandalous. But I didn't hate him. And that was the problem. If I had hated him, I would have had something left to give. But, instead, I felt largely indifferent. But I knew where he was and what he was feeling, that devastation that had taken hold of me weeks earlier. But I had had time to sort through these feelings, to come to terms with the fact that we were over. And he had had no idea.

"So what am I supposed to do now?" he asked.

"Get a lawyer."

"A lawyer?"

"Yeah. You know, to handle your side of the divorce. But, don't worry, I don't want anything from you."

"How can you even say that, Annabelle, when I still want everything from you?"

I shrugged sadly. "I will always love you, Ben, and this will always hurt. But, for now, I just want it to be over."

I turned to walk into the office, feeling so stupid. How could I have been so naïve? How could I have thought that this could possibly work out?

I stood in the hallway for a moment to catch my breath, to swallow the tears back from my throat. I put on my best fake smile and walked into Rob's office. "Good morning, Rob!" I said sunnily.

He pointed to the chair in front of his desk, and I sat down, glancing at the built-in bookcases on either side of the ancient fire-place, wondering if there were any books in there about how to move on after a terrible divorce from a man you trusted completely who cheated on you with the woman who was your biggest fear all along. Probably not. That seemed like a pretty specific topic. "What's going on?"

I smiled brightly. "Oh, nothing. What do you need today?"

He gave me a sideways look. "No, I mean, what's wrong?"

I pursed my lips together in a tight smile and rolled my eyes toward the ceiling. I guess there's no hiding things from a priest. I wanted to tell him, I really did. There was something about him that just made all of your secrets want to come spilling out like stuffing from a ripped teddy bear. But I had two more weeks at my little bed-and-breakfast haven. I had two more weeks before I would have to leave town and face the music. I had two more weeks of getting to be in this cozy office with this wonderful man doing a job that felt really important to me.

So, instead of falling into a pile of distress on his desk, I put my happy face back on and said, "So, what exciting adventure does the Holy Spirit have in store for us this morning?"

He gave me that look that meant he knew I was hiding something, but he was going to let me be, and said, "We're going to go read with some kids at the elementary school."

I said, "Amazing!" But what I thought was that story time with a bunch of precious children wasn't exactly what I needed to take my mind off the one that I had lost only the night before.

Lovey

Weight

The best things in life are the unexpected ones. That's what my momma thought. But me? I'm on the fence about that one. I generally like to be prepared.

And that day, I felt on top of things. I felt ready; I felt like the pieces of life were finally falling back into place. I had graduated from rehab and was out of the nursing home. I could walk, praise the Lord. Dan and I were settling back into our routine, our regular nurses, our assisted living apartment that, while still new, was beginning to feel more like home. I was playing bridge again, seeing my friends.

Things seemed relatively ordinary. I had even managed to forget Annabelle's outburst for a moment or two.

So maybe that's why it didn't happen like I thought it would. I expected some sort of emergency. Ambulance, EMT, defibrillator, extended hospital stay, devastation over pulling the plug . . . So, I guess the reason I didn't cry right away is that I didn't believe it.

When I woke, stretched, listened to the birds chirping outside my window, thought of the delicious French vanilla creamer I had for my coffee, I expected it to be a normal day. Maybe I'd make bacon and eggs for breakfast. Kelly would be there to roll Dan down to lunch while I shuffled behind with the cane I had graduated to, thankful that the cumbersome walker was folded safely in my trunk for long walks and grocery store trips. I would play bridge in the afternoon while Luella sat with Dan, maybe read to him, maybe let him help her with the crossword if he was speaking that day. Then I would come home, have my scotch and we would sit together, probably with a few friends, have dinner, watch the news, and a nurse would put Dan to bed while I read for a while on the couch. That's what I *expected*.

When I sat up and looked at Dan in his bed, my foot nearly touching him in the crowded room, I actually smiled because he looked so peaceful. I got up, taking my robe from the chair beside the bed, rubbed my tight hip just a little and tiptoed as best as one could with a cane so as not to wake my husband. Had a voice in my head not told me to turn back around, I probably would have had another hour or two of normalcy, another hour or two of life the same as it always had been. I would have been happily sipping my first cup of coffee of the morning, whisking the eggs, laying the bacon in the pan.

But I did turn back around, and, when I approached Dan's bedside, I realized that, besides peaceful, he seemed very, very still. When I touched him, he was cold. Perhaps still not understanding what was happening or maybe in denial, I pulled the blanket up around him tighter, touching his chest, which was when I realized it wasn't rising up and down. I put my finger to his neck. No pulse.

Then I sat down beside him in the little chair by his bed and took his hand in mine, staring at him, memorizing the lines of his face, his hairline, his bushy eyebrows.

I had pictured this day in my mind many, many times before. Who wouldn't? In the scope of old age, when you realize that, in all likelihood, you are going to outlive the man you married, it is only practical to imagine how you might feel when he is gone from you. I had pictured hysteria and nausea, tears and screaming. But that supposed that he left me in a flurry of doctors, nurses and hospital workers, syringes and beeping screens.

It was so calm now, a sliver of light rising through the windows and onto his sleeping face. The first thing I did, right then and there, was thank God. Because I was eighty-seven years old, and He had given me the two things I had prayed for most fervently over the last few years. I had outlived my Dan, and it seemed terribly likely that all five of my girls would outlive me. As I exhaled, a tremendous weight lifted off of my shoulders.

And then I screamed like I would never stop. Screamed with the remembrance that this wasn't Dan's sleeping hand I was holding; it was his dead one. Screamed so loud that four nurses came charging into my apartment, as well they should have.

I'm sure they tried to console me and comfort me, hug me and soothe me. But nothing was going to make this better. My entire life had revolved around this man, and now, just as quickly as he had appeared in the school line beside me nearly eighty years before, he was gone.

Annabelle

∞

Drowning

Lovey always says that, when you're in church, being in the front row is a safe bet because you want to make sure that God sees you. It was a joke, of course, but, truth be told, I've never really felt the need to be in any pew every Sunday morning. I knew God was there watching over me, guiding my steps, pointing me in the right direction. But, unlike my Lovey, I didn't feel the need to organize the fall bazaar or shine the chalice over gossip with the other members of the altar guild. Somewhere in that time at Saint Paul's, I had started to realize how good it could feel to be a part of a church, to feel the Holy Spirit in the quiet moments in the pew. I think that little church family contributed to the fact that, though it had been weeks since I left Ben, I was feeling strong and refreshed.

Putting Holden off for that long had required some serious effort, but, practical as ever, he realized I needed some time to myself. To just be. My two weeks at The Oaks had turned to three, three weeks to two months and two months to three months. I had made a good friend in Judy, the owner, and I think we both found comfort in sharing our deepest secrets with a relative stranger.

Lying to my family had been tough, though, and they knew something was up. My daily calls had turned to weekly ones. I spent a lot of time talking about my job and evading questions about what Ben and I were up to. I had asked him to please not try to contact them, and, even though he had hurt me, I knew him well enough to know that he would respect my wishes.

It was hard to believe that it had been nearly five months since I found out about Ben and Laura Anne, all that time carrying around this huge burden. I still hadn't left my husband's hometown, and, even though I hadn't told a soul that really knew me what I was going through, I thought I was feeling strong enough that I might be ready. Ready to face the intense embarrassment that I had failed, ready to know that, everywhere I went, everyone was whispering about me when I left the room. Well, as ready as a person can ever be for something like that.

I knew that I had made the right decision and that I wasn't going back to Ben. It was time to move on with my life.

But the worst part of all of it was having to leave my job. I dreaded not being with Rob every day or getting to be a part of the resurgence of this church's life. And the thing that weighed on me most heavily was that I hadn't made up with Lovey. It was the longest I had ever gone without talking to her. I knew that one moment on the phone and she would know that my life was crumbling around me. And I wasn't ready to admit that they had all been right.

But life was short. And it was time.

I couldn't sleep that night, consumed by the thought that I was going to leave, oddly devastated that I would have to say good-bye to the person I had come to admire and respect the most: Rob. I snuck into the side door of the tiny chapel that morning before the sun had even come up. It was stark and unadorned, the stone floor and the wooden cross and altar rail made plainer by the darkness inside, the stream of light from the streetlamps seeping through the stained-glass windows that dated back to centuries when electricity was yet to be a thought.

Instead of thinking, I just sat. I let the feeling of holy silence that this small space always brought fill me up and bring me the peace that Ben once had. And I realized that no person living or dead was ever going to make me feel whole. I really didn't need a man to do that. But my friends had been wrong too. Because having that great love that I could navigate this life path with was too important to ignore.

I must have fallen asleep sitting up in that pew because the next thing I remember was Rob's voice. "I'm glad I hired you so that I have another person to come with me to morning prayer."

I tried to play it off like I hadn't been there for hours, fallen asleep or been startled awake as he handed me a book open to the lessons for the day that I was to read.

"Hey, you okay?" he asked me for probably the millionth time in those three months. How he got through my being so secretive and him being so sure I was having a bad time, I'll never know.

I nodded and forced a smile. "Sure. Fine. Ready to read."

I knew I had to tell him I was leaving. But surely it could wait a few more minutes.

I don't remember one word of that service, but I'll never forget the beauty of that moment. Our two soft voices, rising and falling together in the stark quiet of the early morning, like a duet sung a cappella. I looked over at Rob and studied the kind lines of his face while he read, the strength of character and purity of heart that drew people to him so instantly. And, instead of reading the Apostles' Creed from the Book of Common Prayer, I looked at him across the pew, where he was staring up at the single brass cross and began to recite from memory, "I believe in one God . . ."

There shouldn't be one thing seductive about the Apostles' Creed. But, somehow, with us all alone in that beautiful chapel, nothing but the raw sound of our voices intermingling, it was like a choir of angels, like our souls and our spirits combining together. I got lost in the sound, even on that first line, and, confusing the words of the Apostles' Creed with those of the Nicene, I heard myself saying, "Maker of heaven and earth, of all that is, seen and unseen."

I heard the pause in Rob's speech, the air lingering where our voices had combined, his eyes meeting mine from the edge of his pew across the aisle. I realized that "of all that is, seen and unseen" wasn't a part of the Apostles' Creed. But it was a part of my creed lately, wasn't it? My husband had given a part of himself to someone else, and He had seen it, hadn't He? My grandmother wasn't at all who I thought she was, but He had seen it. I had lost the baby that I had wanted so much. But He had seen it. It said so, right there in those lines. Seen and unseen.

And the reality of it all floated down and sank in on me, its weight pushing me into the hard wooden pew, the tears I had dammed up for the months and months I had carried these burdens finally escaping.

Father Rob walked the three steps between my pew and his and said, with a half smile, "It's okay. We all get the Apostles' and the Nicene confused every now and then."

I couldn't help but return a flicker of his smile too. And it made me wish that I had confided in him earlier. He always knew what to say. He had such an easy way about him, a comfort level with people's rawest emotions that I've never seen before or since.

"I know you're going through a lot with your family right now . . . ," he started.

But as if he already knew that wasn't what was upsetting me, he stopped. Instead, he sat down beside me and wrapped his strong arms around me, my head involuntarily gravitating toward his chest.

I sniffed, took a deep breath, pulled myself together and said, "I had a miscarriage."

"Oh, Annabelle, no."

I put my hand up to stop him. "It gets worse. Ben and I are separated because he was screwing Laura Anne." I shrugged. "Probably still is."

A reaction that looked more like relief than shock crossed his countenance, like a patient getting bad news but happy for a diagnosis all the same. Then I leaned on his chest again, more to feel its masculine strength and smell his sweet, clean smell again than anything else. "And I just said 'screwing' in church."

Father Rob pushed my head back off his chest, brushed my hair back behind my ears and studied my face. I thought he was going to say something, but, instead, he pulled me into him with just enough force that I knew he was in charge. And he leaned his head into mine. I gasped and pushed him away. "You can't kiss me! We're in church."

He smiled and before I could argue again, I realized that my mouth was on his—and I might have been the one to put it there.

"Rob," I said, pushing him back and gasping. I had never been so shocked.

"I'm sorry—" he started.

I laughed. "Are you completely insane? I'm married."

He cocked his head to the side. "Well . . . married-ish."

I scrunched my nose. "I have been separated for three months. That's pretty long, right?"

I had tasted a bite of something so delicious I didn't care that it was wrong. Like an oversized brownie, I knew I shouldn't have any more, but, all of a sudden, I couldn't care about the calories. So I kissed him again, longer, harder and with more intention this time. Then I leaned back in the pew, fanning myself with my hands, and wiped the sweat off of his blond brow. I looked around, remembering where I was, and said, "This is massively inappropriate." I sighed and said, "I left Ben three months ago, and I haven't told a soul."

He kissed one cheek, then the other, and said, "I have been holding my breath since I met you, just hoping that something like this would happen. I can't explain it, but, from the first time I met you, I just felt like I had known you forever, like you were this part that my life was missing and, suddenly, when you appeared, everything was just better." He looked over his shoulder and said, "I have been counting the minutes until you found out about Ben and Laura Anne so I could tell you how crazy I am about you."

My body clenched and felt frozen to the pew. He leaned toward me, and I put my arm out to keep him from coming any closer. "Wait. You knew about this?"

He paused, and you could see in his face that he realized he had just made the biggest mistake of his life. He scratched his head. "Well, I guess technically I knew."

I could feel the tears of humiliation in my eyes when I whispered, "You knew, and you didn't tell me?"

"I couldn't just come out and tell you, Annabelle. I'm a priest. People tell me their secrets because I'm not allowed to spread them. It's part of the gig."

I stood up, and, though he tried to grab my arm, I scooted past him out of the pew. Before I got to the door, I turned and said, "I can't believe that the person I thought was my best friend would let me walk around all this time looking like a complete idiot, knowing something this huge and not telling me."

"But, Annabelle—"

"You should have figured out a way." I shook my head. "I'm surrounded by people telling me they love me, yet I'm drowning in lies."

"But I tried—"

He never got to finish the sentence. Because, with that, I was stomping out of the church, realizing that slamming the several-hundred-pound door to the chapel was more than a little out of the question.

Lovey

ce

All of Our Prayers

My momma always said that it isn't accurate to say that the death of your partner, who has been by your side for more than three-quarters of your life, is devastating. And, yet, it isn't tragic either, as no one could argue that eighty-nine isn't a life well lived. It is, most of all, a death of the self. I knew how he liked his toast and what his favorite TV shows were better than I knew my own. His social security number came to mind even before mine when filling out tax statements. And then, with no warning whatsoever, where there had been two social security numbers on those federal returns, there was one.

To say that his death was shocking isn't quite correct. I'm sure to the outside world a man who had been in a chair for years was a prime candidate for death, the Grim Reaper surely lurking in those odd hours of the night. I could almost hear friends saying, "Well, it was a blessing. He had been sick for a long time."

But, to me, one minute he was there, breathing, and the next he wasn't. No cancer. No pneumonia. No heart disease. He was simply tired, and his frail and cumbersome body, which had failed him years earlier, decided to throw in the towel.

And, without even a moment's notice, the other part of my soul drifted away on the wings of a shooting star.

And someone had to tell my girls.

This is the worst part of being a parent: the honesty. I waited for a while before I called any of them. I made arrangements at the funeral home, scheduled a time for the church service, gathered the sheet music for the songs that Dan wanted played, submitted the obituary that had been prepared for years to the paper, even wrote a part of a eulogy that I knew I would never have the composure to deliver.

I wanted Louise to enjoy a few more sun salutations in the knowledge that her daddy was right where she left him. I wanted Sally to wallow in the decision between Doug and Kyle a little longer, imagining that her choice would be the hardest thing she would face that day. I wanted Martha to practice consonant sounds with her throng of kindergarteners, that cheerful smile that came from a place of true enthusiasm on her face. I wanted Lauren to fret a little longer over the perfect flowers for the pews of the Presbyterian church at the mercy of her latest bride. And I wanted Jean to feel the strength and support of her father—yes, her father, always her father—behind her on this last day of her campaign.

But death, as in birth, never comes at a convenient time. No matter how prepared you are that the moment is nigh, no matter how anticipatory you have been, there is never a moment where the realization that this is it, my life is changed forever, doesn't come as a bit of a shock.

And then, that's the thing about having five children. Whom do you tell first? Do you roll the die and see where it lands? Do you go in order of birth? Alphabetically by last name? This time, I decided to start with geography.

Jean.

What do you say to your children? How do you soften the blow that their beloved daddy is gone from them forever? And why does a mother bear the burden of having to worry about such things when, for once, she should be allowed a moment to feel her own pain?

But this is life.

And so I picked up the phone.

"Are you okay?" Jean answered breathlessly, and, for a moment, I found myself believing that she already knew.

"No, darling." I heard my voice cracking on the phone. It wasn't intentional, and it was dreadfully uncommon. I never let my children see me cry, always tried to be the steel flagpole in the asphalt that not even a tornado could blow down. Because if you can't count on your mother to stand tall and be brave in a crisis, who can you count on?

I took a deep breath, composing myself, thinking of how difficult this was going to be for Jean. "It's Daddy," I said. "He's no longer with us."

She gasped, as I knew she would, but she surprised me at how quickly she recovered. "No, Momma," she said. "He may be gone, but he will always, always be with us."

And that's when I decided. Then and there. Annabelle may have questions, and I may have been the only living person on earth with the answers, but those secrets would die with me. Because more than answers, more than the truth, every child deserves to have a family. So, so many of us don't get that, one of the paramount blessings in life, but, oh my Lord, don't we all deserve it?

My daughter had been unconditionally, indescribably loved by both of her parents and her sisters. And if you asked this old woman, that mattered a hell of a lot more than the truth.

I could hear the tears in her throat when Jean said, "Do you want me to go to the funeral home and make the arrangements?"

I shook my head, though she couldn't see. "It's already done, darling." I paused, knowing what I wanted to say, but wondering if it was the wrong choice. But today of all days, I deserved to do something that might not make every member of my family unwaveringly happy. And so I said, "Could you please call the others?"

"Of course," Jean said.

And before I could hang up the phone, I heard a key turning in the lock, and Annabelle, tears streaming down her face, ran to me and hugged me so hard it almost knocked me over.

"I'm so sorry, Lovey," she said, over and over again. And I knew logically that she couldn't know about her grandfather's passing and instinctively that it wasn't his death she was sorry about.

I patted her, my own tears falling down on her bare shoulder and said, "There, there, dear."

I pushed her away, and I said what I always said to her mother. "The only thing that matters is that we all know how much we mean to each other. We all know how much we love each other." I could feel those tears clouding my throat again, thickening it and making it difficult to talk. "So if I hadn't woken up this morning, you would have known that none of the other mess was important."

She nodded and hugged me again. "We all love each other. We are family and how we got that way doesn't matter a bit."

I smiled through my tears. "My feelings exactly."

I took her hand and led her to the couch.

She sighed and said, "I have so many things to tell you, Lovey. And they aren't good."

I shook my head, looking down at my crooked finger, resting on top of her perfectly straight, unlined hand. "Me first, darling."

I told her about Dan, and we hugged and cried. As we were sitting, the door flew open again, and I barely took notice because I expected it to be Jean.

Before I even saw a person, I heard a voice. "I tried to tell you, Annabelle." Rob stopped in his tracks when he saw both of our tears.

I didn't have time to wonder what was going on between them because, not a moment later, Annabelle was saying, "D-daddy is gone," and Rob was kissing my cheek, saying, "I'm so sorry for your loss, Lovey."

Then he turned to Annabelle and said, "How could you not tell me?"

"I just found out right this second, Rob," she said, tears and disdain fighting for first place in her voice. "How are you even here so fast?"

"I followed you, obviously," he said. "I followed you out of the church and all the way here because I need a chance to explain . . ." He looked over at me and, as if it registered that something even more important than what was happening between he and Annabelle was happening with me, said, "Lovey, I'd like very much to pray for Dan and your family right now."

It was as beautiful a prayer as I'd ever heard. I patted his knee when he was finished and said, "That was lovely, dear. I'd like it so very much if you'd assist with the service tomorrow."

"No," Annabelle said firmly, standing with purpose. "Rob has to leave now." She pointed to the door.

He stood too, looking down on her, planting his feet and crossing his arms. "I'm not leaving until you let me say my piece."

I looked back and forth between the two of them, so confused that I momentarily forgot my sorrow. If I hadn't known better, I would have guessed they were having some sort of lovers' quarrel.

"I did try to tell you, Annabelle. I saw them at your house that day when I told you to go home." He let his arms fall to his sides. "I couldn't tell you, but I wanted you to know, and that was the only thing I could think of."

I could see the sharp points of her body language relax into curves. "Oh." She paused as though she was thinking. "That is when I found out."

I looked back and forth between them again, and, though I wanted to ask more questions, when you're eighty-eight, it doesn't take too many letters to solve the puzzle. I hadn't liked that Laura Anne since the moment I laid eyes on her at that party. And I would have bet my last bottle of scotch that she was after my granddaughter's husband like a police dog on a drug trail.

When I saw both Annabelle's and Rob's faces shift slightly from angry to relaxed, it was then that I realized that God really does answer all of our prayers, even if He's saying, "Not right now."

Though I had longed, on my knees, for one of my daughters to marry an Episcopal priest, it had never happened. But, I had the sneaking suspicion that God was going to give me another chance with my granddaughter.

Annabelle

∾

Perfect Families

Life is all about being steadfast enough to make a plan and being flexible enough to break it. And that is good because Annabelle the planner had figured out perfectly how she was going to tell her parents and grandparents about the dissolution of her marriage. And Annabelle the planner knew that the blow would be softened a few weeks later by the reunion with Holden, aka, the man of their dreams. It would be horrible and everyone would be talking about it, but they would reason that I was young and scared and now I was just doing what I should have all along. And then one of the women in the neighborhood would be having an affair with her gardener *Desperate Housewives*–style, and everyone would forget about me.

What Annabelle the planner hadn't counted on was D-daddy dying in his sleep. And I hadn't planned on Rob's absurd confession of love. And I hadn't planned on dropping the Ben-affair bomb on Lovey via a fight with Rob in her assisted living apartment. And, most of all, though I had forgiven her outwardly, I hadn't planned on still being so inwardly angry with Lovey. I couldn't stand feeling that way toward her when my entire life she had been my main confidant. But wounds take time to heal.

And that wound that I was so sure had already scabbed over, the devastation of finding out that my marriage wasn't what I thought it was, had opened again and was oozing all over the place. The hardest part was realizing that I was the only person surprised by the dissolution of what I thought would be my forever.

When Mom had asked where Ben was right after we found out about D-daddy, I had mumbled something about him having to work.

She had put her arm around me and said, "So it's over, huh?"

I had been so positive that he was the right decision, that we were going to be a family, that our personalities complemented each other so wonderfully. And all my dad could say was, "Oh, honey. We never, ever trusted him."

The thought of moving on after realizing that I had been so wrong paralyzed me with fear. I thought I knew best. I thought I was mature and reasoned when it came to love. But I had been neither.

Sitting in the third row of Saint Andrew's Church that afternoon, I knew I needed a higher power to help me sort through the avalanche of my life. My handkerchief to my eyes, I waited patiently, thankful that Mom and Lovey had let me forgo the procession, knowing a divorce, a miscarriage and a death in such short order weren't going to equip me for walking stoically behind a casket. I tried to push away the thought that every person in that jam-packed church was whispering about where my husband was.

Well, at least the ones who weren't whispering about Lovey's best friend Katie Jo parading in with her young boyfriend.

Cameron, with absolutely no announcement, as usual, slid into the pew beside me and linked her arm through mine. "I'm so sorry," she whispered.

I could feel the tears spilling over as I nodded. "Thanks."

"I'm most sorry that I ever introduced you to Ben. I was wrong."

I shook my head. "You weren't wrong. If I hadn't tried to steal him from you, all of this would have been happening to you."

I winked, and we both stifled a laugh.

Holden, making like he was genuflecting by my pew, whispered, "I'm so sorry, Ann." He squeezed my hand.

I wiped my eyes, shook my head and said, smiling through my tears, "Thanks, Holden."

He looked at me sadly, still holding my hand. "You coming home tonight?"

I nodded, swallowing hard, wondering if a life with Holden could ever feel like home.

Sitting there in the pew, I longed for a man like D-daddy. A man who was kind and generous, humble and forgiving, faithful and true. A man who knew his values and stuck by them. A man who would give me room to grow to be who I was while trusting me with the truth even when it was hard. That familiar aggravation in the pit of my stomach pinched me again, as I wondered how Lovey could do something so terrible to someone so undeniably good.

Then the lonely echo of the organ turned to triumphant jubilation. I tried to feel happy that D-daddy was in a better place, free from pain and sorrow and suffering. But it's so very difficult to feel happy when you are so sad that you won't be seeing him on earth ever again. My uncles and cousins were carrying the box containing what was once my D-daddy down the aisle with Lovey and my mom and aunts following close behind.

I don't know if it was the swell of the organ or the freshness of the suits or the surge of pride at seeing so many people I loved all clumped together like that. But the aggravation and irritation and annoyance were suddenly replaced by the most ecstatic happiness. As I watched little Lovey make her way with so much grace, I realized that there were no perfect people, not even her. But there are perfect families. And in our crazy, mixed-up way, we just might be one of them.

I glanced toward the altar to see Rob's gaze on me—he had agreed to Lovey's proposal that he assist with the service—but he quickly looked away when my eye caught his. Even in this sad circumstance, his eyes meeting mine made my stomach flip, those bubbles of anticipation filling me up. But that summertime feeling was quickly replaced with dread. Because I had done the butterflies thing. And it had gotten me to this, one of the saddest days of my entire life. No white knight, no happily ever after. Ben, Lovey. The people I had thought infallible had failed me.

Cameron whispered, "I'm aware this is inappropriate, but you know that he's in love with you, right?"

"Holden?"

"No. Rob." She shrugged. "Not that you should take love advice from me of all people, but you might want to look into that."

I shook my head, feeling my eyes burning again. "I'm going back to Holden."

Cameron smirked. "I'm not going to argue with you, but you know how I feel about it."

I nodded. "It's just less . . . complicated."

I looked up, caught Rob's eye again and wiped mine.

Cameron looked at me like I was crazy. "So you don't even want to explore that?"

I shook my head.

It didn't matter that Rob had been the one that I had laughed and joked with, grown up with. It didn't matter that he had helped me navigate these intersecting roads of heartbreak just by being there for me, by greeting me every morning with a smile and a laugh and something fun to do. Because now it was time to think with my head.

I glanced at Rob again, and he turned quickly to defer from my gaze. Then I turned back to look at Holden. He winked at me. He had been there for me when I needed him the very most, I reminded myself. And he had fought for me all this time. The kid deserved a win.

After the ceremony, I went to Lovey and D-daddy's house for what I figured would be one of the last times. While a throng of visitors crowded into the living room, dining room and den, I made my way down the hall, opened the linen closet door, and soothed my tear-stained face with one of Lovey's sunshine pillowcases. I took a few more steps into the empty master bedroom. No Lovey. No D-daddy. No big bed to pile up in and hear bedtime stories. No boxes full of Lovey's jewelry to play dress-up in. No drawers full of neat stacks of D-daddy's handkerchiefs. Just emptiness. It was the exact same feeling that I had.

I felt a hand on my back, where I was leaning on the doorjamb. I turned to see Lovey.

"It looks right empty now, doesn't it?"

I nodded. "Feels it too."

She was strong again, I noticed. Composed and statuesque like always. She had lost the love of her life, and here she was consoling me. "You know, sweetheart. It's going to be hard, but it's going to be okay."

I wiped my eyes with the pillowcase again, its softness taking me back to my childhood. "I know. But it's so hard disappointing everyone when they had these high expectations for me."

She laughed, that great Lovey laugh that I will always hear in my ears. "Yeah. But, on the bright side, that first fall is the hardest. Once everyone realizes you aren't perfect, it's a good deal nicer to go on with the rest of your life."

I smiled, assuming that she had known all about that when she left Ernest Wake for D-daddy. I sighed deeply. "You got awfully lucky, Lovey. Because I followed my heart and now I'm miserable." I stood up a little straighter like she would do. "Now it's time to follow my head."

She raised her eyebrows. "Holden?"

I nodded and shrugged. "Yeah. It just works, you know? He was even going to raise Ben's baby as his own. When do you ever find someone who would do that for you?" She looked at me skeptically, and I paused. I wanted to say *like grandmother, like granddaughter*, but I refrained. "And I mean, I love him." I stood up straighter. "I do." Then I sighed. "I've thought it through. It makes sense. My head says it's a good choice."

Lovey shook her head. "I can't make that decision for you. But I have a secret to tell you, sweetheart. It isn't about your heart or your head."

"No?"

"No. It's about both." She paused. "Look, honey. You've always followed your intuition and your heart. And maybe you took a couple of wrong turns there, but it doesn't mean that you can't trust it now."

"I really don't know that I can." I leaned against the wall. "Maybe I was just kidding myself this entire time to think I had these great instincts."

"Well," she said. "If you were going to trust it one more time, what do you think your intuition would tell you to do?"

That's when I heard, "Can I get you ladies anything?"

Lovey smiled at me broadly and said, "That couldn't have been better if I'd planned it myself." She took Rob's arm and said, "I'd better get back out there."

Then she turned, winked at me, pointed at her head and then her heart.

I laughed. I turned back to that room, blew it a kiss and said, "Good-bye, D-daddy. There really was only one man like you." Then I smiled weakly and said, "But if you're able to send me another, that'd be awfully nice."

I shivered thinking about how hurt D-daddy must have been when he found out that Mom wasn't his child. Then I turned back to the jam-packed living room.

After the funeral and reception and visitors for miles, Lovey pulled me aside and said, "Do you think you could get Rob settled in here tonight? The guest bedroom has clean sheets."

"What do you mean here? Why isn't he just going back to Salisbury?"

I heard his deep voice from behind me. "That's exactly what I said. I promise it will be fine. It's only two hours."

"It is getting dark," Lovey protested. "I won't hear of it, so don't bring it up again."

She kissed Rob's cheek and said, "Thank you for everything you did to make this day tolerable."

Then she kissed me and whispered in my ear, "That combination of heart and head isn't always easy to find . . ."

I smirked at her. "Good night, Lovey. I love you."

"It was a lovely service," I said to Rob as I extracted towels and washcloths out of the linen closet and handed them to him.

"Yeah."

"Look, Rob, I said I was sorry, okay? You don't have to freeze me out."

He smiled. "I'm not freezing you out, Ann. I was just agreeing with you."

"Oh." I could feel my chin starting to quiver, the busyness of the day seeping out and the sadness pouring in. I didn't want to cry, and I didn't want Rob to comfort me, but the man was practically comfort in a bottle. It was like my head couldn't help but want to be on his chest, and I couldn't possibly pull away from those strong arms wrapped around me.

He kissed the top of my head and said, "I know it doesn't help right now, but he's in a better place. He has a brand-new body and he's dining with his savior tonight. So be sad for you, but be so happy for him."

I nodded and pulled away, wiping my eyes. I made my way toward the kitchen and, though it looked different, that kitchen table where I had spent so many fun nights with Lovey and D-daddy, so many of my fondest moments with my family, was still there. I opened the freezer, handed Rob a Klondike bar and extracted a box of Sugar Wafers.

I sat down and he sat down beside me, wordlessly, waiting for my instructions. I rolled the foil on my Klondike bar down, and he did the same. Then I touched my hard chocolate shell to his and said, "To D-daddy and his brand-new body."

Rob smiled. "To D-daddy."

While we ate I told Rob every single memory I ever had with my grandfather, the way he'd always stop and get me Luden's cough drops because candy wasn't allowed at school and how he used to drive me around the yard on the riding lawn mower and how proud he had been at my induction into Phi Beta Kappa.

"You see," Rob said. "He got to be there for all of that. He got to see you grow up and be so amazing and happy." He looked down at his Klondike bar. "And beautiful."

I raised my eyebrow, opened the box of Sugar Wafers, removed one tan pack and handed him a row.

"Frozen?"

"Yup. Frozen. It's the only way, really."

He crunched, little pieces of wafer crumbling onto the table. "This is truly excellent. I mean, really, really good. It's a little like ice cream but with a texture to it."

"Right," I said. "D-daddy didn't mess around."

Even though I smiled, I could feel the tears coming down my cheeks again.

Rob reached over and took my hand. "I'm so sorry."

I shook my head. "No. It's good. See, I thought that I would always remember him the way he's been the past couple of years. That I'd only think of him in the chair or the bed or the wheelchair. That him barely speaking to me and the dimness in his face would be all I would think about." I wiped my tears away and said, "But that's not it. I remember all the really good times too."

He smiled. "I'm so glad, Annie. You deserve all those good memories."

I scooted my chair back, resolving that I would leave the memory of this night, the butterflies in my stomach and the feeling that here was a man, a good man, who got me. It was easy and fun but also felt safe and right. But it was more than that. There was that inexplicable element, that sixth sense that he saw me in a real way that no one else did, and that I did the same for him. But I just didn't know anymore. I had been so, so wrong. How could I ever trust myself to be right again?

"Okay, then. I'd better get going," I said. I could sink into

Holden's memory foam mattress and pull up the thick, fluffy down comforter. Sleep sounded so appealing. Maybe more appealing than Holden.

"You don't have to, you know."

I smiled weakly. "If you want to set the alarm—"

"I love you, Annabelle."

I peered at him. "What?"

"I know what you said," he replied. "But I know that you're in love with me too. I've known it since that first day I met you by the lemonade bowl. You make me feel like I can do and be anything. You make me feel challenged and alive and free and happy, and I know I make you feel the same way. We should be together." Then he put up his finger and, much to my surprise, began rustling around in his pants pocket, producing a diamond so bright it flickered in the dim light of the near-empty kitchen. He got down on his knee.

"Please marry me."

I pulled him up. "You can't be serious. *Marry* you? Rob, we hardly know each other."

He scoffed. "Hardly know each other? Hardly *know* each other?"

It was the first time I had ever heard him raise his voice. He turned to leave the room, and, against all rational, reasonable thought, I found the panic rising inside me. I grabbed his hand. "Well, don't just walk away," I whispered.

He turned, our hands still locked together, his nose mere inches from mine.

"Don't know you," he repeated again, the choke in his voice rising to the surface, the passion with which he regarded everything in his life flowing out and flooding me all the way into my socks. "I know all of you. I know the way you get quiet whenever anyone talks about having a baby because you're so afraid that you never will. I know that the tears gather in your eyes when you thank the Lord aloud in morning prayer. I know that you pretend to love your dad the best, but that, in reality, it is your mother's tenacity that you revere. And I know," he said, taking my other hand in his, drawing even closer to me, "that you act like you always have to have a man in your life, when, in reality, you are always the one calling the shots."

I could feel the slightest tremor in my body, the minor shake that the patient fears most when the words "Parkinson's disease" are mentioned. But I had lost too much this year. Everything that I thought I knew had been taken from me in one way or another. My husband, my baby, my image of Lovey, my D-daddy. For one year, it was enough.

I looked into his eyes quickly, seeing the fervor in them, the conviction.

"You're a priest, Rob. Get serious. You can't marry a divorced woman. Check it out. Says so right there in the Bible."

I turned to walk away and he grabbed my arm. "Why would you do this, Annabelle? You know we should be together."

"What would make you think that this was an appropriate time to ask me to marry you? My D-daddy died, and I'm in the middle of a divorce."

He pointed to the sky. "It was my thing today." He shrugged. "I thought asking you on a date seemed a little more reasonable, but I don't make the rules."

I sighed, wanting not to love that about him. I wanted to tell him about how I had chosen with my heart and it didn't work out. I wanted to tell him that I was choosing with my head this time. Because I was afraid of loving someone truly again, of discovering that another man that took my breath away was nothing like he seemed. But all I could manage was, "Rob, I can't. I have to go."

I turned to walk out the door, and I could feel the tears, so different from those of gratitude in church, spilling over onto my hot cheeks. I had promised Holden. He had been so sweet and so patient. I had told him that leaving Ben had been harder than I expected and that I needed time to heal before I came to live with him. I needed some space. If I was being honest with myself, it was less about needing space and more about realizing what a terrible person I was. I had used Holden. I knew that he would save me from the mess I had gotten myself into. And now that the baby was gone, I didn't need him anymore. And, in all the times we had talked over the past three months, I hadn't had the heart to tell Holden about the baby. He was just so excited.

In the car, a trip toward Holden's house began to feel like a march to the executioner's block. But I had decided. He loved me. Our life would be easy and comfortable and predictable and that was what I needed, I reminded myself.

I didn't even know what I would say when I got there. Holden was so far down the road, sending me crime statistics and shots of houses. It wasn't what I had planned, but, when he whisked me through the door and said, "Hey, pretty girl," I replied, "I lost the baby."

"Oh, Ann," he said. "I'm so sorry." He hugged me. Then he paused.

There was a long silence, with both of us just standing there in the sunroom. It lingered between us like the last appetizer on a plate between polite diners. Finally, he broke it, saying, "So now what?"

I sighed. I wasn't going to call it off again. I wouldn't break his heart a second time. No doubt about it, that would be cruel. So I just said, "Well, I guess you don't have to find a new house now."

I started to say something else, but, before I could, he said, "Annabelle, listen. I love you. And I am always there for you no matter what. You have been my best friend for years, and, if this is what you want, I'll make good on it. I'll do it." Then he paused. "But I met someone."

I could feel the tension melting away, like an ice cream sandwich in the sun. He met someone. I looked up to heaven and said, inwardly, *Thank you.*

"Oh," I said, trying to hide my surprise.

"It was before the baby thing, and, obviously, under those circumstances, you needed me. What we had was more important to me than a couple of weeks with someone else. And I love you, Annabelle. I swear, I really do. But it's . . ."

"It's different," I filled in for him. "It's a different kind of love, the kind of love that people wait for, the kind of love that you dream about all your life."

I knew all about that love. I sat down on the sofa.

He sat down beside me and looked at me earnestly. "I thought that's what we had, Annabelle. I swear I did. And, I'll say it again. If you want to do this, I'm in. I know we'll have a nice life together."

I sat up and turned to face him. "Holden, you deserve more than a nice life. You deserve for your heart to pound. You deserve to be with someone who makes you better, who lifts you up, who makes you feel like you can do anything. You deserve to be with a woman who looks at you and really sees you, who understands you without a single word."

"You won't believe this," he said, hiding a smile. "I think she might be the one."

In spite of myself I laughed quietly through my tears. Holden had always waxed poetic about the mathematical impossibility of there being only one right person for every other one. And, seeing someone with such a good heart be so happy made me a little bit happy.

I felt a pang of nostalgia thinking of those perfect pink peonies that were always waiting for me on his nightstand. He definitely wasn't my one. But he was someone else's.

And, though I didn't want to, I thought of Rob.

Holden had wanted me to stay the night, cuddle up and watch one last movie for old times' sake. But, instead, I found myself kissing Lovey's exhausted forehead, turning off her lamp and slipping into the guest bed at her assisted living apartment. I marveled at her strength, at her ability to get back in that bed, in that room, where she had found him only a few days earlier.

I lay in bed for hours that night thinking. I ached for the baby I had lost, for the love that had slipped through my fingers, for the sadness of all of the losses combined together.

And then I thought of Rob.

I swung my legs over the side of the bed, tied the silk robe draped over the back of the chair around my waist, and marched myself out the door, fuzzy slippers and all.

I don't think I even thought of how ridiculous I must look, walking up Lovey and D-daddy's old driveway in slippers meant for a child, complete with bunnies, and a gown meant for a gentleman's club. But it was one of those rare moments in life where common sense abdicates the throne, losing a near-bloodless battle to pure, unadulterated lack of self-control.

I marched myself right through the front door, slammed it and bounded down the hall to the guest room, Rob's room for the night, flipping on the lights. He bolted up, stunned from the intrusion, rubbing his eyes and squinting at me. I couldn't help but lose my train of thought. I'd never imagined the parish priest I so often shared my cupcake with to have such a toned upper body.

I pointed to the front door and said, "I don't care how much you trust people, I will not, under any circumstances, sleep with my doors unlocked."

He rubbed his eyes again, as if trying to discern if this was the real me or the figment-of-his-imagination me. Those dimples sprang up, and he said, "Okay."

"And if you're going to wake up every fifteen minutes with a message from the Holy Spirit that it's time to move parishes, I absolutely insist on hiring movers to box up all our stuff because you know how much I hate to pack."

"*Our* stuff?"

I sat down on the edge of his bed, my voice finally softening and said, "I know that even though you pretend to be excited when she brings them, you don't like Mrs. Taylor's famous brownies one bit. I know that you purposely give me jobs and send me on errands that you know will make me recognize a skill within me that you see but I don't. I know that you love trashy, prime-time TV even though you'd never admit you watch it." He was half sitting, propped on his elbows now, so I leaned to take both of his cheeks in my hands. "And I know that you are the most selfless, loving, wonderful man that I have ever met."

He sat up now, wrapped his arms around me and enveloped me in a kiss. I closed my eyes and melted into the feel of his body pressed into mine, wanting to do things that one should never think about with a man of God—until he was her husband, that is.

"And you're right," I whispered, "I do love you."

He kissed me again. "I've waited a very long time to hear that."

"This is probably very inappropriate," I said. "Maybe you should get up."

He shook his head. "Can't."

He pointed to his sheet and raised his eyebrows.

"And now I know you sleep naked." I winked at him. "Can't wait for that on the honeymoon."

"The honeymoon . . . ," he whined.

I looked at him and crossed my arms, smiling. "I think we're going to have quite the wedding night."

"When is that again?"

I looked down at the space on my arm where a watch should be and said, "Well, the last time I rushed into something so serious, it didn't end well for me." I sat back down and looked into his kind face. And I knew that he would understand. "I want to do it right this time. I want to take the time to learn how to be an amazing wife, the kind of woman you deserve. I want to go to premarital counseling and know that we're on the same page with everything."

He pushed a loose strand of hair behind my ear and kissed me. Then he rested his forehead on mine and said, "I love that about you, Ann. And I want you to know that you don't have to do anything other than just be who you are. And I can promise you, truly, from the depths of my soul, that I will love you with a vengeance and be faithful to you until the day I die."

Despite what I had been through, despite the disgrace and shame and devastation and indignity of the past year, I knew that I could trust that bridge between my heart and my head. I knew Rob like I hadn't known many people in my life, and I trusted him with every fiber of my being. I knew I could believe him when he made me a promise because he was as faithful a man as I had ever known in every facet of his life.

"Well then, let's just take it slow and see how it goes."

He kissed me again, pulling me down onto him. "I said *slow*, Rob."

He leaned forward and put his head between his knees, slapping his hands on the mattress. Then he looked up. "Help me, Jesus."

"You get dressed and then I'll let you make me a little ice cream." I paused. "Maybe over one of Mrs. Taylor's brownies you brought? She did sort of get us together after all . . ."

"Annabelle, wait—"

"I already said, no, Rob."

"No . . ." He looked nervous. "It's just that I have a secret that I feel like I have to tell you before you can truly make this decision. I want you to have all the information . . ."

I could feel my heart drop through the floor into the furnished basement. "I can't handle any more secrets, Rob."

"Yeah, this one's a doozy." I saw the flash in his eyes. "Mrs. Taylor," he whispered, "is my grandmother."

I burst out laughing. "No, she's not. You're so not funny."

He nodded gravely. "She is."

"She is *not*. You call her Mrs. Taylor, for heaven's sake."

"It's because she makes me call her that." He burst out laughing, and I joined him.

Perfect families, I thought again.

While I was waiting for Rob to dress, eating ice cream straight from the carton, I knew that I couldn't wait to tell Lovey that—though it wouldn't be for some time—someone in her family was finally marrying an Episcopal priest.

Lovey

Safe and Happy

There comes a moment in every marriage when you, as a spouse, are standing at the edge of the steepest precipice one could possibly imagine. It is that moment when you realize that the man or woman you married is perhaps a vestige of the person you thought, but, in reality, bears very little resemblance to the forever you had seen in your mind's eye. The way he mouth breathes on your back in the morning when you are trying to catch the last moments of sleep before one of the babies you have created together issues the morning rooster crow. He refuses to cover his mouth when he coughs and only lifts a finger to assist the children when you are in public and people will see and rave about what a terrific father he is. And then, sometimes, a secret is revealed. Something even more shocking than the fact that this perfect specimen you studied under what you thought was a very fine microscope for years before walking down the aisle, is, in fact, human, comes to the surface in the broad daylight—or maybe in the dead of night.

And you are faced with a choice. He has crossed that giant chasm without you and is standing on the other side. So there you are, waiting, choosing, deciding. Do you cross over and hold the hand that, while not as perfect as you had once imagined, is the one you promised to hold until your last breath? Or do you stay on your side, closed off, unrealistic and utterly unwilling to imagine that perhaps this marriage, this man, this choice is as good as it's going to get?

Some women would have stayed on their side. They would have swept and scrubbed and made it up tidy, steeled their jaw and faced the world alone. But me? I crossed over. Maybe it was the way I was raised by parents who valued hard work and sticking to your vows above all else. Maybe it was that, in reality, I had no good options. I was a mother of five darling girls, but, as beautifully as our package was wrapped, there was no doubt that Dan was the bow atop. And finding another was a risk I wasn't willing to take.

Sometimes, I wonder if maybe choosing the path I did was weakness. But, I'd like to say now, when I know it is almost over, when the man I risked everything for, the man I leapt across that great expanse for, is gone from me, that it was strength.

"Oh, Luella, I don't care for any more tea," I say, after the funeral is over, after the guests have left, after I have slept alone in my room for the first time in sixty-three years, as I am sitting in the living room that has held so many of the most treasured memories of my life.

"Sal, I'm proud of you," Lauren is saying, meaning that my most headstrong girl and my most passive one have mended fences.

Sally smiles sheepishly. "I guess I have you to thank for my current happiness, so thank you."

Lauren tips a fake hat. "And, for the record, I heard there was some speculation over whether I would actually date Kyle. And, just so we're clear, I feel as though I shouldn't have to say this, but, no, I would not date anyone that any of you are or have ever been in love with. So let's just get that straight."

"Sort of ironic," Jean says.

"What?" Martha asks.

"That Lauren would be the one to go to all that trouble to make sure that Sally ended up with the love of her life."

Sally leans over and rests her head on Lauren's shoulder. "Thanks, sis. You really took one for the team."

Lauren puts her arm around Sally and squeezes. "Anytime." She looks up and says, "I would do the same for any of you."

They all laugh. I smile, but I'm not sure where I stand on any of this. I suppose that it's better to divorce and be with the one you're going to be with than to spend your life sneaking around. As has happened so often in my life, I'm not sure whether any of my girls, all chattering around me, notices my silence or lack of contribution to the conversation.

Louise chimes in, as spiritually as one could expect, "You only get one chance to live an authentic life. If this is it, then there's no fighting it."

Jean, predictably the devil's advocate and the voice of unemotional reason, adds, "But, Sally, what about Doug?"

"Yeah," Martha chimes in. "Are you sure it's over?"

I smile, though I'm not sure why. Maybe it is because Sally has stood at her own divide and, instead of taking the hand of her husband, she chose a different path. I would have told her, had she asked, that no one is perfect. I'm sure she thinks she loves Kyle, but give it a few years and he will be just as imperfect as Doug. The newness and the passion will have worn off to an extent. I have seen this so many times in my years. But a mother knows when her daughter won't listen. She knows when to bite her tongue. And so I did and, on this particular issue, will continue to do so.

I want to judge her for abandoning her life or feel embarrassed by what people are going to say as my family is in the midst of yet another scandal, but I am too old, too tired and too sad for all of that. Life is the choices we make, and, I am reminded again, I can't choose for them.

Sally squeezes my knee. I am sitting in the only chair left in the room, a leather wingback that was Dan's favorite. All of my girls are sitting around my feet, and, as if I have rewound the tape fifty-five years, I expect them to argue over what board game to play. I almost look over to Dan, in his chair, grinning behind his newspaper at the world he cocreated. But when I turn my head, he isn't there. And, in some ways, I'm glad he isn't here for this part.

But, as I look around, I know that my girls will take care of Sally. And they will take care of Jean while she takes care of Annabelle. And so on and so forth for the rest of their lives, no matter what the world sends their way. Life will change without us here to bring them all together every holiday, but they are strong. They love each other and they will stick up for each other the way they always have. I'd like to think that I had something to do with that.

"I'm so sorry, Momma," Sally says, the tears filling her eyes. "I know this isn't what you need right now."

But, in truth, I'm happy for the distraction. Worrying about one of my daughters is the only diversion for the void so wide and so thick and so deep that I know the only way out is to close my eyes and not open them again.

"You know what, darlings? My prayer every night was that the

Lord would keep you safe and happy. Safe and happy," I repeated. "Not married to the same man, not free from heartbreak or small-town scandal or away from hard choices. Only safe and happy." I smiled at all of them. "I have to say that, sitting here now, it appears every last one of you is both safe and happy."

And that's when I knew. My job here was done.

Annabelle

∞

Invisible Hand

Lovey always says that, at the end of the day, all a girl really needs to get through this life is a good dose of gumption. And I was trying to gather all of mine as I was sitting in the passenger seat, Rob driving through that same Salisbury historic district that had become my bed-and-breakfast home the past few months.

"Are you sure they're going to be okay with this?" I asked Rob for the thousandth time.

He squeezed my hand. "Annabelle, you are the loveliest person I've ever known. My family isn't going to care that you married some guy who was dumb enough to cheat on you. They're going to love you as much as I do."

I looked over at him. He was so handsome, so sincere. "So, can I still work for you now that we're sort of romantically entangled?"

He looked over. "Hmmm . . . I don't know. I don't think anyone would really care, do you?"

I laughed. "Well, let's see. They cared an awful lot about having a guitarist at the ten thirty service, and I'm still hearing about how a professional chef won the chili cook-off. So, yeah, I'd say this will be on their radar."

He shrugged. "You have to, because otherwise I won't have anyone fun to do my first thing of the day with."

"True."

A wave of sadness that I might not be working with Rob washed over me. And it occurred to me that, while I had taken it as a part-time gig until I found something new, as it turned out, the work of the church fulfilled me. There, I felt like my work had a purpose.

We pulled past Mrs. Taylor's grand, columned home. I sighed, realizing how much I loved this neighborhood's wide sidewalks and shady trees. This town had become a part of my story, and, even though I wanted to get as far away from Ben and his family as I could, I knew that I was going to have to grow up and deal with it.

Mom and Dad pulled into the driveway right behind us. When I told them that I was seeing Rob, Mom gave me the lecture that I thought would never end. "You're rushing into this. You aren't even divorced yet. You're making the same mistake twice."

But Dad had, in his predictably calming way, said, "Jean, for heaven's sake. Let her move on. Could you have handpicked a better man for your daughter than Rob?"

We hadn't exactly dropped the engagement bomb on them yet. We thought that maybe if we told both sets of parents together that it might be a little less of a shock. Well, actually, it would be more of a shock, but no one could make a scene about it because they had the others to save face in front of.

And we would have to do it soon because my engagement ring was more than a little hard to hide.

Rob rang the doorbell, and I handed his grandmother a bouquet of flowers and said, "Hi, Mrs. Taylor. It's so nice to see you." I grinned widely at her, hoping that she couldn't smell my nervousness.

She peered down at my hand, not so much as venturing a smile, and I looked over my shoulder, happy that my mom was still jabbering away on her Bluetooth in the car. "My ring looks good on you."

"Oh, I, um," I stuttered. I didn't know what to say. *Thank you*, felt wrong because she hadn't been the one to give it to me. And I couldn't decide whether she was unhappy that I had been the one to receive the ring.

Before I could decide on a proper response, she looked up at me with that same unflinching stare. "I've known since the minute I laid eyes on you that you two were meant to be."

Then she turned and walked away into the kitchen, my flowers in hand. I looked at Rob, and he shrugged. I was so shocked I didn't know what else to do besides laugh. I thought back to the "You know, we all just always thought he would marry Laura Anne" comment. Maybe it hadn't been said out of malice after all. Maybe it was to plant a seed of doubt in my head that would eventually lead to Rob. Or maybe she already knew something that I didn't. I shuddered wondering how long the whole town had been having a good gossip at my expense.

I heard my parents' footsteps, and I turned with a smile, but, before I could say anything, Mom interrupted, with a pained expression on her face: "I think we need to get to Raleigh."

Mothers know absolutely everything. So I content myself by saying that Lovey knew. She didn't need to read the rest of the chapters because she knew how the book was going to end. I am telling my mother this as I carry the last of the boxes out of the assisted-living apartment that D-daddy and Lovey graced for such a short while.

My mother, the only member of the family who has always seemed completely free of the sentimentality that must be a genetic trait, can barely open her mouth to respond. The funeral may be over, but her dark circles will not be for quite some time.

"How can they be gone?" she whispers.

Louise, a crocheted flower band wrapped across her forehead, reining in the long, dark waves around her shoulders, comes through the door and says, putting her arm around her sister, "They aren't gone." She points to Sally and Lauren and Martha as they pass through the door, "Because we're all here."

I don't think I've grasped that the two people I've always loved best aren't going to be here next week when I want to come visit. D-daddy and Lovey have been a bit like the invisible hand that has guided my life, often showing up or exercising their influence in a moment when I felt like the dead end had come and there was no right way to turn. I had no one left to call when I needed the advice that can only be garnered over years and years of experience. I had no one left to find me dresses at a moment's notice or remind me to always walk tall like I belonged. I ached to remember the arguments that Lovey and I had had in her last weeks of life, the way that I had wasted any of those precious days fretting over something that, while wrong, didn't define or replace everything that my grandmother had been to me. I worried at first that she spent some of her final hours concerned about the safety of her secret. But I rationalize that she knew me well enough to know that I would never tell. She made a choice, and, in her way, I believe she did what she thought was right. Knowing what I know about my family, about how much we all mean to each other, maybe she did do the right thing.

In a similar situation, I thought about making a similar choice. I'd like to think that I would have told Ben about his child, that I wouldn't have cowered from the difficult path. I should be thankful that I didn't have to make that decision, but I don't think a day will ever pass that I don't think of the baby I lost, of the emptiness that replaced that dream. But, if nothing else, that experience made me see Lovey more clearly; it made me understand her choice.

Rob has helped me realize that people make decisions and they have to live with them. And it isn't up to me to judge whether those choices are right or wrong, only to decide how my relationship ebbs and flows in regard to them.

Ben had made a decision that I couldn't move on from. The wall had been built too high and too thick for me to climb over or around or break through. But, even still, I don't regret my time with him. I'll always believe that we truly shared a special kind of love. Special. But not the kind that lasts forever. Not the unconditional, selfless kind. We both made mistakes, and that will always hurt. But the bottom line is that we simply weren't meant to be together.

But, with Lovey and me, the mistakes didn't matter. Because we were bound by something so much deeper. Blood, love and now this towering secret that I would never tell. It was never mine to tell anyway.

My phone rings, breaking the oppressive silence of sorrow surrounding me. I didn't want to smile, but it was that time. That glorious, all-consuming time when the man you have fallen deeply in love with drowns your thoughts with the way his hand feels on the small of your back, and your stomach drops with the memory of his smile on your cheek.

"You will never believe this," Rob said as breathlessly as I'd ever heard.

"I might," I answered wryly.

"I have just been offered the head priest position at Saint Andrew's."

I could feel my pulse tingling with the stunned excitement that, wherever this church was, it meant not only a dream come true for my soon-to-be husband but also equated to an escape from a town that held little for me but heartache and humiliation. "Like, my church Saint Andrew's? Like, in Raleigh?"

"They said they found my new worship style inspirational and were looking to infuse some new lifeblood into the church, perhaps draw a younger membership."

I smiled, my mom and aunts looking at me expectantly. I just mouthed, "Lovey." There it was again, that invisible hand that, even beyond the grave, was still as present in my life as the blinking fluorescent light above my head.

I would never mention the very large bequest to Saint Andrew's in Lovey and D-daddy's will or the fact that Lovey was the head of the search committee for a new rector until the day she died. Just like neither Rob nor I would ever mention those lockbox documents that Melissa met us at the bank before opening hours to retrieve and destroy. Because, like Lovey always taught me, some things in life are better left unsaid.

Smiling into the phone, listening to Rob's voice, the voice of a man I was not only passionate about but that I also loved and trusted, I finally knew that, like those other women in my family, I could be brave and headstrong, I could head off the impending troops with a swipe of my dishcloth. I could comment on the issues that it seemed more sensible to step away from. Walking away from my marriage hadn't been weakness in direct contrast to their strength. It was only that I realized too late that what I had wasn't worth fighting for.

As Rob said, "Are you okay with moving, Annie? Because if you're happy here, we can just stay put."

I thought of the For Sale sign perched in Lovey and D-daddy's yard and how devastated D-daddy would have been that the home he built for his family, the place he loved most in the world, was given away to some stranger. I smiled. "I can't think of anything better. And I know just the house."

It was the first time I had seen my mother smile in a week. She squeezed me to her and said, "Lovey and D-daddy's house, Raleigh and an Episcopal priest. I think you might have gotten it right this time."

I raised my eyebrows. "Well, since you all failed miserably at granting Lovey's lifelong Episcopal priest marriage wish, someone had to step up."

"You never know," Louise said, "it might not be too late for me."

We all started down the hall, I think collectively relieved to never be returning to this place that, while stylish, had equaled death in all of our minds. "You might be a little too Buddhist for that," Sally said.

Louise shrugged. "Ah, so close."

"Maybe I'll go after a priest too," Lauren said.

"Oh," Mom interjected, "so not Doug or John or maybe my husband?"

"That phase over?" Martha asked.

"I think I'll stick to the single ones," Lauren said. "In fact this new guy I'm dating—"

We all laughed, interrupting her sentence, and, as I slammed my car trunk shut and listened to the women remaining in my life banter with each other, I knew that Louise was right: Lovey and D-daddy were absolutely everywhere.

Lovey

Lies That Matter

February 1960

My momma always said that the snow can bury secrets, but, at some point, the frost thaws, the spring comes, and whatever you were hiding comes to light. But sometimes, the truth comes out while the snow is still falling all around you.

"She died," Dan said.

Those two simple words made that panic rise to the surface briskly and painfully enough that I completely ignored the fact that my husband was standing at our back door, at our house in Bath, breath blowing in the winter air, with a whimpering, swaddled child, who, from the sound of it, couldn't have been more than a few hours old. My mind catapulted to my girls, vomit rising in the back of my throat.

But that's impossible, I thought. *You just checked on them.*

Feeling my heart come back into my chest from where it had been racing around the solar system, I stilled my breath and asked, "Who? Who died?"

"Her mother," Dan said, as though that was supposed to clear up anything at all.

The baby began to wail loudly as he shouted over her noise, "Can we keep her?"

"For God's sake, Dan, she's not a kitten." But it registered that I also sounded like I was referring to a stray pet when I said, "I'm sure we can find her a good home."

I took the baby from him and turned to go inside. I sat down beside the hearth in the kitchen, feeling the roaring flames return the heat to my body as he said, "She must be starving. I don't think she's eaten at all."

I looked around the kitchen helplessly, knowing we didn't have any formula or anything else appropriate for a baby to eat. I looked into that beautiful, red, wailing face, and that maternal pull, the tug in your loins that makes mothering feel so right, got the better of me. I knew in the instant I saw that beautiful face, despite what I said, that this little girl belonged to me too, that she would slide seamlessly into the staircase of pigtails that I was raising.

And, without even thinking about it, I did something that was as natural to me as making the beds and boiling the coffee. I opened my shirt and fed this helpless thing that was completely alone in the world save Dan and me.

"Can you do that?" Dan asked.

"Well, I'm still nursing Louise, so, yes, milk is milk, I presume. I don't know what other option we have in the middle of the night in the middle of a farm."

Louise was only ten months old then, and I had breastfed her longer than the other girls, confident that she would be my last child,

wanting to savor those fleeting seconds of babyhood, that deep connection that sharing your body with another can bring, while I could.

"So, could you please explain why I'm nursing someone else's
child in the middle of the night?"

Dan sat down in a chair beside me, put his head in his hands,
and, a moment later, I realized that he was crying. "I was going to
lie to you," he said. "But you have to know the truth. You have to
forgive me, Lynn."

I looked down at the heavy eyelids beside my breast and, more
than my curiosity or the sinking feeling that what was coming next
was an explanation that I wasn't going to want to hear, it occurred
to me how much things change. When Dan and I had reconnected
again and again, our love for each other was like the fire in the hearth.
It was intense, passionate, heated. But, over the years, through childbirth and diapers, scrimping and saving, getting promotions and
losing jobs, the person beside you in the church pew morphs from
the object of your near-addictive love obsession into something more
akin to the sterling silver service on the sideboard. You can always
count on it being there even though you don't really use it in the same
way you once did. And that burning love you had for another person
reshapes itself into the love you have for your family, that united front
against the world that you have become with him at the helm.

And so I made a command decision. Where I had had four
daughters moments earlier, I now had five. "Get the suitcases and
clear as many of the girls' things as you possibly can into them," I
said, stroking the cheek of the now-sleeping baby in my arms.

He looked up from where his head had been in his hands and
asked, "What?"

"Well, we have to move, obviously. There's no way on earth I
can explain this if we're still living in the same town. We'll move on,

start over, and people will just assume we had these five little girls the whole time."

Dan kissed me hurriedly and ran toward the door, like a child on his way for ice cream, afraid that Mother would change her mind. "Wait," he said. "Couldn't we just say she was adopted?"

"Adopted," I spat. "She's your child, for heaven's sake."

Dan was crumbling fast. And I think that's how you know that you're really meant for a person. When, in the trail of their crumbling, you can be upright and unwavering.

"What will we tell our parents?" he practically cried, sitting down again. "Won't they be a little suspicious when we arrive with this child we never told them about?"

I put my finger up to my chin. "We'll tell them the doctor thought the baby was sick, that she wouldn't survive to term. We didn't want them to be hurt by the news, so we never told them."

He looked up at me, his elbows on his knees. "Will they believe that?"

I shrugged. "They don't really have a choice because neither of us is ever, ever going to stray from that story." I raised my eyebrows. "Right?"

"But her birth certificate . . ." Dan trailed off.

"Well, we'll have to get her a new one," I heard myself snap. I took a deep breath and whispered, "I'll have to adopt her, I suppose."

"You would . . ." Dan stood up and wrapped me in the most sincere hug of his life, the tears in his throat choking him, keeping him from finishing a question that didn't need an answer. He already knew the answer because he knew me.

He pulled back and looked at me. "How can I ever deserve you again?"

"You really can't," I said. And I meant it. "But I damn well expect you to spend the rest of your life trying."

And I can truly say that he stood by that promise.

That night is, I believe, the crux of my life. Knowing that my husband had strayed from me broke something inside me. But maybe it was something that needed to be broken. Walking away from the life we had built never even occurred to me. Raising Jean as my own was the best decision I ever made and perhaps the easiest. But those hard decisions, the big ones, the ones that really matter, have always come easily to me, especially in a crisis. I make a decision and I stand by it. Period.

And so, leaving behind most of our worldly possessions, we piled in the car before sunrise and left Bath in the dust, heading up the road toward Raleigh to take the job that the heavens had so benevolently opened for Dan two weeks prior. We had no place to live, no furniture and no idea what the future held. But we had the hurtful, shameful, family-destroying truth to hide. And we had another daughter to raise, a little white lie, a secret that would thread the seven of us together like pearls on a string forever. And, though my husband had once been the one that had made me feel that love like cream rising to the surface, it was my girls now.

And that, as it goes without saying, was more than enough.

I told myself riding into the sunrise that early morning, Jean warm and fast asleep in my arms, that Dan and I could get back to that place of love and trust where we had once resided. After the secrets were buried and a new truth was formed in the lives of our family members, we would repair that fissure and become as strong as we once were. I looked back at my four other little angels, their eyes closed, snoring in the backseat, and then I looked at Dan's profile, the way the sun seemed to radiate off of him less glowingly than it once had. And the thought, though I willed it not to, crossed my mind: *The lies that matter most are the ones we tell ourselves.*

Readers Guide for

Lies and Other Acts of Love

BY KRISTY WOODSON HARVEY

Discussion Questions

1. Throughout the novel, Lovey and Annabelle reflect on the wisdom and life views observed and obtained from the women in their lives. How does this knowledge inform the way both women approach their various personal relationships? How do Lovey and Annabelle relate and differ in this regard?

2. As soon as Ben set his eyes on Annabelle, he immediately believed he had met his wife. Have you ever been this instantly sure of something? Do you believe in love at first sight?

3. Do you think that Ben and Annabelle's whirlwind marriage was an easy escape for her from her previous engagement? If you were Annabelle's friend, would you have tried to talk her out of making this quick decision, or would you advise her to live in the moment?

4. Between college, the war and the disapproval of their parents, Lovey and Dan had to wait a long time until they could be together. Did the wait end up strengthening or weakening their bond? Do you know any other couples that had to delay their relationships because life was in the way?

5. Annabelle notes: "Whether you've been married one year and have just moved to your husband's hometown or you've been married well over half a century and think something is going to unlock the vault of your husband's brain again, it's really the same thing that keeps you going: hope." Do you think that hope sometimes leads people away from reality? What are some examples of how a character's hope was validated in the novel?

6. Annabelle describes her emotions just after meeting Ben: "I'd never felt so totally out of control. I'd never done something so unplanned. And it felt so good I didn't want it to ever stop." At what point, if at all, did you expect the buzz of their relationship to die down? Did you think things would continue indefinitely as Annabelle and Ben believed?

7. Was Annabelle a sympathetic character, or were you frustrated by her choices? Why do you think she jumps into relationships? Could she have benefited from having some time alone?

8. What were your views on Holden's insistence that he and Annabelle belonged together? Did you believe it to be true? At what point, if at all, did you expect Annabelle to respond and agree to see him?

9. Each chapter in the novel begins with a lesson or observation that serves as a theme. Which themes or passage(s) strike you as the most insightful? What lessons or attitudes have been passed down in your family?

10. What does Annabelle's friendship with Rob symbolize, and what does his role as a priest play in their relationship? Do you think that they would have befriended each other if they had met elsewhere?

11. For those who are fortunate, life often presents a choice. Were you surprised that Annabelle and Holden did not end up together? If you were Annabelle, would you have taken the road less familiar, or settled for contentment with Holden?

12. The title of this novel is *Lies and Other Acts of Love*. What are some of the big lies that were told in this book? Do you think that lies must be a part of a relationship in order to keep things afloat, or do you believe that the truth always finds its way?

13. In what ways did both Annabelle and Lovey change by the end of the novel? What are some of the biggest lessons each of these characters learned?

KEEP READING FOR A PREVIEW OF

Dear Carolina

BY KRISTY WOODSON HARVEY
AVAILABLE FROM BERKLEY BOOKS

Khaki

∞

Salad Greens

I designed a special scrapbook for each of my children. A custom-
made blue or pink album with white polka dots and a fat bow
tied down the side, the front center proudly displaying a monogram
that was given to each of you. I take those books out every now
and then. Sometimes I add a new photo or memento. Other times
I gaze at the pictures and marvel at how quickly the eyes-
closed-to-the-world phase of infancy morphs into the headfirst-
plunging alacrity of toddlerhood.

Other times, like tonight, with your book in particular, my sweet
Carolina, I sit on the floor of our family room overlooking my favorite field of corn and simply stare at the cover, running my finger
across the scrolling monogram. *It's only a name*, we have been
reminded since middle school in what has now become perhaps the
most cliché of Shakespeare's musings. But, in what is certainly not
the first exception to a Shakespearean rule, that name means more
than the house your daddy built in this field where we spent so much

time falling in love or the sterling silver service that has been in our family for generations.

It means more because that name wasn't always yours. And you weren't always ours.

I was, just like a mother should be, the first person to hold you when you were born. Your birth mother, after thirty hours of labor, fainted when she saw you, perfect and round and red as a fresh-picked apple. I felt like holding you first would be like stealing money from the offering plate. But as soon as the misty-eyed nurse placed you in the nest of my arms, you quit crying, opened your eyes, and locked your gaze with mine. That instant of serendipity was fleeting because it wasn't more than a few seconds that your birth mother was out.

When she came to, and I was there, cuddling this lighter-than-air you that she had grown inside herself for nine long months, I begged for forgiveness. But she said, "I'm glad you got to hold her first. You've been here this whole dern time too."

I had given birth myself before, and that teary first introduction to a new life after a forty-week hormone roller coaster was fresh in my mind, still damp like the coat of paint on the wall in your nursery. But I'd never been on my feet, outside the bed, when four were breathing the air and then, with one tiny cry, there were five. To experience that kind of wonder is like being born again.

Even in that resurrection moment, I couldn't have known that one day, I would get to hold you, swaddled and warm, all the time. But I did swear that I would do everything in my power to protect you, love you, and make sure you grew up good and slow as salad greens.

And so, my love, if you ever look at your book and think maybe it's a little thicker than your sister's and your brother's, it's only because instead of having one mother to save snapshots and write letters and remind you how much she loves you, you have two: the one who brought you into the world and the one who brought you up in it. And if you ever start feeling like maybe you got dealt a bad hand, that having a mother who raised you and a mother who birthed you is too tough, just remember this: You can never have too many people who love you.

Jodi

Jam Left on
Too Long

Some things in life, they don't even seem right. Like how you can preserve something grown right there in your own backyard and have it sitting on your pantry shelf 'til your kids have kids. And how them women down at the flea mall can write a whole Bible verse on one of them little grains of rice. And then there's the thing I know right good: how ripping-your-finger-off-in-the-combine awful it is for a momma to have to give up her baby.

I think you already got to realizing, looking at me right now, messin' in your momma and daddy's white, shiny kitchen, that I ain't just your daddy's cousin. 'Course, you're still so little now, you cain't know how I grew you in me, how I birthed you, how I loved you and still do. But you give me that same crooked smile my daddy had and squeeze my finger real tight—and it's like you know it all. Whenever I say that to your momma, she says back, "Of course she knows. Babies know everything."

It's a right simple thing to say. And simple is who I am and what

I've been knowing my whole life. I cain't say a lot of fancy things, and I don't believe in making excuses as to why I'm not doing your raisin'. So here's the boiled-down-lower-than-jam-left-on-too-long truth: I gave you up 'cause I loved you more than me. I gave you up 'cause I wanted you to have more. I gave you up 'cause, in some murky way, like that river that runs right through town, my heart knew that it'd take giving you up for us to really be family. I used to tell your momma I was scared that being in your life was gonna hurt you. But then she'd tell me, right simple: You can never have too many people who love you.

Khaki

∞

Other Plans

My favorite interior design clients have always been those who approach me with file folders with magazine clippings seeping over the edges like overfilled cream puffs. They like the feel of this room, the light of this one. They can't live another day without a chaise precisely like that.

I'd always been like one of those clients, totally in touch with what I wanted. So when your daddy Graham and I got married, I knew we'd have lots of babies. I already had your brother, Alex, of course. But when he was born, it was different. I was a very young widow living in Manhattan full-time, my design business and antiques store taking off. In short, I was busier than a Waffle House waitress when third shift let out.

But once I moved back home to North Carolina and married your daddy Graham, his calming demeanor and being so close to nature soothed my soul like a raw potato on a cooking burn. I wanted to breathe deeply, feel the sun on my face, and watch my children grow.

I was dreaming about Graham and me rocking on the porch, watching Alex and his two little sisters—little sisters that he didn't have—play, when I woke up that Sunday morning, my arm tingling numb from being up over my head. I looked down to see Alex nestled in the crook of my body, his arms splayed wide in that unencumbered, worriless sleep of children. He was snoring on one side, Graham snoring on the other, the three of us snuggling like a litter of puppies in the barn hay. I smiled at how the morning sliver of sun peeking through the small opening in the curtains glistened off of my three-year-old's blond strands.

Graham yawned, opened his eyes, and leaned to kiss me. His muscular grip wrapped around me as I shook my practically dead arm, the pins-and-needles feeling burning through me. "Mornin', Khaki," he said.

My name was really Frances, but Graham had changed it nearly two decades earlier when I used to dress in head-to-toe khaki work clothes and ride around the farm with my daddy. It was one of those nicknames that had grown like creeping ivy and been impossible to escape.

I looked back down at Alex's closed eyes, smiled at his legs propped on mine, and whispered to Graham, "Do you have any idea how many times we've had sex in the past two and a half years?"

"Mmmm," he hummed, nuzzling his face into my hair, his unshaven chin pricking my cheek. "I like where this conversation is going."

"No, I'm serious," I said. "Four hundred sixty-two times."

He nodded. "I'm glad to know that someone is keeping track. Are you saying that's too much or not enough?" He grinned that boyish grin at me, his blue eyes flashing, and said, "Because I'd err on the side of not enough, personally."

338 *Kristy Woodson Harvey*

I rolled my eyes. "Come on, Graham. Why the hell am I not pregnant? I mean, how hard can it be? I wasn't even trying for Alex, and 'bam!' just like that." I snapped my fingers, ignoring the fact that I had been only twenty-six then. I tried to push away the thought of that declining fertility chart the OB-GYN had shown me at my last appointment. He had said, "Well, at your age it just takes a little longer." He'd made Graham and me feel like a couple of forty-eight-year-olds asking for some sort of miracle, not thirty-one-year-olds on a very reasonable quest for their second child.

Graham shrugged and yawned. "Maybe my guys don't want to swim in the winter. Maybe it's too cold. Maybe we should wait until summer."

I crossed my arms, my nostrils flaring. He pulled me in closer and kissed my cheek.

"Oh, come on, pretty girl, you know I'm just teasing you. We're going to have lots more babies and fill this house up."

I looked up at him, my lower lip protruding the slightest bit. He kissed it back in place, leaned his forehead on mine, and whispered, "I promise. I'd never let my girl go 'round not getting something she wanted."

I smiled, my heart feeling that familiar, practically lifelong surge of love for my childhood sweetheart, when Alex rolled over, looked around sleepily, and laid his head on my lap. "Hey, Mommy?" he asked.

"Yeah, sweetie?"

"Can we have bacon for breakfast?"

I laughed and ran my hand through his shaggy hair. "You can take the boy out of the hog farm, but you can't take the hog farm out of the boy." I pulled him up and gave him a firm kiss on the cheek that was still plump and juicy as a ripe tomato.

"I think we might be out of bacon, but I know some grandparents who never run out of pork." I pinched his side and said, "You go brush your teeth, and we'll go over there."

Graham perked up, and, rubbing his tight stomach, said, "I need a big ole Pauline country breakfast."

Pauline had worked for Mother and Daddy my whole life on the farm, and she made the best homemade biscuits and gravy in the world. I shook my head. "I will take Alex to Mother and Daddy's. Then, when I get home, if you impregnate me, you may have a Pauline breakfast as a reward."

He whistled and rubbed his hand down the back of my silk gown. "Oh, baby, I love it when you get so romantic with me."

I slapped his thigh and pointed my finger at him. "I'm not teasing you. I'm getting Alex ready, and you better concentrate on producing some of that fine Jacobs baby-making sperm."

When we pulled up to the end of Mother and Daddy's driveway, I took a moment to marvel at how the giant oaks, each of them having been there for centuries longer than the home itself, grew together into a green canopy, the ideal frame for the white plantation home that graced their ending. I had an entirely new feeling about this house now, its white columns of Pantheonic proportion that were so quintessentially Southern.

When I was younger, coming home equated to poorly chosen words and hurtful digs from my mother. Maybe it was becoming a grandmother or the general smoldering of temper fire that comes with aging, but my once impossible-to-please mother—though still a force to be reckoned with—had become much, much more pleasant.

Alex unsnapped his booster, jumped out of the car, and flew through the front door before I could even say, "Hey, wait up!" or wrangle him into his coat.

He always got as excited as a jewelry collector at a Christie's auction to see his grandparents. It was the same way I felt when I saw Daddy, that mixture of love and pride that swirls together like a backroom science project. Mother stepped out onto the front porch, her sassy hair perfectly styled in keeping with the same Chanel suit she'd been wearing for decades. I felt myself unwittingly roll my eyes. She leaned over to hug my son. We still didn't always see eye to eye, but Mother could have slapped some butter on Alex and eaten him right up like one of Pauline's homemade biscuits.

Instead of following Alex through the front door, I walked around to the side, smiling at Pauline's imposing figure turning bacon on the griddle at the opposite side of the blue-and-white tiled kitchen while she hummed "A Mighty Fortress Is Our God." When she heard the screen door slam, Pauline wiped her molasses-colored hands, almost the same size as the eye on the antique stove, on the apron puckering over her thick waist. She wrapped me in a hug and said, "What's wrong with my baby?"

I had a smile on my face and hugged her back as hard as I could, and Pauline still knew something was wrong with me. "I was just wondering why you're back here frying bacon when I tried my damnedest to bust you out."

She laughed heartily and shrugged. "Had to come back. You was the one that introduced me and Benny, after all."

Pauline had met her second husband and late-life love when she, Mother, and Daddy had come to New York to help after Alex was born. They had started their life together there, but, as I knew all too well, you simply can't take the South out of the girl. Much as I would imagine one would want to escape the claws of my momma, not a year later, Pauline was back like a homing pigeon, Benny in tow. When I confronted her, jaw agape, about why she hadn't run far, far away, she said simply, "You know, baby girl: You and Miz Mason and Daddy Mason's my family."

And so we were, which was even more evident when Pauline said, "Come on, baby. You can tell Pauline."

I sat down on the stool beside the range, my lifelong Pauline-talking perch, and said, "I can't get pregnant."

She looked me up and down. "'Course you cain't."

I crossed my arms. "Why on earth not?"

"Girl like you cain't get pregnant. You ain't nothing but skin and bones."

I looked down at myself. I was naturally thin. But maybe the stress of traveling back and forth to New York for work was getting to me. Or perhaps the vegan diet and yoga kick I'd been on was too much. The hormone-balancing book I read said it would help me conceive. But every month I was more disappointed than the last when that minus sign appeared on the EPT. "You think that's all it is?"

"'Course," she said. "You was lookin' healthy when you got pregnant with little man."

I nodded, thinking that, who knows, maybe I was just too thin. Pauline might not have been a doctor, but she was always right. Feeling sorry that I was kissing three months of sprouts, flaxseed, and leafy greens good-bye, I grabbed two crispy pieces of bacon off Pauline's drip pan and crunched. I was a hog farmer's daughter, after all. Bacon was my birthright.

"Good girl." She nodded. "Now you get on outta here and come back for some breakfast when you're good and pregnant."

I laughed, and she added, "I'll keep an eye on little man."

Lying in bed an hour later with my legs propped on the headboard—I had read somewhere that elevating your legs helps the sperm find their target—Graham kissed me and said, "I just feel like it took that time, babydoll."

I smiled weakly. "I sure hope so."

He nodded. "I'm going to go get ready for church while you . . ." He paused, circled his finger around where I was lying, and said, "While you do whatever it is that you're doing there."

An hour later, sitting in church, light streaming through stained-glass windows, Graham's arm around me, Daddy beside me, and Alex playing down the dark wood pew, I felt the strongest message from heaven that I had before or since: I was going to be a mother again. Of course, I thought, naturally, that I was pregnant. Turns out, God had other plans.